~ The Devil in Blue ~

This book is intended for audiences 18+. It contains dark themes such as mental illness, references to torture and brainwashing, dub con, sexual abuse (not by MMC), violence, and graphic sex.

He will look for you.

He will find you.

He will destroy you.

Words ingrained in my mind, spoken to me every morning and every night. He will *look* for you. He will *find* you. He will *destroy* you.

They never told me who *he* was, only that he would be my demise. I didn't know what he would do to me if I ever saw him. Whether he would hurt me or imprison me. Hate me or use me. Kill me or damn me. I didn't even know what he would look like. A man? A shadow? A demon?

After my parents died and the world came for me, I almost wished he would find me. Destruction would be the ultimate escape. Oblivion would be the final door I had to walk through to meet the darkness. Instead, I watched every year pass with agonizing sluggishness, trapped in a prison. But this prison had no bars. This prison was made of flesh and bone and was filled with voices that whispered horrid things to me. Bloody things. Violent things.

Violent things some minds could not fathom.

Those who see only when they're awake could never imagine the worlds I wander when I sleep and therefore cannot understand fear. Fear had become my blanket and it cradled me. It cradled me and nurtured me until I created something else. Something I will never escape. Something bound to me like my bones and skin. I cannot exist without them and yet they ache, split, and bleed. I am a house of pain.

And the creature fear pulled forth from my soul enjoys it. She's sadistic and punishing. She hates me for giving in except I don't know what I gave in to.

Nothing in my life has made sense for a long, long time.

I was absently stroking my brush through my unruly golden tresses when I heard the cathedral bell toll. I bristled every time that deep, brass tone sang from town. A town close enough to hear and yet far enough away that prying eyes could not see past the hedges of willow trees surrounding the manor in which I lived.

Aedon Heights was a fourteen-acre estate packed full of foliage inside high brick walls covered in vines. In the winter, the trees and plants turned to gray, scraggly things that looked like the starved beggars on the streets of Cragborough. The cathedral took up a ridiculous amount of space and despite the drab style of the buildings surrounding it, it was made of fancy brick with meticulous mosaics on the domed ceilings and bright stained glass windows.

It was an eyesore. I could see its steeple from my window and as the bell continued to chime, I stood from my small vanity with the cracked mirror and walked over to stare blankly at the gaudy thing. From my room, it was vague, but I knew too well what it looked like up close and inside. I'd been on my knees praying to statues many times before on the hard, stone floors.

I was still dressed in my nightgown at that early hour. I had no need to change out of it since there were no plans to leave the manor that day. Autumn made the air cold and my fire had gone out, leaving nothing but a pile of gray ash on my hearth. But the cold did not bother me. Not like it used to. Frost salted my windowsill so I knew the snow would be coming soon. I liked the snow. It made everything seem pure when I knew all too well how impure everything was underneath.

Including me.

But Lucien liked to pretend I was not tainted by the shadows. He liked to pretend I could be cleansed, but he had no idea how wrong he was. I knew one day his assumptions would damn him. And perhaps I'd be the one waking with blood on my hands.

Looking down at my pale, long fingers, I wondered what they would look like painted red and dripping coppery warmth. I wondered what my dress would look like stained with such filth. The slightest spot on any of my dresses prompted Lucien to buy me something new. I'd gone through so many gowns that I'd lost count, but Lucien enjoyed buying me clothes. I was a doll of sorts. I had enough garments to spare.

The heavens are watching you, a voice inside me said. *Be good lest you attract the wrath of Malvec.*

"No," I muttered to myself, leaning against the wall to stare once more at that ugly cathedral through the autumn mist. "He doesn't exist. Nothing does outside of this."

I didn't enjoy the voices in my head. Not that I could ignore them. I also couldn't dismiss the possibility that they would one day be more than voices. Maybe one day they would drive me back into the insanity from which I was pulled. All people warred with themselves. All people had wretched minds that they kept

3

locked away. But not all people had memories of things that weren't their own and yet felt like their past was missing at the same time.

Perhaps I was a devil in the pale, cold skin of a woman. Perhaps one day, torturing it out of me would work. But not yet. Pain had only enticed it to stay thus far. It had grown to love it.

Maybe I had too in a twisted, sick way.

There was a knock at the door and a raspy woman's voice on the other side, making my head turn.

"Briar," Catlyn said. She was the only one to brave venturing to the top of my lonely tower to retrieve me. Lucien didn't dare climb those stairs. "Lucien would like you to dine with him this morning."

I took in a breath of the crisp morning air as a frigid breeze wrapped itself around my throat. I begged it to squeeze, but it only teased.

"Should he not be at the cathedral already?" I asked.

He went to worship twice a week. He used to drag me with him, but when he noticed how it affected my mood, he left me at home.

"He has taken today off," Catlyn said. She hesitated a beat before solemnly saying, "It is your birthday."

I'd forgotten...

Which birthday was it?

Sighing, I said, "Fine."

Catlyn wasn't leaving. I could hear her heavy breaths still in the hall. She was a little plump and climbing my stairs made her quite fatigued. I waited, wondering what else she had to say.

"You have read all your books," she said.

I glanced at my bedside table where my books were sitting in a neat stack. I had read them all... twice.

"Yes," I answered. "I wish I could read more history books. They fascinate me."

"I will see what I can do," she whispered. She paused a moment, looking around like she was trying to figure out her next sentence. But she didn't have to. I sensed what she was going to say by her body language alone. "Um, he has requested your white dress," she finally said.

My heart stopped. It had been a while since I'd worn *the* white dress. I had many in cream and ivory, but only one in white. I didn't enjoy it. In fact, the garment sickened me.

But I would not have to endure it for long.

"Very well," I said, still staring out toward Cragborough with a mix of disgust and longing.

Finally, Catlyn's footsteps could be heard waddling down the stairs to leave me be. I basked in the cold for a moment longer before walking toward the foot of my bed where a trunk wrapped in leather sat latched. I flipped the metal lock up and opened the heavy lid. It creaked in protest, its hinges sticking.

Inside the chest were some trinkets. Nothing important. I had so few important things and I certainly did not keep them somewhere so easily found. Among the trinkets was the white dress. It was an old thing all wrapped up in silk. I reached in and pulled the folded gown from its confines, placing it on the bed. It was torturously prominent on my blue-gray sheets. Tugging at the tiny bow on the top, I untied the silk and pulled the dress up by the shoulders to look at it.

It was magnificent with its lace and beads and embroidered bodice. Magnificent for an innocent woman to attend a day of prayer in some holy place.

But I wasn't an innocent woman. Maybe I never really was. Inside, my soul was black as onyx and just as hard. Just as heavy. But I would cover that blackness with white if that was what

Lucien wanted because despite all that felt wrong, he had saved me from a worse fate.

I owed a lot to him.

Which only amplified the guilt I felt every time that voice in my head told me to drive a knife through his gut...

Lucien was dull company on the most boring of days. He was not fond of conversation and I was not fond of him in general.

Shame racked my brain every time I told myself that...

Lucien deserved all my love and respect and still, something in me itched around him like I was allergic to the air he occupied.

I'd put on his dress. Despite its beauty, it was not a comfortable thing. It squeezed me too tight and some kind of fiber on the inside scratched at my skin. Had I not been practiced in being uncomfortable in corsets and bustles, I would have been audibly squirming with irritation.

In front of me was a cooked steak slathered in butter and onion. I cut into it soundlessly, every stroke of my knife precise and gentle while Lucien made no such efforts across from me. The table was long with six mahogany chairs on either side while we sat at each head, new candles burning along its length. In the very center was a fresh vase full of white carnations, a flower Lucien swore was my favorite, though I couldn't remember telling him that. In fact, I didn't much like the sight of them.

Not that I knew what my favorite flower was.

The gardens behind the estate had many different kinds and they were all beautiful. I would have chosen any of them over the fluff of petals that was a carnation.

Lucien valued new and shiny things. He never let candles burn past one meal. Never let me wear the same dress twice besides my special white gown. He despised dirty dishes and dusty sills or charred logs sitting on the hearth. It was a wonder he'd kept me so long. I had certainly been used more than once.

I swallowed a bite of tender steak and reached forward to take my wine glass. In it was a dark cranberry concoction with a sour taste, but it wasn't wine. Lucien denied me adult luxuries. Which didn't bother be much because the taste of wine was too sour and overpowering for my pallet. He still kept the hems of my skirts off the ground when we were in private like unmarried girls had them and he liked when I curled my already wavy hair and adorned it with silk bows.

There was always something wrong with that for me. I was locked behind a veil that only showed me glimpses of the outside world, but I knew enough. I knew that after my maidenhood had been taken, I should not have been wearing so much white. My hair should have been styled however I liked it. I should have been able to drink whatever I wanted and go to town with friends, but Lucien had his own traditions.

"Did you paint today?" he said, picking food out of his teeth with a chicken bone. Each time he did, I caught of glimpse of his gold molars. He had three. "Father Eli was adamant about you painting when I took you in."

I lifted my eyes over the rim of my cup as he leaned back in his chair, his bodyweight straining the solid wood. He was not fat, but he was not muscled like the men who tended the chores outside. He had clean skin that was shaved smooth every morning, but his eyes had yellowed through the years. Too much drink, I suspected. And his teeth were following suit, likely because he smoked his pipe every night.

"I did not want to paint today," I said, putting my cup down. "So I read."

"You read? Have you new books since last I bought you some?"

"No," I sighed. "I reread the one about the ghostly sailor from the coast."

"The Blind Coast? You are reading nonsense then," he laughed.

I'd always hated his laugh. It was wheezy and gruff and made his whole body shake and ripple. And usually, he used it to mock me in some underhanded way. Not that I could do anything about it.

"Nonsense or not, I find the idea of a coast in perpetual mist fascinating. And even more so, a sailor's spirit who collects souls for—"

"Why don't you play me a song," he said with a yawn.

I had a bite of food on my fork and, looking down. I hadn't even finished half my meal, but Lucien was bored and he'd devoured every bit of his food so quickly.

In the corner of the dining room was a cello. It was a gorgeous piece. Its red wood was inlaid with gold flecks and it was polished to glossy perfection. Lucien had it made special for me, for the moments that he wanted to hear music. He had me learn many instruments. The harp. Violine. Piano. But the cello was his favorite. I had to admit, the deep, haunting sound sang to my soul in a way no other instrument did. It pulled me into a familiar darkness.

I stood from my chair, walking slowly toward the beautiful piece. Pulling up my skirts, I sat down and propped the thing between my legs, poising the bow over the tight strings. I'd memorized every piece of music Lucien had in his manor and sifted through my mind to find one that suited me that day.

Lucien lounged back in his chair at the dining table, lighting his ivory pipe. He began to puff on the scented smoke, staring off into empty space as I slid the bow across the strings. A deep, slow melody took form and echoed through the large chamber. Closing my eyes, I let the music coil around my bones and soak my muscles. That particular song always pulled me under the waves into a place where I was drowning. A place so dark, I couldn't see which way was up. But in that place, I always felt like I was close to something. I reached out, my fingertips just barely skimming some unseen shadow in the black. An answer. One I could never quite reach.

Somehow, feeling closer to it was addicting, even if I could never unveil what it was.

The music ventured deeper, filling me and plunging me further into that dark maze of mystery. There was so much missing there. Perhaps that was why it was so dark. It was an empty void where something once was.

And as I descended into that void, searching endlessly as I had done a thousand times before, I began to sing.

Elise in a field of thorns.
Her steps made red with blood.
She wails in fear, her dress is torn.
But on and on she walks.

The mist doth veil her eyes.
The dirt doth flood her ears.
The night is thick and the field is vast
But on and on she walks

Elise is far from found
Her heart and breath silent
She bears the cold beneath the mound
But on and on she walks

The night is very long
The trail does not appear
This is the maze, there's no way out
But on and on she walks

By the end of the song, I nearly forgot the music was coming from me. I opened my eyes to a silent, still dining room that smelled of Lucien's tobacco and carefully placed the cello and the bow aside, letting my reality come back to me. My stagnant, empty reality.

"Why do you always choose that song?" Lucien said, keeping his back to me.

"Because I enjoy the melody," I said.

But that wasn't the reason.

"It's such a depressing song. Next time, choose another."

"Of course," I said obediently.

"We will have to bleed you soon. Perhaps it will help your state of mind."

I stroked the small dotted scars that littered the inside of my elbow through the sleeve of my dress where needles had pierced me a hundred times before.

"Yes, sir."

Lucien took a few more puffs of his pipe. "There is a masquerade this Friday at the catacombs to celebrate Allhalloween. I received a very formal invitation from a Count of Norbrooke."

I wasn't expecting much after that considering Lucien did not often bring me to social gatherings. But... perhaps... a masquerade where faces were covered and identities were skewed would be different.

"Come here," he said, motioning for me to approach him.

I stood and walked slowly toward the dining table, straightening my skirts before I came to stand be his side.

"I would like to attend and I'd like you to come with me," he said. "For your birthday, of course. And I've never heard of this count before. He is an outsider. It's always smart to know new faces."

"If that is what you wish," I said, folding my hands properly in front of me.

Lucien stared at my interlocked fingers and then gently pried my hands apart, taking one and kissing my knuckles.

"We shall have to find you a new dress," he said. "We will go to the modiste tomorrow. We will buy you a mask as well. Are you excited? I thought you would be."

"Of course."

"And," he stroked my hand with his thumb, putting his pip down on a plate. "Will you be a good girl until then?"

"Yes, I will be a good girl," I said flatly.

Lucien slowly stood, his eyes everywhere but on my face. An uncomfortable shiver rolled down my spine. The same shiver that racked me every time he was about to indulge. Many years of the same routine had not made it easier.

Lucien was never rough. Never cruel. He was simply... Lucien. I'd never fought him before. I wasn't sure why, but I never tried to protest even when it made me feel cold and sick inside.

My fight had been taken from me over the years I supposed.

When he stepped behind me and began lifting my skirts, I allowed it, staring across the room at the cream-colored wallpaper. I felt the chill of air on my bare thighs. The gentle pressure of Lucien's hand on the middle of my back urged me to bend over the table. Taking a deep breath, I folded, turning my head to the side to stare at the candles burning in the middle of the table and those ugly carnations.

There was no escaping to my void in those moments. There was no going to sleep or thinking of other things. There was just an overwhelming numbness to those moments when Lucien wanted me. I heard his fingers fumbling with the buttons of his pants. Felt him slide my undergarments down to my knees. Felt his clammy flesh press to my backside. I even allowed my mind to feel his spit-soaked fingers toy with my entrance.

I'd never gotten wet for him. Not once. But it never deterred him. He thought I was broken as it was, so of course that was just another of my many flaws.

Then I stopped thinking. I stopped feeling. I stopped caring.

Those moments weren't me. Those moments were nothing. Those were the moments that collected in some dark corner of my mind, feeding the monster slumbering there. That monster was fat off forgotten things, for I'd forgotten so, so much.

3
BRIAR

My pale hair was braided over my shoulder and decorated with a small hat that had a thin veil of mesh to cover my eyes. Lucien had gifted me another gown, this time in pale rose with pastel pink trim along the high collar. It itched, but I would never tell him that. Lace gloves covered my fair hands and a fur-lined cloak draped over my shoulders. The dress was unnecessarily heavy, the bustle thick with layers and trailing a step behind me. It was not a traveling dress by any means, but Lucien enjoyed how I turned heads.

So long as eyes did not look too long.

I was a trophy. One Lucien flaunted in public from time to time only to put me behind closed doors for months following. I was not to speak much lest I say something that gave away my lunacy. But that was fine because talking was no treat. People never seemed to have any depth anyways once words escaped their mouths.

It was rare for me to venture around town with Lucien and I subtly took in the sights with silent excitement. I loved the town. Contrary to the gray buildings and hazy atmosphere, the people of Cragborough seemed to always try to offset the drab setting with colorful clothes. It was bustling with people of all kinds. Dark hair. Pale hair. Dark skin. Pink skin. Wrinkled faces and young faces. The smells were blissfully overwhelming, too. Perfumes, food, and even the simple odor of burning wood from chimneys all tickled my senses in a way the drab interior of Lucien's manor never could. If I avoided the cathedral, I actually enjoyed the town very much.

I wanted to visit a bookstore to replenish my collections. I wanted to have tea in one of the beautiful cafes. And when a light drizzle graced the brick streets of Cragborough, I wanted to dance in it. I stepped out of our carriage with intentions to do just that, but I had no hopes of succeeding.

Lucien opened my umbrella for me, ensuring no drop hit my delicate skin.

We headed down the street, Lucien two strides ahead of me. I was not his wife and people knew. I was his ward. His prize. His prize for what, I never understood. People knew the stories around the manor. Stories about a young woman plucked from the horrors of an asylum by a selfless baron who simply wanted to give her a better life.

I was that woman. His charitable act.

With so few memories past my time with Lucien, I had to accept that I was broken. My head was not right. There were too many black spots. Too many voices. Too many shattered pieces for me to be sane.

And insane people needed others to take care of them. Lucien was that person for me.

So, I was not his wife. I did not hang on his arm with a smile as other women did with the men accompanying them. I ate what I was given, I wore what I was gifted, and I spoke the way Lucien enjoyed, if at all. Obediently and softly.

None of it made a difference to me. I stopped feeling—truly feeling—long ago. Small bursts of happiness, or something resembling it, teased my thoughts from time to time, but otherwise, I was just a feather floating where the wind took me. And that wind was Lucien.

Entering a familiar dress shop, the owner, a woman with a deep, copper-colored complexion, greeted us with a heavy accent. I didn't know where she was from and I desperately wanted to know, but I had never asked.

Ethel pinned her dark curls up and smiled brightly. She was always excited over Lucien, who never hesitated to spend his money on a gorgeous gown to dress me in. I stood near the wall, hands clasped in front of me, as Lucien and Ethel talked over an appropriate design for me.

Ethel looked me over, squinting her eyes at me as Lucien hung over her shoulder, hands behind his back. She tilted her head to one side and then the other and hummed thoughtfully.

"You always put her in these pale colors, but it is Allhalloween, Baron," she said, crossing her arms over her bosom.

Ethel had a full figure and wore complimentary colors without fail. As a dressmaker, her fashion was always forward and detailed with beads, delicate trims, and stitching that seemed ahead of our time. Her bustles were always a bit flatter and her jewelry was exaggerated, leaving no eye unturned.

I wished I could dress how I wanted. Then again, I wouldn't even know how to dress differently. I didn't even truly know what I liked.

Ethel and Lucien had been talking amongst themselves in front of me as if I was not there for some time. When they came to an agreement, it was clear Lucien was a bit uneasy about it.

"She will be in a mask," Ethel argued. "No one will even know it is your little flower."

"Red is such a flashy color for her, do you not think so?" Lucien said. "Perhaps a color less exaggerated."

Ethel sighed. I had to be her most boring customer aside from the amount of money Lucien was willing to spend.

"Perhaps I can compromise." She bit her lip in thought. "Yes."

Without another word, she retreated to the back room, leaving Lucien and me in the dress shop alone. I let my eyes wander the shop and all the clothing on display. There was a beautiful, emerald green dress by the window draped over a mannequin made of wood. The layers of jewel-toned fabric were mesmerizing, but it was the lovely jewelry hanging around the neck of the mannequin that truly caught my gaze.

I inched toward it as Lucien pulled out his gold pocket watch to stare at the time.

On a silver chain was an arrangement of metal twists that shaped a pair of moth wings, each adorned with gems that glistened like peacock feathers. The colors shifted as I changed my angle of view. Between the gems was a silver skull with rubies for eyes. It was subtle, beautiful, and a bit eerie. Every element together made poetry for my sheltered eyes and I almost reached out to touch it when a figure passed in front of the window and snapped me out of my mild trance. The figure had been standing at the corner of the building outside, so still my eyes did not catch him until he moved.

The figure didn't walk particularly fast, but it was fast enough for me to lose sight as soon as I noticed him. All I could tell was that it was a man, tall and broad, with a long, blue coat that faded to black at the hem. I saw nothing else, but something about the instant made my heart stop for a blink. There was a sliver of suspicion that the man was watching me through that window long before I noticed his presence, but it was forgotten quickly when I heard Lucien's voice pull me back from the display.

"You will wear your diamonds," he said flatly, eyeing the necklace I'd been admiring.

Flashy jewelry distracted from the innocence of my face, he always said.

Although, I wasn't sure how someone's face could look innocent. Nor did I understand why it mattered if we were going to be wearing masks.

When Ethel returned from the back room with a large box, Lucien moved to an oak table in the middle of the shop to judge the contents she so eagerly brought out for him. I stayed back, watching from afar as Ethel opened the box and unfolded a deep gold gown made of layers and layers of red-trimmed silk. Swirls were hand embroidered along the hem of each layer and trailed upward, fading into the cinched waistline of the sleeveless marvel. A rounded neckline plunged a little deeper than I knew Lucien liked, but with some thought, I was surprised to see him nod with approval.

"This color is sure to do wonders for her brown eyes," Ethel said. "They'll light right up."

I withheld my shock as she folded the dress back into its box. It was so unlike Lucien to allow me to wear something so extravagant. But when I caught him paying her, I knew it was real.

But we weren't done.

Lucien carried the large box out of the shop, handing it to a footman near our parked carriage before we headed a little further down the street to an artist's den. I'd heard of such places where people indulged and freely explored the expanse of free thought in manners "unbecoming of the upper class," Lucien always said. So it confused me that we stopped in front of one.

There was no sign or indication that we were at an exclusive artist gathering. Only the smell of tobacco and Absenth gave it away. Lucien looked rather peeved when he descended the steps to a red door off the path. He motioned for me to stay on the sidewalk like he thought my getting too close would corrupt and bend me into an undesirable version of myself in seconds.

Lucien knocked twice on the red door and almost immediately, it opened. A man with disheveled black hair, a skinny frame, and his white shirt unbuttoned to display his flat torso stood with a very content smile on his face. He brushed his hair back with a sniff and looked Lucien up and down before realizing what was going on.

"Right," he said, ducking back into the den.

Smoke trickled out from inside smelling sweet and warm and I found myself leaning a bit to try and see past the entrance. Then the man was back with a sloppy stack of masks in his arms. He giggled at the way they balanced in his hands and began to show them to Lucien. I watched as Lucien sifted through one after another. Black lace, molded leather painted into colorful designs, half-masks on sticks. There were many, but Lucien settled quickly on a full-faced mask and a half-mask in black.

He paid the man and quickly returned to the sidewalk with the masks in hand, eager to leave that smoky corner of town. I was interested to see the masks he'd chosen but kept my interest bottled up for the time being. I'd see soon enough.

And that was when reality set in. I was going to a masquerade. The last time I went to any sort of gathering, it was Lucien's birthday and I was hardly allowed to dress up, speak, or dance.

I wondered if I'd be so tightly leashed at the masquerade. I couldn't imagine Lucien going through so much trouble to dress me if I was not going to be allowed to celebrate like everyone else attending. It was Allhalloween, after all. It was a night I had never gotten the chance to experience but one I'd been fond of for years. A night when people said the walls dividing the realms could be crossed. When spirits from other worlds came out to play and cause mischief. It was a festive concept in current times, but there was an era when it was not. When sacrifices were made, violence plagued the streets, and zealots disrupted all manners of peace. Fae, devils, and evil spirits walked among mortals, and at one time, it had caused a war. A war I was lucky to have never seen.

If I was being honest, all of the old art I'd ever seen of the supposedly evil half-world seemed quite beautiful. Glowing trees. Iridescent waters. A moon almost as bright as the sun. But there were also terrifying creatures. Dark things. Demons. Monsters no nightmare could accurately conjure.

I wasn't sure which part of it appealed to me the most.

But Allhalloween was the day people felt closest to realms most didn't even believe existed anymore. It all sounded tremendously entertaining and now I was finally going to see the festivities firsthand. Excitement fluttered in my veins.

I only hoped Lucien wouldn't lose his nerve and cancel our attendance. I was used to disappointment and had always tried to avoid it by thinking the worst, but this was different. I truly didn't want to miss out. Something about it felt… right.

Catlyn barely spoke a word to me as she helped me into my new gown. She cinched my corset tight, coiled my silver blonde hair into a beautiful updo with spirals hanging on either side of my face, and then laced me into the gold masterpiece from Ethel.

I had never worn anything so lavish. And the way the neckline plunged to the top of my breasts made me feel naked. But... it was a good feeling. To not be constricted by high, modest collars and itchy trims was so different from the everyday wardrobe Lucien chose for me.

I stared into a floor-length mirror at the woman in front of me, barely able to recognize her. My arms, though they'd thickened a bit since my stay at Southminster, were still thin and pale. A pair of lace, fingerless gloves covered half of them, but somehow it only seemed to accentuate how frail I was. My collarbones protruded, but that was not new.

Folding my hands together in front of me, I regarded the gold dress I was wearing. A train fell behind me, decorated with intricate swirls that tangled up the dress in the most meticulous embroidery and beading. I brushed the front with my hands as

Catlyn stepped up and handed me a string of tiny diamonds on a silver chain. It was the only piece of jewelry Lucien had ever gifted me. I lifted it, clasping the tiny lock behind my neck, and sighed.

"You look stunning," Catlyn said.

"Thank you," I said emptily.

"Color truly suits you."

I almost smiled at that. Almost. But after the masquerade, I was certain Lucien would have a whole new wardrobe of dull dresses with high collars waiting for me.

I decided I was going to savor this night. I was going to remember every second of it and relive it every moment I could.

Not to say I was not thankful for Lucien's generosity. Taking me out of that horrible place was the biggest kindness anyone could have done. I would have rotted in that place, I was sure of it. He always treated me well. Fed me. Clothed me. Kept me safe.

And he's used you every day since to appease his twisted desires…

There was no telling where I would have ended up if not for him, though.

"The world is full of monsters that want to destroy innocent things like you," he would say.

And I believed him because one of those monsters ruined me. He drove me to insanity. Took everything from me.

He will look for you.

He will find you.

He will destroy you.

Lucien and I stepped into his nicest carriage that night. The interior was blood-red with velvet cushions. I'd only ever ridden in it once before when he wanted me to accompany him to lunch with the Duke of Halesworth. I wasn't sure why he wanted me at such important events. I'd always suspected my presence would be an embarrassment considering where I was from.

But the elite loved people who did charitable things and taking care of a woman like me was certainly charitable.

"I want you to keep your mask on all night," he said flatly. "And should anyone ask your name, I shall answer for you."

"Yes, sir," I said.

I was used to not speaking for myself. There was no telling what would come out of my mouth if I was allowed the freedom to converse with others, so the fact that Lucien had taken up that burden was a kindness.

The town of Cragburough passed us by rather quickly. It was quiet until we arrived at the cathedral. I looked up at the stained glass windows and bristled. Artistic as those giant, multicolored windows were, they depicted things that didn't sit right with me.

I'd been inside the cathedral before and it was an uneasy experience every time. It was dark and the candles shed light in all the wrong places. Mainly, on a giant monument that sat in the middle of the main hall. It showed an angel with great big wings that spread across the entire space. The angel was meant to be beautiful, I was sure, but he was anything but. His features were too soft. His eyes were too empty. His body was too perfect. Such perfection was a ruse. A way to lure people in. Beauty so flawless was far more terrifying than the things people often said lurked in the dark. Those things I'd become good friends with. Those things were true.

The stained glass portrayed similarly beautiful images with roses, angels in different poses, and light. It was all too good. Too wonderful. Every time Lucien disappeared for his worship, I was glad he never asked me to come along anymore. I feared the cathedral would undo me one day.

The masquerade, to my luck, was not held at the cathedral where many holidays were celebrated. The masquerade was being held in the catacombs. I'd never been to the catacombs, but it was a vast underground chamber with equally intricate décor if the stories I'd heard were true. Every fallen hero from the war was kept there in the marble walls. Heroes who fought many great enemies and brought down corrupt kingdoms, ensuring the magic that had enslaved so many people hundreds of years ago could not do it again.

Excitement fluttered inside me because being in the presence of hundreds of dead was far more appealing than being inside a well-crafted cathedral surrounded by the living. *Death* brought me peace. The stillness. The end. The dark silence and the promise of nothing was the greatest harmony there could be.

"Strange to hold the Allhalloween masquerade in the catacombs," Lucien said, toying with the house ring he wore on his thumb. "The war has been over for fifty years and yet he wants to remind us of the bloodshed by hosting this event among the dead."

"Perhaps where he comes from, it's honorable to celebrate with the dead," I said. "We want to remember the war, after all. Those who drove the fae back into their realms and out of ours should be honored, should they not?"

Lucien and most others didn't like talking about the war. It seemed many wanted to believe it never happened, but I was always eager to learn. Not that Lucien allowed many books into Aedon heights for me to read about the events. Everything I knew was from listening to others talk or from the books Catlyn snuck into my possession. Or... from what I'd been told in Southminster.

I wished I could remember who I was before the asylum, but all I had were the words of others. I was found with dirt on my feet and blood on my face spewing stories of a devil and a land shrouded in shadows and evil. Shadows some said would consume our world if we allowed them to walk in our realm unshackled. The very same evil that had killed everyone I knew and left me alone with a broken mind and body.

They said it was fae. After the war, some fae had been left behind and like demons, they preyed on humans until they were all hunted down. It was a horrible chance that the very last of the fae found my family's farm and slaughtered everyone, stealing my life from me. But I supposed it was a better chance that my mind had chosen to forget it all anyway, even though the effects remained.

Beliefs about a world between life and death were so scattered now. It almost made me eager to find it while most feared its existence. People wanted to believe that the half-world and all its demons disappeared after the war. Magic was sparse and the creatures made from it even more rare. The heathenistic idea of fae, sorcery, and monsters residing in a world we couldn't see was destroyed and society swore to a deity that promoted good behavior, control, and rules. The Church of Phariel. Our guardian. The protector of the mortal realm.

But I'd never seen him and all we had were his words. Or what people said were his words.

Coming to the large mausoleum a mile from the cathedral, the carriage stopped, pulling up behind a line of others just arriving at the event. Already, I could see intricately carved pumpkins lining the brick walkway, their mouths stuffed with small candles. The autumn leaves blew across the path with gusts of gentle wind, carrying the scent of orange and cloves through the carriage windows.

I was glad my face was concealed behind a mask. I was smiling much too brightly. Lucien might have thought it childish of me.

When the carriage stopped and a footman opened the door, Lucien stepped out first in his gold, velvet tailcoat and top hat, his face half-covered in a black mask with amber jewels. Turning, he held out a hand to me and I reached out with my gloved hand, placing my fingers gently in his. My shoes had small heals, but they were easy to walk in. They did, however, make me as tall as Lucien. I was tall to begin with and Lucien was not, but that night, he didn't seem to mind.

I stepped down onto the brick ground and the small train of my dress followed me into the crisp fall air. My mask was leafed in dark gold with strings of red vines tracing the outer edges. On the forehead was a leather mold of a dragonfly with tiny rubies inlaid across its body. The rest of the detail was hand-painted. It was a gorgeous creation. One I was glad to wear so I could enjoy my night unhindered, attracting no more attention than anyone else.

Holding out his arm, Lucien beckoned me to walk with him. If he was offering, then I didn't want to deny him. I slid my hand over his bicep, looking around at the other attendees to see the largest variety of fashion I'd ever seen. Some were in dresses with full, layered skirts. Others were in smaller ensembles that hugged their legs. The men wore waistcoats, trench coats with expensive embroidery, and cloaks. The masks ranged from tiny lace eye covers to full, horned masterpieces, jester masks, and beautiful face coverings that extended into equally beautiful headdresses. I wanted to squeeze Lucien's arm with excitement but tampered that impulse down, acting the role of an obedient companion.

Coming to the arched entrance down into the catacombs, Lucien pulled a black parchment invitation from his coat pocket and handed it to one of the identical staff members at the top of a wide, descending stairway. The staff in his black skeleton mask took the invitation, opened it, and inclined his head, allowing us passage.

And down we went.

I could hear the sound around us changing. No longer was the wind fluttering in my ears. Now the distant hum of music was bleeding toward us from deep underground, singing off the walls with haunting grace. Candles lined the walls, the wax layered in hardened trails over stone shelving.

When we came to the bottom of the steps, the passage opened up into a massive underground hall with polished stone floors, twisting pillars, and marble walls filled with hundreds of golden plaques where the dead had been laid to rest. There was a red carpet stretched through the length of the catacomb-turned-ballroom that ended at a dais where a band of harpists, cellists, and violinists played a beautiful melody.

Lining one wall was a long table filled with food from apples in hot cider, stacked towers of aged cheese and black grapes, and ham slices slathered in dark cherry glaze. On the other wall was a long table arranged with crystal glasses filled with the darkest wine I'd ever seen. The mix of cinnamon and apples and wine filled the ballroom with the most pleasant aromas.

Rose petals and fall leaves were lightly scattered on the floor, swirling under full skirts as people spun through the hall in a slow dance.

It was all the most magnificent thing I'd ever seen and I wanted to stop to take it all in, but Lucien raised his chin at the extravagant display as if it meant nothing. I knew that even he had never been to an event so brilliant, though. The thing was,

27

with nobles, they never wanted to appear impressed by each other. They were in a constant, deceptively polite battle to upstage one another.

As we began walking the hall, I noticed a few people standing at the food tables, their masks lifted onto their heads so they could snack on the lavish foods.

If the Count of Norbrook wanted to make a statement, he was getting his point across. I was not well-socialized, but I was a reader and a listener and I knew that most of the attendees were there for one reason. To meet the mysterious count and gain his favor. Lucien was one of those people. Me? I just wanted to see every inch of the beautiful masquerade and listen to the music

Lucien stopped just short of the dance area, looking over people's heads as if searching for something.

"I'd like to meet this count," he said. "But how could I possibly know who he is with all these masks about?"

I didn't answer him. Most of the time I knew that if he was asking a question, it was simply him thinking out loud.

"Ah, Father Eli," Lucien said, heading over to talk to a man whose mask was raised to take a drink.

The name made my breath catch in my throat.

Father Eli had a face I'd never forget and it made my gut wrench. It was one no mask could cover. I gripped Lucien's arm a little tighter, but luckily he was distracted by his surroundings that night and didn't react. He stood in front of Father Eli, who wore a white robe with a gold collar. His white and gold mask sat on the wide brim of his hat while he sipped on wine. A clean-shaven face looked down at Lucien, his lips so full they looked too heavy for his plump face, caught in a perpetual frown.

Father Eli could not see my face, but I still felt a need to look down to hide it.

"Ahh, Baron," he said, his voice booming and deep. His gaze flicked toward me and I felt small. Smaller than I had in a long time. With Lucien, I was obedient but never small. Father Eli made me feel like I was getting crushed under a giant boot. "This must be the lovely Briar."

His eyes fell to my exposed chest and, unwilling to appear as meek as I felt, I held onto my composure with all my might and politely bowed my head.

"Father," I greeted kindly.

The man had done nothing but care for me during my time at Southminster. I wasn't sure why he made my skin crawl. Perhaps because I associated him with all the pain he forced me to work through when I was recovering from my trauma.

And the welts and the cold and the torment of his presence.

"She's become quite the educated young lady, Father," Lucien said proudly. "You should hear her play. Her music is simply divine."

"I do not doubt it. She always had great potential. We all knew she could not go to waste. Have you bled her recently?"

"After tonight. I wanted her energetic for the event."

Thankfully, the two did not discuss me for long. They started a boring conversation. One I easily ignored as I continued to look around. I watched the dancers for a while, wishing I could be twirling with them, but unless Lucien agreed to join me, he was unlikely to allow me to indulge. And perhaps it was for the best. If I lost myself in the crowd, I might become overwhelmed.

All around me, the colors ranged in a variety of red, gold, and copper. There was some purple about and a few shades of autumn green, but it all fit the theme of Allhalloween, a fall holiday filled with earthy colors. But as the music picked up a little, the crowd of dancers suddenly parted, the two halves dividing like a flock of birds that just had a stone thrown through it. My eyes were drawn to the dramatic movement and traced the long red carpet on the floor to a giant, marble fireplace clear across the catacombs.

Standing near the orange fire was a man in the most terrifying costume I'd seen so far. He was broad-shouldered and tall with a long, tailored coat the color of midnight. Silver and black embroidery made thorned vines across the bottom and the hems of his slightly flared sleeves and even his shoulders. A thick collar stood behind his neck and folded over his chest, decorated with giant black feathers. On his face was a glossy black mask shaped like an elk skull with the finest detail etched into its gleaming surface.

I could not see his gaze, but somehow, I knew he was looking at me and it stopped my heart for a beat. On his hands were black leather gloves tipped with silver jewelry to mimic talons and in one hand he was holding a silver chalice. He was leaning against the hearth, booted ankles crossed, just staring. He could have passed for a statue, but just before the crowd of dancers married again in the center of the dance floor, his head canted ever so slightly.

I quickly diverted my attention, my cheeks flaming beneath my mask. I dared not look back, fearing what I would do if the crowds parted once more to reveal him to me.

5
BRIAR

Lucien and Father Eli were still talking about boring business affairs, so I continued to absorb the party. I did not try to look back at the fireplace, but my eyes made it there anyway after a slow scan of the room.

The man was gone.

I should have ignored the fact, but instead, I found my eyes surveying the crowds for him. He was horrifying. Most attendees had chosen the elegant, lovely route in terms of style, but he took elegance and turned it into a beautiful nightmare.

And I liked it.

If my demon in the dark was real, I imagined he would look like the man in the elk mask.

"Sweet," a sensual voice said near my ear.

I whipped my head around to see a woman in a black gown standing beside me, close enough for me to smell the rose perfume behind her ears. She had a mask shaped like the face of a raven with real feathers covering it. What skin I could see was white as snow and a head of tight, silky curls the color of coal was piled neatly with a thin lock hanging over her shoulder. A pair of vivid blue eyes peered through the mask. In her hands were two glasses of wine.

"A lady should never be forced to endure the boring conversations of men talking money," she said, her full, black lips slanting. "Come," she said, holding a glass out to me. "Let us walk the room."

I shook my head. "I should not leave my—"

"Nonsense," she said over me, holding the other glass out to Lucien just when his attention turned to us. She stepped in close to him, tipping her chin up. "You would not mind, my lord, if I stole your lovely companion away, would you?"

Her voice was velvety and seductive. Though hesitant, Lucien nodded once, his half-covered expression seeming conflicted but he did not argue with her.

I was in shock.

The woman's cold, long fingers brushed over the top of mine, sliding it away from Lucien's arm.

"Come, sweet," she said, leading me away from him.

There was a slight sense of panic deep down in my chest when I realized I was being led away from Lucien. Though I was eager to enjoy the festivities, I never did anything outside of the manor without his company. Being around so many others without the anchor of his presence was a bit jolting. The woman took my hand and squeezed tight. Perhaps because she sensed I was anxious or perhaps she did not want me to go back to him. Either way, it grounded me, despite that she was a stranger.

"I must say, your gown is exquisite," she spoke as we strolled along the outside of the dance floor.

"Thank you."

"Are you enjoying yourself? I understand that Allhalloween is not as celebrated here as it is in other places."

"I have not yet had a chance to explore the place entirely. But you are right. Allhalloween is a bit of a whispered holiday."

"Yes. I've visited your cathedral. It is a dreary place. Your days of worship must be quite depressing."

I wanted to tell her that I did not attend worship, but I wasn't fond of talking about myself. So instead, I chose to talk about her.

"So you are not from Cragborough?"

"Oh, no. I am from a much more vibrant place. Perhaps it is why I do not wear color," she chuckled. "So much of it back home hurts my eyes."

"And do you have a place for religion where you are from?"

"In a way. We pray to something much different than your magnificent angel. What is his name?"

"You're talking about Phariel?"

"Yes, Phariel." She said the name like it was a bit of a joke and sighed, hooking her arm in mine. "Well, we do not pray to an angel. We serve Rune of the Glyn."

That name she said with confidence and pride.

"I do not know the name." Though I felt as if the syllable was familiar to my tongue.

"Not many do, sweet. Not after the war. Perhaps you've heard his name differently. Merikoth? The Devil in Blue? He goes by so many."

Chills rolled down my spine and I didn't know why. Catlyn had smuggled small bundles of books into the manor past Lucien's attention many times. One of them was a thin book of old myths and one of those myths was called *The Devil in Blue*. It told of a cruel god who commanded both death and life with childlike carelessness. I swallowed, recalling the way the book illustrated his shadowy domain like it was the hell Phariel warned his followers about.

"You *have* heard the name," the woman said, a wide smile slowly spreading across her lips. Looking at it, I almost thought it looked too big and unnatural on her face. "Do not fear. I believe that deep down, none of us truly believe our gods and angels exist. They remain a crutch we lean on when we cannot stand on our own. A concept we look to so we can discover our own advice."

Her philosophy brought me back and I blinked with surprise. To say such things in Cragborough was sacrilege and those guilty of having such free thoughts were met with ostracization or worse.

"Do not fret," the woman said. "The music and the strength of the wine combined keep prying ears far from our conversation." She paused, pulling me closer. "You seem nervous."

"Perhaps I am. It is not often I get to have conversations at all." I turned to look at her. "Can I ask your name?"

"You may ask me anything you'd like. My name is Naevys. Naeve to most. And yours?"

"Briar."

I was about to ask something else when we came to a wall where Naevys stopped us both to look at a giant, gold-framed painting that looked to have been hung for the event. On it was a depiction of a ghostly white woman with mist for hair and robes made of white smoke. In her hands was a lantern emitting bright bluish light across half the canvas. On the other half was a sea of shadows and among them was a darker cloaked figure with his hand outstretched. But his hand was cut in half by the barrier of light between them.

Something about it was horribly tragic and ominous, but I could not stop looking at it.

"The Death of Love," Naeve said. "A story where I'm from."

My heart hurt at those words. "What is the story?"

"There is always a guardian of light. Always a guardian of the dark. One cannot exist without the other. They love each other deeply, but they may never touch." Her head turned toward me, her gray eyes darkening. "For light is the death of darkness and darkness the death of light."

"But they must suffer existing in the same space," I muttered, almost feeling the painting come to life before me. "Yet never close enough."

Naeve was staring at me. I could tell, but I dared not look at her. Instead, I breathed deeply and let the story sink in. It was tragic. It made my heart heavy, but a heavy heart was better than an empty one. I learned that a long time ago, so whether it was happiness, pain, sadness, or anger, I never let it go to waste.

Glancing to my left, there was another painting. I knew the image well from one of the books Catlyn had gifted me. Three circular images were stacked atop one another, each depicting a different world. A dark, ominous realm with clouds and no sun, a world of sunlight and rich with life, and a world with two moons and a maze covering the bottom half of the circle.

"Mmm," Naeve hummed. "The Quendalier. A depiction of the realms."

"Has no one thought to report this to the authorities? It's heresy to promote the realms," I whispered.

Naeve leaned in to whisper back. "I will tell you a secret. Phariel doesn't give a shit." She giggled. "In fact, he's probably laughing. You understand each realm has its own sovereign. Brothers, the three of them. And Phariel is the youngest. And the most irresponsible," she sighed.

I threw her a surprised glance, but in truth, it wasn't Phariel I was anxious about. It was the zealots that did things in his name.

People who would have cursed Naeve's presence at the masquerade for even talking about the other realms.

"You have an appreciation for art," Naeve sighed. "I can tell. The count does as well."

"You know the count?"

"Of course. I am one of his most trusted advisors."

A woman? I furrowed my brows, though my mask concealed it.

"Will he be appearing here tonight?"

She smiled wide again, that strange grin catching me off guard just as it did the first time."

"Sweet," she said, leaning in and lowering her voice to a near whisper. "He is already here."

Somehow, that sounded chilling. My pulse quickened a bit as she unhooked my arm and stepped away.

"Admire the art," she said. "My tongue is bored. I need something to eat."

It was then that I remembered I had a glass of wine in my hand. I looked down at it, brought it up to my mask, and smelled it. It smelled rich and aromatic, but I still wasn't a fan of wine's sour, jaw-clenching taste. Not wanting to be rude, I walked over to a nearby table filled with more wine cups and set it down for someone else to enjoy. Besides, Lucien had instructed me not to take off my mask and to drink, I would have to do just that.

Lifting my head to look across the long line of cups and platters of fruit, I noticed the man in black walking among the crowd. He was taller than most, his antlers giving him even more height. He was not lounging on the outskirts of the celebration that time. He was roaming, his long coat flaring out behind his legs a bit, but I only caught a brief glimpse before he disappeared into the masses again.

"What is that perfume you're wearing, darling?" a voice said. It was equally sensual to Naeve's but with a higher pitch. "It smells divine."

I turned around to see another woman in black standing just behind me, her face shrouded in a veil of fine, silver chains attached to a beautiful headdress of black roses and twigs. Her skin was the richest shade of brown with gold dust along her collarbones and the tops of her pushed-up breasts.

"I am not wearing any," I said.

Her wine-colored lips curled up in a wide grin and I swore that her teeth were sharpened to points. Every one of them.

"Even better," she said, beginning to circle me. Her deep-blue eyes skimmed over my entire body from hem to head. "Love this dress as well. It does nothing for your skin, though, love."

I was taken aback by the forwardness of her comment and folded my hands neatly in front of me.

"Well, I did not choose it," I slipped.

I regretted the boldness of my words immediately, but it didn't stop the woman from hearing them.

"Oh? Well, who chose this for you, then?"

"My guardian. And the dressmaker who created it."

"Were you sick, love? Could you not pick your own gown?"

I shrugged my shoulders. "I had no interest."

That part was true. While I enjoyed fashion, I had no need to choose my own.

When the woman held out a hand, I almost forgot to take it in greeting.

"The name is Lura," she said, her smile persisting.

"I'm—"

"Briar. Yes, my sister told me."

Sister? I took notice of her dark complexion again but brushed off the notion thinking perhaps they were adopted siblings and Lura didn't say anything to clarify.

Picking a grape off the table, Lura slid it between her lush lips and sucked, her polished black nails like little claws. As she peered up at me, her black eyes almost seemed too dark to be real. When she bit into the grape, a small drip of juice trailed down her chin and her tongue darted out to catch it, but she never broke eye contact. In fact, she squinted like she was waiting for me to say or do something.

My gaze immediately raised over her head in search of Lucien. I hated that I was looking for him. The twisted security he provided made my gut turn, but I was becoming so anxious in his absence now.

"You nervous, love?" Lura said, pouting her lips.

"Not at all," I lied.

"Just excited, then." Suddenly, her hand jutted out to curl around my wrist. She raised it between us, her thumb pressing on the vein hard enough that I could feel the sharp prick her of nail. "Your pulse is rather fast."

"Lura," Naeve's familiar tone slipped between us. I saw her waltzing in our direction with a handful of black cherries in one palm. She was chewing on one as she approached and flicked the stem over her shoulder just as Lura dropped my wrist. "You mustn't frighten the girl. Elanor is watching."

Lura rolled her big, round eyes and stole one of Naeve's cherries, ripping it from the stem with her teeth.

"Elanor is always watching," she sighed.

"And when Elanor is watching, *he* is watching."

My pulse fluttered at the sound of that and suddenly my skin was cold like the autumn air had come rushing into the catacombs. As the two women giggled amongst each other and ate their cherries, I took another slow look at the crowds just as another song began to play. Some left the dance floor, allowing room for many more to take their place. Skirts swept across the floor. Feet pirouetted in all directions in perfect unison. The string instruments filled the hall with a beautiful melody... and yet, I was feeling chilled by something unseen.

Lura and Naeve stayed by my side for some time. They indulged in the extravagant foods set out for guests while I refrained, unwilling to unmask myself. Except for one time. I just couldn't resist tasting one of the dark chocolate cherry pastries. They were bite-sized so, turning my back for a split second, I lifted my mask just enough to slip the pastry into my mouth without anyone noticing.

Except for one person...

My eyes fell upon a woman in the crowd like she was a light in the darkness, only she was dressed in the deepest of black gowns. It was so black it almost looked like a void. She had the mask of a skeleton on her face, painted in white with black shadows and silver filigree on the outer edges. Long, straight black hair fell over her shoulders in perfectly combed locks. Big, puffed sleeves made her look broad whereas her corset tapered her waist to unbelievable narrowness. A high collar of black feathers sat around her long neck and, as if she was a wax sculpture, she stood there staring at me in the middle of the dance floor, unmoving.

Everyone around her seemed to avoid her like she had an invisible barrier around her.

I thought that maybe, like the other women in black, she would come to speak to me. Her attention certainly was fastened to me. Pale-blue eyes cut into me from twenty paces away and yet she did not approach.

I was getting uncomfortable under her scrutiny when she finally turned and glided through the crowd and out of sight. I was frozen, feeling the weight of a thousand gazes on me even though no one was even paying attention. Then I turned to see both Lura and Naeve had stopped talking and were staring at me.

"He's seen you now, love," Lura said. "He'll want you to dance with him."

"Who?" I asked.

6
BRIAR

Both girls retreated, arm in arm, their chins raised high as they lost themselves in the mobs of attendees.

"There you are," a familiar voice said, drawing my attention.

Lucien stood behind me, his complexion a bit paler than I recalled it being moments ago. And, I couldn't be sure with his face half covered, but I swore that there was a slight sheen of sweat on his skin.

I prepared to endure a mild scolding for walking off with strangers without him, but he had nothing for me.

The music changed again, encouraging a new dance. Looking at the beginning stance for the dance, I realized it was the Peros. It was a beautifully provocative piece. Not too many people included it at their gatherings for the intimate nature of it, but the fact that the masquerade was featuring it excited me. I listened to the haunting violins and shuddered, feeling a wonderful heat on my skin.

When red silks were unrolled from the ceiling, I was hypnotized. Even more so when two women in black bodysuits skipped gracefully through the crowds like pixies, their suits studded with white gems that made them look like they were shrouded in the night sky. They took hold of the silks and began to climb, their legs and arms gracefully hooking the fabric as they ascended. The crowds began to clap and nod in approval at the beautiful dancers as they began a perfectly synchronized dance above the floor.

"What a strange dance to include," Lucien commented. He looked around to see that many had left the dance area, opting out of the waltz. "Well," he said. "If I know men, and I do, the count included this dance as a challenge to us modest folk of Cragborough." He held out his hand to me, not even looking at my face. "Let us accept the challenge."

I took his offer, but I wasn't particularly keen on dancing the Peros with him. It was a long dance and I was still suspicious of his condition.

He escorted me onto the dance floor and we took position beside each other, shoulder to shoulder. When the music changed tempo, it was delightfully slow, setting the pace for something to be savored. I raised my hand up to meet Lucien's palm and we walked carefully around each other before switching partners to do the same thing. My blood froze when I found myself palm-to-palm with Father Eli. He was masked now in his long-nosed visage lined in gold, but it did not help the bugs from crawling under my skin.

"What a gift to find you here, so adapted and obedient," he said before I spun to partner with Lucien again.

As soon as Lucien's hand met mine, that woman with the skull mask caught my eye as she walked the outer edge of the room, staring. Seeing her stole the chill from my blood that Father Eli had left behind simply because I was so curious. She was far away, but I just knew she was looking at me and it caused me to lose a step. When I met up with Lucien again, he was looking at my feet.

"Are you well?" he asked, more out of embarrassment than concern. I knew he wanted to make a good impression on the count, wherever he was.

"Yes, sir," he said. "My toe caught my skirt is all."

We continued through the dance when I saw Lucien shake his head as if to brush off a bout of dizziness. The beat of the music picked up, which included more twirls and spins and I was beginning to wonder if they were getting to him.

Halfway through the song, it was clear Lucien was not well. I kept on, unsure whether to tend to him or not and risk embarrassing him when he was so clearly invested in impressing the mysterious count.

But his condition only seemed to worsen. I leaned in as we spun across the length of the dance floor behind a long line of others.

"Are you alright, Lucien?" I whispered.

He didn't like me to call him that, but at the moment, I doubted he would notice much.

"Do not speak," he said. "Just da—"

He could not finish his sentence.

Lucien finally succumbed to whatever it was he was feeling and hunched, clutching his stomach. He shoved me back, slapping a hand over his mouth as he darted off the dance floor and shoved through the crowds.

He'd never left me like that. He'd never abandoned me to the mercy of a crowd of strangers and now he'd done it twice in one night. I would have been alright navigating the party alone for a while more if Father Eli's white figure had not immediately caught my attention. He saw me alone and began to move in my direction, sewing threads of discomfort down my spine. I was so confused and caught off guard, standing without a partner in a sea of people when the dance had not finished.

Before I could think of a way to escape, a body moved up behind me, pressing lightly to my back. Father Eli immediately diverted to another partner, skipping into the steps of the waltz and away from me. Time slowed to let me feel the body behind me. His chest was hard and warm and when I whipped my head to the side, I could see dark fabric over broad shoulders. His hand slid down my arm, gloved in thin, black leather with those silver talons on the ends. His fingers coiled around mine, lifting my arm out to take a position in the dance where Lucien had left it empty.

"It seems your partner has abandoned you," he said, his voice barely above a whisper.

The stranger spun me, rejoining the dance. His other hand slid around my waist, his palm pressing to the middle of my stomach. I slid my hand over the top, my fingers sinking between his. Stepping slightly to the side, I was able to see his elk mask, but his eyes were swallowed by shadows. I could see nothing of his real face.

"I know you saw me from across the room." His whisper was a caress.

Staring into the crowded ballroom, I tried to call on every ounce of my practiced composure only to feel my control slipping through my fingers like fine sand. The stranger twirled me to face him as the music changed tempo again. Our palms pressed together as we waltzed in a careful circle in time with the others. Still, I could not see past the darkness veiling his stare. I wished to, though. Desperately.

This man made me feel small, but not in the same way Father Eli did. As we moved, I let my eyes roam the length of his form. He wore knee-high boots in dark leather. His pants conformed to his long legs, and the black material covering his body was littered with designs in a dark blue brocade. I could see no trace of his skin. All I could see of him was the long, smoke-blue braid of hair that slithered down his back when we both spun. But even that might not have been real. Everyone, including him, was in costume for a reason.

The man canted his head. "What is your name, beautiful little bird?"

"Beautiful?" I said, finding my voice. "You cannot see my face."

He leaned in. "I do not need to see your face."

I smiled under my mask at the sultry tone of his words.

I pivoted again until my back was to his front, following the intricate steps of the dance. Dipping his head, the man continued to talk to me, his hot breath escaping through thin slits in his mask and tickling my neck.

"Tell me," he said. "What drew your eyes to me when you spotted me by the hearth earlier?"

"Your mask," I admitted. "It is terrifying."

"You feel fear and your first instinct is to make eye contact with it?"

"Fear, my lord, has been my most constant company since I can remember." I unconsciously rested my head back against the man's firm chest. "When I can feel nothing else, fear is there to remind me I am still breathing. There have been times I thought I was incapable of feeling anything at all, but that dread always finds its way back to me."

"It makes you feel alive."

"It does. It reminds me I *want* to be alive. For fleeting moments, at least. It suppose it's a bit thrilling."

His hands reached around to the front of me where I could see his gloved fingers uncoil a piece of jewelry. My eyes dropped to the pendant dangling on the ice-silver chain. Gems encased in molded metal the shape of a moth with a skull in the middle reflected the light in a rainbow of hues, taking my breath away.

The stranger first used one hand to unclasp the diamond necklace, letting it fall down my front into his waiting palm. Then he brought the new necklace up over my chest. It carried the warmth of his hands and as he clasped the chain around the back of my bare neck, my heart sighed with pleasure. Relief. Excitement. A million things ignited inside of me and as I reached up to touch the pendant hanging just below my throat with my fingertips, I remembered the emotions I'd felt in the dress shop when I found the necklace in the first place. It was the same way I was feeling now.

Slowly, I turned to face the man, forgetting the steps of the dance entirely. He was so close. I could smell the cloves and leather on him wafting toward me with his intoxicating heat. Even when I could not see his face, I could feel him and his presence rippling through the air around us. My fingers still clutched the pendant and, like a hawk watching a fish swim circles in a pond, he stared down at me with a hunger I should have feared.

And maybe part of me did fear it. But a bigger part of me believed he was a key to a lock that had kept me prisoner for so long. There were hooks in me. Gleaming, polished hooks that had pierced right through and were pulling me in. And this masked man was the lure. His coat seemed iridescent as he walked in a slow, calculated circle around me so his shadowed eyes could soak me in.

"You were in the market," I said, recalling the figure outside the window.

"I am everywhere, Briar. But the only place that matters right now is here."

I had not told him my name...

When he circled to my back where I could not see him again, I noticed the song in the ballroom had changed. String instruments took on a new melody that sang through the whole building like a choir of sirens. The stranger's hand snaked around my waist, his palm pressing against my stomach once more to pull my back against his chest. His other hand wrapped around mine, pulling it to the side as we began to sway to the music.

I knew all of the dances. Lucien made sure of it. But I didn't know this one. Still, he led me so perfectly that my feet never missed a step and our movements fell in line with the melody like the dance and song were one and the same.

When at last the stranger spun me around to face him, our bodies fit together like two links in a broken chain. With one hand in his and my other resting on his shoulder, we twirled, filling the space with our waltz like we were the only two there. The wind from the open doorways kissed my bare shoulders and neck and still, my skin was hot. My heart was racing. I could sense every bit of the stranger from his scent to the calm thud of his heart to every little twitch of his muscles under his clothes as we moved.

"Who are you?" I whispered.

"Everything you'll ever need. Everything you'll ever want, hate, and love." He leaned in close, his breath caressing the shell of my ear. "I am your madness as much as you are mine. And you know it all too well."

The music changed again, becoming slow and quiet like a whisper of what it had been all night. Someone near the stage where all of the musicians were arranged raised a glass with the reddest wine nearly overflowing from the rim. The woman with the straight, inky hair. When she stepped up, she lifted her skull mask up over her head, managing not to disturb a single strand of hair as she revealed her eerily beautiful face. High cheekbones sharper than blades held up large, almond-shaped eyes. Thin and elegant lips had a perfect, graceful curve to them and were painted such a dark shade of red they were almost black.

The stranger and I stopped and turned our attention to the woman. Oddly, he did not release my hand. I took a quick glance around the room in search of Lucien's tailcoat but saw no sign of him.

If he were there, the sight of the man with the elk skull mask holding my hand would unravel him.

"Lords and ladies of Cragborough," the woman spoke, her voice just as flawless as I imagined it would be. "I hope you are all having the most wonderful time on this Allhallowcen night. Now, it is nearly midnight and we have more to give during this memorable time. But first, I am certain you're all eager to meet the count himself. The one responsible for this lavish and darkly entertaining event."

There was seductiveness to her tone that made everyone in the room go still as stone. Not one person could take their eyes off of her while she slowly paced from one side of the dais to the other on feet so nimble it was like she was floating.

"May I present," the woman continued, raising her glass. "Count Gaelin Mortis."

The stranger stepped away from me and I turned with a start. He lifted my hand as he moved back, inclining his head before he began to glide through the crowd toward the dais.

My heart stopped. The woman's lips curved into a smirk as she gave the man a shallow curtsy. The whole room filled with applause as the count greeted his guests.

"I would like to formally thank all of you for coming at my invitation," he said, standing tall and proper. "To not know who I am and still attend a masquerade in the catacombs on the most mischievous night of the year takes great courage."

I felt like cold fingers were tracing the bare length of my back.

"But this night is far from over," he continued, capturing my gaze. "Midnight has struck. The moon is full." He paused, taking a glass filled with wine from Naeve as she slid up beside him. "Now, do tell me. What do you all think of my precious wine?"

The crowds began to hum and nod approval to each other. Those with glasses in their hands took a sip and raised their glasses with appreciation. I looked around at all of them, a bit envious that they could enjoy the elegant drink.

"Good," the count said. "Please, if you have not had any, I insist you have some now. It is my family's pride. You'll taste nothing like it no matter how far you travel."

I watched Lura weave through the crowds, refilling people's cups with a stylish silver pitcher filled with the rich-smelling drink. When she came to me and noticed I was without a glass, instead of offering one, she simply let her eyes roam my body and smiled crookedly before moving on.

The count gave everyone a few moments to take another swig of the wine before he took a sip of his and set the glass aside.

"Now, I am sure you are wondering what else I have in store for you tonight." The crowd expressed their excitement with more nods and words of anticipation. "But that will come soon. For now, eat, dance, and enjoy yourselves for the spirits, good and evil, that are lurking about. Do not deprive them of their entertainment. They only come out for one week a year, after all."

It took a while for the attendees to reengage in the celebrations. It wasn't until the orchestra started playing again that people began to disperse and the count stepped off the dais, disappearing into the crowd.

I looked for him. I tried not to seem like I was searching, but I was. His figure had dissolved into the clusters of costumed patrons. I told myself our encounter was simply by chance. That he thought me a joke. I was someone to dance with and taunt for a small moment. There was no other reason he even would have noticed me among so many other extravagant fashions and flashy masks.

The music felt louder now. People clustered on the dance floor with new enthusiasm, their wine glasses in hand and their drinks trickling over onto the stone floors. I was suddenly overwhelmed by the mixed odor of drinks, food, and perfumes and felt like I couldn't breathe.

Walking off the dance floor to the side of the room, I found a hallway leading away from the main festivities. I knew hallways in catacombs were just passages filled with more dead, but the dead were silent at least.

Why was I suddenly uneasy anyway? I'd been doing fine until that moment. I was quite proud of myself actually, especially since Lucien and I had been separated all night.

Coming to the hall, I realized it was dimly lit with a few half-melted candles. That was alright. The darkness didn't bother me. The noise was growing more distant and the passage opened up into a circular chamber, the walls lined with more plaques. In the center of the room was a small platform, on top of which was a stone casquet with the top removed and propped up against the side. I eyed it curiously before starting a slow circle around the outside of the chamber. My heels clicked softly on the stone floor, echoing in the mostly open space and reminding me how alone I was.

It felt good.

I was often alone in my tower, but not like this. The catacombs were a graveyard and as I lost myself reading the names on the plaques, I wondered what, if anything, the dead could hear. Perhaps they heard nothing, but if they did, it would be distant music and voices. Perhaps it made them feel less alone. Or perhaps they hated the ruckus and longed for everlasting peace.

I glanced at the casquet again once I reached a halfway point along the wall. There was an oil torch lit on one of the pillars which made that portion of the room a bit brighter. The plaques seemed a little older there. The faces were not as pristine and some of the etching was worn and illegible. I reached out a gloved hand and ran my fingers along the stone as I continued to walk. Ten steps later, my eyes were on the casquet again and I unconsciously veered away from the wall to approach it.

My heart thumped a bit at the idea of seeing a body inside. I'd never seen a body. At least, none that I could remember. I couldn't imagine they'd leave one in the open, though.

Unless it was far beyond decomposition and just bones.

Which was exactly what I saw when I peered over the edge of the casquet and set my eyes on a skeleton. It was a woman by the look of her elegant, embroidered gown. Once it was a deep red with silvery trim, but now it was practically brown, red only showing in the least stained places. Strings of gray hair fanned out around her skull and her skeleton hands were crossed over her stomach, a bouquet of long-dead flowers crushed beneath her bony fingers.

She was beautiful.

Agony couldn't show on the face of a skeleton with no expression. She seemed so peaceful. So finished. I canted my head at her remains, reaching slowly into the oversized casquet to touch some of the beautiful jewelry and keepsakes that had been left with her remains. When I found a gold necklace, I pinched the oval locket on the end of it and brought it to my face, glimpsing the name on the back of the dusty trinket.

Lady Edenholm

Looking down at the small carving on the edge of her casquet, I read her full name.

Lady Ellee Edenholm, High Priestess of the Orkivian Order.

I was a reader. I knew what the Orkivian Order was. It was an organization sworn and trained to kill half-worlders during the war. Monsters. Mages. Shifters. Anything that did not fit had a target on its back. I thought it was a cruel and hateful concept, to kill things simply because they were different, but wars had been fought many times and the supernatural always seemed to be in the middle. Even after the war, there were stories that the half-worlders left behind were captured and sold in underground markets.

But I wasn't there during the war. I had not seen the horrors. Perhaps it was natural to try and eliminate the dangers, even if it was cruel.

Like putting the insane in a place where they cannot touch or harm people...

The battles between classes, species, and beliefs were one of the many consistencies in the world and Lucien always tried to protect me from it all since he took me as his ward. But historical struggles always intrigued me.

I kept staring at the woman in the casquet, placing her necklace neatly back in its place. She must have fought many battles. Seen a lot of death. But now she was silent. A state I often longed for.

Unsure how much time had passed, I felt fatigue creeping up on me. I was tempted to remove my mask and breathe, despite what Lucien said about taking it off. I nearly did, but decided against it when I glanced at the woman's face again. With no skin and no features to make her different from every other skeleton in the world, she was wearing a mask, too. Without the etching on the casquet, she was no one.

And with no real memories, I felt I was no one, too. It was a horrifying idea but one I had lived with for a long time.

I squeezed my skirts, taking a deep breath of the stale, dusty air of the room. Slowly, I hiked up the layers of fabric and found myself stepping over into the roomy casquet, careful not to break any of Ellee's bones. When I stretched out alongside her, I laid back and stared up at the domed ceiling where the light of the candles just barely reached.

It was dark. Raw. No fancy tiles or mosaics. No pretty paintings. Just stone. I put my hands on my stomach and tried to imagine which flowers I'd be holding if I were dead.

Definitely not carnations.

I let the faint music from the main hall fade from my mind until there was silence. Silence like a grave. My grave. A place where lost memories no longer mattered. Where my identity didn't need to be known. Where pain no longer existed.

I nearly fell asleep in that casquet. I found it quite comfortable, but when I realized how long I'd been absent from the party, I slowly sat up. I was still alone in that room and as I climbed out, I became aware of the music again. The gentle strings and harps were a melody that soothed me and I was excited to join the celebrations after I'd gotten a moment to myself. I wasn't sure why I'd left in the first place.

Something about the count.

Just thinking about the count made my skin prickle. I rolled my shoulders back to chase away the feeling as I headed for the hall leading to the main chamber. I could smell the cinnamon and spices again as I neared, but just as I saw the glow of the ballroom at the mouth of the passage, the silhouette of a man took up the space. Tall, broad shouldered, and dawning a long coat. Unale to see his features when he was backlit the way he was, he looked like the antlers of his mask were fused right to his head.

I stopped, hands gently clasped in front of me as the count approached. As if my thoughts of him had manifested his presence, he started toward me with a confident and almost threatening gait. When he came into the candlelight of the narrow hall, the fire glistened off his polished mask making it almost look like he was on fire.

I dipped my head in greeting. "Count Mortis."

He halted a couple steps from me and leaned up against the wall, crossing his ankles. When I straightened again, he was just staring, head cocked.

"What brings you to the lonely halls when your masquerade is such a wonderous success?" I asked. "I know many would love to speak with you."

"Yes, it is," he said, his deep voice carrying in the hollow passage like a gentle touch. "And yes, they would. But here I am."

We stood in silence for a moment until I glanced around him and saw Lucien roaming the crowd, probably searching for me. I knew the right thing to do would be to go to him, but I was not in a rush. Especially when the count had shown up to distract my thoughts. Even from behind a mask, he was the most interesting thing at that party.

And that was saying a lot.

"You seem quite comfortable surrounded by the dead," the count said. "Most ladies here seemed uneasy before the wine loosened their nerves."

"Of course, it is the wine for me as well," I said.

"But you haven't even had a sip."

Something in his voice told me he was smiling behind his mask. I blinked, wondering how he knew I wasn't drinking, and inclined my head again.

"You caught me. I do not favor the taste of the drink."

"What tastes do you favor?"

"I don't quite know."

That was somewhat true. Food had never been a luxury to me. It was just a means to keep living. But when I really thought of it, one thing came to mind. My eyes wandered into nothingness as I recalled the taste from the last time I'd eaten it over a year prior.

"Chocolate," I said.

"Chocolate," the count repeated.

I glanced up at him again and met his dark, empty eyes. "And you?" I said.

"You already know the answer to that."

He pushed off the wall and took a step toward me.

I stood my ground, not wanting to seem afraid. It was a well-mannered encounter and Lucien wanted so badly to be noticed by the count. If I embarrassed his name by reacting poorly to the count's company, I knew it would make my life miserable for months to follow until he focused on some other prospect.

"If you are referring to rumors, I do not keep up with social gossip," I admitted.

He slowly shook his head, taking another step and reaching out a hand to dust off some dirt from the shoulder of my dress. Something about that gesture told me he knew what I was doing deep in the catacombs, though that was impossible.

"I am not talking about gossip. *You*, Briar, already know me."

I almost laughed because I most certainly did not.

At least... not since Southminster.

"You know my desires. My favorite things. My needs," he continued. "And things I cannot forgive."

I shook my head. "You are mistaken. And you, my lord, don't know me either. I assure you." I bent again in a shallow bow and skirted past the count toward the ballroom.

"Running will do no good," he said, his voice following me into the main chamber. I skimmed the crowd for Lucien and found no trace of him. In one direction, I saw Naeve watching me, a cherry between her lips. In another direction, I saw Lura licking a drip of wine from her long finger. "Your soul is mine, Briar," the count whispered.

He was so close to my ear that it made my skin prickle. I whipped around and found myself staring at the empty hallway. My heart leapt at the shock of it. He was right there, his breath on my neck when he spoke, and yet he was gone. I swung my head back around, but not even a hint of his presence remained.

And then his booming voice came from the dais in front of the orchestra.

"The witching hour has struck!" he announced boisterously, drawing everyone's attention to him like magic.

Had I really been gone within the catacombs for three hours?

I blinked at my lost time and felt my head starting to spin a little. Reaching out, I placed a palm on the nearest pillar, watching the count address everyone for a second time.

"I know you people of Cragborough are partial to your angelic beauty, Phariel, who doesn't quite like the idea of this holiday. But where I am from, Allhalloween is a most celebrated event. One that demands not only fun and festivities," he paused a moment, scanning the crowd. "But sacrifice."

Finally catching my breath, I moved to a table filled with water glasses and lifted my mask only enough to take a few sips.

"Allhalloween has another name if you remember," the count continued. The crowd went dead silent in anticipation of what he was going to say. "Devil's Night. It is a night most special. A night where things are not as they seem. Where the realms and all things residing in them may cross paths. Are you not afraid to know that fae and goblins and perhaps even demons walk among you as I speak? As you were dancing and eating and laughing to excess?"

A woman in the crowd laughed at the idea, her lips stained red from her excessive wine drinking. Her husband started to laugh with her and then looked up at the count.

"What reason do we have to fear myths and legends?" he said. "Even if you believe in those tales of other worlds and magic, they are simply ghost stories. Phariel is our savior and putting stock in other realms only drives us further from his guidance."

A few people nodded and spoke quiet words of approval.

"Phariel is a cunt," the count said, his voice just loud enough for me to hear, but many seemed to have missed it.

His eyeless mask moved about the room like he was studying each and every face in front of him.

"Faceless," he said like he wasn't talking to us anymore. "All of you." He slowly began to pace, elegance and danger filling every step. "So easy to tempt with riches and luxury." A woman in the back stumbled into someone, laughing at her mishap. She was drunk. So were many others. "I have a special gift for you all tonight." He stopped and raised his hands to the sides as if presenting something.

Another bout of silence fell over us all until another bold man finally spoke up.

"My lord," he said. "What is it you are presenting besides what's already been given?"

If I had to imagine the count's face, I imagined it with a sinister smirk. The atmosphere had changed. A different sort of chill fell upon us and I seemed to be the only one sober enough to feel it. I shivered, looking around again for Lucien. Perhaps now was a good time to leave the festivities.

"Oh," the count said. "I was not speaking to you. The gift I am presenting is to my lovely ravens."

It took a while for people to catch on. They all glanced around, confused and lost. I was doing the same, but my sober eyes were the first to fall upon the three beautiful women in black standing evenly spaced on the outskirts of the crowd. Lura, Naeve, and the woman whose name I assumed was Elanor. They'd removed their masks and each of them had faces more beautiful than I even expected. They were like three wraiths under the golden candlelight. Their eyes, however, were from another world when under the light of the full moon. They were black as onyx now with no whites to be seen, mirroring the perplexed and fearful expressions of the crowd.

Slowly, each of the women's mouths curled up into grins too wide for their slender faces.

Much too wide.

"Legends," the count continued, a casualness to his voice that made things seem even more alarming like he didn't care at all that the women were staring at us all with horrifying, ravenous gazes. "Myths. Call it what you will, but the veil is much too thin tonight to believe in anything outside of what's happening right now." He stepped down from the dais and slowly began walking through the throngs of people. "And right now, I am reminding you what you've all forgotten. The other realms exist, whether you deny them or not. And until now, there's been no reason for anything or anyone to meddle. Giants do not care that bugs live in their basements. But when bugs forget that giants exist, they stop being careful. They *meddle*."

I realized then that he was slowly making his way toward me. The crowds parted gradually, letting him pass. When he reached me, I felt the weight of his stare like an ice-cold wave.

"And when they meddle, the giants who did not mind them living their tiny, little meaningless lives, get angry. And bugs are reminded that all a giant must do is step on them."

I gulped, noticing everyone had backed away to give us space. But I didn't want space. Not if it was occupied by the count.

Something was terribly wrong.

"Ladies and gentlemen," the count said. "Meet my ravens."

When I saw Naeve show her teeth, they were sharpened to beastly points. The tall one let her long tongue slide over the front of her fangs, allowing her breath to leave her in a pleasured sigh like she'd just scented something delectable.

"We do love the smell of these ones," she said, her voice layered with many tones.

"Yes, like fine wine," Lura added.

"So clean, the lot of them," Naeve said, her now long, sharp nails trailing down the front of her slender neck.

The crowd did not react at first. Perhaps it was a trick to get everyone in the mood on Allhalloween. I'd heard of some towns putting on shows of such nature or decorating mansions in macabre ways for the entertainment of their patrons.

But sheltered as I was, something about the situation felt too real. Only a fool would not realize something was off.

My skin tingled with uncomfortable awareness. The feeling was familiar in a way that made me sick. My heart knew something my mind did not. A memory. Something awful inside me wept at the danger I now knew we were all in. Panic sat in the pit of my stomach waiting to grip me and pull me under. The people around me slowly began to tighten up, inching closer to one another as if they were finally beginning to feel the danger as well.

But being in a large cluster felt counterproductive.

The night was about to end in a nightmare.

I could feel it in my bones.

9
BRIAR

People used the word "numb" so freely without truly understanding what it was not to feel. To be hollow and weightless and cold was a void I never wished to enter again.

And I remembered it all too well.

Even more than that, I remembered the pain that led me to that emptiness. Immense pain. Scalding, slithering, burning, slicing agony. In my spine, my skin, my lungs. All of it ached.

I was young when I was taken in by the sisters at Southminster Asylum. A child, they told me. Dirty and injured, I was the face of madness and despair, saved from such horrors that I could not distinguish the help from the demons. Half the sisters bore scars from my fingernails before they chose to dock them so short my fingers bled.

I deserved it.

They were only trying to help and I'd lashed out at them, again and again and again.

But the pain from my past always surged forward when they were in the room and it was like I was reliving it all again. Something lanced down my back like red-hot blades cutting into my skin. Then I heard the deafening screams. I couldn't remember whose they were, but my Father Eli suggested the screams were the people of my village as they burned under the devil's thumb. Every time he spoke to me about it, I would find a new way to act out.

I began biting.

So they began binding me. They found new different to do it every time until my sessions at the asylum had me buckled into a jacket, a leather strap across my mouth. I thought it was humiliating for a short while and then my soul began to die.

And dead people could not be humiliated.

I did not speak. I did not eat.

So they forced the food down my throat with tubes, my ankles and wrists strapped to an uncomfortable chair so I could not thrash.

I wanted to die.

But they kept me alive.

They cared...

My throat burned every day. The tubes scratched the sensitive insides and each morning my esophagus was on fire. So I began eating again to save myself from that agony. Soup at first. And then soggy oats and bread.

And back to Father Eli I went. I found it strange that I did so little talking in our sessions and he barely asked me to. I suppose it was because he was trying to help me and I didn't have much to say outside profanities and insults. I don't know why I hated them all so much. Perhaps because when my soul was dying, I didn't care to save it and they did. They kept me from the sweet oblivion I longed for.

I'd become so empty. They tried to fix my silence and emptiness with methods that only got more extreme. The lines were blurred. Day after day, more of me died, and soon... I didn't care whether or not my heart still beat. I was already gone.

• • •

The numbness I knew so well grew inside me and I felt the world fading away into bitter silence. Looking down, the hems of my golden skirts were soaked with blood. I knew it was blood because I could smell the coppery tang of it in the air. It had never bothered me before. Blood fascinated me. Everyone needed it to survive and yet it was always so eager to leave the body. So vivid against any drab background. Enticing and so uncomfortably beautiful.

My head canted at the realization that everyone around me was dead. Their corpses were spread throughout the large chamber, laid in grotesque, twisted positions like they were marionettes after someone had cut their strings.

My ears were ringing. My heart had slowed so much that I barely knew if it was beating. Perhaps this time I would not find my way out of the void. Perhaps this time it would swallow me whole and I would finally parish the way I longed to so many times.

Figures that it would eat me alive on the only night I had found any enjoyment in a long time. But such was life. An endless struggle. A never-ending race in pursuit of happiness. The illusion that we'd one day win the race was all we had.

But I wasn't so ignorant.

Before I faded, there was a sound. One that led me back from the void into the very real and chilly moment I was standing in. It was a man's voice. A whimper. A fearful one that made me blink. Suddenly I was returned to a place where I could feel. See. Breathe. I slowly looked up and I saw the count with his horrifying mask still clean and polished despite the massacre around me. My breath shuddered out of me when I felt a twinge of fear tease my pulse. A fear that coaxed me back to my body and reminded me I was not empty, spent, and shriveled. I was alive. And, for some reason, I was scared.

Standing in front of the count was Father Eli, his white robes no longer pristine and instead splattered with fresh blood. His mask was on the ground in a puddle of blood along with his wide-brimmed hat. And, like three ghosts from the shadows, the trio of women in black, Naeve, Lura, and Elanor, emerged from behind the count and came to stand on either side of him. One of the count's claw-tipped fingers was pressed under Father Eli's chin, poised against his jugular.

I felt sick. My head was swimming. I had no choice in the matter as my feet stumbled back and I turned on wobbly legs to walk away. Lura appeared in front of me to block my slow and unstable retreat. Her footsteps were soundless. I moved my eyes slowly up to her now unmasked face and she just smiled at me, blood dripping sloppily down her chin and chest. Like a child, she put her hands behind her back and made a *tsk* sound with her tongue.

"You reject the count's gift?" she said.

"What gift?" I said flatly.

She gently placed a hand on my cheek and turned me to look at the count again as he shoved Father Eli to the ground. He fell to his hands and knees, blood making an audible splash beneath his palms. Father Eli let out a shaky cry and cowered on the ground, head tucked in.

The count was pacing, one hand rested behind his back as he raised his other to click his metal claws together in a slow rhythm.

"I don't understand," I muttered.

The count's masked face snapped in my direction and the deepest most haunting chuckle filled the space between us.

"You do not understand?" he said. He gestured toward Father Eli. "He is yours to kill, little bird."

"K—Kill?" I stuttered. "I don't... I can't do that."

Yes, you can.

Something cold slid into my hand. So cold I could feel it through my thin glove. I raised my hand up to find a dagger clutched in my fist. I dropped it to the ground with a clank, taking a step back. Delicate hands caught my shoulders and I heard a woman's voice gently shush me.

Slowly, Elanor circled around to my front, her unblinking eyes so radiantly blue again that they were almost blinding. She was a hand taller than me, her neck swanlike in her feathery collar.

"Perhaps she truly loves these people, my lord," she spoke, looking at me but clearly speaking to the count. Her eyes moved slowly down my body and back up. "So much so that she's forgotten."

Without any idea what that meant, I glanced over Elanor's shoulder at the count. I could see his broad chest heaving with tense breaths. Whether it was disappointment, anger, or something else was beyond me, but it made my whole body rigid. There was an uncomfortable silence that spread across the room, broken momentarily by the wind as it whistled through the stairway leading to the streets of Cragborough. It was disrupted again when Lura inched toward Father Eli with a hesitant step.

"I could finish him for you, my—"

"No," the count hissed.

Lura cowered away, dipping her head as she moved to the side.

What was this? My mind was shattered. I understood nothing and expected to wake from my psychotic episode at any moment, but I didn't.

"Take him to Ferrothorn," the count said more calmly. "He'll serve a purpose yet."

"We should just kill him now," Elanor said.

The count gave her one elongated look and she and the others complied.

Naeve bowed her head and then, before my eyes, disappeared into misty shadows. Those shadows spread like smoke until Father Eli disappeared within them as well. I expected the shadows to fade and reveal an empty space like a magic trick, but they remained and only continued to spread.

"Shall I fetch the other, my lord?" Elanor said, her voice deep and monotone.

The count ignored her, slowly advancing in my direction. I felt rooted in place. My feet were sewn to the ground, weighted and trapped. Elanor slipped into the growing shadows as they began to consume each corner of the catacombs. I watched the count getting closer and gripped my skirts in my fists, trying to breathe.

Perhaps I was still napping beside Ellee and this was all a nightmare.

But I knew better than to truly believe that...

Without any words, Lura disappeared into the darkness next. Slowly, the shadows ate everything and left the count and me in complete and utter darkness. Silence surrounded us and the wind had faded. I couldn't say I was cold or warm. I was simply in between. The count took one last step until he was half a stride away and I could smell the warm scent of cloves and leather. Both of his hands were rested behind his back like a true gentleman and I thought perhaps he would be one for a brief moment.

But then I remembered the bodies around us, all dressed in their Allhalloween garments covered in blood. I could no longer see them, but they were there. I looked up into the black elk mask. Then, one hand slowly slipped from behind his back and lifted in front of me. I kept staring into the black eyes as his fingers gripped the bottom of my mask. He hesitated briefly and then began to lift it, pulling it off my face.

It felt strange to be free of the mask I'd been wearing for hours, especially when such a mysterious man was the first to look upon me. He paused and then tilted his head to one side, dropping the mask to the ground and into the devouring shadows. My eyes stung and I realized I hadn't blinked in a long while. When I finally did, they only stung more, bringing tears to my eyes and blurring my vision.

Gently, the count raised both hands between us and he removed one of his gloves, revealing a pale, moon-white hand. My heart began to race as he used that hand to stroke his fingers lightly across one cheek.

That light touch consumed me.

His fingers sent a ripple of heat across my body. One that burst through my veins and circled back to consume my heart with fire. I swallowed and when I did, his thumb brushed down my throat and trailed over the necklace he'd placed on my neck earlier that night.

With one hand still resting against me, half on my neck and half on my chest, the count used his other to cup his mask. My pulse fluttered again as he lifted the elk skull away.

But he looked no more human without it.

I was not staring at the face of a man. Men did not look like the count. The count's face was chiseled and strong. Sharp cheekbones and a square jaw with the subtlest dimple made him look like a mythical illustration. Almond-shaped eyes with an exaggerated slant looked down at me, bluer than I thought blue could be with a pale center that almost seemed to glow. And his ears, both with a slight point at the top, were adorned with silver chains and cuffs.

A breath quivered out of me at the sight of him. There was no way that he was real. My thoughts were overwhelmed at the sight of him and the phantom pain on my back responded as if I was physically agitated by his presence.

I had to know.

Without thinking, my hand slowly lifted, my fingers reaching for his face. The count watched me but abruptly caught my wrist before I could make contact. I gasped softly before he pinched the fingertips of my glove with his other hand and slowly pulled the fabric off my arm. I took a deep breath, filling my lungs with his scent as my hand met the air. Then... he released me, allowing me to continue. So I did.

I gradually stretched forward, my fingertips meeting his cheek. He was warm. Soft. He was *real*.

Why was he real?

And then those words whispered back at me with warning.

He will find you.

He will kill you.

He will destroy you.

I snapped my hand back and the count caught it, anger washing over his once handsome face. His eyes lit up with blue fire and I felt a familiar shock course through my body. One that was telling me to run. To hide. To do anything I could to get away. But the count held my wrist with one hand and cupped his hand around the back of my neck with the other, his lip peeling back to reveal sharp fangs.

"No, little bird," he hissed. "You do not get to flee. Not again."

"Who are you?" I asked, blinking away the blur in my eyes just to feel a tear slide down my cheek, hot as fire.

"I told you. I am your madness, Briar. And you are *absolutely* mine."

10

BRIAR

Memories were a funny thing. They were the past. Answers. A way of recalling your life, bad and good. A way to learn lessons and to keep from repeating the same mistakes twice. But all mine ever did was flee into the deep, impenetrable recesses of my thoughts and they were doing it again. All I remembered was blackness. Dancing shadows that swirled like smoke, alive and conscious as they surrounded us, and the bodies that littered the ground.

Us.

The count and me.

He was there, dressed in his elegant coat. After he took off his mask, everything felt different. The air itself was thicker. My whole body trembled with a strange, horrifying warning.

I am your madness. And you are absolutely mine.

As those words repeated in my head, my eyes peeled open. I didn't remember going to sleep.

I stilled for a long moment to let my vision adjust and found a canopy above me made of purplish-black silk. Squinting, I could see tiny gems embedded in the fabric like stars and could almost smile at the beauty of it if I wasn't so confused. Slowly, I lifted onto my elbows to find that I wasn't injured. I'd woken many times to terrible stiffness, sore muscles, and sickness when I was at Southminster and did not fancy the idea of repeating that, so I was glad to feel refreshed.

When I scanned the room I was in, I knew I wasn't back in an asylum. Asylums had white walls, tiny mattresses indented with the memories of the many others who slept in them, stains on the floors, and no furniture, sharp edges, or unbarred windows. This place was elegant and surreal with hanging lights that looked like upside-down tulips with fireflies in the middle. There was a fireplace that looked as if it was made of crystal, which mirrored the firelight into the room in beautiful flickering rainbow patterns. But somehow, the room still appeared dark and ominous. It smelled of rain and crushed orange peel, a smell I didn't know I liked until that moment.

To my left, across the big room, were double glass doors with silver, swirling patterns throughout, and outside that glass barrier was a cloudless, moonlit night.

I swung my legs over the edge of the mattress, realizing that I was wearing a thin silk dress with colors that seemed to change at different angles of light.

I didn't even know fabric could be that way…

I half expected to have trouble standing. At Southminster, if I was particularly rowdy, I was forced into sleep and was moved to my "special" chamber. Every time I woke from such an instance, I was plagued with terrible headaches, dizziness, and a foggy mind. When I stood off the bed, I had none of those symptoms.

So where was I and how did I get there?

Perhaps Lucien found me in a mad stupor and escorted me somewhere.

No, nothing in Aedon Heights looked anything like the enchanting chamber I was in. Lucien's manor was drab, dull, and smelled of soap and musty fabric.

Barefoot, I walked to the glass doors and carefully wrapped my fingers around the coiling silver handles.

Locked.

I turned around and glimpsed a tall, maroon door across the room, the wood of which was carved into the image of a lion. I strolled toward it, noticing the plush fur rug under my feet. Whatever the creature was that had provided the pelt was giant. Big enough to cover most of the floor in the room, but without a head, I couldn't even guess what it had been before it was a fancy rug.

My black dress tied at my waist and fell comfortably loose from there with a slight train. The sleeves were fitted all the way down and flared at the wrists. Intricate little silver buttons were sewn up the forearm and a "v" plunged to the top of my breasts. Around my neck was the same necklace the count had given me at the masquerade. I fingered it with surprise when I reached the door, pausing for a moment before grabbing hold of the knob and pulling.

The door opened with a sorrowful moan and let in a light gust of fresh, flowery scents. My hair lifted off my neck at the breeze and I sucked in a breath, chilled. Peering out, I saw a wide hallway with a deep blue carpet extending in both directions. The walls were lined with more tulip-shaped lights, giving the passage a strange, ethereal glow.

I stood in the doorway for a moment, listening and soaking in my new surroundings. There were doors in both directions, all of them different and all of them equally stunning. I stepped hesitantly out of the room and chose a direction, walking so silently that I wondered if my feet were hitting the ground. When I came to a silver railing, I realized I'd found stairs.

Stairs were good.

I looked down the wide steps to see that they curved toward a vast foyer. The ground was black marble with silver inlaid into it like thin veins of ice. There were crystal columns spiraling upward all the way to a domed glass ceiling that gave me a perfect view of the moon, only it looked so much bigger and closer than I'd ever seen it before.

Before I was too distracted, I started to descend the steps. At that point, it was most likely that I was inside some crazed dream, but dreams could be interesting. So long as they didn't take a mad turn into something sinister and horrid.

When I reached the bottom of the steps, I was in awe of the walls. They were covered in vines and on the vines were purple flowers with starbursts of white in the middle. I stopped, immediately inching toward the flowers as if they weren't real. If I was in a dream, then they weren't.

I needed to touch one.

I reached out, my finger brushing over the velvety petals of the biggest one. I snapped back when I realized I could feel it. It was cool to the touch and soft.

"This is real," I whispered to myself.

Turning, I saw an archway leading into another section of what I was beginning to think was a palace. The light from that passage danced across the glossy marble in orange and golden hues, a stark contrast from the black and silver of the foyer I was in. I ventured toward it, enthralled.

From that golden room came the scent of sunlight and warm grass. I crossed the threshold into a massive chamber with a ceiling three stories high and blazing with moving light as if a fire had been captured behind glass and was raging silently above. I expected I'd feel hot, but the room was cool and dry, strings of lights weaving up the walls like climbing vines. It was so bizarre and magnificent.

At the other side of the long, golden room was a massive globe. I walked toward it across a floor so shiny that the ceiling seemed to dance on its surface. When I came to the globe, it was twice as tall as I was on a swirling copper stand, and inside, light and designs were moving as if alive. The strange, fiery glimmer was singing. It was faint, but there was a slight hum coming from the glowing orb and I couldn't help reaching out to touch it like I had the flower.

My fingers were mere inches from it when a voice cut through the silence.

"I wouldn't," it said.

I spun around to see the count.

Only he wasn't the count. Under the amber light of the strange ceiling, he was more menacing. Taller, perhaps. Or maybe it was because I wasn't wearing my heels. His skin reflected whatever light he stood under and accentuated the shadows of his chiseled face. He had on a blue robe and beneath his robe was nothing but his bare chest, tattooed with glowing, iridescent designs in thin, swirling lines. They crept down his chest and plunged into his low-hanging leather pants, drawing my eyes downward.

I was far too used to being unimportant in the presence of people more powerful than me, so when his form strode my way, I stood my ground, locking my fingers loosely in front of me like I would if I were greeting Lucien's important guests.

But even with my experience bottling up my emotions and reactions, the count made it difficult to remain composed.

I was definitely dreaming…

When he was only a few steps away, he stopped, lifting his chin as if he were a nobleman looking down on a servant. His eyes were like glass marbles, the light of the globe reflecting off of them like a storm.

"The power of a sun is contained in that globe," he said. "And it can burn you where you stand."

I swallowed, completely oblivious to his meaning. How could the sun be contained? I had no idea what to say to him, either. I had so many questions and yet none of them made it to my lips. He cocked his head, watching me too closely. He lifted his hand a little as if he was going to reach out and touch me again, but he stopped. His stern expression gave away so little about what he was thinking until his brows twitched. He was... sad.

But the flash of expression was so subtle and so brief that I was forced to dismiss it entirely. He drew back his hand and cleared his throat. His gaze dropped momentarily to my neck where I still wore the necklace he'd given me. I hadn't thought to take it off. I loved it too much.

No one had ever given me anything I actually wanted before. No one had paid attention enough to even know what I liked.

Realizing I wasn't going to speak, he sighed, dropping his hand back at his side. He was exasperated, but if my suspicions were correct, he kidnapped me. Why would he be frustrated about that?

Spinning on his heels, the count began walking briskly out of the long room, his robe flaring out behind him.

"Follow me," he demanded.

He was rude. But I was no stranger to rude men or doing what I was told. I started after him, confused, a little afraid, and entirely entranced by everything. When I was able to pull my thoughts together, I watched the count walking ahead of me and wondered what he was. *Who* he was. Why did he want me and how the hell did he get me? I wished I could remember something for once.

We kept moving through other equally enchanting passages, which gave me a better idea of how giant the place was.

Sometimes, I found my steps slowing just so I could take in the sights, but when I realized the count was getting further away, I jogged to catch up. The toe of my foot caught the edge of his robe and he hissed, spinning around to face me. It was so abrupt that I almost crashed into him and had to rear back to avoid doing so. The count's nostrils flared, his blue eyes piercing as he towered over me.

I wasn't the cowering type. I never had been. Even when Father Eli finally declared me tame, I never curled into a ball or whimpered in a corner. I simply went quiet and still. I wasn't sure it could be considered defiance. Acceptance of what might come, perhaps. And that moment was no different. I stared up at the count's irritated gaze and forced steel into my spine, hands firmly by my sides.

We became locked in a sudden and heated stare for a moment before his eyes slowly softened, gradually tracing over the rest of my face like he didn't think I was real either.

Strange.

"I'm sorry," I muttered.

That flash of sadness washed across his gaze again but he swallowed it down, replacing it with a stony hardness that made his jaw clench.

"Come," he said, turning around to keep going.

"Where are we going?" I asked. "Where are we? How'd I get here?" I stopped for a breath, wondering if Lucien would be looking for me, but the sight of the count's pointed ears and strange eyes distracted me. "*What* are you?"

We came to a tall set of double doors. The count pushed one open with one hand, but I could tell by the way it moved that it weighed a lot. I slipped into the room behind him to see a long table made of frosted glass. On it was a feast of foods unlike anything I'd ever seen. Crystal cups of water sat at two place settings while glasses filled to the brim with dark red liquid sat at another three. At those settings were three familiar women dressed in black.

Naeve, Lura, and Elanor lounged in blue cushioned chairs picking at small, red fruits with their sharp teeth. I was almost relieved to see them, but then again, they were as much strangers as the count was. And if I remembered correctly at all, they slaughtered everyone from the masquerade right in front of me. I recalled the smell and the blood staining the hem of my gown.

No wonder someone changed me...

The count sat himself in an oversized seat at the head of the table and when I looked around, I found only one more place left to sit and it was across from him. I walked over and I slipped into place in front of a plate filled with fruits I'd never seen and hot, buttered toast with jam on the side. Only then did I realize how starving I was.

Suspicious, I looked up at the three women, who all watched me with fixed stares. Elanor was the only one who never seemed to give away any sense of what she was thinking. Her face was straight and unreadable, but her eyes were sharp.

The count sat back lazily and twirled a grape between his fingers, his eyes on the table in front of him as if he were in deep thought. Reaching out, I took one of the bite-sized fruits and popped it into my mouth, chewing carefully.

The fruit was tangy and sweet like a tiny orange, but it wasn't an orange. The whole time I was chewing, Elanor's eyes felt like needles on me.

"Are you certain, my lord, that it was a good idea to bring her here?" she said.

Naeve and Lura whipped their heads toward her like they were surprised to hear her speak. The count, however, said and did nothing. He had one of his knives upright with the tip of the blade on the table while he slowly spun the handle with his fingertips.

"It was a mistake," I said. Everyone's eyes came for me at that moment, even the count's, and I felt like I was being crushed by them. "You don't understand. I'm not stable around others. This was surely a misunderstanding."

Lura let out a childish giggle. "She is not what I expected."

"What did you expect?" I asked.

"Nothing," Elanor cut in. Finally, she turned her eyes to the count, raising her sharp chin. "We should put her in—"

"Silence, Elanor," he said, his voice tense but quiet.

"Yes," Naeve said. "Silence. You're scaring the poor girl, I'm sure." She looked at me, a too-sweet smile on her rouge lips. "Eat. You're too thin. A body like that won't survive here for long."

Lura let out another girlish laugh.

"I'm sorry... where am I?" I asked.

"You're at Farrothorn," Naeve said.

"Enough, Naeve," the count said. "She knows perfectly well where she is. Do not treat her as if she doesn't."

"I'm not sure she does, my lord."

Her brows creased with confusion. She must have caught the blatant shock on my face. I most certainly did not know where I was.

Or maybe I did... but I could not remember.

So many memories were lost to whatever horrors I faced before Southminster and perhaps more were lost in the asylum itself. I was an incomplete puzzle, half my life missing in the depths of some trauma-based amnesia. I was miles past frustration. Not knowing had been the biggest constant in my life.

That didn't make it less jarring to be told I knew something I didn't. Panic was creeping up on me. I couldn't know these people or this place. There was no way.

"Where is Lucien?" I asked, suddenly feeling like I needed him there to ground me.

He takes care of me.

You've longed to be free of him. Don't lie.

My heart started to beat a little faster, confusion gripping me too tightly. Its claws were deep and I needed someone to tell me what to do. What to think.

You can't think for yourself. You're too broken.

The count's eyes snapped toward me at the sound of Lucien's name. Even from across the table, I could see his pupils shrink like he was a predator fixed on a wounded animal. My breath caught in my throat. I felt his stare like an arrow to my chest.

"You dare speak his name in my presence," he said.

The three women's faces stilled and the whole room suddenly felt colder.

I needed Lucien.

"Please," I muttered. "He'll know what to do. I'm not equipped to have this conversation."

"Not equipped?" He spit the syllables with disdain.

"I mean… I am unwell. I shouldn't be here."

And that was all it took.

I had tipped the scale and not in my favor.

"Get out," the count said.

"My lord," Elanor interceded, her voice careful and low as if any other tone would get her killed.

"Get out!"

~ The Devil in Blue ~

BRIAR

The whole room vibrated with the count's rage as he stood, knocking his heavy chair back so hard it toppled to the ground. Naeve and Lura whined and darted from their chairs, their bodies bursting into puffs of swirling black smoke. From the smoke appeared two ravens, their wings flapping frantically to pull from the table as fast as they could. Elanor was the last to move away, but her face was stern and defiant. She didn't like being scared off, but she surrendered just like the other two, her body shrieking into coiling shadows and reforming into a raven so she could leave.

I was gripping the wooden arms of my chair with white-knuckled force. When the women disappeared through a small, round window high above the dining room, I turned back to look at the count. He stood at the head of the table, staring down at me with eyes bright as moonlit snow.

My heart stopped for a breath and I felt my body shiver with unease. Not because I feared death. I stopped fearing death a long time ago. I was stricken with a sense that I was lost, aimlessly wandering. And that was the worst feeling.

"I don't know what's going on," I muttered shakily. "But I'm sure Lucien has answers for—"

The name triggered something in the count once more. He tilted his head like he was hearing something high-pitched and uncomfortable. Then he gripped the edge of the table with both hands and tossed the whole thing to the side as if it was not made of thick glass and piled with plates and candles. I jumped from my seat as the table and all its contents flew across the room, crashing into the wall. Plates shattered. Food soiled the marble.

My spine went painfully rigid when I turned to look at the count again to see two giant black wings unfold from behind him. They nearly spanned the width of the dining hall. Iridescent onyx feathers blocked out the light of the hallway and were tipped with a talon as large as my hand on each peak.

With one beat of his wings, he was on me. His hand coiled around my throat and he shoved me backward, kicking my chair to the side with his foot. I clawed at his wrist as he forced me against the wall. My blood turned to ice. I was pinned between a marble barrier and a winged demon. I hadn't felt so helpless in a long time, but the feeling was all too familiar. Waves of anxiety rippled through me at the sudden vision of being restrained, gagged, and fed words that I didn't understand. And though the count wasn't quite cutting off my air, I still felt like I was suffocating.

"Stop with this act, Briar," he hissed, showing me his sharp fangs as he spoke. "These lies. You are a witch. A fraud. A deceptive cunt. A traitor." He squeezed a little tighter, pressing his body into mine. "Did you think I wouldn't find you? Did you think you were safe in that little town? From *me*?"

It was making sense now.

"I will end you before I let you tear me in half the way you did when you left!"

His grip was unyielding and I was helpless against it. If he wanted to, he could twist his wrist and snap my neck. The words he was saying made me wish for it, in a way. He was saying things I was supposed to know. A past I was supposed to remember. It was all anyone had ever done.

"You're him," I forced through my lips. "The one they told me about. The one who will destroy me."

Tears stung my eyes and suddenly he was squeezing too tight. I couldn't breathe. I wanted to welcome it, but my damn body had other plans. My body didn't want to die and I began to writhe, kicking my legs and tugging at his fingers, scratching my own skin with my nails just to pry him off of me. I needed air.

When darkness started to come, he released me. I sucked in a painful breath, collapsing onto my hands and knees. Rubbing my throat, I came to terms with what I'd just realized. This man—this count—was the thing they'd all warned me about. The one who helped slaughter the family my mind could not even do me the courtesy of remembering. He was real.

Slowly, I found his boots standing in front of me and panned up to see his face staring down at me. His wings were folded back, but he was no less menacing.

"I *will* destroy you," he said. "For you have destroyed me. *You*, a flame, and I, a moth, and you have burned me." He slowly crouched in front of me and instinct forced my head down like a submissive dog. Reaching out, he snatched the necklace from my neck and crushed it in his fist, letting the pieces shatter to the ground like dust. "I would have burned the whole world for you. But now I might burn it because of you."

Staring at the pieces of the necklace, something in me cracked. I tilted my head at the multicolored mess of broken crystals and twisted metal.

I wanted that necklace. I loved it. I'd chosen it and he'd given it to me. Lucien had never given me anything of my choosing. He never cared to ask. Seeing that trinket broken on the floor tore my tired heart to pieces and I couldn't begin to understand why. It was only a thing...

I hadn't lashed out in anger in so long. Like an alcoholic resisting wine, I had resisted letting my emotions free. It had only ever served to condemn me. How easy it was to submit to the anger and pain and despair that once made me. Southminster had leached that part of me away... but not entirely. The bore of Lucien's company and the drab style of his house had tempered the need to explode.

But the count had the opposite effect. His ramblings of another past I didn't know twisted me inside. I was shattering like that little moth made of jewels.

"Why would you do that?" I muttered, sweeping my hands over the twisted pieces of jewelry.

A shard of metal sliced into my finger and immediately it bled, adding crimson droplets to the mess. I didn't care. Physical pain was a feeling at least. One I'd used many times in the past to distract from the other kinds of pain. The pain of not knowing.

"It was a gift," I said, my vision blurring.

Tears filled my eyes and dripped into the blood. Brows furrowed, I looked at the odd combination and accepted that it was all me. Blood, broken pieces, and tears.

The count stood, his leather boots stressing as he moved.

"You don't even like necklaces," he scoffed. "You hate anything around your neck."

He turned to walk away and fury ran its cold hands down my face, stealing my self-control. I jumped to my feet, the frustration I felt at Southminster coming at me like a flood full of debris. The rage I'd bottled up around Lucien thrust itself forth and only made it all worse. It knocked me one way and then the other, making me feel unstable and out of control and lost in my ire. I bolted toward the count, nails out. I was going to jump on his back, but he spun to face me. I slapped and punched and wildly tried to beat him only to feel his hands around my slender wrists, holding me at bay.

"That was mine!" I screamed. "You gave it to me! It was mine and I loved it!"

In all my struggling, I managed to swipe his face with my hand, smearing blood across his cheek. His eyes burned with irritation and he knocked me back with both hands. I stumbled, tripping on the hem of my dress. Reaching out, the count grabbed the front of my dress and I thrashed to pull free.

"Let me go!" I screamed.

I was a young woman in that asylum again. I felt trapped behind a tight jacket, arms folded uncomfortably. My throat burned at the memory of food being forced into my stomach when I just wanted to starve.

They cared. They were helping me.

No, they tricked me into believing I wanted to live.

They loved me.

Tears stung my eyes and my whole body ached with fatigue and hot anger and sorrow all at once.

I was trapped in a prison of bones and flesh.

I jerked backward and felt the thin material of my dress rip. Something gave and I toppled onto the floor, my head slamming on the hard marble. I didn't even feel the pain before darkness took hold, plunging me into nothingness. With any luck, that was the end of it. No more wondering. No more fighting. No more rage and confusion and helplessness. No more pretending.

RUNE

The giant crystal sculpture in the greenhouse toppled over with the force of my swing and shattered on the tile floor into a thousand blue pieces. Pacing, I balled my hands into tight fists, my fingers itching to be around her neck again but also stinging at the fact that I'd done it at all.

Briar.

The name that made my blood boil and my cock stiffen. The one who made my heart whole and then ripped it in two. My salvation turned madness.

I'd lost my temper in the dining hall. I didn't intend to, but I also didn't intend to bring Briar to Ferrothorn. My aim was to find her, remind her of her slights against me, and kill her all in the same night. Instead, when I heard her voice, my resolve turned to ash in my hands and I couldn't do it. K

Weak. I was weak. It only proved how much power she had over me, the witch. The conniving, selfish witch. She deserved to suffer and yet when I saw those tears in her eyes when her necklace was shattered, my heart split in two all over again. The pain that lanced through my chest when I saw her weep over a mere trinket thrust me back fifteen years to a different time. A time that wasn't so tainted by betrayal and hate.

Why? It was a necklace. A bobble with no real value. The gems were not even real. They were simply specks of colored glass. And yet she looked so broken.

And it killed me.

"My king," a voice said, calm and collected.

She was always calm and collected, my Elanor. The ice to my fire, especially since Briar had left. I spun to find her at the entrance to the greenhouse, hands neatly clasped in front of her. No amount of rage and destruction deterred my oldest raven. She knew me inside and out and was surprised by nothing.

As it should have been. I had done well with her.

"She will live," Elanor said. "It was only a cut to the back of her head, but the skull is intact."

"I am better than that," I hissed, scrubbing my face with my hands. "For her mere presence to send me into a rage like that... she remains to have this control over me after all these years. It's sickening."

"It was to be expected. We all thought she was dead."

"To see her with that man," I ground out, seeing that baron's sour, aging face in my head. "To see her living in luxury as a mortal. She chose him over me." Turning, I drove my fist down onto a long, glass table and watched a web of cracks burst out in all directions. "What could he have possibly given her that was better than all that we had together?"

"Mortals are fickle," she said coldly. "They are constantly seeking more no matter how much they have. She was seduced by it, as I said she would be. Even souls wiped clean of their previous lives in the Labyrinth remain the base characters they were before. And she's proven that. She must have been selfish in life."

"She was better than that," I sighed, feeling defeated. "I *thought* she was better than that. But to rip me open with words scribbled on paper rather than facing me herself... it's unforgivable. If she'd have come to me, I would have... I gave her everything. And for fifteen years, she's been masquerading as a rich noble."

There was a stretch of silence in the greenhouse, allowing the faint howl of the wind outside to sing around us. I took a deep breath, letting the herbs and floral scents soothe my burning lungs.

"Then what do you plan to do with her? Forgive me, but if her presence torments you so much, then it should be obvious what your next step should be."

"Should it be, Elanor?" I said with a glare, daring her to elaborate. "Because nothing about this seems obvious."

"You've never let anyone live who's wronged you, my king. And she's wronged you more than anyone."

"I thought it was simple, but it is not."

"I can feel you, Rune. You forget that. I am closer to you than anyone and I feel the pain. I have felt it all these years and it was forgotten for a time until you saw her again. Relieve yourself of her, once and for all."

"There is more to this, Elanor," I barked.

"She is playing a game and you are falling into her web. Do not make me follow you into that poisonous trap again because you know that if you tangle your limbs in her silk, I will have to follow. If you are too warm to her deceptions, I will do it for you. You simply have to ask. I will do *anything* for you."

I spun to face her, my hand jutting out to grasp her chin. Elanor, of all my ravens, never flinched at my violence. She never shed a tear or yelped with dread. She didn't even unclasp her hands from in front of her and in turn, I didn't drive her back against the glass wall. I held her there, fingers biting into her cheeks.

"If it is a game she's playing, then I will play," I snarled. "And if I fall into her web, you *will* follow because it is the reason I made you. Do not assume you have a choice."

Teeth clenched, she stared up at me. "Yes, my king. Always."

A twinge of guilt stabbed my soul but I swallowed it down. I didn't have time to battle my own ravens when I had finally found Briar. I was having enough of a struggle when it came to her. Years of thinking I would never see her again. Years of searching. Of suspecting she'd taken my gifts, my love, and my soul with her to the human realm. She lied to me. She used me and she abandoned me. Elanor should have known better than to poke a beast who was already rabid and I was practically foaming at the mouth.

I released Elanor and stepped away.

"She pretends not to know me," I said, gaining control of myself. "I want to know what she's playing at. So alive she will remain until I know more. Neither you nor anyone else at Ferrothorn will touch her. understand?"

"Of course," she inclined her head. "And the prisoner?"

The mere mention of him made me have to stretch my tense neck from side to side with a groan. "Get what you can out of him. I know you still know how. And I know you will enjoy it. Just tell me when he breaks. I want to be there to see it."

"And the other one? The baron?"

My nose twitched at the mention of him. So much murderous energy was flowing through me, but I needed to be patient. I could not crack under the pressure. If I did, then I had no right to call myself the King of the Glyn.

"Leave him for now," I said. "I will pay him a visit when the time calls for it. I have a week to do so before the veil falls again.

Until then…" I turned to peer up at the palace through the glass walls of the greenhouse. "Briar will be my focus. I need answers."

"Your focus," Elanor sighed quietly. "What a dangerous place to be."

"Indeed."

"And how will you get answers? She fears you now. Her tears said as much."

"As she should. I want her to fear me. But I know there is someone else she will not fear. Someone she has yet to meet."

I felt so much pain when I finally opened my eyes again and not because I'd bashed my head on the marble floor. No, this pain was different and it was the kind I hadn't felt in years. A debilitating sensation like I'd lost something important. Like I was missing something. Like someone without an arm still felt the ache where that limb once was, I felt the agony of something that was ripped away from me.

And I couldn't remember what it was.

Father Eli always told me it was better not to remember. To experience such horrors is a curse. To forget them is a blessing. He would tell me those things every day and it kept me from even trying to uncover a past that had destroyed me. But after I woke up in the count's palace, those phantom wounds were opening up again and I didn't even know what they were from.

I felt myself slipping into the madness that had gotten me locked inside Southminster in the first place. Without Lucien to keep me sealed out of those memories, I felt the madness stalking me again. And I would fall to it eventually. I knew I would. I already started. I remembered attacking the count and it sickened me. That rage had boiled over so fast and without warning and I'd given into the violent urges that had always been festering in me. If left unchecked, they always told me it would hurt people. Perhaps even kill them.

That wouldn't be such a bad thing...

But the count had broken something I loved. Something that was mine. The necklace.

It was a stupid trinket and one he gifted me. I shouldn't have loved it so much when it was given by a man who very clearly hated me for reasons I couldn't fathom... but I did. Tears stung my eyes when I remembered it shattered on the floor, ripped from me like everything else in my life.

I was staring up at the canopy above me when I heard the heavy door click. I rose up on my elbows to see a man enter my room. I thought it might be the count for a moment, but he held himself differently. Tall with a similar build, the man slid into my chamber with a small tray in one hand. He was humming something that I could hardly hear, but I could tell it was a gentle, soothing melody. A lullaby, perhaps. He wore leather pants with brown boots and a copper-colored tunic hung to his thighs, cinched with a leather belt that wrapped twice around his slender waist.

But the thing that caught my eye the most was the metal mask that covered his face. It looked old and was littered with scrapes and chips, the designs on one side misshapen from what I assumed was years of use. Shaggy black hair was tied into a low ponytail with loose strands framing his covered features.

When the man saw me, he stopped humming and nearly dropped his tray. A dish of food slid to one side and he barely caught it before it fell.

"You're awake," he said.

"Yes," I said.

The stranger walked briskly to my bedside and set the tray down on the nightstand. I saw a bowl of porridge, some toast, and a wooden cup of tea that smelled like citrus and honey.

"Are you in pain?" he asked, reaching out toward my head.

I recoiled, feeling cautious, and scooted across the mattress. Standing, I found a small, round mirror on the wall and approached it, seeing myself for the first time in days. My hair was loose around my face. Without Catlyn to braid it every morning, it was a bit of a mess. My hair had always been a bit untamed with a mix of waves and curls that got tangled easily. But I didn't mind it. I hadn't truly looked at my hair in its natural state in years. Light brown eyes with red tones stared back at me, dull and underlined in tired shadows.

There was a soreness on the back of my skull that made me wince as soon as I started combing my fingers through my curls. I hissed and prodded the stinging bump.

"You should let me check your head," the man said.

But his voice felt distant. Looking down at myself, I noticed I was wearing a new dress. One made with green silk in layers of flowing fabric. The neckline was low enough for me to see the bare spot on my chest where the moth necklace had once been. Such a little thing and I'd grown so attached overnight.

Pathetic.

I brushed the naked skin there and slowly turned to look at my visitor.

"Who are you?"

"My name is Petris, my lady."

"I'm no lady," I said softly, stroking my neck with the tips of my fingers.

"All the same, I've been assigned to serve you."

"Why?"

He hesitated, his shrouded eyes wandering. "I suppose the lord of the castle thinks his presence would disturb you."

He wasn't wrong. But why would he care?

"He tried to kill me," I whispered, looking at my gaunt face in the mirror again.

"Pardon me. I don't think that was his intention."

"He crushed my necklace."

I was mostly speaking to myself, but Petris seemed to hear everything and I could feel him inching closer.

"Rune can let his anger get the best of him sometimes."

I turned to look at him when I heard his name. "Rune? I thought he was Count Mortis."

"When he needs to be, he is the count. Here, he is Rune. The King of the Glyn."

"The Devil in Blue," I muttered.

"To some." There was a long pause. I was still absently touching my neck, my other arm crossed under my breasts to cradle myself. "Briar is your name, yes?"

"Yes."

"Well, Briar. I'd like it if you ate something. I saw the dining hall. I doubt you ate much last night."

Slowly, I turned around and walked to the bed, sitting on the edge of the mattress near the food. I grabbed a piece of toast first and took a bite. The jam smeared over it was divine. Lucien was never fond of sweet things. The jam was almost overly sweet, teetering on the line between too sour and too sugary, but it was doused by the bread.

Taking another bite, I looked up at Petris. He was standing a few steps away now, hands clasped behind his back. He was just watching me and something in my gut told me why. I was no stranger to being monitored. I casually took another bite of toast.

"He asked you to make sure I ate, didn't he?" I said.

95

Petris cleared his throat uncomfortably. "Yes."

"Why? He expressed nothing but hate last night. Why should he care if I starve to death?"

"I don't want to assume I know what happened, but Rune's anger is often confused for hate."

"Are you defending him because you love him or because he forces you to?"

"I've never been forced to do anything."

Those words sounded true. Firm, like he didn't want me to question them.

I placed the toast on the tray and took the bowl of porridge in my hands, soothed by the lingering warmth on the metal. It smelled like rosemary and garlic. Taking a spoonful into my mouth, I tasted sharp cheddar and herbs on my tongue. It was perfect. So perfect, I felt instantly content. Which was something I was not used to. I almost didn't trust it.

"He said it would be your favorite," Petris said, a hint of sorrow in his words.

"What?"

"The herbs in the porridge. He said you'd like it."

"I do."

"Then you've had it before."

"I..." I couldn't remember. I knew the taste. It was familiar, but I only recalled Lucien having one meal prepared with rosemary and it was otherwise stale and forgettable. I shook my head. "I must have."

Petris canted his head at me.

"What other foods do you like?" he asked. "I can inform the kitchen staff."

I took another bite of porridge and shrugged. "I don't care much for food."

That was a lie. I greatly enjoyed tastes but had yet to explore enough properly to deduce what was my favorite. Aside from chocolate. And evidently, rosemary porridge. Everything else I'd eaten was for the benefit of others, not me.

I polished off half the bowl and moved to the sweet bread again to balance the savory taste. Feeling a little restless, I stood and slowly strolled the room while I ate, all the while side-eying Petris and his strange mask.

"Why do you wear that?" I asked.

His head dipped like the question was uncomfortable. "I just do, my lady."

"Please, don't call me that."

"What should I call you?"

"Briar?"

"Of course. Well... I am hideous beneath this mask, you see. Beastly, I've been told."

"You can't be more hideous than the beast that tore apart the dining room last night."

"You would be surprised. I am a collection of wounds that have disfigured me."

"So he makes you wear the mask?"

"No, on the contrary. My king enjoys the strange and the weird and the horrifying. His kingdom is built on the things the world does not want to see. The mask is for me. Perhaps one day I will remove it, but today, it gives me comfort."

"Why?"

"One can see the world more clearly sometimes when the world can't see them."

I felt myself shiver at those words. Swells of doubt and fear crept up inside me and made my skin cold. The food lost its taste and I set the last bite of toast back down on the tray with the rest of the leftovers, taking the cup of tea and downing the whole thing.

"Forgive me. Did I say something?" Petris asked.

"No," I said, straight-faced and composed. "I'm simply finding my footing."

"Well, I hope I can help. Rune said you'd probably like to dine alone for a while. I'll bring you dinner when it's time. Until then, you're free to roam the castle. Just... don't go where any door is locked."

"How can I if the doors are locked?"

He shrugged. "There are always ways. This place has a mind of its own, you'll find."

He turned to leave, but my tongue got away from me. Petris was easy to talk to and I didn't want him to go. Not yet.

"Wait," I said. "Tell me why I'm here."

He paused, staring at me for a long moment. "I'm not sure it's my place to speak of—"

"Please. I have been passed from one place to another with no control. If you tell me not to ask again, I won't. I'm good at complying, but... the things he said to me. I can't stand them. I need to know."

He hesitated a long while before turning to face me again, sighing softly.

"Rune is the King of the Glyn. You must know what that means. He controls the half-world and sees all the souls that pass through it into the afterlife. It is a taxing existence. One that drove him mad for a time. And a mad King of the Glyn is a dangerous one. He was unhinged... until he fell in love with a mortal. She gave him joy and joy stifled his dark urges. He gave her everything... and she ripped him in half in return."

"I don't understand. What does that have to do with me?"

"The king believes you *are* her."

I stared for a while, waiting for him to tell me he was jesting. When he didn't say anything more, I shook my head.

"No. I'm an orphan. My family was killed in a massacre when I was young. Fae caught in our realm slaughtered everyone I knew and the sisters at Southminster took me in."

"Where did you come from then?"

"Haydenside. My family bred horses. My mother looked just like me. My brother looked like my father. We lived in a small cottage and then... and then..." I couldn't see it. I had never been able to see it. I just knew it. I'd repressed the memories, but over and over, Father Eli told me everything. Told me why I needed help. Why I was a danger to others. I felt a twinge in my chest as I spoke of the horrors, trying to keep calm, but my voice was already shaking. "Half-worlders came and destroyed everything. My home. My family."

"Half-worlders do not venture into the mortal realm without consent from its sovereign. The laws made after the war forbid them. They cannot even cross if it is not the week of Allhalloween," he scoffed.

"Well, that is what happened. They slaughtered many. I escaped, but not without wounds of my own."

"Wounds?"

Father Eli's voice spoke to me and I closed my eyes. He helped me. He helped me put those memories in a box where they became just words instead of violent, terrible visions. I was lucky. He made me hate him in order to lock it all away so I could live. He sacrificed my affection to fix me and I was thankful.

He twisted you up, inside and out.

He saved me. They all did.

"Briar."

My eyes shot open. I knew how close I was to sinking into that dark pit where my memories from Southminster waited for me and Petris had pulled me back. I would have pulled myself out eventually, but he'd saved me the time and discomfort. I looked at the empty shadows that were his mask's eyes and took a long, deep breath.

"I have a past," I whispered. "And it wasn't with your king."

14
BRIAR

Perhaps the king and his castle were all in my head. Perhaps I'd finally broken and fallen victim to my insanity for good. If I was being honest, it was far more interesting to be a prisoner in the madness of Rune's castle than it was to be trapped in the bore that was life at Aedon Heights. It was a stagnant life there.

But I could not forget that Lucien, uninteresting as he was, saved me. Like so many others, he had sacrificed his time and expenses to take care of me. Speaking ill of his company made a knot of guilt form in my stomach. I shook off the feeling, slowly pacing circles in my room. Lucien wasn't fond of letting me take any walks outside unless it was around the groves and well within the walls of his estate. Otherwise, he was always with me and the path was always his, not mine.

But that was for the best when my path had led me so far down dangerous roads before. I was liable to walk right off a cliff just to find out what it felt like to freefall for a few seconds.

Staring out the glass doors to the balcony, I felt a need to spread my wings a little. There was a garden beneath my room and when I opened the now unlocked doors, the floral scent wafted toward me, so pleasing I couldn't help smiling a little. I walked out into the night with a moon so large and so full that it lit up a vast courtyard in a cerulean glow. There were willow trees far in the distance. I saw apple trees filled with white apples. Flowers lined a cobblestone path, the grooves of which were packed with veins of green grass. There were things glowing in the yard, but from the second floor, I couldn't make out what any of it was.

I wanted to see it.

Petris told me I was allowed to go anywhere as long as I didn't walk through any locked doors. Seemed easy enough to avoid.

The air outside was neither cold nor hot, so there was no need for a cloak or a coat. I did, however, need shoes, which I found in a small armoire across from my bed. A pair of black, leather slippers were just my size so I slipped them on and walked out into the hall. I looked both ways as if I'd see guard dogs at my door. There was nothing.

Biting my lip, I started down the hall to the stairs, descending to the first floor. There had to be a door to the outside somewhere and I wanted to find it.

As I passed through the foyer filled with flowers, my lungs flooded with their fresh scent. It triggered something in me. Something comfortable. I could have stayed there for hours just breathing in their cool aromas, but I still wanted fresh air, so I continued searching.

It didn't take long for me to find a pair of giant double doors. The kind of doors. I approached, lifting a hand to grip a thick, glass handle. Pulling, I realized the door was latched and searched for something to free it. I found a long, barred bolt running across it with a teardrop-shaped handle at one end. I took it and slid the latch out of place with all my weight. The loud glide of wood and metal scraping together echoed along the walls and I paused as if someone was going to catch me and tell me I wasn't allowed to leave.

When no one came, I continued toying with the heavy doors, tugging once more on the handle. It started to give, but it weighed so much. There was no way that those heavy things were a main entrance for someone to freely walk in and out. I put my entire body's weight into pulling it ajar and heard the wood moan like the doors hadn't been opened in years. A crisp breeze smelling of rain and flowers wafted toward me.

Winded just from pulling the door open, I kept it cracked just enough for me to fit and slipped through the space into the courtyard. From there, the view was entirely different from the one I had from my balcony.

It was beautiful. Dreamlike.

Though it was night (I thought), the moon was like a drop of sunlight in the sky, shedding enough light for me to see everything. I walked a bit further along the cobblestone path, noticing little lightning bugs fluttering up from the plants growing along the edges. There were white roses on thorny vines that coiled around metal fences. Moss-covered stones were stacked into knee-high walls with tiny bell-shaped flowers tucked into the grooves. And the way the moon touched everything made it all seem to glow. In fact, patches of small mushrooms *were* glowing, growing in circles that varied in size.

I strolled further into the yard, approaching what looked like tall hedges of greenery with arches of vines marking the entrance into a maze. Or perhaps just another part of the courtyard. Either way, I wanted to see what was beyond it, so I ventured forward, catching the sound of running water in the distance. I was almost to it when I heard the sound of a raven squawking behind me. I turned around, scanning the area only to find myself completely captivated by the sight of the palace itself from the outside.

It took my breath away.

Towers and rounded walls made of both glass and metal created a mosaic of sharp and almost violent shapes, creating something so hauntingly beautiful that I hardly believed it was real. It looked like a painting. It reflected the moonlight on its slick surface like water.

And it was massive. It was so much larger than I suspected and I had already suspected it was large from what little I'd explored of the inside.

Panning upward, I caught a glimpse of the third story where the moon's light did not reach. It was odd. There was nothing to obscure the light, but it looked dull in comparison to the rest of the palace. Even the balconies seemed shrouded in darkness like the whole floor was dead.

It seemed strange to refer to a part of the palace as dead, but the way the light danced on some parts and not on others gave it an eerie sense of personality. At any moment, I expected to hear it sigh with contentment. The third story just seemed like a lame limb no one had the heart to sever.

When I heard a faint whisper nearby, I almost thought the palace *had* breathed. I whipped my head around to see the entrance to the maze had suddenly gotten darker. So dark I couldn't see a single thing beyond it. At my feet, a thin fog crept out toward the path I stood on like hands trying to pull free from tar. I wasn't afraid of that darkness. Not in the least. I was curious but a sliver of warning kept me from going toward it. My spine stiffened and I felt a ripple of emotions tickle my senses. Sorrow, grief, frustration, confusion. They tangled inside my head and brought me back to a time when I felt all those things in a constant, mangled loop. I stepped back, unwilling to fall into that endless routine again.

Then again, as the layers of whispers grew louder, I sensed something else within that darkness. Nothing. Absolute nothingness. And nothingness was freedom. I'd often fantasized about nothingness and my foot inched forward thinking about it. A cold chill coated my skin and I listened harder to the strange whispers, trying to make out words.

"What are you doing?" a voice said.

I turned once more to see Elanor standing in the path ten paces away. Her black dress was fitted so perfectly to her slender form. Her long neck was covered with a black, lace collar that crept right up under her sharp chin.

"Petris said I could wander," I said.

"Who?"

"The servant? The man in the mask?"

I almost thought her eyes rolled and I suspected from the smug look on her face that she was not the type to recall the names of servants.

"Of course," she said. "Well, he was not wrong. The king doesn't wish for you to be a prisoner here. Petris should have been clearer, though." Her eyes flitted to the arched entrance past the hedges. "Venturing in there will only get you lost and no one can come out of there unless they find their own way."

"Is it enchanted?"

"Everything here is enchanted. It's the Glyn."

I knew the Glyn was magical, but I never knew what that truly entailed since all I'd ever heard or read about was made out to be mythology and nothing more. I wanted to ask what it meant, but I didn't want to ask Elanor. She reminded me of the sisters at Southminster. Stern, disciplined, and vacant of the tells most people had when they felt any emotions at all. I was certain that happiness and a plot to murder looked the same on her face. People like that did not inspire me to relax.

"Are you not afraid?" she asked.

"Of what?"

"You stand with your back turned to the Labyrinth and you're not even flinching."

The question caught me off guard. I hadn't thought of it. Not that way.

"I don't fear the things people should."

"Why?"

Every question sounded so demanding.

"I don't know," I shrugged. For a moment, I thought of leaving it at that, but my words kept coming. "I believe I'm running out of things to fear."

"There are *always* things to fear."

She stared, analyzing me too deeply. I let her gawk. Weighty as her stare was, she was no different from everyone else.

"Did you come here seeking me?" I asked. "Did the count... did Rune tell you to watch me, too?"

Father Eli always had one of the sisters watching over me at all times. If I was some kind of captive, I suspected Rune would be no different.

"I did not come out here for you," she said flatly.

I furrowed my brows at that until a gust of cool wind hit me in the back, driving a thick cloud of fog toward the path. It enveloped me for a moment and then swirled away. The faint scent of roses and cedar touched my nose and a familiar shudder rolled through me. Turning, I saw the man himself. Rune.

Rune's long, blue hair was braided tightly back, displaying his pointed ears. His black wings were folded behind him.

I almost thought I imagined his wings in the dining hall.

His sapphire eyes fell on me, piercing and cold, and I froze beneath his gaze. He marched forward a couple of steps and stopped, lips slightly parted like he was surprised to see me. Then his gaze lifted to Elanor.

"What's this?" he asked, his deep voice reminding me of the man who'd crushed my necklace, flipped a table, and pinned me to a wall by my throat in a fit of rage.

I swallowed but held my ground, recalling how many times running had not worked in the past.

Running doesn't work when you're surrounded by walls.

"She decided to take a walk," Elanor said. "*Petris* assured her it was allowed."

I looked between Elanor and Rune with subtle turns of my head until both of them fell silent. Then, Elanor glided forward, the short train of her black dress dragging on the stone. She passed me, reaching out and handing Rune a small vial of clear liquid. He uncorked it with his thumb and downed the contents in one gulp before handing it back to her empty.

"You stayed too long this time," Elanor said. "In your current state, lengthy treks can slow you."

"My treks of late have not been long enough," Rune said. "The Labyrinth is far too crowded and their wailing is keeping me up late."

Elanor nodded in agreement. "Shall I prepare your bath?"

Rune's eyes caught mine and I missed a breath when I realized he still knew I was there. I had hoped I was forgotten. I was used to it and as much as I shouldn't have liked it, being forgotten came in handy many times before.

"Yes," he said, still looking at me. "I'll need one. There's far too much filth in my realm these days."

Elanor gave him another nod and spun gracefully, walking away and leaving me alone with him. I bristled at the memory of the dining room and felt my fingers tighten.

Being alone with men stronger than me was not unusual, but Rune was different. His presence alone was stifling and he wasn't even touching me. I lowered my eyes, standing quietly. When he didn't say anything, I thought perhaps he'd leave me to my wanderings in the courtyard.

But he didn't.

He shifted, coming around to my front and facing me. Slowly, I lifted my eyes and met his icy stare.

"You should not wander these grounds alone," he said.

"I was told I could."

"The palace, perhaps. Everything surrounding it is hungry and you wreak of emotions they'd find very addictive."

I had no idea what that meant but it made my pulse jump.

"Then why bring me here?" I said. "This place isn't meant for humans. Living humans, I mean."

"It's not really meant for the dead, either."

"Precisely. I know what the half-world is. It's the place in between." I looked past him toward the misty, dark maze. "Is that place filled with souls?"

His slow nod answered that question. "They will wander for a long time, most of them. Until they either deal with their pain or let it devour them."

"What happens then?"

"Then, they leave through the door they create. There's no telling what's on the other side. Only they know."

I wondered what my door would look like. Would it be built from my pain? Hatred? Hope? I wanted to know so badly that I almost moved toward that dark, ominous maze entrance, but Rune was in my way and something told me he wouldn't let me find out.

"What were you doing in there?" I asked softly.

"Helping."

"But you said souls must do it on their own."

"I don't show them the way. I simply light candles so they can better find it themselves." He sighed heavily. "The maze gets full and the songs of the damned incessant."

I strained to hear what he was talking about and barely even heard whispers.

"I can't hear it," I said.

"Lucky you."

His bored tone drew my interest. I stared at his face, stricken once more by how handsome it was. He barely looked real. He was a painting in a book. A figure in my dreams. But he'd also wounded me.

He was the man I danced with at the masquerade. Even then I sensed something odd about him. Something uncomfortable and overpowering.

"Why did you crush my necklace?" I whispered, uncertain why I'd spoken the question aloud.

Rune tilted his head like he was as confused as I was.

"Why ask such a foolish question when you should be asking more important things?"

"I've already asked you the important questions. You nearly killed me over them."

He blinked like the statement had hit him in the gut. I didn't expect that. I didn't expect to see any hint of regret in him, but I did. For a split second, it darted over his expression and was immediately cut with tension.

"I refuse to believe you don't remember," he muttered. "But it would be too cruel of you to fabricate a lie so powerful that you believe it. And if I wanted you dead, you'd already be in that Labyrinth with the rest of the damned. Again."

"I haven't fabricated anything. I cannot be whoever it is that you think I am."

"Then who are you?"

"I told you."

He stepped forward, invading my space. I wanted to back away, but Lucien had taught me never to shy from his touch and I suppose that lesson was what kept me grounded. I stood firm and let him get close, even if it made my muscles seize.

"You told me lies," he hissed.

"They were not lies." I paused a moment, trying to bite my tongue, but something about Rune made me want to speak up. To challenge his words. "Do I look like her? Is that what this is about?" He hissed and started to pace, scrubbing his face with his hands. "Whoever this woman is that you think I am, do I look like her? Am I being used to fulfill some vengeance? Some fantasy?"

"You look *nothing* like her," he said bitterly, eyeing me with the same disdain I saw in the dining hall. "There's not a single hint of blue in your eyes. There isn't even…"

He trailed off.

I repeated Petris's words in my head about his anger being confused with hate and did my best to see it that way, but his eyes were so disdainful.

"My eyes have always been brown," I said." Like my mother's."

"of course they have," he sighed.

"Then…" I said. "I don't understand."

"I found you, Briar. I found you because I've been searching. To discover you under the thumb of a man—a mortal man—my gifts squandered and spent, was enough to damn me to hell. Humans are greedy. I thought you better than that."

"You speak of Lucien."

"Do not say his name."

"He saved me. Though his needs sometimes were undesirable, he took me in when no one else would. I owe him small bouts of my time at the very least. He saw a sparrow with a broken wing and cared for me when he could have drowned me."

I wish he had sometimes.

"I said don't speak of him," he said through his teeth.

"Why? Does it hurt you so much to hear me speak kindly of the man who pulled me from the brink of my own destruction?" I should have shut up. "Does it pain you so much to even hear another man's name? What have you done to earn my cooperation except separate me from the thing that grounded me in the world and take from me the only gift anyone has ever given me that meant something!"

He turned abruptly and took a long stride toward me, appearing so close I nearly fell backward.

"I loved you!" he roared.

My eyes wide, I stared up into his burning gaze, breathless and at a loss. But those words hit me hard, winding through me like a thread of lightning zapping every nerve.

"I am not the woman you think I am," I forced. "I can't be. I grew up in Haydenside. My family bred horses. My mother looked just like me. My brother looked like my father. We lived—"

Breathing like a dog hungering for a bite, he reached around my head and grabbed a clump of my hair, tugging at the still-sensitive abrasion on the back of my scalp. I winced, but never took my eyes off of him. His other hand slithered down my body to my hip and he gripped me, pulling me flush with him. I planted my hands on his chest, trying to keep some space between us. His heart beat wildly under my palms and filled me with heat.

"You have a scar on your hip," he whispered harshly. "Where is it from?"

I was surprised he knew about the scar at all but tried to reason that it was because whoever changed my clothes had told him.

"I got it when my home was burned. It's a burn scar."

"From what?"

"From the hilt of my father's sword. The house was burning. It was hot and I fell on it."

His angry expression suddenly relaxed and he shook his head, releasing me only to grab my wrist and lead me toward the palace. His hold was harsh and forceful when it didn't need to be. I was complying all the same, but if he needed to take out some anger on me by gripping me that firmly, I would let him to avoid another outburst later.

At least, that was what I convinced myself I was doing.

Rune stormed through the giant double doors, pushing the heavy barrier open with one hand like it weighed nothing, and then dragged me through the foyer and into the very room where that large globe burned with its golden glow. His pace was difficult to keep up with. I stumbled and tripped, every time regaining my balance so I could keep going.

That room was enchanting when I found it initially. Now, it was daunting. The air felt hot and the roof too bright. Rune pulled me with him to what looked like a tall column made of gold that was carved with intricate swirling designs.

"Every Summer Solstice, this room becomes unbearably hot," Rune said. "It tracks the sun and lets me know when the ways are open for me to travel the realms."

I was almost too distracted by the images on the pillar when he spun me around and slammed me into the column. Something protruding from the wall jabbed my lower back and I flinched, sucking in a breath through my teeth just as he planted his hands on either side of my head.

Rune was on me before I could move, his body pressed close to mine and his dark wings spread like a shadowy cage around us. His scent infected me, filling my lungs and melting something deep inside. Something I didn't know was there until that moment. Not fear. Not shock. Excitement, perhaps. Desire.

"Many times, our passion grew nearly as hot," he whispered roughly, his hot breath spanning across my cheeks. "It was your idea." His hand slid down to my hip, pressing me up against the protrusion still poking my back. "To do it here. To see how long it would take before neither of us could stand it."

I couldn't take my eyes off of him. Blue as his eyes were, they seared hotter than embers. He held my gaze for a while and then slowly dropped his eyes to my lips.

Many men had stared at my lips. Usually, because they wanted to use them or they were afraid of the teeth behind them. But the way Rune looked at my mouth made a fire within lick across my cheeks. His fingers kneaded into my hip, pulling me forward until our bodies were touching and I could feel the rapid, storming sound of his heartbeat filling the space around us.

"I put you here," he whispered. "Against this column. On the hottest day. You winced then as you did just now, but by the gods, all it did was feed that passion." He pushed me back again, closing his eyes and speaking against the side of my forehead. "You smiled so wickedly and then you kissed me, hard and deep, and you *begged* me to fuck you."

I should not have closed my eyes, but I did. I could see it. Not because I remembered, but because of the way he spoke and the things he said, they built the moment in my mind as well as any memory would have. My heart was racing. My skin was hot and begging for relief. My ears were ringing and my cheeks were aflame. I didn't even know that I'd moved my hands until I felt the fabric of Rune's tunic in my fists. I wasn't pushing him away, though. I was pulling him closer.

"I took you by your thighs," he said, his hand sinking lower until he was cupping my backside. "And I wrapped your legs around me." His other hand suddenly took a handful of my hair and tugged my head back. His mouth hovered so close to mine and the way I was craning back to look at him sent a shock of pain through my shoulders. Panic teased my senses, but it wasn't the panic I was used to. It was panic over something I feared I wouldn't get. Something I needed. "And I fucked you for hours until your screams had torn your throat raw."

My eyes had been dry, but suddenly they stung with tears. The way he looked down at me, pinned and at his mercy, was so predatory. So feral. So filled with want.

The threat of men forcing themselves on me had never occurred. Southminster was filled with sisters and Father Eli and he never touched me like that. Never expressed the desire. Even Lucien had never forced me. I'd always complied out of gratitude and obligation. He saved me. I was his. I owed him.

This was different. Rune was strong. Otherworldly. The way he was holding me and trapping me there against him made me feel like I was being pierced by hooked chains from all directions.

Those stinging tears left my eyes and I felt the heat of them glide down my cheeks. I was looking at him, but I was seeing past him. I was staring far beyond his blue eyes and gazing into the void where something was waiting to eat me. Where some giant beast was hungering to finally get me and tear me apart. Father Eli kept me from that beast. Then Lucien took on that role.

He will look for you.

He will find you.

He will destroy you.

My madness was the beast. My destruction. The thing they'd all tried to protect me from.

Rune was the beast. *He* was the demon in the dark. My madness.

Upon seeing my tears, all of Rune's aggression was leached away. The harshness in his face softened and he shook his head, slowly releasing me and stepping back. I regarded him with a version of fear I didn't understand. One I hadn't felt in ages.

It was the way I used to look at myself in the mirror.

He could absolutely destroy me and there was a large part of me that wanted to let him. I could see him ripping out my heart and soul because I was completely at his mercy.

Being at my own mercy had never served me well.

Rune took a few slow steps backward, recollecting himself. The further he moved from me, the more confused I felt. I didn't know if I wanted him closer or if I never wanted to see him again. What he made me feel certainly left a mark and I didn't even truly know what it was.

"Passion like that is hard to forget, Briar," he whispered softly, taking a deep breath.

He folded his wings once he was nearly halfway across the room and then turned, marching out the door and leaving me there alone against that golden pillar.

It took me a few breaths to come to my senses again. I was shaking. My whole body felt cold, and not because the room was chilly. The room was quite warm, but something had sucked the heat from my skin. I took a slow step away from the pillar and reached around to the sore spot on my lower back where I'd hit something. Turning, I saw a small, oval handle of some kind engraved with a sun, its rays stretched on two sides.

The handle was the same size. The same shape. The image matched. My heart stopped because it wasn't possible.

I reached out and touched the handle again, hand trembling. It fit perfectly in my palm and as I pulled it, small portions of the pillar flipped open and the light from the globe flooded through, sending shadows in the shapes of elaborate designs across the slick floor. It was beautiful... but it wasn't why I was standing there in shock and puzzlement.

That handle was the very image branded on the back of my hip.

Impossible.

My sanity was such a fragile thing, constantly fighting against a hundred fissures that had been growing bigger over the years. I feared I was about to fall through into whatever hell lay below the breaking glass I was standing on.

So I ran.

I sprinted through the palace, up the steps, and into my room. I closed the door quietly, in the habit of not making noise and attracting attention to myself lest someone throw me into a straitjacket or a dark room. Then I fell onto the bed and pulled the blankets over me, staring up at the canopy.

I knew what it felt like to let my nerves win. To let my mind take me places outside of reality. It was sheer panic. I hated it. I would have rather met the void and that silent, eternal darkness I believed waited for me on the other side, but what I wanted and what I got had never lined up. I hadn't blinked in what felt like hours until the panic started to pass. My heart was pounding painfully against my ribs, filling my ears with ceaseless noise. My tears had dried up and my fingers and toes had become ice cold.

It will pass, Sister Harriot always said.

She was always the gentlest. When the others were quick to restrain me after my outbursts, she was always there to stroke my hair back when I was buckled in too tightly to do it myself. I didn't really remember my mother, but I wanted to think she would have been like Harriot. She taught me to breathe through the attacks. To endure the times when my mind and body couldn't align. When the puzzle pieces didn't fit and my thoughts were falling apart, she was there to tell me it would all come together eventually.

But Sister Harriot was also the one who shaved my head the day they baptized me. She knew I loved my hair, but she took it from me, even after I begged her not to.

Today is your new birthday, she told me.

I resented her for taking my hair for weeks, but that was the day that everything started to change. I bit less. I scratched less. I talked less. And eventually, my hair grew back.

Everything grows back.

Only my memories—my true memories—never did.

Madness was a demon that followed me everywhere. It hid in my own shadow. And the king—Rune—was either the demon himself or he was tempting it, using my own flesh and soul to lure it out of the shade.

I could almost feel its claws.

I fell to sleep waiting for its venomous bite.

But I'd slept with the demon many times. In a horrific way, he kept me warm when my blankets weren't enough.

My body always knew when someone was coming, even if I was sleeping. It came from living at Southminster for so long. Someone was always at my door.

This time, I didn't know who it was, but I knew they were there. I sat up slowly and stared at the door through the darkness, wondering when they'd announce their presence. When there was a soft knock, I pulled my knees to my chest and sighed.

"Come in," I said.

If it was Rune, I'd endure whatever torment he had for me.

The door opened, letting the light of the hallway bleed into the chamber. A tall man's silhouette cast itself in front of me and when the faint blue light from the balcony doors covered him, I saw the glint of metal on his face. A mask.

Petris.

I didn't even know him and yet his presence instantly soothed me. Maybe because he wasn't Rune. Whatever the reason, I was glad to see him.

"My lady," he greeted, a tenderness in his tone. "I mean, Briar."

He slid further into the room, opening the door wide to let more light in. There was a long stretch of silence and I wondered, considering the lack of food in his hands, why he was there if not to feed me.

"I wanted to check on you," he said kindly.

"Check on me?" I asked.

"Yes." He took another step into the room. "I spoke to Rune." Even his name made me tremble. "He wanted me to tell you—"

"I didn't mean to upset him again."

"That he was sorry."

I furrowed my brows at that.

Petris walked closer, coming to stand a few strides from the bed. I didn't know how to reply to that so I stayed silent, waiting for Petris to say more.

People never apologized to me.

He cleared his throat. "He wanted to ask if you were hurt at all."

"Hurt?"

He gestured to his back and I immediately thought of the knob jabbing into me.

"Oh," I said, reaching back to prod at the sore spot near my spine. "A bit sore, perhaps, but not hurt. Thank you."

He took another step forward, placing his hands behind his back like he was starting to relax.

"He was rough with you again," he implied.

I nodded. "He was. But if he truly thinks I'm this person he keeps talking about, I suppose I can understand his frustration."

I was disoriented thinking of all the things he said to me. When I recalled the scar on my hip that matched the handle on the pillar. It didn't make sense.

"Where is your mind wandering, my... Briar?" Petris asked.

I barely realized it was wandering.

"Do you tell the king everything? I mean, you knew about what happened. So you've spoken to him. Are you close?"

"Quite close. I've known him my whole life. I know him better than anyone."

I dropped my eyes, giving our conversation some thought. I had never really confided in anyone before. I had always wanted to, but my secrets were never valuable enough for people not to share. The sisters shared them. Father Eli shared them. By the time Lucien took me in, I stopped sharing all together.

"If you feel the need to tell me something," Petris said, taking another step. He was right next to the bed now. "Something you don't want me relaying to the king. I can do that." He paused for a moment to let that sink in. "You look like you need a listening ear."

I looked up at him, internally pleading for him to stay and listen. When he slowly sat down on the bed, I didn't flinch away with unease. I wanted to scoot closer. He was far enough away so that we wouldn't touch if we reached out to each other and it felt like he did that on purpose. Like he was trying to give me space.

"I can't tell day from night here," I said softly. "I don't even know how long it's been."

"Only a few days."

"I don't know that I care, really. But... I can't remember a time when my thoughts were truly my own. I've been told what's real and what isn't for so long. Father Eli told me about my family. The slaughter. The horrors that drove me to madness. I don't truly remember any of it, but I went mad for a reason. That must be it." I felt my hands shaking and clasped them together tightly to keep the shudders at bay. "But now Rune tells me I am a liar. That none of that is true and that I am this traitorous person." I felt a lump forming in my throat. "How could that be true? And yet... things do not line up. How could I have that mark on my body? It is a trick, yes? A trick crafted by your king. He is fae. They're tricksters. Demons. There is magic here. He could manipulate me any way he wants."

There was a feeling I felt often when reality and dreams came too close to one another. When madness twisted reality, I needed something to pull me back. Something to remind me not to drown or to float away. Oftentimes, that thing was pain. Father Eli taught me that pain could ground me. Keep me focused. Pain was shocking enough to wake me from those maddening stupors. Nails to my skin. Teeth to my lip. Heat to my hands. My ability to hurt myself in so many ways served me well after I left the asylum. I needed the pain. Southminster tortured me into needing it. It was a dark and necessary gift.

It was abuse. Heartless, sadistic abuse.

It's kept me going this long...

That sense of being utterly out of control was coiling its fingers around me and dragging me in too many directions.

I barely realized what I was doing until Petris's voice broke through the barrier of my scattered thoughts. My fingers were in my hair, pulling and ripping at the delicate strands. My breath was coming in rugged, almost painful gasps.

"Briar, stop," he said.

He was right in front of me. He'd shifted close, his hands gently tugging at my wrists to get my fingers out of my hair. Tears stung my raw eyes and when I looked at him, he was a blurry mask with no expression. No judgment. I took a deep breath, eyes wide and crazed, and tried to realize his company. I tried to appreciate that I wasn't alone in a cell with padded walls, tied and immobilized.

Petris folded my hands into my lap and cupped his own over them, letting his warmth soothe the chill that had made a home in my body. I looked at the dark shadows of his eyes and tried to find my balance without the pain I craved.

"Tighter," I whispered.

He canted his head, his thumb lightly brushing over my knuckles.

"What?"

"Hold me tighter," I said. "I... I will hurt myself if you don't."

He inched closer to me, his knee pressing against my leg, and he squeezed my hands tighter. And tighter. He squeezed so tight, I felt my joints crack. It was painful and I loved it. I needed it. I closed my eyes and I nodded, leaning toward him.

"Briar, you will not wander that far. I will not allow it."

I wasn't sure when I had fallen asleep again, but somehow I stayed that way. No dreaming. No uncomfortable tossing. I was warm and I was comfortable and as I came to, I understood why.

Curled on my side with the thin top sheet draped over me and my head on a down-filled pillow was enough to put me into a nice slumber, but it was the heavy arm wrapped around my waist that was the true culprit. That and the long, muscled body fit to the bends of mine and pressed to my back.

No one had ever slept beside me like that. It was protective and comforting.

We were both fully dressed, me under the sheet and him on top of it. The steady drum of Petris's heart tapped against my shoulder blades and the almost completely silent sound of his breath tickled my ear. He was sleeping.

Slowly, I turned my head to see the aged silver of his mask in my peripheral.

Petris had stayed with me.

I remembered him holding my hands. I recalled him saying things to me but I hardly knew what they were. But whatever he did had taken away the confusion and panic. How long we sat there talking and simply being in each other's presence was another foggy instance to add to the many that littered my mind, but I was glad for it. I hadn't felt so rested in ages. Something about the way he embraced me felt reassuring.

No one had ever offered that. Not in that way.

Lucien offered walls. Food. Clothing. Simple conversation and education. He never offered his embrace. His company on days when he had nothing else to do was so rare.

I slid my hand down Petris's forearm to his fingers and slid mine between them. He was soft and warm and gentle, a stark contrast to the master he served.

What would Rune think of him being in my bed? He'd been so furious about Lucien's mere name before. Perhaps the two were so close that he would not care or be mad over it.

I could only hope. The last thing I wanted was to get Petris in trouble for consoling me after the king brought me to tears.

I lay there in silence for some time before I carefully rolled over onto my other side, sliding my hands under my cheek to stare at the mask in front of me. I couldn't even tell if his eyes were opened or closed. Some strange magic seemed to conceal them in blackness no matter what angle I was staring from. I wanted to assume he was sleeping so I could simply watch him. Not that the mask would move or twitch like a real face would, but it fascinated me to know someone was behind that veil. Someone claiming to be hideous and yet kinder than anyone I'd ever known.

I lifted my hand, my fingers skimming over the shape of his lips, up along his cheek, and down the straight bridge of his nose.

"Don't take it off," he whispered.

I wasn't even startled by his voice. It fit into the silence so easily.

"I won't," I said, my fingers moving along the outer edge and down to his chin. "I don't mind your mask." I took a few deep breaths, tucking my hand under my cheek again. "I do wish I could see your eyes, though."

"You wouldn't like them."

"Are they hideous, too?"

"Perhaps."

"Hideous things don't bother me."

"What about beautiful things?"

"Maybe I think hideous things are beautiful."

I thought of the casquet in the catacombs. The way Ellee's skeleton looked, so aged and still and dusty. And then I thought of how calming it was to lay next to her. She was hideous and macabre to most, but to me, she was gorgeous in her peaceful silence.

What was wrong with me?

My eyes must have betrayed my thoughts because Petris shifted, drawing my attention.

"Your mind is wandering again," he whispered. "Where is it going?"

"I'm worried about something."

"What?"

"I'm worried the king is right. There's... something missing inside me. So many dark spaces where memories should be."

"You said you remember your parents. The farm. The massacre."

"I remember being told about them. They showed me every scar from that day. Told me I was refusing to revisit the incident. It was too violent. Too awful. I thought that was the part of me that's been missing. My parents' faces. Our house. I can see them... but I can't touch any of it. They're like pictures in a book. Vague pictures. They don't even have color."

"Who told you about your parents?"

"Father Eli did. At Southminster Asylum. That's where they put me. I was too dangerous to be around others at the time. But every time he spoke to me about my family, I had... episodes. I was angry and vengeful, he said. So he helped me bury those memories. And then he helped me heal."

I must have looked like I was teetering on the edge of control again because Petris reached out and wrapped a hand around my wrist, squeezing hard.

"I was sick," I muttered. "They took the sick part out, but... what if I needed the sick part? What if it was a part of me and now I'm just broken?"

"You were not sick, Briar."

I sniveled and sat up in the bed, head hanging low. "I was. I truly was. If you'd seen how out of control I was, you'd have committed me, too. I hurt people. But, when I left, something in me was gone. Sick or not, I think I needed it. And Rune only makes me feel more broken. He says these things and I don't know what's real. It's Southminster all over again. And until I believe him, I fear he'll lock me away. Hurt me. Force me to live like this until I bend the way he wants me to."

Petris sat up in front of me, hand still on my wrist like he thought I might float away. Heavens, I felt like I was about to.

"He would never do that. Despite the way he acts, he wants your freedom over anything else."

"Why?"

"It's complicated."

"No," I shook my head. "It's not complicated. I am not myself. I never have been. And people keep trying to make me into something and I don't know what it is."

He paused a moment, watching me break apart. I hated it. I wished I could just hold it together like I had been taught to, but the screws were too loose.

"What did they do to you there?"

"They…" I hesitated, desperately trying not to revisit it in detail. "They helped me. Using any method they could."

"What methods?"

I shrugged. "I don't quite remember them all." I stared across the room at the unlit fireplace and let my mind tiptoe through the halls of Southminster for a moment. "They hit me sometimes. Only when I would not let them speak. I fought back, but it slowed their progress, so they took steps to still me. Calming herbs. Tea. Then these horrible cold baths for hours until my teeth were chattering and I couldn't feel my body. It was demons, they said. Demons from my past. When they could not control me, they put me in small rooms. Small cages. For their protection, they said."

I stopped, letting myself breathe. I could still feel the icy water on my skin, sucking the life out of me slowly. I could feel my limbs stiffening from the tiny cages where they put me to calm down.

"I drew so much blood fighting them, but they never gave up on me. I scratched them, bit them, and screamed awful things at them. But they never gave up."

"They hurt you that much and you think they were helping you?"

I didn't answer that. I didn't know how. No one had ever asked me a question like that.

"And Father Eli?" Petris continued, realizing I didn't know what to say.

"He told everyone I would get better. He kept the sisters in line when they wanted to leave. He talked to me the most. Helped me to chase the bad memories away. He even brought the doctor."

"The doctor?"

"The one who took my blood. They thought my madness was a disease for a time. It worried the sisters every time I hurt them. Every week, they took blood, cleansing me of the sickness more and more each time. And then Father Eli brought Lucien to me and Lucien took me out of that place, assuming full responsibility."

"And the bleeding? What did they do with the blood?"

"Got rid of it, I suppose. It was sick blood."

Petris went quiet for a moment, his masked face shifting to the side as if in thought. The silence stretched too long. I was beginning to imagine the expressions on his face. Doubt. Regret. Judgement. All the things that made me want to shrink away into the darkness. But then my stomach made a soft grumbling sound and broke the tension.

"You're hungry," Petris said. "I didn't get a chance to bring you food last night. Come."

He slid off the bed and stood, holding out his hand to me. I regarded it for a moment, astounded at how kind he was in contrast to the others. Not that Naeve and Lura were particularly unkind, but they'd been friendly at the masquerade and had since avoided me it seemed. I reached out and clasped his hand, standing off the bed.

Petris led me downstairs and through another hall I had not ventured down into a large kitchen. It was bigger than the one at Aedon Heights with the same beautiful marble and glass that made most of the other rooms in the palace. Vines grew along the walls on the inside of the large chamber and a long, polished wood table stretched from the entrance to another door on the other side of the room. Cabinets and storage pantries were arranged along one side and racks of drying herbs and other items hung so neatly they looked like part of the décor.

There were no servants or cooks and everything was meticulous like the place had barely been used. Petris kept hold of my hand as he led me to the pantries.

"What would you like?" he asked.

I looked around at the emptiness of the room. "There are no cooks."

"Not at this hour, no. They sleep until the king takes his dinner. Other times, we all fend for ourselves. So? What would you like to eat?"

I bit my lip, staring at the pantry when Petris opened the door. I saw flour and dried meat. Dried fruits. Biscuits. Jars of loose-leaf tea. Jams and preserves.

It was a lot.

It smelled amazing, like sugar and spices, but I couldn't begin to tell him what I wanted.

"I don't know," I said. "Whatever is convenient I suppose."

"If you cannot decide, then we will eat one of my favorites," Petris said, not lingering any longer on the question.

I was grateful for that.

Letting go of my hand, he walked into the pantry and pulled out a cloth bag. When he set it on the table and opened the drawstring top, I saw purple potatoes the size of my fist spill out. He walked to a stone sink and rinsed them before filling a pot of water and dropping them inside. I stood patiently watching as he tossed some small logs into an iron oven unit and set the pot on one of the burners.

There was no need for conversation. Petris was so concentrated on what he was doing like he was creating some masterpiece and I was enthralled by it. I sat on one of the wooden stools to soak it in as he prepared diced mushrooms, diced carrots, thin slices of aged cheese, yogurt from a cold cabinet in the corner, and strips of cured ham. By the time the potatoes were done, the kitchen was beginning to smell divine.

Petris placed one of the potatoes on a plate and cut it in half. Steam billowed from the fluffy white inside as he mashed a fork into the meat. Then he layered the other ingredients into the potato and topped it off with sprinkles of dried garlic, lemon juice, pepper, and rosemary.

"Sorry, that took so long," he said, sliding the plate over to me and taking a seat across the table.

"You are not eating?" I asked.

He leaned forward on the table and tapped a finger to the metal of his mask. I wanted to tell him I didn't mind, but it was his choice and I wanted to respect that.

I stared over the food, admiring the melted cheese and the perfect arrangement of herbs. Taking a deep breath, I savored the smell of it and then took my fork and started to dig in.

When I took the first bite, an explosion of flavor completely overtook my tongue. My eyes widened and I glanced at Petris, chewing the perfectly cooked potato and savoring the taste.

"Do you like it?" he asked.

I nodded. "It's amazing. I've never had potatoes prepared like this. It's no wonder that it's your favorite."

He chuckled. The sound, though a bit muffled behind the mask, was so handsome and gentle. I looked up at him as he poured some red liquid into a cup from a glass pitcher and walked the cup to me. When I brought it to my mouth, I smelled cranberry and honey. Excited, I took a sip and was not surprised to find that I loved it as much as I loved the potatoes.

"Well, well," a voice said.

I glanced at the doorway to see Lura and Naeve standing arm in arm, their black dresses less extravagant, but still just as beautiful as the last time I saw them.

"Getting friendly with the help, are we?" Naeve said with a mischievous smile.

They waltzed toward the table, finding the board where Petris had sliced up the ham. Each of them took a piece and slid it into their mouths.

Looking at Petris, I noticed he was looking down at the table while both their eyes were narrowed on him.

Lura chuckled childishly as she chewed. "Interesting dish to prepare, isn't it, Naeve?"

"Quite."

"I think it's quite good," I said, feeling like I needed to defend Petris somehow.

"Of course, you do, love," Lura said with a pout, sliding her long-nailed finger across my cheek.

"Finding time to wander today, ladies?" Petris said, lifting his head.

Looking at him, his demeanor had changed. I had thought that his hanging his head was submissive, but now he seemed almost annoyed. Lura's smile drooped, but Naeve just rolled her eyes playfully.

"We're only teasing. You know how we get bored."

"Then perhaps you should be on patrol. It's your job, after all."

Both of them sighed, taking a bit more meat as they strolled toward the door on the opposite side of the kitchen. And the whole time they were leaving, Petris had his gaze on them. I stopped eating, feeling like there was some kind of tension in the room.

When the girls had gone, I found myself staring at Petris, wondering so many things. He let out a deep breath and ran a hand back through his black hair like he was annoyed.

"They irritate you?" I said, scraping another fork full of soft potato into my mouth.

"Not exactly," Petris said. "They tease me. And sometimes I feel a need to tease them back."

"Who are they?"

"What do you mean?"

"I mean, I saw them turn into ravens the other day. And... at the masquerade, they did things. Horribly violent things."

"They're the king's ravens. They're whatever he needs them to be. Messengers. Scouts. Companions."

"And they serve him?"

"They do. Very loyally. Any sovereign can make familiars."

"Sovereign?"

"Each of the three realms has a sovereign. Rune rules the Glyn."

"And, they make familiars?"

"It is a risky art. Witchcraft, humans would call it. A sacrifice of blood, tears, and bone will create a familiar and they're different for every sovereign. For Rune, they are ravens. A reflection of his soul. Not quite living. Not quite dead. Born from him at different stages in his life. That is why they all dawn different personalities, you see. Sides of him so few really understand. They're his tools when he needs them to be. A long time ago, it was said that the King of Malvec, Rune's brother, created so many of his own that he could fight wars with them. But he lost control of most of them many centuries ago, the fool."

"And they have their own minds? Free will, I mean?"

"They are a part of their creator, but individuals nonetheless." He took a deep breath and sighed. "Unfortunately, those hundreds of creations escaped across the realms. Familiars aren't bound by the laws sovereigns are. They can cross worlds whenever they want because the rules only apply to those who have a soul. Some are here in the Glyn. Some are in Forlahn where mortals live. Their foul nature is what made humans want to eradicate all supernatural creatures to begin with. Magic users. Fae. All who were different were destroyed."

"The wars. They started because of Malvec's king?"

He nodded.

"I cannot blame humans for their fear. Runc's ravens... they devoured all those people at the masquerade."

"Ahh, yes. They do that sometimes," he chuckled. "To those who were never alive, the essence of the living is a welcome treat."

"And you? Are you a tool? A raven, I mean?"

He scoffed and I could almost see his smile in my mind's eye. "I was created by the king, but I am not the same."

I didn't know what that meant, but I didn't ask for more. I simply accepted that I'd understand someday or I never would and that was alright.

I took the last bite of food and finished my serving of juice, finding myself aptly satisfied. Petris was gazing at me, his head tilted slightly to one side. A flush hit my cheeks and I felt my lips curling into a smile.

Smiles were rare. I couldn't remember the last time I truly smiled. Practiced smiles were one thing. Genuine ones were rare. It felt... good.

"Tomorrow, I can make you something new," he said. "We'll find your favorite food soon enough."

"Today, it is this," I gestured at the empty plate.

Another bout of silence fell over us. I thought he might have to leave me soon. Being a servant of the palace probably came with many responsibilities. But if he left me, what would I do? Explore the grounds more?

"What is it you like to do, Briar?" Petris asked.

I shrugged. "I used to play music. And I painted. Anything that keeps my mind calm, I suppose."

"Were you told to keep your mind calm or was it a choice?"

"Nothing is a choice," I chuckled.

It was a disturbing thought. One that had bothered me for so long that it was now just amusing. But Petris wasn't amused. His lack of response made me pause.

"Everything is a choice," he said softly, an air of frustration in his words.

"Well, I do enjoy reading. Escapism is my greatest joy. Stories with action. Love. Horror. All of it, really. Lucien worried books would cloud my mind and make me skew reality. He worried it would inspire defiance or violent outbursts."

"But he allowed you to read anyways?"

"Occasionally. He liked me reading educational books, mostly. Religious texts."

"But you like the stories."

"I always have."

He lowered his head for a beat and cleared his throat. "I know you might not want to hear this," he said gently. "But so did she."

I stiffened, my expression frozen in time when I heard that. When it processed, I felt my fingers go cold and squeezed them together against my skirt to keep warm.

"She," I muttered. "Thank you."

"For what?"

I dropped my gaze, biting my lip. "For referring to her as a different person. Do you believe that she is?"

"I don't know what I believe, my lady. Briar. We're all as confused as you are. In a different way, perhaps, but still so very puzzled."

"You knew her, then?"

"I did."

"What was she like?"

"Demanding. Fiery. She challenged the king like no one else could. Made him feel alive. And for someone like Rune, feeling alive is so very important."

"Was she like him?"

"Not at all. She stumbled from the Labyrinth, but things were different between them. She chose to stay and he allowed it."

"Stumbled from the Labyrinth? What do you mean?"

"Sometimes, a soul stumbles out of the mist. It doesn't often turn out too well for them. Lucky for her, Rune found her. He could have tossed her back and let her wander away to find another path, but he kept her instead. Fate is tricky sometimes, and he believed she was his fate. She lit up an otherwise dark eternity for the king. She brought life to this place. When you cannot die, you forget that you can live. You can forget the joys existence can bring. The sorrows. All the things that make a soul. And the man who governs the realm in between *must* understand what makes a soul or he would not care to guide them. He would see no point in protecting their journeys."

"She was human, then."

"Until he gave her eternity."

"And then what?"

That question made me so uncomfortable. A stinging chill rolled down my spine and I stiffened at my own words.

"And then... she took what he'd given her and she left. Tore his heart out of his chest."

"Why would she do that?"

"She was curious. He loved her curiosity, but it led her to places he could not follow. She wanted the joys of being human." He was beginning to speak with more tension like his jaw was clenched. I could tell he was bitter about it. Perhaps he didn't have the same rage in him that the king did, but he was deeply upset. "It was all in the note she left before she disappeared. Her remorse. Her confessions. Her betrayal. But none of it stopped her from leaving."

"You love your king," I whispered.

"Sometimes. Most of the time I hate him."

"I don't understand."

"He is a fool. He left himself without armor when it came to her and he was destroyed for it. This place was once impenetrable and since she happened, it's fallen to pieces. He goes into the Labyrinth and more and more souls lose themselves to the endless wandering because he spent so long denying his responsibilities here. Too long pining for a woman who only betrayed him. The sounds they make... I hear them at night. They're loud and consuming and it would not be that way if he'd just kept lighting the candles and helping them move on like he's supposed to. Then, maybe fewer souls would wander out to be devoured by the hungry beasts prowling this world. But he believed too strongly in his love for her so when it was gone, he believed too strongly in vengeance."

I felt shame for whatever happened between the king and the woman he loved and I didn't know why because I couldn't be her. There was no way. It was too fantastical a story. It was impossible and yet... I felt guilty for her transgressions.

"I can't hear them," I said. "The souls, I mean."

"No, only he can. And me, of course."

"Why you?"

"Because, in a way, the king and I are the same. It's very hard to explain. We were both created here and so we are both this place. Him, the king, and me, the slave."

Words escaped me. The conversation had stumped me and I could add nothing else to its progression when my mind was too tangled up in the strangeness of it all.

"Enough of that," Petris said, slapping the table with his hands and standing. "It's not my place to tell you these things. But seeing as the king lets his emotions dictate his conversations, perhaps it was better that the story came from me."

"I imagine he would have shouted it all and thrown something," I said, amused when I should have been scared of the idea.

Petris let out that handsome chuckle again and circled around the table to me.

"Come with me," he said. "I want to show you something. If you're going to be here for a while, you should have a way to pass the time."

I followed Petris through the kitchen to the other door and found myself standing at the bottom of another stairway. This one spiraled upward and the narrower path was almost secretive. We climbed and climbed, past the second floor to a hallway that opened into a dark, gloomy level of the palace. It was then that I realized where we were. We were on the floor that I'd seen when I visited the courtyard. The dark windows and the quiet stillness gave it away.

The hall smelled like dust and candle wax like it had gone untouched for years. A few strides down the passage, Petris stopped and looked back at me. I was busy ogling the high walls and unlit sconces and nearly collided with him before I realized he wasn't moving anymore. He held out a hand to me and I took it without hesitation.

We strolled further. Balconies with glass doors were all along the path allowing the bright blue moonlight in. Glancing at the floor, I saw purple carpeting with swirling silver designs.

"Everything about this place is like a dream," I said.

"It was built by the first sovereign. And each king following added to it in some way."

My interest piqued. "How many kings have there been?"

"Many. Each turning of the ages, the king is reincarnated."

"So... it is the same king in a different body?"

"The same soul. Different minds. Different hearts. Different desires, dislikes, and ideals."

"Can a king be corrupt?"

"Yes. But not for long. There is always a balance. The realms see to that." He took a few breaths before continuing. "Some of us believe *she* was his balance. Before she appeared, Rune was on the brink of something very dark. Something that could have destroyed a lot of this world. And others, if he had gone unchecked." He glanced over his shoulder at me. "If that delicate little bird hadn't shown up, the realms might have been at war by now. A much more brutal one than the one you've heard of."

"He must be very lonely," I said under my breath, knowing loneliness all too well.

Even with all the sisters, Father Eli, and Lucien, I felt more alone than I would have buried in a coffin six feet under. At least in a grave, there were no whispers in my ear. No punishments. No expectations.

Petris stopped outside a pair of mahogany doors and looked at me.

"You have no idea," he spoke softly.

Petris was being polite referring to the king's lover as "she," but I knew that he didn't believe himself when he said it. He thought I was that woman, too. But it was too heavy a weight to bear.

I dropped my eyes in shame and tucked my hair behind my ear until I heard Petris pushing one of the doors open.

"Ah," he said. "Unlocked. I thought it might be."

"What do you mean?"

"These doors locked themselves the day she disappeared."

I didn't like that...

The more signs appeared that I could have anything to do with Rune's lost love—the woman who betrayed him—the more I was squirming in my skin.

But I swallowed my unease, eager to know what was behind that door.

The old hinges whined like the knees of an old woman standing from her seat. I peered into the room and saw a burst of moonlight from across the chamber. Leaves and dried flower petals blew toward us from inside and carried the scent of leather, paper, and wood.

"The king may not like the idea of you coming in here," he said, lowering his voice to a whisper. "But it hasn't seen visitors for many years."

Petris led me inside and I found myself standing in a giant, circular room with shining glass floors. In the middle was a massive tree with branches that fanned out like an umbrella over the whole room. I could tell that it used to be lush with leaves and flowers, but the branches were bare and brown now, the poor thing forgotten.

Along the walls were shelves taller than four of me and they were filled with books in pristine leather binding. Petris let go of my hand and walked across the room from me while I stared at the collection of books in utter amazement. Before long, I heard a match strike and glanced toward Petris where he was lighting something on the wall. I expected candles but instead, veins of white light suddenly burst through the wall like quiet lightening and climbed into the ceiling, creating a dome over us that lit up the entire chamber.

"Is that magic?" I asked.

Petris returned to me and slid his hands neatly behind his back. "Something of the sort. This room is alive, you see. The whole palace is, in a way. It just needed to be woken up."

There was a smile on my lips and it wasn't leaving. I was enthralled by the ceiling. The tree. The floors that looked like frosted glass. Looking at the now illuminated shelves, I saw so many titles. My mind was overwhelmed with a need to look at every one of them. I skipped toward the nearest one and ran my fingers across the leather spine, reading the gold lettering.

"*Sveric Memoriatum*," I said, unsure what language it was but so eager to know. "*The Dragon and the Sky. A Marriage to Winter.* How many are here?"

"Thousands. I've never counted. Kings have been collecting them for centuries."

"He reads, then?" I asked, excited to find something about him that I could relate to."

"Of course, he did," Petris said gently like he didn't want to upset me by mentioning her again. "But she did even more."

My smile drooped and I bit into my lip, trying not to feel that weight return.

"Don't," Petris said, stepping toward me. "I prefer your smile over your frown."

I veiled my emotions as I always did, with straight shoulders and my hands neatly locked in front of me.

"You're the first to have seen it in a very long time," I said.

"That's a pity. It's a beautiful smile."

My cheeks flamed and I had to press my lips together to keep from smiling again. A bout of silence made my blood rush and I had to wonder why Petris was such wonderful company. I didn't even know his face, but he'd been so good to me. If it wasn't for him, I might have sunk back into that cold, silent darkness I knew so well and just drifted away like ashes on the wind. Especially with the way the king had prodded me so aggressively about a past that wasn't mine.

"I must attend to other things," Petris said vaguely, clearing his throat. "This library is yours. No one comes here."

"I can come here whenever I want?"

"Yes. Provided you remember the way."

"I do," I said excitedly. Petris inclined his head a bit and then spun on his heels, heading toward the door. "Thank you," I said after him.

He halted and glanced back toward me, silent for a long moment as if he was hesitating to say something. And then he nodded his head again and left the library.

I watched the door where he disappeared, listening to his steps fade down the hall. Part of me would have rather kept his company, but when I looked at the endless collection of books at my disposal, I could think of nothing else. I turned around and grabbed the first one with the most beautiful lettering. *Elven Legends.* I'd never read anything about elves. To Lucien, they were a myth, like so many other things. Perhaps they were, but that only made the idea of reading about them even more enticing.

Near the balcony doors, I saw a round, cushioned seating area with embroidered pillows and a glass table that was cut into a raw shape that resembled ice.

If there was seating and a table, I would need more books.

I began skimming the ones I could reach and pulled out three more. *Songs of the Sea, The Ruthless History of the Eastern Pirate Cove,* and one in a language I couldn't even read. I hauled them all to the sitting area and prepared to dive in.

143

The Labyrinth was a dreary place. No other plane in the universe held so much emotion and I'd learned over the years to build strong walls around myself so the grief did not slither into my conscience.

It took too long for me to erect those barriers, though. Being without them had taken its toll. I'd paid a hefty price for allowing rage, hate, and revenge to infect me. A price I would never forget.

The past

• • •

Many humans adopted a bogus idea that their actions in life dictated where they went when they passed on. They worked hard to make themselves believe that if they lived good lives—charitable lives—they'd enter the afterlife through pearl gates.

Phariel had done that. He was a viciously manipulative cunt and he liked seeing what people would do under the threat of punishment. Would they fold or would they rebel? But Phariel didn't have to see their souls afterward. He only had to see the foolish humans prancing around, ignorant and so moldable. After a century or two, he'd get bored and find some other way to bend humans to his will just so he could laugh about it.

But no matter his promises, I knew it was all false. No god or gods dictated where mortals would end up after their last breath left them. They dictated that themselves, in *my* Labyrinth. In the Glyn. I ruled the final gate through which they had to walk. There were no sweet fantasies in my Glyn. I knew the truth. The soul of a murderer could walk into the most perfect eternal dream from my Labyrinth the same as a child who only knew life for a few days simply because neither of them possessed a guilty conscience. For guilt was the ultimate hell and those carrying too much of it rarely escaped into the heavens they wished for.

It was unjust. It sickened me to see rapists, killers, and sadistic monsters create a rapturous afterlife for themselves because they had no remorse. It irked me more to see some of the worst souls somehow find their way into the mortal realm again and grow into the same monstrous fucks they were before.

I wanted to destroy them. It wasn't right that they were allowed to live free of remorse and inflict harm on others. It wasn't right that they could roam my Labyrinth without answering for their misdeeds. And I knew Malvec would never take them unless they disrupted the balance enough. His prison realm was meant for the most wicked. Those who defied the balance and turned things too upside down to ever fix. He would never turn his attention to the evildoers in my Labyrinth unless I made him.

So, I found loopholes in the rules. I started to interfere. I was not to touch a soul wandering in my Labyrinth, but I could do as I pleased with those who wandered out. Left too long to their own devices with no memories of their mortality, souls outside of the Labyrinth became terrible, primal creatures with no sense to them. I *had* to destroy them. It was my job.

Cutting a hole in the Labyrinth's hedges helped me do that. And when the bad souls started to filter out, I let them get lost in my woods. I *let* the monster grow and eat its way out of them to show what they truly were. Because if they became monsters, then I would have an excuse. An excuse to hunt them, slaughter them, and wipe the world clean of their existence, ensuring they'd never be granted another chance or another life.

Too many times, I'd seen mothers, children, and innocents wandering in my Labyrinth, lost and confused and condemned to endless turmoil. I could see all of their memories. The Labyrinth stores every single one for every single soul and keeps them long after they pass on.

It's hard not to judge when you see all that people are and all that they've done.

I was sick of the imbalance. I was powerful. All three of us were. We could destroy or remake the realms if we wanted to. We could burn the laws and shape the world however we liked. Phariel certainly liked toying with the humans in his charge.

So why was I sitting around letting awful souls experience heaven and watching innocents wade through confusion for eternity?

• • •

So many...

I had destroyed so many over the years since I created the breach in those hedges. Every soul that wandered out into the forest of the Glyn became something awful and I slaughtered each and every one of them.

But my forests became places of danger and fear and the terrible escapees had chased away so much of the beauty in my Glyn.

I was king and it was a necessary sacrifice to see filth get cleansed.

Blood, guts, and dirt were caked onto my tunic, but my coat was fairly clean. I always took it off before a kill, discarding the extra fabric that could wind around my legs in a fight. A long day in the woods hunting and slicing and destroying ugly beasts had left me grimy. Every day, it left me filthy and I knew the filth was going deeper every time I swung my sword, but I had to endure. I had been neglecting the Labyrinth. What was the point of lighting candles so awful souls could find their way to a rapturous afterlife? I'd rather they found their way into my woods. There were so few worth helping those days. Mortal souls kept getting more twisted and I just. Kept. Destroying them.

And I enjoyed it. One swipe of my sword could cut a kelpher in half. One flick of my wrist could snap the neck of a roglyn. It was so easy to destroy. So easy to focus my anger on corrupted things.

And so fucking satisfying for all of two minutes before the revulsion set in.

"Seven," a voice said. "A good hunt. Wonderful job, my king."

Elanor. My raven. I had never created a familiar before her. I did not even know she'd be a raven. Or a woman. But she was a striking one and she was always so eager to aid in my hunts. To find the hundreds that had escaped the Labyrinth, I needed help, so I birthed her from my very blood to patrol the woods for me.

And she did her job so well. She had a nose for wicked souls and sniffed them out so quickly, always so keen to see me take them apart.

But now my day was done.

"Fly ahead," I ordered. "Draw me a bath. I need to wash this stink away."

"Of course. A bath is well deserved. I will make you one of my elixirs, too. For your nerves."

Elanor took on her raven form in a blink and disappeared toward the palace.

Alone, I was able to think. Every time I destroyed a soul, the high lasted for mere moments. It was a high that came and went and was followed by guilt and sickness. But part of me always thought it was worth it.

The thrill of the kill made me want more. Every day I wanted more and I let more souls escape the Labyrinth, eager to shower in their screams, their blood, and their fear. If they would not punish themselves, then I would. Happily.

And if I went too far, the realms would balance it all. Perhaps the realms would find a way to destroy me and a new king would take my place. One that was too much of a coward to do what I was doing. But until then, I was going to do my part. They could call me anything they wanted after I was gone, but I was going to wash the Glyn in the blood of those who did not deserve release.

Sticky with the remnants of my most recent hunt, I strolled toward the palace. I was lost in stirred-up hate and bitterness when something caught my eye just outside the big arch leading into my Labyrinth. Another escaped soul to cut to pieces, I presumed. I squeezed the hilt of my sword, excitement shooting through my veins.

But I paused when I realized I was not looking at a monster. There was no dark aura hanging over her head like a storm cloud. No guilt. No horrors lingering like parasites on her soul. No stench of evil.

Odd. All souls were haunted by something, even if they didn't know what it was.

She was lost, but she wasn't acting lost. If she had wandered out of my Labyrinth, then I should have been cutting her in two. But I couldn't. I didn't want to.

She was tall, slender, and naked with pale blonde hair like spun silver and gold in tight ringlets and waves. She had eyes like burnt umber and a face that leeched the cold right out of my heart. When she saw me, I could hear her blood rush. Whether it was fear or excitement, I didn't know, but it made mine mimic the rhythm.

I was covered in gore and she did not flinch away. Even the blade clutched tightly in my hand did not make her run.

"What is this place?" she asked me.

Her voice was melodic and sweet, vacant of whatever life she led before she ended up in the Glyn. She was new. Bright. Innocent. A clean slate.

"This is the Glyn," I said.

Her smile flattened at the sound of my voice and she blinked her beautiful eyes at me. Her long hair covered her small breasts, though she didn't seem worried about her lack of clothes. Why would she have been? Once free from the Labyrinth, most souls were stripped of almost everything they were in life. The memories belonged to the misty maze.

Although, that fact did not deter me from slaughtering all the other escapees.

This woman barely even knew what modesty was and it was a beautiful thing.

In her delicate fingers, she held something. A pink flower, which was still attached to a thin twig of the plant she'd plucked it from. The twig was covered in thorns and had pierced her skin in multiple places. Blood trickled down her hand and wrist and a bit was on her thigh where she likely rubbed against the bush to take her pretty flower.

"Sweetbriar," I muttered.

She smiled and looked down at her flower, touching the soft petals with bloody fingers. When the red smeared across the flower, her brows knitted and she opened her hand to see the stains across her palm. I took a breath, smelling the metallic tang of her blood mixed with the sweet floral aroma, and slowly walked toward her.

"You're bleeding," I said.

"I didn't…" she said, still puzzled. "I didn't feel it. When we bleed, there should be pain, right?"

Slowly, I reached out and I took the flower from her hands, watching her rub the blood over her fingers as if she'd never seen it before.

"The sweetbriar roses are covered in thorns," I said, tugging the flower off the top of the twig and discarding the rest. "Did you not see them?"

Sticking the end of the short rose stem gently between my teeth, I took the woman's hands and wiped the still-wet blood from her fingers and palms with the cuff of my coat sleeve. Once she was thoroughly wiped clean, I could see the dozen little cuts and punctures littering her hands. She canted her head at the minor wounds, unconcerned. But when I placed that little flower in the center of her palm, a bright smile spread across her lips.

"I just saw the flowers," she muttered, lifting the rose up in front of her to gleam at its beauty.

Despite her not being concerned over her nakedness, it felt intrusive to stare at her bare form so I put away my sword and slid my coat off my shoulders. She was distracted by the rose as I maneuvered her arms carefully into the sleeves.

"What is your name, little bird? Or do you not remember?"

"My name?" The question caught her off guard like I'd snapped my fingers in front of her eyes. She drew back, her forehead creasing. "I... I don't know. Should I know?"

I delivered her a soft smirk and shook my head. "It's no surprise that you don't." Glimpsing the flower in her hand, I said the first thing I could think of. I will call you Briar."

"Briar," she whispered, savoring the name on her tongue. Her eyes flashed up at me, emphasized by the red forming on her cheeks. "I love it."

Once more, I looked up at the Labyrinth just beyond the courtyard. It was right to put her back on her journey and let her discover where she would go next. A woman like her could have heaven waiting for her. Paradise.

Or perhaps hell was waiting to be built with bricks of her past deeds. Looks could be deceiving.

But she hadn't found her heaven or her hell. She had stumbled out onto my doorstep. She found *me.*

I looked down at her again and instantly I imagined her being mine. I could keep her. A king could keep anything. I governed the Labyrinth and all of the Glyn.

The sound of feathered wings flapping caught my attention. With a whisper of gentle wind, Elanor transformed into a beautiful woman behind me wearing a black dress formed straight from the shadows, as always.

"Your bath is nearly ready," she said with a smile, striding up to me and dusting off her skirts. She hesitated when she saw Briar wrapped in my coat ogling the flower. "What's this?"

"She wandered out," I said.

"Out of the Labyrinth? Should you not—"

I shook my head. "She is not part of the hunt," I said. "She's..."

I didn't know what she was. I didn't know what I wanted to do with her. All I knew was that I'd sheathed my sword to put my coat around her.

Briar finally tucked the flower away into the cuff of my coat sleeve as if to hide it for safekeeping and noticed Elanor standing beside me. She raised her brows as if about to introduce herself when she was distracted by a statue deeper in the courtyard. It was an old thing that had been standing since before I was king. Two large hands made of crystal and stone stood upright and interlocked. Moss and the glisten of morning dew made the thing look quite enchanting. I'd always thought so, but Briar regarded it like it was the most beautiful thing in the world. She crawled up onto the thick stone base and slowly ran her hands up the curved sides with fascination.

"So childish," Elanor said.

"Not childish. Fascinated."

I couldn't take my eyes off of her and Elanor noticed. She noticed everything.

She huffed, crossing her arm. "You should put her back. You destroy the bad ones. She's clearly not bad."

"I can't."

I tossed a glance at Elanor to see her narrowing her eyes up at me.

"Why not?"

"I don't know."

"If you keep her, you'll have to take care of her. It will interfere with your duties. She—"

"It will interfere with nothing."

"The hunts will—"

"I am king, Elanor. I can do as I please. And if she truly does interfere, I will close the wall."

"Then the bad ones will stop wandering out and there will be no hunts. No justice."

"There will always be hunts. Souls have been escaping all along. I only made it easier for them."

"But—"

"If you cannot handle it, I will make another who can," I hissed, growing tired of her defiance already.

She glared and then took a deep, centering breath and nodded. I created her when I had a thirst for the hunts. I knew why she was unwilling to see me stray from them, but she would learn to focus on other things. I knew she would.

"Of course, my king. Whatever you want," she finally said.

The Past

Briar's laughter was infectious. If she was laughing, then eventually, so was I. What did her in was Gordon's face when he bit into her undercooked, oversalted sweet buns. His cakes were the best and Briar would never deny it, but she was always so eager to try things she'd never done before. That day, she chose to make sweet buns and I sat back to watch, anxious to see how she would mess up the entire recipe.

Epically. She messed it up *epically*.

Gordon was in the process of trying to swallow down what he'd bitten off. The old man was polite if nothing else. He choked down the bit of bun, dissatisfaction deepening in the wrinkles of his face. Briar was doubled over against the table in the kitchen, hands covering her face as she guffawed over Gordon's effort.

"Don't swallow, old man," I finally laughed. "I saw her put the eggs in. I swear to the heavens half of it was the shells."

"I fished them out!" Briar defended.

"And…" Gordon wheezed, finally getting the chewy bite down. "Did you use a pinch of salt?"

"Yes."

154

"She spilled it in."

Our simultaneous answers made Gordon's face pale. Kind as he was, it wasn't easy for him to see other people cooking. Especially when their cooking wasn't up to par.

Briar smacked my shoulder with the back of her hand, her cheeks bright red with amused embarrassment. Biting her lip, she chucked one of the rolls at me. I shifted casually out of its way and grinned.

"If you'd have tasted it before Gordon got here, you could have warned me!"

I cocked a brow. "Me? Taste *that*? I'm a king. I only eat the best. And my refusing to eat it should have told you enough."

She grumbled, taking one of the buns and biting off a good portion. The way she pretended to like it made me chew my lip, waiting for the moment she would realize her mistake. To her credit, she choked it down just as Gordon had... but almost immediately afterward, she dumped the rest into the waste bucket with a sigh.

"Don't fret," Gordon said, waving a hand and retreating toward the door. "I've made fresh ones with the missus. I'll fetch them if that's what you're craving, girl."

Briar's smile remained, but she hung her head low, pinching the bridge of her nose.

"Cooking is not your strong suit," I said.

"What *is* my strong suit?"

"Ahh, this again." I stepped around the table toward her. She suppressed a giggle as I placed my fists on either side of her. "You'll figure it out eventually, little bird."

"How many years will it take for me to figure it out?" She huffed out a sigh. "I wonder what I was good at in life."

"Don't wonder that," I said, brushing a strand of her hair behind her ear. "That's not you anymore."

Briar had always been fascinated with mortality. Being in the Glyn, she was no longer quite mortal. No longer quite dead. No longer quite alive. But she never ceased to keep wondering what and who she was before she died. Perhaps I would show her one day. Memories remained in the Labyrinth even when souls left it, but I wasn't sure it would be best for her to find them. I could lose her. Or worse, she could lose herself.

She was with me in my world and every day that passed made her more beautiful in my eyes, with or without the memories of her human existence. She was so full of life. So full of curiosity. She was too trusting for her own good, which made it so easy to play pranks on her, which Elanor took full advantage of.

Sometimes her pranks were close to going too far, but Elanor was an intense woman and Briar seemed to have learned to handle herself.

"What are you staring at?" she asked.

I'd been staring...

I hadn't even realized.

"You," I said.

The word just came out and I held my gaze steady, watching as my presence changed her. I'd been playing with Briar lately, seeing how far I could push her and what she would think of it. I liked how she bit her bottom lip to keep from smiling. I liked the way her cheeks grew pink and the way her pulse thrummed so loudly.

"Me?" she said, her tone entirely too flirtatious for the innocent act she always put on.

I narrowed my eyes at her. This was the first time she seemed to be playing along. The first time she was fighting back a little and gods it made my body respond. I almost felt guilty for it. When she showed up, she was a handful, always getting lost. I had to care for her and teach her like she was a child. But over the years, she developed her personality. Her voice. She matured and became a woman with questions. Opinions. Needs.

And holy heavens, the way she was looking at me at that moment sent heat trickling south. I cleared my throat, internally admitting that if she ever chose to play my game and make a move, I would be on my knees surrendering.

"I will make us something to eat," I said, licking my tongue across my lips.

"Potatoes?" she said. "With cured meat? Perhaps some rosemary?"

"How did you know?"

"Maybe I was a fortune teller before. Maybe I had abilities like Elanor does. Like a witch."

"She prefers to think she was an enchantress. She inherited some interesting traits when I made her, I will admit."

"I prefer to tease her. She can be a real witch at times." Her eyes dropped to my lips and that simple little shift in her expression made my pulse stutter. "Almost as much as I enjoy teasing you."

"And how do you think you tease me?"

"Evidently by existing," she chuckled. "You always look at me like you want to..." she trailed off but the suspense had my hands twitching to touch her.

"Want to what?" I whispered, leaning in closer.

The way her hair was twisted off her neck, leaving the soft, milky skin exposed, made heat swell in my belly. She smelled like honey, baked bread, and flowers and it was irresistible. Perhaps fate put her on my doorstep. For me. Because I found everything about her so wonderfully addicting. From her beauty to the bright way she saw a world that I'd lost hope in long ago, it was all so damn perfect.

I'd all but forgotten about the hunts since I found her. I'd closed the hole and I'd left the Labyrinth to the souls that wandered it. I wasn't sure it was a good thing, but Briar made me forget the violence. The thirst for the slaughter. All of it.

"Want to…" she said, suddenly swiping her fingers across my cheek and smearing it with honey.

My lips parted with shock and I stilled, processing her assault. She spit out a laugh that she had tried desperately to contain and slapped her other hand over her mouth.

"You just left yourself so vulnerable," she said, her voice muffled behind her palm. "I'm sorry. That's for letting me feed those salty buns to poor Gordon."

Reaching over, I slapped a hand into the flour piled on the rolling board and she stiffened.

"No. This is my favorite dress. You wouldn't."

I raised my hand and let my white palm hover over her. She shook her head, but instead of cowering, her eyes were challenging.

"Don't," she said.

"I'm very vengeful, Briar."

"I'll clean it off."

"Not good enough."

I was about to smear the flour across her top when she stepped into me, her hot breath against my jaw seizing my movements.

And then her tongue was gliding up my cheek, licking the sweet honey from my face in one long swipe.

Gods and hell and whatever else I could swear to filled my mind and I cursed to myself as my breaches tightened around my groin.

Fuck.

Briar's tongue stopped just before my ear and she took the honey into her mouth, breathing deeply as she slowly stepped away.

So she was playing my game. It really wasn't fair. One move and she had already won.

"You," I groaned. "Are evil."

"I am smart," she whispered, looking up at me with those big, piercing eyes.

"Are you?" I reached down, taking her hand in mine and slowly lifting it between us.

She watched me bring her honey-covered fingers to my lips and slide them into my mouth. The quiver that shuddered through her reached my cock and I loved it. I watched her eyes as I gradually licked the honey off her fingers and dragged them slowly out of my mouth. She was enthralled, her teeth gliding over her bottom lip again but in a much more sensual manner.

She was as hungry as I was.

"That's not fair," she muttered. "I'm not as good at this as you are."

"You're plenty good, Briar."

The heat of her body seeped through my clothes and with it came the scent of her sweet, genuine arousal. I took a deep breath to soak it all in and wanted so badly to press my lips to hers. I had longed to feel her mouth on mine since I saw her. I never thought it right. Now, I hardly knew if I could resist.

But I didn't have to wonder anymore because Briar and her curious mind chose for me. She glimpsed my lips as I licked the remaining honey off the corner of my mouth and rose up on her toes, kissing the edge of my smirk.

I was finished.

"Not good enough, little bird," I rasped, shaking my head. "I want all of you."

With a delirious nod, she slid her fingers around the back of my neck and pulled me down to her, her mouth crashing into mine like she'd been just as starved for my kiss as I had been for hers. How long had she been waiting? Wanting?

I didn't care. I wrapped my arms around her waist, bringing her tight against me. She moaned and I devoured that sensual sound, sliding my tongue deep into her welcoming mouth. There was no hesitation in her. No indication that she was afraid. Nervous. She held me as greedily as I held her, but it didn't distract from the fact she was untouched. Perhaps in life, she could have been anything. She could have been a whore in a brothel or on the streets for all I knew, but in my realm, her past life was a mere flicker to the roaring flames of what she'd become over the years with me.

She was as innocent as they came, her body pure and untainted by men like me. It had been one of the things keeping me from taking her like I wanted to.

"My king," she whispered when we finally parted for a breath.

I growled softly at that. "You never call me that."

I kissed her again, grazing her lip with my teeth and eliciting a sweet little whimper.

"But you are my king," she said. "And I quiver at the thought of what you might do to me if I said..." She kissed me again, her fingernails scraping over my scalp. "Do whatever you want."

I swore silently at the temptation, gripping her hips and hoisting her onto the edge of the table. She squeaked when I devoured her mouth in another kiss and tossed her legs apart. Fabric draped between her knees and I desperately wanted to lift it away and feel her, but I bit back those urges, reminding myself that she had always been curious. Curious to almost dangerous extents. Curious, irresistible, and perfect, but untouched all the same.

"You've never done this with anyone," I pointed out.

"You don't know that."

"Your mortal life doesn't count." I slid my hands down the curves of her sides, my cock straining behind my leathers. "You were relieved of that when you walked through my Labyrinth. Death is the ultimate rebirth, Briar."

She kissed me again, hooking the back of my legs with her ankles to pull me closer. I held my breath for a moment, doing all that I could to resist stripping her and plunging deep into her virgin body. It was all I wanted.

"So, what are you saying?" she panted.

"I'm saying I want you to be sure."

Drawing back, she peered up at me with the slightest hint of a pout that made her kiss-swollen lips bow adorably.

"For years, I've yearned for you," she confessed. "Don't ask me why my heart beats faster when you're near. Don't ask me why the thought of you stealing that innocence from me only excites me. I don't know the answers to any of those questions. I just know that you've woken me from a dream I didn't know I was trapped inside. I see more than I ever have. I don't know who I was in life, but in my gut, I know it doesn't matter. Here, I'm happy. And I hunger for you, Rune of the Glyn." Her nails raked lightly down my neck, reminding me that my cock could get harder still. "My king."

"Fuck, Briar," I whispered, pressing my forehead to hers. "You could have me on my knees if you asked. Do you know what you do to me?"

"I want to. You've given me so many experiences since I've been here with you. The only one I lack is *you*."

I clutched her wrist, dragging her hand down my chest, over my stomach, to the hard erection trapped behind my clothes. She sucked in a shivering breath and boldly cupped me, her heart exploding with passion so quickly the sound was flooding my ears.

"This is what you do to me," I said. "This and so much more, Briar. Tell me again that you want it. Tell me with absolute certainty and I will make you mine. I'll take all of you and I'll give you all of me. Now."

She nodded, her breath fast and deep as she stroked my cock through my pants. Clutching her hair, I tugged her head back to get my point across, desperate to devour her.

"I need more," I said. "Say it."

"I'm already yours, Rune," she breathed. "I always have been."

Those words—those simple words—destroyed and rebuilt me all in one breath. Briar was mine. A little rose that fell at my feet. My empty existence no longer felt hollow and it was all because of her.

Present

For days, I found my way to the library and lost myself in the pages of old books. I learned new things, wandered through exciting stories, and found a new appreciation for macabre charcoal art. Lucien had brought me a dozen books throughout our time together and while I was thankful for them all, I never imagined having so many to choose from. The glass table was stacked every day and by the end, I did my best to put the books back where I found them.

Eventually, I decided to start using the rolling ladder to find books on the higher shelves and discovered an entirely new world of literature. It was overwhelming in a way that I never wanted to give up. Petris, who seemed to get increasingly busy over the days, eventually caught on that I was not leaving the library and began bringing my food there rather than to my bed chambers.

On the fourth or fifth day, I finally fell asleep on the comfy sofa near the balcony with a book about an enchanted pair of boots splayed across my stomach. I hadn't meant to but without an ability to tell time the way I was used to, I barely even knew how long I stayed awake.

I was so comfortable against the embroidered cushions, not ever wanting to wake from what was possibly the best sleep I'd had in months. I heard the faint sound of the library doors opening but was too tired to open my eyes. I was just barely entering the dream space, which, for me, was usually empty darkness or a horrible nightmare, when something soft was draped over my body. I kept my eyes closed, a sense of peace washing over me and encouraging me to fall deeper into my slumber, when a warm hand lightly slid across mine, taking the book I held against my stomach from my lax grip.

I took a long, deep breath and smelled cedar and rain and the faint scent of roses. Perhaps the balcony door had been left open.

Then that warm hand moved to my cheek.

I must have been dreaming. It would be the first time in a long time and I was thankful that the dream was pleasant. And if it was a dream, I could savor it. So I did.

I slowly turned my head into the gentle hand, a breath escaping my lips in a soft hum.

"Sleep well, little bird," a voice said, deep and tender.

And then warm, velvety lips were on my cheek.

It felt too real and I didn't want it to end.

But then the hand was gone. The kiss was gone. I drifted deeper into the dream until the dream turned to the sweet nothingness of a quiet sleep.

And then the music started. Beautiful music. Haunting music. It would have sung me further into my slumber, but I chased it instead. I chased it out of my dreams, reaching for the wonderful, sorrowful sound until my eyes were opening. I was awake... and the music was still playing.

I was curled up on the sofa, a fluffy cushion under my head and a plush, woven blanket draped over my body. I hadn't put the blanket on myself so immediately I began to question what had been a tired hallucination and what had been real.

Looking at the table I'd stacked with books, I recalled an empty plate being there from the lunch Petris had brought me earlier. It was gone. So he must have ventured into the library to see me and kindly cleaned my space and put the blanket on me. My cheeks flushed at the thought of him caring for me like that. Not even Lucien had ever been so thoughtful. He always had Catlyn do those things and still, it was always out of duty more than anything because Lucien had employed her.

Perhaps it was the same with Petris. He worked for the king, after all.

Except, the things he did and the things he said were far more than obligatory acts. He didn't need to show me the library, bring me food from halfway across the palace, or talk to me the way he did.

Rubbing my eyes, I noticed the music again. It was faint, coming from somewhere deep inside the building. The melody was easy to recognize. It was strings. A viola.

I rose from the sofa, feeling a bit of a chill that night, so I wrapped the blanket around myself and walked quietly toward the door. Barefoot since my only trips were from my bed chamber to the library over the past few days, I tiptoed in the direction I thought the music was coming from. At first, I had no idea if I was going the right way, but after trekking clear to the other end of the vast third floor, I found another set of stairs leading to yet another story. The music was louder there, echoing through the halls like the melancholy voice of a woman.

I gripped the metal railing and started to ascend.

The stairs curved and opened up into a shorter hallway with stone walls and sconces burning brightly down the length. A blue carpet stretched across the middle of a stone floor and I followed it, my feet silent.

Louder and louder the music grew. I passed a few big doors but refrained from looking inside. I was easily sidetracked and I wanted to find the source of the tune.

Then, turning a corner, I saw one door that was cracked and letting faint light bleed through. The music was just inside and when I began moving closer to it, the mournful melody became a bit angry. Intense. Then it shifted to something energetic but just as strong. The tangle of emotions was torturing the strings of a viola and it was intoxicating.

I crept toward the door and took the silver handle, pushing it open just enough to peek inside. I saw pale wooden beams and arches throughout a vast bedroom. Blue marble floors. A fireplace as tall as I was with disciplined flames dancing on a stack of logs. A giant bed with silver and blue silk sheets sat a little disheveled in the middle of the chamber like someone had just climbed out of it. The ceiling was a gorgeous mess of vines with tiny white flowers dangling like little dew drops. Tables were stacked with books and candles were fused to wall shelves with melted wax.

The music enveloped the room, bouncing off the walls so the chamber was flooded with the hypnotic sound. I crept inside, heart pounding because something told me exactly whose room I was in. It smelled like him. It *felt* like him. Part of me was screaming for me to run and another part of me was too overcome by the music to heed those warnings.

Passing a smaller table, I glimpsed a half-eaten plate of food and a half-drunk glass of red wine. What was left of the food was familiar. Boiled potatoes with cured meat, cheese, and herbs.

So Petris cooked the dish for the king as well.

The corner of my mouth quirked at the thought and remembering Petris and his kindness made me stop walking. Perhaps it wasn't worth it to catch the king's attention, no matter how much the music lured me in. He hadn't called for me or even passed me in the hall for days. I nearly forgot I was residing in his palace.

And seeking him out in his rooms would only break that comfortable cycle. I decided it was best to leave.

But then the music stopped and my heart with it.

He already knew I was there.

22
BRIAR

The bedroom fell deathly silent and then there he was. The King of the Glyn moved into view from an adjacent room as if he sensed my presence. He rounded the corner and stood there with a viola blacker than coal in one hand and his bow in the other. His long, smoke-blue hair hung over his shoulders and he wore nothing aside from a pair of low-hanging silk pants. His pale chest was bare, a sculpted canvas of muscle and iridescent markings that only emphasized his masculine beauty. His wings were tucked away out of view, making him marginally less intimidating than he was the last time we saw each other.

Silence stretched between us. Rune looked at me with a sense of suspicion like he wasn't quite sure if I was there or not and I was feeling that in my bones. Why was I there? Was I really so weak to an enticing melody?

"Forgive me," I muttered, clutching the blanket around myself like a protective barrier. "I heard the music and... my feet got away from me."

His eyes soaked me in thoughtfully and then he shifted, leaning his instrument against a bookshelf and placing the bow on a cluttered table. I followed the bow as he set it down and knocked a booklet to the floor. It flipped open and I caught a brief glimpse of sketches inside, one of which was of a woman with unruly pale hair and a pair of large wings spread out behind her.

Rune picked up the book, snapped it closed, and tossed it on the table with the others before I could get a good look, but something about that image seared into my mind.

"How did you get in here?"

"The door was open," I said.

He glanced at the open door quizzically. "Was it now." He refocused his attention on me. "You like the melody, then."

It wasn't a question.

"I suppose I did. I enjoy music. It distracts my thoughts."

Our eyes locked and I felt a wave of warmth flood my skin. Maybe it was because he was without a shirt and we were standing in his bed chamber. It seemed awfully intimate for two people who didn't know each other. Well... one person that didn't know the other, at least.

"Do you recognize the piece?" Rune asked.

"Should I?"

Slowly, he cocked his head to one side and studied me. His gaze moved from my head to the blanket wrapped around me and then to my bare feet and back up.

"You've been in the library," he said. "*Your* library."

"Mine?" I vaguely recalled Petris saying something similar.

But he also said the library was *hers*. Rune was not as gentle about the subject as Petris was and I could feel him wanting to push me again about memories I didn't have. I needed to leave, but as soon as I slid my foot back a step, Rune advanced to keep the distance between us the same.

"I enjoy the books very much," I said. "I hope it's alright that I spend time there."

He shrugged. "It was your favorite place in the world. I built it for you, after all. My own addition to this palace. Before, it was simply a dusty room with piles of disheveled books."

"You mean... you built it for *her*."

I didn't sound nearly as stern as I had hoped.

Rune scoffed, rolling his head back and staring at the ceiling for a moment in mild frustration.

"I suppose your scar means nothing," he said, still smiling, but there was no humor behind it.

"I don't understand the magic here. You could have conjured something to match my scar."

Deep down, I was starting to accept it wasn't a coincidence, though.

"That room has been here since before I was king. There was no conjuring—"

"Then it is some kind of trick," I cut him off, feeling cornered. "I've had this scar since I was young. Since my father's sword was dropped into a fire and he pulled it out to fight, burning his hands to protect me before being cut down. I rolled onto the hilt and that's the story of it."

"Is it what they told you?"

"They?"

"In that pitiful asylum you resided in for so many years."

"Petris told you..."

"Is that what they told you to say to me if I should ever get my hands on you again?"

I furrowed my brows at the implication. "Get your hands on me again? What is it that I truly am to you?"

He shook his head with a sigh like he regretted his own words. As always, Rune was heated, letting his emotions eat him alive. I couldn't blame him. I often longed for my emotions to do the same. I'd always bottled them up and they festered like a rotting wound, decaying more every day.

"I'm tired, Briar," he said. "So tired of longing. Of holding back. Of wanting to burn the world."

I felt something at those words. Something I didn't expect. Pity. But more than that, I felt sorrow. For both of us. He imagined I was someone I wasn't and I barely even knew who I was. We were both lost.

"I am sorry for you, Rune," I said.

"Sorry for me?"

He was growing angry again. I needed to quell it. Soothe it. Break the cycle where I would scream in confusion and he would push me toward the edge of my madness. When he stepped forward, hands curling into fists, I clutched the blanket and forced words from my lips.

"What was the song?" I asked, stopping him. He lifted his head, taken aback. "I really did enjoy it."

My heart was racing, but somehow, I managed to get my words out evenly and calmly.

Rune blinked and took a deep breath as if trying to calm himself. "It is called *Bell Ringer*. It is about a man cursed to ring the bells at the gates of eternity. But eternity turned him bitter. Then sad. Then angry and hateful."

"And hateful he remained?" I asked.

Rune's eyes softened a bit, his shoulders relaxing. "No."

"The end of the song seemed a bit aggressive. I assumed—"

"I didn't finish," he whispered.

"Oh." I glimpsed the viola sitting behind him and then shifted my gaze back to Rune, taken by the way his eyes tore into me, digging deep and mercilessly. "Can I hear the end?"

I didn't intend to give myself an excuse to stay longer, but my mouth got away from me. And perhaps part of me truly wanted to hear the end of the song.

Rune hesitated as if he was just as surprised as I was that I'd asked. But eventually, he backstepped toward the viola and picked it up. He watched me as he tucked the end under his chin and poised the bow over the strings. After his eyes had finished stripping my armor from my body and leaving me defenseless, he began to play.

I remembered the aggression and anger in the tune, but where he picked up was nothing like that. It was gentle, slow, and beautiful. The walls bounced the sound back like we were inside an opera house and I was entranced by it. I wanted to stay near the door so I felt like I could escape if I needed to, but I felt a pull leading me further into the room. I watched Rune play, his fingers dancing across the strings with grace and precision.

And the way the firelight caught every curve and dip in his sculpted body made him look like a moving statue, every part of him pure perfection. He was a dream. The melody was a dream. All of it was a dream.

Before I knew it, my foot had moved forward. I stared at his hands as he played the instrument, bending it to his will. I was inching closer and closer, wanting to get nearer to the music. The blanket, my thin security, fell off my shoulders and draped over my arms like a shawl as I stood at the cluttered table, keeping it between myself and Rune as a last-ditch effort not to get too close.

But I wanted to be close. The music was like a siren to my soul and I loved it, even if I knew it could crush me. It was more than a melody and somehow, I knew it was because *he* was playing it.

When the song finished, the echo of it remained for a while, slowly dissipating and leaving us both in silence once more. I blinked, coming back to reality—or a version of it—and looked up at Rune to see his eyes peering down at me with a tenderness I had not yet seen from him.

"You see?" he said softly. "It ends with hope."

"It's beautiful."

He gently placed the viola on the table with its bow and sighed.

"When this room echoes the music, it does not echo the wailing."

"Wailing? The souls, you mean."

He nodded. "There was a time they weren't so loud."

"When was that?"

His eyes met mine and he smirked devilishly. "You don't want to know."

Something in me did want to know, but I didn't push it. Rune was studying me again and it made me feel naked, so I pulled the blanket up once more, pretending to get a chill.

"You've been spending time with Petris," he said.

"He's been kind to me," I said, uncertain how the king would react.

Strangely, instead of acting the part of a jealous lord, he dipped his head with a long exhale, rubbing tension from the back of his neck.

"He's often the things I cannot be."

"He said the two of you are close. What does that mean?"

"It means just that. We're close."

I wasn't going to get answers from him. I wasn't going to get answers from anyone. Not ones I could accept. But I was used to not having answers and even more used to having questions, so I bit my tongue and let it go. But as I was thinking of what else to say, Rune moved slowly around the table toward me. My body went rigid as I backed up a step. But then I decided I needed to hold my ground and wondered if running would only make things worse. It always did at Southminster.

But this isn't Southminster.

"I've made you fear me," he whispered. His hand came up to brush my cheek with the backs of his fingers. I flinched a bit but tried not to turn from his touch. It didn't stop my heart from galloping in my chest. "But at the masquerade, you mentioned how terror was a comfort. What has changed, I wonder."

"I woke from one dream and fell into another," I admitted. "Nothing is ever real. But something about this place scares me more than dreams or nightmares ever could. I suppose it's a different fear. One that does not let me breathe."

His fingers skimmed my jaw and slid gently down the side of my neck to the place my necklace would have been if he hadn't crushed it to dust.

"Because your demons are here," he whispered. "All you left behind remains in these walls. You know it."

"I know nothing."

My heart ached at the confession. I knew nothing. I never had and I never would. I was stuck in limbo as much as the souls in that Labyrinth were. Everything he said—everything Father Eli ever said—trapped me behind another lock I had no key for.

"Still as beautiful as ever."

"Stop," I pleaded.

Rune moved toward me, his hand cupping my cheek. Heat flooded my skin and I shivered, not wanting to feel that way. I didn't want to feel that tug. That strange temptation. I wanted no part of it.

No matter how good it felt…

I closed my eyes and turned my face into his hand, letting my lips skim over his palm. I heard a soft intake of breath when I did that and for some reason, it made that pull even harder to resist. I opened my eyes and looked up at Rune, enveloped in the warmth of his body and the scent of his skin. With his other hand, he took my wrist and raised my palm to his chest.

"I want you to touch me," he whispered. "What your mind has forgotten, your body has not."

I should have pulled away, but I didn't. Even when he released my wrist, I left my hand against his bare chest. Rune stepped in closer until our bodies were nearly pressed together and when he did, I moved my hand down to the hard plain of his stomach, feeling his naked skin under my fingers. His hand slid back, cupping the back of my head. His fingers combed into my hair and he gently tilted my face up, forcing our gazes to meet.

His eyes could melt ice in seconds.

"Something in you recognizes this feeling," he said. "You may have given up what we had, but no amount of effort can completely kill what we were, Briar."

"What were we?" I sighed, unable to stop myself.

"In love."

The word hit me like a brick. It nearly broke the trance, but then Rune dragged me back under when he leaned down toward me, his lips brushing softly against mine. I sucked in a breath, expecting him to be forceful, but he remained gentle, his fingers lightly kneading the back of my head for a moment before he fisted my hair.

"What I wouldn't give to feel you touch me. To feel you kiss me." He moved forward, driving me slowly toward the wall. "To feel your nails tearing at the skin of my back again."

"Stop," I said weakly, my back hitting the wall.

"You don't want me to. I can feel your heart skipping with every word I say."

"You make me nervous."

"Or do I make you crazy? You feel something when I'm around you. Don't lie to me. Don't lie to yourself."

"I don't know what I feel. You're scaring me."

"Because I feel real." His palm pressed to my chest where my heart was thrumming wild and out of control. "Because you want me."

I shook my head, but no words came out. He fisted my hair tighter and tugged, forcing my head back again.

And then his other hand was wrapped around my throat...

He didn't squeeze, but I felt utterly at his mercy.

"As much as I want you wrapped around my cock and your heart around my finger, a part of me wants to end it all," he rasped, sucking the heat out of the moment and replacing it with a cold reminder that he was a monster. "To end the thing that has tormented me all these years."

My brows furrowed and I looked into his darkening eyes with suspense.

"Perhaps you should," I said flatly. He tilted his head, his eyes flitting rapidly back and forth between mine. "If your wish is to put me out of this world, then doing so would grant us both relief. You, relief from me, and me, relief from this existence."

He finally squeezed, barely leaving me air to breathe. "Why are you so eager to leave this world? You were so full of life. So eager to make the best of what was given to you."

"I am *not* her," I said, finally finding a tone fitting for the words. "What I am is a shell stripped of everything that makes a person. *Stop* wishing for more. I am *nothing.*"

Saying it out loud made me lightheaded, but it was my deepest truth.

He shook his head with denial. "No one is nothing."

"We are all nothing. I only discovered it sooner than most."

"Stop."

"Destroy me, Rune. They all said you would."

"Stop."

"If you must hurt me to feel something then do it. I've learned how sweet pain can be. It's man's greatest tool as well as mine. It distracts me from the madness nipping at my heels. Madness feels nothing and too much all at once and it haunts me, so hurt me, Rune. Do me that kindness. Be like all the rest."

Rune shook his head, brows creased like he could not find words to respond. But he did, eventually.

"Perhaps I should hurt you," he said, squeezing my throat a bit harder. "Perhaps I should finally be rid of the thorn in my side. I nearly burned the world for you, Briar. Only to find that you don't even know who I am," he said through his teeth.

I watched him, drowning in his eyes as the air was choked out of me. I didn't need it. I'd always told myself that the moment death licked my neck I would revel in the idea that it was finally noticing me. Finally paying attention.

But then he released me. The rush of oxygen to my brain made me see stars. I lost track of where I was for a split second and the king allowed me no time to process before his lips were crushing mine.

23
BRIAR

Lucien had never kissed me.

His lips never touched mine or any other part of my body for that matter. I wasn't sure I'd ever been kissed, but when Rune's lips were on me, the whole room faded behind a foggy veil. My ears were ringing and my heart was sputtering so wildly I thought I might choke on the vibration.

The hand on the back of my neck held me firm and forced me to crane my head back as Rune ravaged my mouth. His tongue parted my lips and delved inside and I let him invade me. Even when his hand left my throat, I could hardly breathe.

But... something about it felt so terrifyingly good.

I knew Lucien and Lucien only. I knew his clammy hands and his disconnected stares and fleeting feelings of being used and discarded.

This was entirely different. My body felt everything. Even if my mind couldn't recognize it, I felt like my body did.

My palms pressed to Rune's bare chest and I moaned. I didn't mean to. The sound egged him on and he pulled me closer. Heat rose inside me like my skirts had caught fire. I was disappearing.

Fearing that kiss would crack me open for good and I would never be able to fuse myself back together, I tried to pull away. Rune wrapped me in his arms, his strength a prison I wanted desperately to escape and stay inside at the same time. I pulled harder, my fingers curling so my nails were biting into his skin. He groaned and slammed me against the wall, deepening the kiss. I trembled, terrified of the way he was making me feel. Of the way I loved his smell. His power. The taste of him on my tongue. The heat of him on my skin.

I needed to leave. I needed to breathe. To scream.

I shoved against him again and he pushed forward, his knee sliding between my legs. Fire slithered up my thighs and gathered in my core.

It wasn't right.

I'd been taught to be modest. Guarded. Silent.

But I was feeling so vulnerable in that moment. Vulnerable and willing.

Craving a man so cruel was a shameful thought and yet my body was enjoying his harsh touch.

Madness truly was a monster and it was biting into me so hard that if I didn't stop things, I was going to disintegrate under the weight.

So I sucked Rune's bottom lip between my teeth and I bit down. He pulled in a sharp breath and growled, but it wasn't until I tasted blood that he pulled away. Blazing hot eyes tore into me when I looked up at him. Blood wept down his chin. I had bitten him harder than I thought. I could taste the sickening copper tones on my tongue as I panted for breath.

Lucien would have locked me in my room.

Father Eli would have done worse. Much worse.

But Rune just stared at me, breathing heavily as he lifted a hand to swipe at the blood with his thumb.

I needed to flee. Something burned between my thighs and it was disgraceful. Horrifying.

Wonderful.

I ducked under Rune's arm and headed for the door. The blanket had slipped off my shoulders and I felt the cold chill of the palace air on my skin.

Rune did not attempt to stop me as I stormed out of his room. Once in the hall, the dam inside my body began to crack. I knew it would burst soon, so I pressed a hand to my chest and I sped up. Looking back, he was not following me, but that didn't stop my panic from clawing its way up to the surface. It would smother me soon.

I needed Petris.

Of all the people in that place, he somehow had a way of calming me down. Of talking to me in ways that distracted me from the demons playing at my mind. Were I still with Lucien, he would have bled me to expel such horrible things from my thoughts. But I wasn't with Lucien and I was beginning to doubt I ever would be again.

I was beginning to doubt my "sickness" had anything to do with my blood, either.

I didn't know what to think.

I needed to find Petris.

I headed for the kitchen, hoping I'd find him there preparing something delicious. But just as I turned the corner, Elanor was there in the shadows. I nearly crashed into her.

Her gaze was pointed and stern. The way she looked down her nose at me would have made me shrink away any other time, but in the state I was in, I just wanted to hit her. She wrinkled her nose at the blood on my lips and sniffed like she smelled something foul.

"You wreak of greed and indecision," she said, stepping forward.

I held my ground, planting my feet and balling my fists like she was one of the sisters come to buckle me into my cloth prison.

"What are you talking about?" I asked.

She moved toward me again, her lips pressing into a flat line as if she were angry with me.

"My king did not bring you here to give you luxuries and leave you to wander and waste time."

"No, he brought me here thinking I'm someone I'm not."

She moved further into my space. A full hand taller than me, she had a demanding and overbearing presence. Her sharp cheekbones made her face a canvas of shadows and dips.

"What do you want?" I asked.

"I was his first. I'm closer to Rune than anyone. I can feel almost everything he does. The way he pines after you is nauseating. Especially after seeing what you've become." Her gaze moved over me once, dissecting me.

I growled out my frustration and tried to skirt past her. "I can take no more of this. I know I am mad, but I'm beginning to think you all are equally so."

A cold hand coiled around my wrist. Thin as Elanor was, when I tugged against her grip, she was unmoving. I nearly tripped over myself when she started walking, dragging me behind her like a child.

"I will show you what madness truly looks like, little one."

"Stop," I said, my voice much too meek to persuade anyone.

Elanor walked with purpose, holding her black skirt with one hand and pulling me along with the other. I didn't know where we were going. I recognized the halls for a while and then suddenly we were descending a stairway deep underground to a place I didn't even know existed. The steps were rough stone and scratched at my bare feet. Wooden torches lined the walls in such a rugged fashion that it was like we'd entered an entirely new building. The air was cold and smelled of dust and mold. To keep my balance as we rapidly descended the narrow stairwell, I dragged my hand along the wall, barely avoiding tripping on my skirts.

"Where are we going?" I asked. "Stop this. Please."

"You'll find that being gentle and delicate is not in my nature. Neither is waiting. I know what the king desires and he desires the truth. So should you."

I wanted to scream at the top of my lungs that I knew the truth, but if I was being honest with myself, I knew nothing. I was doubting everything I had ever been told since meeting Rune. It made it all so much worse. My mind was a bog. Tar was everywhere and I couldn't make sense of the mess nor could I move through it to find my way.

"Elanor, please," I said, realizing the further we went, the darker the place became.

The rooms where the sisters locked me in were always dark as if the moment they closed the doors, they forgot about me. I'd learned to love the darkness for a while, but the longer they left me, the more I hated the silence. Now, those awful feelings were coming back. I tried to pry at Elanor's fingers, but her grip remained too firm.

"Please," I repeated.

We came to a door. It was simple and wooden with a round metal handle. When Elanor shoved it open, the wood cracked and squeaked on rusted hinges.

Utter darkness lay beyond it.

"Do not put me in a cell," I said, really starting to fight her but to no avail. "Stop this!"

She pulled me further and further into the basement where the stone floor turned to frigid, damp grittiness.

"I cannot break him," Elanor said, catching me off guard. "Maybe you can."

She snapped her fingers and a row of hanging lanterns along the wall burst to life, lighting the basement with orange light. I smelled piss and filth and pressed the back of my wrist to my nose, pressing my back against the wall as the firelight flooded a small cell in front of me. There was someone inside divided by a row of steel bars that seemed much too intricate for such a dank dungeon.

Panting, both from fear of being thrown in a cell and exerting myself to get away from Elanor, I peered into the space and saw a figure dressed in white. Or what used to be white. His garments were now stained with dirt and other excrements and tattered nearly beyond recognition. He was curled up on a few wool blankets against the wall and stirred when he noticed us. I saw his face when he rolled onto his side and my breath turned to ice in my lungs.

"Father Eli?" I muttered.

Elanor grabbed my shoulders and shoved me toward the bars.

"Oh, my little beauty," he rasped, smiling at me as if he wasn't locked in a filthy cell rotting away.

I gripped the bars in front of me, not knowing what I was supposed to do.

"What have they done to you?" I asked.

Like an animal, he crawled to the bars, dragging his white robes behind him.

"Oh, nothing I did not expect," he said through another smile. His hands clamped over both of mine and squeezed. "I wanted to see you. They said I could not." His cold lips pressed to my knuckles. It was something he'd never done and I stared, taken aback. In fact, he barely ever touched me at Southminster. He had mostly ordered others to do it. "I must bleed you. To keep the sickness at bay."

"I—I thought the same. I have not been well, but... you said I was better."

"Oh, did I?" He laughed. The sound was maniacal and high-pitched.

Whatever they'd done to him, it had driven him past his brink. I turned to Elanor to see that she'd backed into the shadows, giving me plenty of space.

"Let him go. It's me you all want. Why is he here?"

Before Elanor could refuse me, I felt a blunt pain on my fingers and jumped back, holding my hand where Father Eli's teeth had almost broken the skin. He reached for me, smiling again, and then completely descended into a pained, sorrow-filled whimper, shaking his head.

"We must bleed you," he said under his breath.

"Father Eli," I said. "What is it they want? Perhaps you can tell them and they'll let you go."

I didn't believe that for a second.

"What they want is the truth."

"What do you mean? What truth?"

His bloodshot eyes met mine and I saw something in them. Something wicked and awful. I'd seen him look at me like that before. Every time he was mad at my lack of progress, he gave me those eyes. I inched backward, catching another whiff of urine and dirt.

"So stupid," he said, staring right into my eyes. "So perfectly, horribly stupid you are."

"Father…"

"It was so perfect while it lasted. Now look. I'm in a shit-covered cell beneath the very palace you came from."

I felt my stomach turn at the implication and shook my head slowly, wishing I hadn't just heard what he said.

"You've been beaten into saying what they want you to say," I muttered.

He laughed, but that time it sounded dark and mocking. "And *you* were tortured into believing what we wanted *you* to believe. For fifteen. Fucking. Years."

My head was on fire. My ears were pounding. My heart had completely stopped and my breath was a ball in my throat. I'd been struck with words I didn't want to hear... again. Father Eli's chuckle was a distant sound until I came back to the world and was able to process what he said.

"Don't," I said. "Tell them the truth. Tell them what you did for me at Southminster. Perhaps then we can both leave this place."

"I'm not leaving this place. Whether I speak the truth or not, the king will kill me. Slowly if he decides he has the time for it."

"Why? I—I don't understand. Father—"

"Because we took something of his. We took the heart right out of the devil's impenetrable chest." He turned to face the bars more directly, pressing his forehead between two of them to look up at me. "We sliced off her pretty wings. Then we cut off her pretty hair. Her pretty nails. We almost took her pretty teeth, but she'd grown smart by then. She stopped biting."

"No... that was to protect the sisters. To protect you. So you could help me."

I completely disregarded the part about "wings." Father Eli wasn't well…

"Help you? Because your family was slaughtered and you witnessed the whole thing? Stupid girl. We had to think of something to tell you. Something horrible. Something that you wouldn't *want* to remember. And every time you questioned it, we showed you the reasons why you shouldn't."

Pain lanced down my back where two rigid scars had always been. I was told they were from the incident that had taken my family from me. Just like the brand on my hip.

"I don't understand," I whispered.

"We tortured you, Briar!" he roared, pounding his hands against the bars like he wanted to lunge at me. "The slicing. The drowning you and reviving you. The solitary rooms bound and buckled. The breaking of your bones. Can't you remember!" He laughed his last words like he was teasing me and it twisted my insides into knots. "You tried, poor thing. You tried to kill yourself. First, you tried to bite off your tongue. So we gagged you. Then you tried to cut open your wrists. So we bound you. You tried to starve, but we couldn't have that. So down your throat, the tubes went. Every time you whined 'Where is Rune! Where is he?'" He spoke in a high-pitched, mocking tone to mimic a woman. "Do you know how crazy you sounded? 'The King of the Glyn will find me. Ooohhh!' No one wanted to help you. You *belonged* at Southminster with the psychos and the lunatics."

"You're lying!" I screamed.

"There she is. 'You're lying. You're lying.' You said it all the time, every day I told you about your parents dying in that massacre. Half-worlders? Half-worlders never come onto our plane anymore. Except, of course, to retrieve something that belongs to them." Another loud, raspy laugh. "We thought we'd have to just kill you, but you came around. It worked. It *finally* worked..." He stopped, staring right into my eyes. "Once Dr. Matthers cut into your head. Oh, after that, you complied. More and more every day you believed everything we said and more and more you forgot about *him*. It finally. Fucking. Worked."

He pulled on the bars and lurched to his feet. "We tamed the devil's love," he said through his teeth. "We practically skinned you alive and we put something else inside. Something perfectly wrecked."

"No," I whimpered. "No, I'm... I'm a.."

"A what? A sad little orphan who came running to us? Barefoot and traumatized? Stupid! If you'd have asked anyone, no one has ever heard of Haydenside. It docsn't fucking exist."

"This... this is my madness coming to taunt me." I shoved my fingers into my hair, pulling at my scalp. The pain helped to ground me. It led me back from my nightmares. Only it wasn't working. "I am not—"

"You are *nothing*."

"No... Lucien. He took me from that place to give me a better life. To take care of me."

"Lucien was the worst of them. He visited you long before he became your guardian. I advised against it. Fucking a girl while she's brain-dead and strapped to a bed is low, even for me, but he did fund the entire thing, so who was I to question him? He hired the doctor. The sisters. He bought my institute so we could focus solely on you and no one else."

"Stop."

"He loved that pretty cunt of yours. So much that he wanted you all to himself."

"Stop!"

I pulled at my hair again, craving the sting. But that demon was biting at my ankles. The one telling me to seek violence.

Blood. I spun and caught Elanor staring at me, her expression unchanged. Then, like she knew exactly what I wanted—what I needed—she snapped her fingers and I heard a metallic click. I spun around to see the gate crack open like the lock had been dislodged. My eyes rose to see Father Eli stepping away from the bars, his eyes tired but his smile remaining.

"Grant me what I denied you all these years," he said, lifting his hands out to his sides to present himself.

No longer was he the big man in robes waiting for me to enter his study. No longer was he the man who'd slapped my hands with a wooden stick when I did not recite his words the right way.

No longer was he my savior.

Deep down, I knew he never had been.

His constant whispers veered me down the wrong path. And now I was lost, likely never to be found again. All because of him. Because of Lucien.

"Why?" I asked, stepping toward the bars.

"Why?" he whispered. "For immortality. For the thing everyone wants but is unwilling to stoop for. Your blood was the answer to that."

"Sick blood."

"Immortal blood. Sweeter than plums and richer than wine. It can add years to a mortal life or it can cure incurable disease." Finally, his smile fell and his shoulder drooped. "But I am spent. Do as you wish."

Slice him. Hurt him.

I shook my head. "I am not a killer. I am not cruel." I looked back at Elanor, tears stinging my eyes. "Not like everyone else here."

I spun to leave when Father Eli's voice followed my retreat.

"You finally agreed, you know," he said. I stopped, my nails cutting into my palms. "You agreed to forget. Your way of taking the pain away, I suppose. You sacrificed all that you knew just so the pain would stop. You let Dr. Matthers pierce your brain. And your last words? 'I found my way before and I will again.'" He laughed lightly at that as if it was a joke. "Looks like you'll never find your way now, stupid girl."

Rage. Fire. Blood. My vision turned red. The air smelled of copper and filth now. I wanted to stop breathing but instead, I was panting. Still, I couldn't get enough air. My fingers itched to feel flesh ripping beneath them. Father Eli's flesh. I'd felt that rage before and it nearly destroyed me.

Use it.

Kill him.

Lost, confused, and shattered, I needed something to sink my hatred into. Someone to take the fury and disdain that was about to eat me alive. I turned, slowly that time, and I looked at Father Eli. The man who'd fooled me into thinking he was helping me. The man who filled my head with so many lies. The one who'd taken everything from me. Everything. And now I didn't even know what everything was. I had nothing.

I thought I knew madness. I thought I had finally begun to understand it, but in that moment, I was madness itself. I was crazed. Bloodthirsty. My heart beat in a rhythm I hardly recognized as if lunging for Father Eli before my feet even moved. I marched toward the cell, my eyes seeing him and only him.

I flung the gate open, preparing to wrestle him to the ground where I'd likely lose in a battle of strength. But he didn't move at all. He stood there, closed his eyes, and let my fingers clamp around his throat. I dug my nails in, feeling hot, sticky blood against my hands as I drove him back into the wall. I screamed, the sound broken and shrill. It instantly ripped my throat to shreds, but there was no helping it. I'd never felt the way I was feeling then.

I shoved Father Eli's head against the rough stone. Once. Twice. I heard his skull crack and screamed again through clenched teeth, pulling him to the ground. He moaned in pain, curling in on himself as if he was having second thoughts about letting me touch him. Perhaps he didn't truly want to die. Or perhaps he'd never known true pain until then. But he had denied me the chance so many times to end things for myself, so I was going to deny his chance to live.

I walked into the hall, taking one of the lanterns from its wall hook, and swung it down on his head. Again on his arm. His leg. Blood spilled from his split skin when the hot glass shattered across us both. I felt some of it hit me but I used the pain. I used it like a weapon and I hit him again. The lantern oil spilled over his robes and caught fire, eliciting a high-pitched shriek that went on forever as he rolled in the flames.

"You took everything from me!" I cried, my voice ragged.

I tossed the broken lantern aside and just watched him burn, screaming. Crying. I wished I could keep hitting him, but I couldn't The way the flames had claimed his body made it impossible. Burning flesh filled the cell with an acrid odor as Father Eli staggered to his feet, skin peeling in paper-thin layers as the fire devoured his face. And when he scraped at it in a feeble attempt to wipe the flames away, only flesh and melting fat came away on his fingers until he was practically dripping pieces of his own body.

I watched with sadistic satisfaction as he burned. He yelled louder than my ears could take, but I forced myself to listen. I forced myself to memorize those sounds. He'd robbed me of my memories and so I'd fill that empty space with my vengeance.

I dodged him as he stumbled across the cell and hit the wall. I could have finished it, but I didn't. I watched until the flames engulfed his mouth and nose. His cries were choked when the fire flooded his lungs and he convulsed, collapsing to the floor. His voice turned to wet gurgles and finally, he stopped moving. His body was a twitching, burning heap on the floor at my feet and I felt... nothing.

I stared, searching for remorse. For disgust. For anything that could remind me I was human and had a soul, but all I found was gratification. Pieces of undeveloped emotions were scattered inside me, just as broken as they were before Father Eli was a corpse. I'd accomplished nothing except surrendering to my wrath and hate and confusion.

Madness had become me and it was unforgiving.

Covered in blood and dirt, I turned and walked slowly out of the smoke-filled cell, shaking and dazed. I barely knew where I was but a part of me knew, without a doubt, that I'd been wanting to do that for years. I finally had and I felt emptier than ever.

And then *he* was there.

He was standing in the shadowed hallway, clothed in a blue tunic cinched tightly at his narrow waist. Rune. Pristine and handsome and absolutely aware of what I'd just done. I shouldn't have cared at all what he thought of me, but I still felt shame. Embarrassment. Resentment over the fact that he was right about me to some capacity and part of me knew all along.

Tears touched my eyes, but they had yet to fall. Perhaps they were from the smoke because I couldn't feel a damn thing at that moment.

It's finally happening. You're drowning.

Maybe it was for the best. Maybe I needed to let go because no matter what, I was still lost without memories to guide me.

The past I thought was real was a lic and my real past was shrouded and unobtainable. I was nothing.

I ran.

My dress was covered in soot and my hands were sticky with blood.

"Briar, stop," his voice called to me.

But I didn't. No more following orders. No more doing what others told me. No. More.

I hoisted my skirts off the floor and I sprinted up the steps, dizzy with emotions. When I came to the foyer, I ran for the heavy doors and gripped the thick handle.

"Do not go outside like this," Rune demanded. "Briar."

Vision blurred behind tears, I hauled the door open a crack and squeezed through to the outside. Where I was going, I didn't know. All I knew was that I needed to leave. I needed to get away and free myself from the cage. All of the cages.

The moment my feet hit the cobblestone, the chill of the outside devoured me. I didn't care. I retreated down the path, through a vast garden, past the maze entrance, and into the darkness. I didn't know how far the darkness went, but I was certain it wasn't far enough.

The cobblestone disappeared and my bare feet hit damp soil. Moss. Sticks and dried leaves. Black trees came into view and I ran straight toward them, careless of the increasingly cold air. I was breathing heavily. So heavy that my head was spinning. I felt nausea bubbling in my stomach and swallowed it down. I would *not* let Father Eli's death make me sick.

But maybe it wasn't the burnt flesh and blood that made me ill. It was all the things he said. All the things I already knew and foolishly denied.

Stupid girl. Stupid, stupid girl.

Something was behind me. Heavy footfalls quickly rose up in my wake followed by the eerie, growling breath of something in pursuit. The demon of my insanity perhaps… or something else. I didn't care. It could eat me alive and I would thank it for doing what I could not.

Branches grabbed at my hair and dress. Stones and roots dug into my heels. The air chilled my lungs and chapped my lips but I just kept going, begging the darkness to swallow me whole. But then I reached a clearing and my foot snagged on a log. I went tumbling forward and rolled across a mossy knoll. Once I was on my back, the massive shadow of a winged creature rose into view, silhouetted against the full, bright moon. Claws and teeth glinted in the light as fleshy white wings beat to lift the creature into the air. A spine-wrenching growl flooded my ears and red eyes bore down on me like two glowing drops of blood.

Fear shoved me out of my stupor, reminding me that my heart was still beating and some twisted sliver of me desired that it kept doing so. I leapt up, grabbing a big rock on my way to my feet. I lifted it and threw it at the beast with all my strength, hitting it in its ugly snout. It hunched forward in anger, its jaw unhinging to open wide and bear its long teeth. It was so pale that I could see every vein and bone through almost transparent skin. Its spine was too long for its limbs, curving in a way that made every vertebra protrude.

Fury and frustration and sadness over my own existence burst out of me in an ear-piercing scream as the creature lunged, its open jaw showing more rows of teeth. The eyes rounded with madness, bugging out of its head. It rose on two legs, stalking toward me and audibly snapping its teeth over and over again. Strings of drool slid from its lips and I braced, bearing my own blunt teeth at the monster in response.

At least this creature did not pretend to be anything more than a hungry, nightmarish fiend.

It raised its hand, uncurling long, bony fingers. I silently begged it to aim for the heart when a symphony of howls rose up all around the clearing. The creature paused, its nostrils flaring wide as dozens of padded feet sprinted toward the clearing.

Would I be torn to bits by wild hounds, too? I couldn't even be surprised by that luck.

Just as I thought the worst, I saw a large animal appear from the shadows. It was a hound, yes, but not one I'd ever seen. Its body was rippling with lean muscle hugged in short, shiny black hair. A long snout was wrinkled into a snarl as it shot forth on four legs with feet that had long, almost finger-like toes. On its head were two ram's horns that coiled back from its face and glowing red eyes stared straight forward. I was certain the beast was going to lunge right for me and fight over the spoils of my death, but it didn't.

The hound raced toward the pale, winged creature, its jaws clamping down on its wrist. More hounds darted from the trees and attacked ferociously, scratching and biting. I watched in horror as they fought, but the creature flung its attackers off one by one. The six of them could only slow it down, but they couldn't take it to the ground. I needed to move away, but I couldn't find my balance.

A break in the hounds' attack made the beast turn its voracious attention back on me. It reared its head back with a screech that could have broken glass and then stilled, its eyes widening again with shock. I pressed my palms over my ears, my eyes focusing on the bloody tip of a sword through the creature's stomach. It stumbled backward and as it did, two giant black wings spread from behind it. Wings that were not its own.

With one beat, Rune was in the air, yanking the sword from the beast's belly. Guts and entrails spilled from the cavity sounding like dead fish flopping onto a deck. The smell was like meat that had been sitting in the summer sun for five days. I backed away as Rune landed on the ground between me and the creature, fury burnt across his perfect features. He marched toward me, bloody sword in hand, and took my wrist.

He was going to take me back.

Flashes my many attempts to escape the asylum ravaged my mind. The beating. The dragging. The tears. The feeling of hope being ripped away, layer by agonizing layer.

I tried to free myself from Rune the same as I had those burly guards at Southminster, but he was unyielding. His grip was so harsh that I nearly felt my bone break. Just when he turned around, the beast had recovered, barely aware that its entrails were tangling around its feet as it walked. Its horrifying, toothy grin returned. Like a hellish hyena, it laughed, the sound sending needles through my insides until the nausea returned. It swiped at Rune, but he blocked, slicing the creature's hand clean off with his blade. The severed appendage flopped to the ground, long fingers twitching.

Unfolding its wings, the creature opened its jaws again and stretched to its full height, towering over Rune. It could have swallowed his whole head. With its other hand, it swung and Rune cleaved that one off too, but not cleanly. It dangled on tendons, the sharp bone shard exposed. It bit down on Rune's sword and ripped it from his hand, cutting its cheeks on the blade, but it didn't care. It tossed the sword aside and before I knew it, Rune was spinning around and using his body as a barrier between the beast and me. He jolted, letting out a loud growl through clenched teeth.

Rune turned around again, pulling his shoulder off of the creature's sharp wrist bone. He'd been impaled. Blood soaked his tunic, but he paid it no mind. His wings fanned out and he leaped into the air again, coming down on the beast's back. I watched as Rune took the creature's smiling head in his hands and twisted it to one side at such a sharp angle that the spine audibly snapped in two. The creature went silent. Its big eyes rolled back in its skull. Its jaw dropped open and one last wheezing breath sighed from its corpse.

Rune released the creature's jaw and let the body droop to the ground in a heap of white flesh, blood, and guts. His wings folded back but one of them looked a bit limp. I watched him stretch his shoulders and wince, hissing as three crows sored into the clearing. They dropped to the ground like black droplets of smoke and landed, appearing as three beautiful women.

Lura was immediately at Rune's side, babying him and pouting like seeing him hurt could bring her to tears. Naeve glimpsed the corpse, her eyes widening when she realized I was standing on the other side of it. When she saw a couple of the horned hounds limping and licking at their wounds, she moved to beckon them to her side. She began petting them and examining the minor damage with love. Elanor, however, regarded everything with her chin high and her hands rested by her sides like nothing about it fazed her.

"Take our king back," she said, her eyes piercing into me.

"Come, my king," Lura said.

"What about the kelpher?" Naeve asked, pointing at the carcass. "It will attract more shades."

"Disgusting thing," Lura grimaced.

"And… what happened to you, sweet?" Naeve asked me.

"She murdered our prisoner," Elanor said coldly.

"She—"

"Enough," Rune barked. "Let the hounds feast on the kelpher. They earned it. And take Briar back to Ferrothorn."

"What about you, my dear king?" Lura whimpered, hanging on his shoulder like an attention-starved cat.

He turned to her, gently placing his hand on her cheek. "I will be fine. You know I will. Now, do as you're told."

And just like that, Rune turned his back, groaning quietly as he stretched his wings, and launched himself out of the clearing.

"Where's he going?" I asked.

Elanor stepped forward and looked at the bloody beast on the ground. Wrinkling her nose, she snapped her fingers, and the hounds, forgetting their injuries, trotted toward the thing and began to eat, ripping at flesh and breaking bone. The sound was unnerving, but I dared not look away. Violence was no stranger and watching the skin tear only reminded me that I'd survived yet another horrible fate. It was like death was mocking me.

"Come, sweet," Naeve said. "They smell even worse when they're dead."

Lura walked beside us as we headed back to the palace, her arms hugging her torso.

"He's hurt," she whined.

"Stop your crying," Naeve said. "He's been hurt worse. Much worse." She said the last part under her breath as if recalling something awful.

"Where did he go?" I asked.

Naeve wrapped an arm around my shoulders and pulled me close. "Our instructions weren't to wonder where he's gone. They were to bring you back. Gods, you're shaking." She rubbed her hands up and down my arms. "We'll get you all better. Won't we, Lura?"

"He needs us," she pouted.

"Ugh." Naeve rolled her eyes.

We returned to the palace sometime later, which made me realize how far I'd run. My feet were bleeding and my throat burned and I could still feel the blood on my hands and smell Father Eli's burning body in my nose. It was disgusting and foul.

When we arrived on the second floor, Lura was still pouting. Naeve brought me to a door only a couple of rooms down from my chamber and walked inside. Scented floral oils were strong in the air. Lura, still frowning, walked over to a footed bathtub and turned a little faucet handle on the spout, letting the metal tub fill with steaming water.

Since I'd arrived, I had been bathing with cloth and wash bowls. I hadn't even thought of having a real bath. I'd been too overwhelmed.

Like every other part of the palace, the bathroom was like a dream. Fresh vines covered the walls. Tall windows let in the light from outside and flooded the whole chamber with it. Preoccupied, Lura sprinkled the filling tub with oils and then sighed sorrowfully as she started to pace.

"Don't mind her," Naeve said, helping me to undress. "She's rather attached to the king. We all are, but poor Lura has been infatuated for many years."

"Infatuated?" I said.

"It's hard not to be when a man like him decides to make you when he needs care the most," she chuckled. "Lura just wants to see him happy because he made her when he was at his saddest."

"And you? When did he make you?"

She sighed. "Just before you disappeared." Her smile was hesitant. "He made me when he was happiest. Mostly to be your friend," she chuckled.

"And... Elanor?" I didn't want to ask about her, but since we were on the subject.

"Elanor is the oldest. Neither of us even know how old she is, but I do know he made her when he was... how should I put this... his most violent self."

"I don't understand."

Naeve started helping me out of my garments.

"Rune was damn near ruining this place before you came along. Slaughtering souls." She winced. "Terrible, vicious business."

"He slaughtered them?"

"Didn't think they were getting a just afterlife. Evildoers don't often get what they deserve. Law says he can't interfere with a soul's journey inside the mist. But he can do whatever he likes to souls if they leave the Labyrinth. So..." She lowered her voice. "He coaxed the bad ones out so he could kill them before they reached their afterlife or found another body to occupy."

"That doesn't sound so bad," I said, thinking about all the people I wanted to kill at Southminster now that the blindfold was starting to tear and I knew what they were truly doing.

"No, it doesn't. But fury is a powerful thing and Rune didn't stop at the bad ones. When a soul escapes into the Glyn, it changes. Bad, good, innocent, guilty. It's all the same if they get loose. They all turn into beasts looking to feed on what they don't have. So he started slaughtering them all. And he liked it... which was the problem. Thought he was doing good work. Thought he was the only one who could make those hard choices."

I shuddered at the idea. Innocent souls and bad souls, all wrapped up in monstrous transformations. Images of Rune hunting them down and killing them put him in an entirely new light.

"But that was nearly a century ago," Naeve said, trying to make light of things. "When he found you, it all changed." She sighed sharply. "Sometimes I think Elanor doesn't like that he changed, though."

When my dress slid off my shoulders and pooled at my feet, I started to come back and realize what had happened. What had *truly* happened. I lifted my hands in front of me and glimpsed the dried blood under my nails and in the grooves of my palms.

"Gods," Naeve gasped. She cleared the hair from my back and gawked at the scars I knew I had there. "So it's true, then. Elanor was the one to change you when you arrived. She said what you looked like, but—"

I spun around, catching the shocked look on Naeve's face. I said nothing. I just processed it and then took a deep breath, straightening my spine.

Truly, I didn't care who saw my scars. My body was far from sacred. Less so now that I'd heard the truth of things from Father Eli. Being bent over a table and fucked by Lucien was one thing. Knowing he did it while I was strapped to a bed, practically dead, made the acid in my stomach boil.

Nothing about me was sacred.

I faced away from Naeve just as the tub had filled up and I turned off the water. I knew how to bathe on my own. I often didn't like Catlyn to help me since most of my baths followed moments of Lucien's indulgence and I was always eager to wash parts of myself Catlyn probably didn't want to see. In this case, I wasn't washing Lucien away, but I was washing something much worse from my body. Shame, regret, and disgust to name a few.

Naeve stepped forward as I sank into the steaming water. I curled my knees to my chest and stared blankly at the vine-covered wall in front of me.

"I can bathe myself," I said.

Naeve and Lura both paused like the statement surprised them. They were probably expecting to have to help me through my turmoil and nurture me, but I needed no nurturing. What I needed was a moment to soak it all in. To realize how utterly fucked I was. I just needed time to process how wrong it all was so I could at least mend my thoughts.

But who was I kidding? If I could not mend my thoughts before, I certainly couldn't now.

26
RUNE

It was the last day of the autumn crossing. The week of Allhalloween made the walls between worlds as thin as lace veils and I had one night and one night only to do the thing I'd wanted to do since the moment I saw *him* at the masquerade.

Lucien Van Lock. The monster who'd defiled one of the most beautiful souls I'd ever met. My Briar. The way she spoke of him as if she needed him—as if she loved him—made me sick, but I couldn't bring myself to tear a man apart if she felt so strongly for him. Not in the beginning. Now, after what I heard Father Eli say in that piss and shit-covered cell, there was no holding back. No more trying to remain good. I was rigid and bloodthirsty, through and through. I'd given my sweet Briar my fae blood. I'd given her wings to fly. Freedom to be curious. I'd promised her love and protection and I failed.

They took everything from her. They took her from *me*.

I would burn the whole world for her.

I could, and that should have terrified people.

I stood inside the manor where Briar had been residing for the past couple of years, according to my findings. It was so far from the place I'd lost her initially. If only I had found her sooner. Even Elanor's constant trips to the mortal world did not yield any results and waiting to be granted passage every year was torture.

But I would have ripped the world apart if I had been allowed to roam freely among mortals. Phariel knew it, the bastard, and yet he never once aided in my search. He was too caught up in how humans adored him to care that his brother was on the verge of tearing everything to shreds right under his feet. He hadn't even complained about the slaughter at the Allhalloween masquerade yet. The masquerade I held right under one of his beloved cathedrals where humans sang their misplaced adoration for him on the daily.

The narcissistic cunt.

Maybe he was too afraid to complain. Murdering and bleeding dozens of his precious humans was a breach of our guidelines, but for me, it was simple revenge for him allowing humans to violate and break my sweet Briar right under his nose.

If he ever built up the nerve to face me, I would burn his heart right out of his chest and send it to Malvec to rot. And perhaps he knew it.

But none of it mattered now.

The manor was dull and smelled old and outdated. It was nothing like her. No part of that place reflected the colorful, vibrant soul that I knew was trapped inside the prison they'd built around it.

Lucien wasn't home. Good. I wanted time to absorb the filth of it all. Time to be disgusted and furious. I needed to feel it all, to let it choke me so I could pour all of that disdain into Lucien when I killed him.

Aedon Heights was drab and cold and the more I walked, the more the place felt dead. Sadness gripped me knowing I did not find Briar sooner. Years of hating her felt like the biggest sin I had ever committed because while I was hating her, she was suffering immeasurable pain and torment.

Father Eli's words echoed in my head. The way he said she called for me. How she wished I would come for her. How she allowed herself to forget only to save her from a fate that I could not rescue her from.

Had I known the truth, I would have cursed all the laws of the realms. I would have found a way to cross plains—to defy the order of things—to pull her from that hell. And I would take whatever punishment the universe bestowed on me if it meant she was safe.

Instead, I had been gullible and foolish.

My nose twitched when I caught a familiar scent. Briar's scent. I followed her flowery smell up worn steps to a second floor, only it was leading me further up a narrow corridor and into a small room at the very top of the manor's tower. It overlooked orchards and the ugly cathedral in town. A large chest sat at the foot of the bed, the lid open like someone had recently sifted through it. A white dress was draped over the lid and when I touched it, I could smell his filth all over it. His sweat. His spend. I bared my teeth and hissed, tossing the over-worn fabric.

He'd fucked her in that dress. How many times, I didn't know. Sickness rolled inside me again.

Good. I was going to use it. I deserved to feel every ounce of it until the day I was dust.

Walking around the bed, I smelled Briar on the sheets. On the pillow. I saw her sorrowful strokes on a painting of an apple tree near the window. A stack of dusty books sat on the nightstand and another was on a desk opposite the bed.

She did love to read.

After exploring her tight, drab confines and finding myself wound up with more emotions than I wanted to ever experience, I found myself standing in front of that window. I stared at the view that I was certain Briar stared at every day during her time with the wicked Lucien. Even with a broken mind, I knew in my gut that she would have wanted to look into the world and imagine what she'd do if she was ever truly free to explore it.

My breath trembled at the thought. The rage was building, one fiery drop at a time, waiting for Lucien to return. I would wait until the Glyn ripped me back from the mortal plane if I had to. And I would wait in front of that window where my Briar once stood, breathing in the filthy air of the realm that stole her from me. The realm that had twisted her and cut her up into tiny, discernable pieces, all for greed. All for the fae blood *I'd* given her.

Guilt had a bitter taste, like blood and acid combined, and I used it to stoke the flames of my wrath when I heard the door downstairs creek open.

He was home.

The day was late. The house was dim. Lucien's manor was far off the beaten path, isolated from prying ears. Silently, I glided downstairs and sat myself at a long dining table in what was clearly Lucien's seat. I heard two voices. A woman and the snake himself. When the woman came into the dining room and headed for a few lanterns to give the room light, I waited, watching her plump form waddle around.

She was just a servant. Guiltless, I suspected, and likely better off without her employer. When she lit the first lantern and the light passed over me, she gasped, nearly leaping out of her skin when she saw me lounging in her master's chair. Quietly, I raised a finger to my lips and she clamped her mouth shut. Lucien entered the room behind her, holding his pocket watch in one hand like he was tight on time.

"Mr. Tilken said they'll continue questioning—"

He choked on the rest of the sentence when he saw me and froze. It took everything in me not to stand and lunge forward to rip out his throat, but that was too easy. I recalled his sickly face at the masquerade. Naeve had been kind enough to put mushroom powder in his drink, ensuring he'd be out of the way most of the night while I circled my prey. At the time, it was Briar. Now, I wished I'd focused on Lucien.

"Who are you?" he demanded, looking me up and down.

I remained seated and looked once more at the help. "Go on," I said softly. "Tell your peelers that Baron Van Lock is dead."

"What?" she gasped, pressing a hand to her chest.

"You heard me." My eyes went back to Lucien, watching them round in fear. "You found him, mutilated on the floor of his estate."

"I—"

"Now," I cut her off.

She quickly spun and sprinted out the door.

As I suspected. She held no love for him. Who ever could?

Lucien tried to follow, but as soon as he moved, I was behind him. I gripped his throat, pulling him up and off his feet before slamming him down onto the dining table. Candlesticks crashed to the floor and the noise made the woman yelp as she scurried out of the house. I could hear her muffled voice screaming for help as she ran. Hearing it made Lucien scream for help as well. I would have covered his mouth to conceal the shrill noise, but I loved it. So, instead, I soaked it all in, smiling maniacally.

"Scream," I snarled. "Scream all you want." I grabbed the front of his coat and pulled him toward me, eyes glowing with hatred. "Lucien Van Lock." I emphasized every word with disgust before moving my nose over his face, taking in the stink of tobacco and bourbon. "Do you know who I am?"

"Y—You're him. The one they said would come for her."

"So, you don't know. Not really."

"I—I—"

"How did you get Briar in the first place? Did you see a young woman alone and snatch her up? A young woman like her must have looked perfect for the taking."

"No. I didn't. That was Father Eli's business. I wasn't there."

I picked him up again and threw him into his too-fancy chair. "Did you know she was mine?"

"I didn't know! Father Eli said he acquired a fae girl from a woman. I didn't believe him at first. Fae haven't been around since the war. You can't even find them in the dark market these days. But then I saw her. Sh—She needed tending, poor thing."

I blinked at that strange comment, but I didn't let it distract from my resolve.

"Tending? Like a fucking stray animal?"

"Look, I only provided the funding."

"Why?" I snarled.

"I..."

"Why!"

"I—I was dying! No doctor could save me. I needed fae blood. That's what all the old books said. Fae blood can make you better. Make you live longer."

The idea made me shake with repulsion. Fae blood. Dark market. Harvesting immortal blood to buy a few measly years of a pathetic, empty life. It was sickening.

"I didn't touch her when she was in the asylum," he continued. "That was all Father Eli. He's the one you should talk to. He had his methods."

I laughed darkly at that. "Father Eli is dead. And before he died, he confessed a few things."

I propped my foot against the chair between Lucien's knees and knocked the whole thing back onto the floor. He screamed again, a sound much too high-pitched for a grown man. Circling around, I crouched down by his head and gripped his chin, hovering over his fear-stricken face.

"Such as how you defiled her body," I continued, those words stinging my throat. My claws protruded from the tips of my fingers, eager to tear and maim as I stroked his stubbly cheek. "While she was immobile and restrained. Your filth and perversion are all over this house. I can feel it." My talon cut into his flesh and he writhed, trying to escape the pain. "*My* Briar."

"Wh—What are you going to do?" he said with a shiver, his hands grasping the arms of his overturned seat.

I lifted my bloody talon to my mouth and swiped the acrid blood over my tongue, tasting his deceit all over it.

"I'm going to relieve you of your wrongdoings," I muttered, a cold chill overtaking me. "For her. For me. For you, Lucien."

I gripped his head and with a hard tug, I slid him off his chair and swung around to straddle his body.

"You always knew I'd come for her, but I don't think you fully understood. I am Merikoth. The Keeper of the Dead. The King of the Glyn. The Devil in Blue. Call me what you want for the next few moments that I allow you to live, but it makes no difference."

"Phariel, save me!" he shrieked before tensing his jaw.

I chuckled at that and shook my head. "He really does have you all believing in his horse shit lies."

210

Slowly, I gripped his jaw again and dug my nails into his cheeks, forcing him to unclench his teeth. Then I shoved my fingers into his mouth, prying his top jaw from the bottom one. I ignored the ache in my shoulder where the kelpher had stabbed me. It was nothing compared to the satisfaction I was feeling as I tore into Lucien.

"I'd say sorry, but the truth is, after seeing what Briar did to Father Eli when she discovered the truth, I'm saving you," I said, watching Lucien's cheeks slowly split as he squirmed and shrieked in horror. "I thought of bringing you to her so you two could sort this out yourselves, but I suppose I'm merciful. I won't burn you alive like she did Eli. No... but I will make you look like the monster you are. When I'm through with you, you'll barely look human."

Finally, his jaw snapped and the blood that filled his throat turned his screams to gurgles. Blood sprayed across my cheek and I reveled in the coppery heat. Leaning back, I got a good look at the monster before me, thinking, for a brief moment, that I was no better. But at least I could admit it and the difference was, I was a monster for Briar. I always would be. He was a monster for himself.

Arms pinned beneath my knees, Lucien's struggles did little to help him. I was done looking at him. Done listening to him. I glanced down at his chest and my nose twitched with hate.

"May your sins be washed away in my Labyrinth, Lucien. You can thank the beautiful woman you destroyed for keeping me from just destroying you when you get there."

I sighed, plunging my talon-tipped fingers into his chest so hard that the bones snapped. His gurgling screams immediately went silent, his lax jaw and flailing tongue flopping to the side as his head fell. I curled my fingers over his heart and squeezed, piercing it. Hot blood soaked my sleeve and the front of my clothes. My wings uncurled from my back and encased me in a temporary tomb with the dead Lucien as I pulled back my hand. Arteries and veins snapped as I plucked it from his chest and, standing, I dropped it like a weed I'd torn from my gardens.

I stood over the carcass beneath me, looking down at the foul sight. It did nothing to relieve the guilt I was feeling. I'd let Lucien and all the others destroy the woman I loved and I hated her for it. *I* was the monster and I'd never forget it. She was too good for me. Too good for Lucien.

But I didn't have the best track record when it came to morals.

Visions of Briar's tearful eyes when I ripped her necklace off of her burned inside my head. The way I treated her... it was unforgivable.

On Lucien's bottom jaw, I saw a glint of gold drowning in the pooling blood. A gold tooth.

I might not have been able to recover the necklace I'd destroyed, but I would give Briar another gift. Something more meaningful. Whether or not she accepted it would be up to her.

All I knew was that I would not live long enough to eradicate the blame I felt for not finding her sooner. She was my everything. I encouraged her to fly and then I had let her fall.

27
BRIAR

I soaked in that bath until the water had turned to ice, listening to the palace. The creaking of its wooden beams. The wind shaking the windows. The occasional droplets that fell from the faucet and into the tub. The palace was indeed alive in some way. Part of me wanted to ask it if it remembered me like everyone else evidently did. But, if the palace said yes, it would only wound me further.

Why couldn't I remember?

I managed to wash most of the blood off my body and dunked my hair into the scented bath, doing my best to finger-comb the knots and twigs out of it. All the while, I kept replaying Father Eli's confession in my head. None of it was news to me. I knew all that they'd done to me at Southminster. But now I was seeing it all through a different lens. None of it was to help me. Not a single moment of torture was for my benefit. It was to collar me. Wreck me. Ruin me so I was so beyond repair that I could not fight back.

And I never did once I was broken. I was made to think I was mad. I was treated as if I was until I had been pushed beyond my limits. I really was mad. What little bits of my sanity I had left had been torn out of me by some doctor whose face I couldn't even see.

When I was sick of seeing Father Eli's burned corpse in my head, I let my mind venture past it to the clearing where Rune had appeared and slayed the beast. I saw it in much greater detail. His strong wings. His harsh grip as he pulled me away. The swing of his long sword and even the way he shielded me from the creature's lethal blow and took it upon himself.

I wondered if he was alright.

Even if my life meant little to me in that moment, he'd saved it. He put himself between me and something monstrous. Something out of my nightmares. A kelpher. I didn't know what it was, but it was horrifying. Everything past the courtyard was horrifying.

Shivering, I realized just how cold I'd let the bath get. I slowly rose out of the water, letting it slide off my naked skin a bit before stepping out and taking a thick cotton towel off a wall hook. I patted my hair dry first before looking up at a full-body mirror mounted on the wall. Seeing myself sent another shiver right through me. My eyes were puffy, whether from lack of rest or from all the chaos that had transpired in the last few hours, I didn't know. My skin was too pale and my expression too heavy. I looked dead.

Maybe I was in all the ways that counted. I couldn't tell anymore.

I was about to pull the towel up around my body when I paused again, my eyes dropping to my hips. I hesitated for a long moment before slowly turning to glimpse the very specific scar on the back of my hip in the shape of that damn handle Rune had shoved me against. It made no sense and yet it made all the sense in the world. *His* world.

My eyes panned upward and I turned my body as far as I could without pulling my gaze away from my reflection. There, between my shoulder blades, a place I hadn't looked at for years, were two rigid scars. Father Eli's sickening confession was salt on a very old wound and I wondered what had been there that they'd stolen. What else did he cut away besides pieces of my mind?

I couldn't look at myself for long. I was ashamed of the body I'd allowed to get battered, bruised, and violated. I couldn't recall the fight I put up completely, but I wanted to think that I would have fought to the death if I had been able.

I remembered some of my attempts to retaliate at least. I tried to starve. I tried to hurt myself. I tried to end it all by ending myself.

How hopeless of me...

Naeve had brought me fresh clothes before she and Lura left me in the bath to soak. She had draped it over the back of a sofa that sat near the wall. When I picked it up, I saw a beautiful green dress with long sleeves. It was nothing fancy and I was thankful for that. Remembering the corsets and bustles and hats Lucian always dressed me in made me cringe. Not only because they were uncomfortable, but because he was no longer my self-sacrificing guardian but a sick, demented, villain.

How could I have been so stupid? How could I have let myself get so twisted and out of shape? I was used to shame but not like this. Not so deep and penetrating and infectious. I wanted desperately to remember my past. My real past. But the more I thought about it, the further it got away from me.

I slid the new dress on and braided my hair over my shoulder and out of the way before quietly leaving the bathing room and heading down the hall to my bedroom. I knew being alone would allow so many voices in, but I also didn't feel fit to be around anyone at the moment. I slid into the room, locked the door behind me, and curled under the blankets of my bed.

I wished Petris was there.

Of everyone in that palace, he had treated me with the most respect. The most humanity. And even if I had nothing to say to him, the memory of his body curled against mine urged me to close my eyes. Slowly, I drifted, losing myself to exhaustion.

I rose from my bed and curled my legs beneath me, feeling exposed and cold despite the layers of blankets. I was starting to sense a difference in the times of day even if there wasn't a sun. There was a certain stillness to the nighttime hours and I was feeling it at the moment. I woke up much too early and wanted to go back to sleep, but the shadows were creeping in on me like my madness demon knew I'd shed blood and it smelled it on me. The darkness that always haunted me was reminded I existed and now it was taunting me, proud and vicious.

I felt cornered despite the size of my room. I felt like there were hands reaching out from every dark corner where I couldn't see. From under my bed. From behind the curtains.

I killed Father Eli. I did it out of wrath and I did it without thinking, but after the fact, I hoped it would alleviate some of the pressure I was feeling over the years. A pressure to be a certain way. To let foreign hands shape me and dictate my thoughts. My emotions. My everything.

It hadn't. I was glad he was gone, but it didn't heal the wound he'd opened up. Not by a long shot.

Standing, I headed for my bedroom door, eager to get some air. My mind and body were too restless to stay in one place if I could not go back to sleep. When I opened the door, a tall, masked figure was looking down at me, hand poised in a loose fist by his head like he had been about to knock.

Petris.

I knew I wanted to see him. I didn't know how badly until he was standing in front of me.

On any other day, I would have smiled, but smiles were foreign at the moment. Instantly, I felt tears welling in my eyes and a lump growing in my throat.

He made me feel like I could have emotions and my body was eager to let loose.

"They told me what happened," he said. "Are you—"

I stepped into him, burying my face against his broad chest. His warmth soothed my skin and I curled my arms between us trying to soak it all up. Without even questioning me, Petris wrapped me in his embrace. Heavens, he was everything.

"Where have you been?" I asked.

No tears had fallen yet, but they teetered so close to the edge.

"That's not important," he said.

He turned his face toward my forehead, careful not to rub the hard metal of his mask too hard against my skin. I sighed, relaxing into his body. When I felt thoroughly warmed, I slid my arms out from between us and wrapped them around his waist, savoring the touch of someone who did not expect anything in return.

"I think I was wrong," I said, my voice muffled against his chest. "About everything."

"What do you mean?"

"Everything—everyone—they were lying to me."

"Then... you believe the king?"

"I can't believe anyone. Not Father Eli. Not Lucien. Not the king. I can only believe myself, but unfortunately, I know nothing," I laughed humorlessly.

"Perhaps memories will come with time."

"I don't care if they do," I sighed. I pulled back and looked up at him. "I mean, part of me wants it all to come back, but what if I remember and it makes losing what I had that much worse?" I paused and took a deep breath. "Perhaps I should long for new ones. Memories that are mine and no one else's."

He hesitated and then slowly lifted his fingers to stroke the line of my jaw with the backs of his knuckles.

"Then start your first memories with rest," he whispered. "You need it."

"I've been trying. The thoughts chase me from sleep."

"You must try harder."

I spoke quickly, nearly cutting him off. "Stay with me?"

He regarded me for a moment like the question had stunned him. I didn't want to alarm him with the request. It was terribly inappropriate for a woman to ask a man to share her bed, but we'd done it already. And, without Lucien—without that society and that hideous steeple looming over town—I didn't care about what was appropriate. And I couldn't imagine climbing under the covers alone again.

I waited and then finally, Petris nodded.

• • •

The last thing I remembered from that awful day was Petris climbing into bed with me, respectfully staying on top of the blankets while I was curled beneath them. His body fit so well with mine, taller by just the right amount so he could cradle the curve of my back as I slept on my side. His heat lulled me to sleep and the gentle tap of his heart on my shoulders kept me that way until my eyes finally opened again.

I knew by the cold chill on my back that Petris had left before I woke. I didn't mind. He probably had plenty to do and I'd kept him from it all. I slowly rolled over and brushed my arm across the empty space where he'd slept.

Rising, I brushed my hair back from my face and swung my legs over the edge of the bed. My bare toes touched the cool marble and I almost yelped, looking around for a pair of house slippers. I saw my little leather ones by the door and walked toward them, sliding my feet inside before freshening up with a washbowl near my bed. It was filled with fresh water sprinkled with rose petals and I suspected that was all Petris. His thoughtfulness was a godsend.

I walked out of my room, not keen on keeping myself cooped up all day. I'd been cooped up my whole life—at least, the life I could remember—and I refused to self-inflict that loneliness.

My first instinct was to head to the kitchen where I knew I'd be able to find some kind of snack to fill my empty stomach. Until someone outright told me I was a prisoner, I assumed I still had the freedom to do as I pleased in Rune's palace, and that included feeding myself when I felt the need.

When I entered the kitchen, I smelled something divine being prepared. I expected to finally see the kitchen staff, but still, no one was around. There was stew on the stove though and I smelled the fresh scent of bread in the oven. I took a deep breath only to feel my stomach rumble.

Near the very end of the table with his back turned was Petris with half a pig and a cleaver in his hand. He drew it back and slammed it against its thigh once. Twice. He severed it and then rolled his shoulders back as if he was stiff. Specifically, he stretched his right shoulder like it was truly bothering him and it made me pause.

Suddenly, I didn't want him to know I was there. I watched him, standing quietly around the corner as he dismembered the pork. Then he removed the cloth apron he was wearing and draped it over a stool before he walked over to a wash bin to scrub his hands clean. His head turned in my direction and the way his body changed, I could envision a smile on his face, which soothed any tension I was feeling.

He turned fully toward me as he dried his hands.

"Briar," he greeted. "You hungry?"

"Of course," I admitted, slowly making my way toward the table where more cooking ingredients were spread out.

Just as I sat down, two women and an older man with a long, braided gray beard, entered the kitchen. They each wore work clothes, so I assumed I was finally seeing the kitchen workers. When they spotted us, they all paused, whatever chatty smiles they had on their faces slipping away.

"Oh," one of the women said, her plump, freckled cheeks glistening in the orange firelight of the wood-burning stove. "Well, this is a surprise."

The other two cooks watched Petris with mild suspicion, which raised my own, and then headed toward me with friendly smiles.

"You must be the lovely Briar," the freckled woman said, her auburn hair pinned up into a tight bun so her slightly pointed ears could peek out from the curls. "I'm Tessa. This is Gordon and Audrey."

I stood and greeted them all with a polite bow of my head. For a moment, all three of them just stood there... staring. Their smiles slowly fell again one by one they appeared to be saddened by something. Especially Gordon. Something in his eyes seemed on the verge of tears and it wounded me. Then Petris spoke up to break the silence.

"She's hungry," he said.

Tessa blinked like someone had clapped their hands in her face. "Of course. What would you like, dear?"

"Oh, I don't really know," I said.

Gordon let out a wheezing chuckle and headed toward the table where Petris had left the pig. He started to collect the parts and arrange them on cooking platters while Audrey began tending to the veggies.

"I think some boiled quail eggs and buttered rolls would do wonderfully," Tessa said. "I'll get that for you right away."

Petris was at my side soon after Tess left it and I looked up at him with relief. The staff was kind, but they were still strangers and I didn't want to think about speaking with strangers after the previous day I had.

"How are you feeling?" Petris asked.

"Better," I said. It was a half-truth. I felt physically refreshed, but my mind was still in such a state of disrepair, I didn't rightfully know how to act. "Is this food for something in particular? It looks like you're making a feast."

"The king requested it. He'd like to dine with you tonight. The stew is for everyone else in the palace."

I stiffened a little. Seeing him again would allow me to thank him. After everything, I didn't get the chance. Then again, he was beginning to trigger things in me that I wasn't sure I was ready to face.

"Does that bother you?" Petris asked.

I blinked up at him. "No. Not in the way it might seem. I was a fool to run off like I did. And I was too stunned to thank him before he left."

"You'd just killed a man," he said. "I think you had the right to be stunned."

The words hit me like a fist and I dropped my head, looking at my hands like they were still covered in blood.

"Forgive me. That came out colder than I intended," Petris said. "Speaking of the incident, though," he continued, being more careful with his words. "I can't imagine what's going through your mind. If dining with the king tonight is too soon, then—"

"No," I cut him off. "Father Eli is dead. There is no sense in still letting him dictate my life. I don't feel sorry for him nor am I sorry I did it. My whole life, I've wanted to burn the world in one way or another." I let my volume drop to a whisper. "I'm capable of killing so many others and no one has ever known how easily I would swallow the guilt… if there was any to begin with."

The words surprised me. I knew I had rage in me. I always had. To hear myself admit what I wanted to do with it—how bitter I'd become over a world I felt was a prison—was jarring.

A warm hand was on my face before I fell too deep down that hole. I looked up to meet the shadows of Petris's eyes.

"Not one bone in my body blames you for what you did. I only wish I was there to see it."

The dark implications of those words caught me off guard. But… I liked it. There was pride in his voice like what I'd done was an achievement. Maybe it was.

"Would you judge me if I said it felt good?" I asked, knowing full well that if he said yes, I wouldn't care. "To watch him burn."

"Never."

He didn't even have to think about his answer.

It was clear that Petris was a busy man preparing for the feast the king had asked for. And I had plenty of thoughts to keep me company. Not all of them were pleasant. In fact, most of them weren't, but I had an entire library to occupy my mind. After I'd eaten the delicious little meal Tessa had made for me, I headed there and stacked my little glass table full of books. Curling up on the sofa, I dove into the pages, ready to lose myself somewhere that wasn't my head.

Hours and hours passed with no disturbances and I'd worked my way through two storybooks filled with wonderful, romantic anthologies. Tales of princesses being taken from their towers and saved by princes and knights. Stories of tragic love. Happy endings and sad endings. Had I the capacity to cry anymore, I suspected the pages would be stained with my tears, but I'd shed so many the past few days that I doubted I had much left.

Stupid girl.

Father Eli's voice kept echoing back at me. *Stupid girl.*

I closed my book and set it on the table, folding my legs beneath me on the sofa. I managed to keep my mood fairly even since leaving the kitchen, but the later the day became, the more I started to wander. Father Eli was nothing but a burnt corpse now. Magots would find him eventually if they hadn't already. I wasn't sure what had been done with him, but I hoped he'd been tossed to the wild things beyond the courtyard. Imagining a kelpher ripping into him with that sinister, disturbing smile full of teeth was morbidly comforting.

After what he told me about Lucien, I wouldn't mind adding him to the scenario. I wasn't even sure what had become of him. He'd fallen ill at the masquerade and after he and I got separated, I knew nothing. He could have been one of the many bodies left behind by the ravens or he could have escaped the slaughter.

It would be like him to escape retribution. He'd avoided debt collectors enough times to tell me he was good at slithering away from the consequences of his actions.

Restless, I stood and began to pace, my arms hugged across my stomach. I walked circles around the big tree in the center of the library, never able to truly fix my mind on one thought. Instead, I bounced between many, which caused a headache to form in my temples.

"There you are, love," a voice said.

I spun around to look at the door and saw both Naeve and Lura walking in, hand-in-hand.

"Have you lost track of time?" Naeve said.

I wasn't keeping track of it in the first place...

"You need to get ready for dinner with the king," Lura added.

The two came right up to me and sandwiched me between them, herding me to the door.

I had thought we were heading to my room before I realized we were going in the opposite direction once we came to the second floor. I didn't ask why, though. They seemed to have a plan and I was in no mood to argue.

Coming to a black door, Naeve pushed it open and I was faced with rows of dress forms dawning beautiful, intricate gowns. They were nothing like the ones at Ethel's shop in Cragborough. Each one was vastly different from the next. Ivory with lace. Red with silver trim and layers of sheer fabric. Gold with endless embroidery. I skimmed them all, wondering where to start.

"Pick one, love," Lura said with a giggle.

I wasn't used to picking. I sighed and slowly walked into the room, weaving between dress forms to look at and touch every single dress. My mind was overflowing with choices and I almost doubted I'd be able to choose one.

Until a dark silhouette caught my eye.

Standing in front of a large floor-to-ceiling window, backlit by the bright moonlight, was a dress like no other.

The deep teal that faded to black at the hem was both seductive and sophisticated. Off-the-shoulder straps trimmed in fabric roses created a swooping neckline on a perfectly tailored corset that extended into layers and layers of flowing fabric.

I stepped up to the gown and lightly slid my fingers down the front of the gown. I never thought I would want to wear another corset, but for that dress, I'd make an exception. It was a masterpiece.

"It's decided then," Naeve said, lightly clapping her hands together.

I blinked with surprise and whipped my head toward her. "What?"

"Sweet, you came straight for this dress. Go with your gut. You love this one."

"Hmm," Lura said. "I thought for sure you'd pick the red one. Everyone said it was your favorite color and—"

"Lura," Naeve hissed. "Our king requested we not mention anything about that." She turned and smiled kindly at me. "This dress is the one she likes. This is the one she'll wear."

BRIAR

Looking at myself in the mirror, I saw a different woman than the one I was in Cragborough. The deep blue-green of the dress fell around me like liquid jewels. The pleats on the bustle crowded with roses at the back, hips, and on the straps, which hung just barely off the peaks of my shoulders, emphasized every feminine aspect of my form. The train trailed two steps behind me, embroidered with vines and more roses where the material faded to black.

It was nothing like the dresses Lucien made me wear and it was everything I could have dreamed of. Perhaps it wasn't corsets and bustles that I hated. Perhaps it was the ones Lucien made me wear. My new gown flattered my pale skin and brought out the rich brown shade of my eyes. Cragborough had made my eyes dull and colorless, but now... I didn't even know who I was looking at.

Coal lined my eyes and a deep red tint painted my lips, making them seem fuller than I knew they were. And Lura had twisted my hair into a beautiful spiral over one shoulder, leaving half of my neck bare. And on my arms were lace fingerless gloves that reached just past my elbows.

"Stunning, love," Lura said, joining me in the mirror's reflection.

"Absolutely," Naeve added. "Now, come. Our king is very punctual."

"No, he's not," Lura giggled.

"Well, we are."

Naeve took my hand and began leading me to the door. Suddenly, my heart was racing. Was it because I was walking too fast or was it because I was about to dine alone with the king? I didn't want to admit it was the latter.

When we came to the bottom of the steps into the foyer, I could see the doors to the dining hall ahead and took a deep, shuddering breath. I focused on the doors, seeing the incident on my first night in the palace sweep across my vision. The flipping of the table. The anger. The necklace crushed to dust on the floor.

But maybe none of that mattered anymore. Things were changing.

Naeve pushed the doors into the dining hall open and the delicious smell of dinner wafted out toward me. We entered, our shoes clicking on the marble floors. The table was not the same as it was before. It was smaller and only two chairs sat on either end of it. Candles were stacked between a reef of purple flowers beside a platter loaded with baked pork, fruit, and blackened veggies. The bread I smelled cooking that morning was sliced thickly and slathered in butter with small bowls of jam and cheese spreads sitting out.

It was far too much for two people to eat.

I slowly approached the arrangement and ran my fingers along the silk cloth laid out across the table. When I heard the doors close, I realized the ladies had gone, leaving me alone. The silence was overwhelming. I looked around, my eyes fixed on the place where Rune had put his hands on my throat and ripped my necklace off in one swipe.

And now I was dining with him.

But I had to remember the wound he'd taken for me. That was worth more than a little jeweled moth on a chain. So were the truths that had been revealing themselves to me, despite how unwilling I'd been to hear them.

I didn't have to endure the silence for too long before the doors flew open again. I spun to see Rune stepping into the room, one hand on each door for a grand entrance. He looked as if he'd been rushing. But when he saw me, he stopped like he'd hit a wall.

His hair was braided in three neat rows along the sides of his scalp, leaving the middle swept back and loose down his back. His tunic, an onyx black with iridescent blue embroidery, hung just above his knees and leather pants and boots covered the rest of him. His wings had been tucked away with whatever magic he possessed, but black feathers decorated the shoulders of his outfit as if to remind me they still existed.

He looked so similar to the day I met him at the masquerade, but there was no longer a mask between us. My heart sputtered in my chest and I had to bite my lip to keep from gasping at the harsh beat of it.

Rune regarded me wordlessly for a moment, his gaze soaking me in like he was in a mild trance. I wasn't used to it. I smoothed my hands down the front of my dress and cleared my throat, feeling much too exposed all of a sudden as he closed the doors behind him and began walking toward me with a slow, careful stride. Of course, I could be dressed in layers of fabric and a winter coat and still feel exposed in front of Rune. He knack for making me feel naked in all ways.

"You look…" he said, pausing for a moment to look me over again. "Absolutely stunning, Briar."

"Thank you, Rune… my king." I curtsied awkwardly, forgetting all my formal training from Lucien.

The corner of his lips curled up handsomely at that.

He continued to approach, fixing the cuff of his tunic.

"How is your shoulder?" I asked. "I meant to ask yesterday, but I didn't see you."

"Better." He came around, being sure to walk close enough to me that I could smell the cedar and roses on him. He pulled out the chair at my end of the table and I turned to sit down. "I told you not to go outside in your state," he said, walking to the other seat across from me. "Now you know why."

"Do I?"

"The woods here. They know when you're vulnerable. When you're weak. And every beast within them smells it and they're always hungry."

"What are they exactly?"

"Souls come out of the Labyrinth in different ways, but left in my realm too long, they each turn into something else. Usually something vicious. Rotten souls are capable of growing a rotten form."

"How many are there, then?"

I recalled what Petris had told me about the king and his issues with balance and controlling his anger. I wanted to hear it from him, though.

"It is an entire world parallel to the mortal one," he shrugged, lounging back in his chair. "There are many. Especially since I allowed them to roam free."

I swallowed hard and dropped my eyes to my lap. "Petris told me about you." I hoped I wasn't tossing him to the wolves by telling the king about our private conversations.

"Did he?" he said calmly, eyes fixed on me.

"He said you cut a hole in the Labyrinth so you'd have an excuse to hunt the souls that escaped."

"I did."

I was a bit stunned that he didn't even try to deny it.

"I'm thousands of years old, Briar. Cutting a hole in my Labyrinth is not the worst of my crimes."

I blinked with shock and found myself staring at him like he wasn't real again.

"That's the first time you've said that," I said.

"Said what?"

"How old you are. I suppose I haven't really thought of it."

"Well, when you exist as long as I have, you make many mistakes."

"So, you think cutting open the Labyrinth was a mistake?"

"I didn't say that."

Everything he said seemed so certain. I wasn't sure if it was a lack of remorse or mere acceptance that he'd done things and there was no going back whether or not he regretted them.

When our conversation started to slow, I remembered I was famished. I looked down at my plate and the perfect slices of pork slathered in some kind of sauce. I cut into it and brought the smallest bite to my lips.

Cranberry gravy.

It was beyond delicious. I savored it, chewing slowly when my eyes trailed across the table and up to meet Rune's stare again. He had the faintest hint of a smile on his lips before he brought a piece of fruit to his mouth and bit it in half. It was far too sensual a gesture. My cheeks flamed and I swallowed my small bite of food.

"Do you like it?" he asked.

"Of course, I do. Your cooks have a knack for flavors."

"It's why I keep them."

I stuck my fork into a small pearl onion. It tasted just as divine drenched in the same seasoning as the pork.

"Is that how you think of everyone here?" I said. "As something to keep or discard?"

"Yes."

His answer was so certain and lacked shame. But I didn't mind it. The king was sure of himself and that was something I envied.

"But everyone here has a choice," he continued. "Of whether or not to be kept."

"You must treat them well if they've all chosen to stay."

"They didn't all stay."

He spoke softly that time, eyes fixed on me. I had a piece of pork in front of my open mouth when he said that and I stopped. I could have put the fork down and consoled him. Tried to alleviate the blame he had put on me. Instead, I ate the pork and chewed, sitting up straight with a sigh.

"If this was a lavish dinner prepared to accuse me of more lies and deceptions, can it wait until after I've eaten?"

His lips stretched into an amused grin. One I found utterly beautiful. Then, a small bout of gentle laughter rose from his chest and it sent warmth shooting through me. Why was I so weak to that sound? Those eyes. Every contour of his face.

"There's your spirit," he said. "And I don't plan to accuse you of anything." His smile fell away and he sat forward, elbows on the table and his fingers folded and covering his chin. "I was there when Father Eli confessed to you. The lovely Elanor had been working on getting the truth from him for days before she dragged you down there. I'm sorry seeing you is what it took."

"I'm not," I said. "Hearing him say it confirmed what part of me has always believed. And that is that he was never telling me the truth. Not once. But I didn't have another truth to turn to, so I foolishly believed him."

Stupid girl.

I dropped my head, shame pressing in on my skull.

"He tortured you," Rune whispered.

I watched him, trying to understand what he was feeling. I knew what I was feeling. I was enraged and violated, but he was feeling something just as potent. I just couldn't quite read it.

"He tortured you for years and I wasn't there," he said, his voice so soft I could barely hear it.

It was then that I realized what I was seeing was guilt. Incredible amounts of it. Regret. His certainty had dissipated and left him looking defeated.

"Yes," I said. "He did. In ways you cannot fathom."

His expression was unchanged. He watched me like he was waiting for me to elaborate, but I didn't want to. Then again, Father Eli had always advised against me remembering the ugly parts of my past. He may have been talking of a fake past, but it still gutted me to know why he always told me to forget. Because it made convincing me of other things that much easier.

So even if I wasn't going to tell Rune exactly what they did, I needed to hold those memories close and never let them get lost inside the madness of my twisted mind.

"I'll remember what he did forever," I said. "Most of it, anyways. And I have to hang onto what I know. It's *all* I know. The only memories that are mine."

"Those cannot be your only memories."

"They are for now. Pain, chaos, destruction, and vengeance. It's all I am."

I reached out and took a crystal glass filled with some kind of sweet, herbal drink mixed with honey.

Someone remembered that I did not like wine.

My lips quirked knowing it was probably Petris and I took a sip.

"Are you enjoying the library?" Rune said.

I nodded, setting my glass down. "It's been a welcome distraction after the latest events. There are so many books. I long to read them all."

"Then you've decided to stay. You'll need a lot of time to read them all."

My eyes shot up at that. I hadn't even thought of leaving or staying.

"I... didn't know I had a choice."

"Now you do." He watched me, waiting, but there was nothing for me to tell him. Not yet. "There's no need to answer. Not yet."

"I don't know where I would go if not here. I have no home in Cragborough. Or anywhere, for that matter. And the thought of returning to Lucien makes me sick to—"

"You won't be going back to him," he said, eyes focused elsewhere as if he was seeing something in the room that I could not. When his gaze found me again, he blinked his way slowly out of his vision. "Ever."

That word was possessive and confident. I wasn't sure exactly how he meant it, but it was reassuring nonetheless. I took another sip of my drink, swallowing quietly.

"At the masquerade," Rune spoke again. "When you saw me for the first time. What did you feel? Aside from the terror you admitted to me."

"I felt... curious."

"Curious?" The corner of his lip quirked. "Of a man with an elk skull mask?"

I nodded. "I have many demons. They've only ever shown themselves in the form of my lunacy. I thought you might be one of them. I thought perhaps you'd come to free me somehow."

"Free you?"

"I've had fantasies since I can recall. Of escaping my prison. Not just Southminster. Myself. Most days, I feel *I* am a prison. One my soul has been aching to escape for many, many years. I am battered and bruised and yet I breathe. And while I still breathe, I am still trapped."

Rune went quiet, leaning back in his chair with one elbow propped on the arm, his fingers stroking across his lips in thought. Anyone else would have been quick to tell me to stop those thoughts. To focus on other things, store them away, and feign stability. Not him. He allowed me to have them and part of me was thankful for that freedom.

"I wish so badly that I could bear the pain for you, but I can't," he whispered. "It is yours to experience. Father Eli took something from you. No apology could ever be deep enough to relieve that burn. He twisted your mind. He erased me from it." He clenched his teeth and cleared his throat like he was giving himself a moment to breathe. "Through your blood, he used the life I gave you to chase away time. To live longer years. Healthy years at your expense. At the cost of your mind and body." He stopped to take another breath. "And Lucien. Your blood saved him from death. From a disease that would have taken him otherwise."

I swallowed, the information somehow unsurprising, but it still stung. The bloodletting was as much a lie as everything else. It was not to cure my insanity. It was to steal something magical from my blood. Something I didn't know I had.

"I am not surprised to know they've stolen even more than I thought. My mind... It is a wasteland where I'm certain there were lush fields thriving with memories."

Rune took a deep breath and slowly scooted his chair back to stand.

"A wasteland with plenty of space to create new memories," he said, stepping around the table. He held out his hand in offering. "Dance with me, Briar. No mask this time."

I wasn't sure which was more frightening. His elk mask or the beautiful face looking down at me. Either way, something was pulling me to him and the chaotic danger he was beginning to represent. My pulse fluttered, eyes wandering the quiet dining room when a faint melody echoed across the walls out of thin air. Harps. Violine. The sounds harmonized and filled the room with music.

"How..."

"Does it matter?" Rune said.

It didn't. Not in the least.

I reached up with my gloved hand and placed it in his, standing from my chair. Without the long table, the large dining hall was spacious and empty, leaving us plenty of room to move. This time, no one was around to crowd us. The stifling noise of a hundred feet was absent and there was only us.

He pulled me toward him until my front was pressed against his. His free hand slid around my waist and held me close, his eyes pinning me more securely than any chain or jacket ever could. But it felt good.

We began to move. There was no practiced choreography. There was only us swaying and spinning together in perfect unison. Every time his foot moved forward, mine moved back. Every time I felt the slightest tug, I spun with him. It was a strange partnership to make sure neither of our steps faltered and... I loved it.

"Eyes on me, little bird," he whispered, never looking away.

"When I asked who you were at the masquerade, you said you were everything I needed. Everything I would ever want, hate, and love."

"I remember."

"Did you mean that?"

"Every word."

"And... what do you think I feel now?"

He spun us around, pulling me harder against him. "I know you hated me. Maybe you still do."

I shook my head, boldly meeting his gaze with my own. "I don't think I ever did. I was—I am—afraid of what you do to my thoughts."

"And what do I do to your thoughts?"

"You free them. You urge my emotions to the surface." I thought of the way Petris urged me to be vulnerable. It contrasted the way Rune made me feel like I wanted—like I could—lash out. Be violent. Bold. "And I don't quite know how to navigate the world with so many free thoughts." I paused a moment to recall the necklace he'd crushed so easily in his fist and bit my lip. "Perhaps I hated you for a night. When you crushed my necklace."

He canted his head at me. "Why was it so important to you?"

I shrugged. "I'd never gotten a gift before that someone didn't force on me or assume I wanted. People have always told me what I should like and what I should wear. I never said I wanted the necklace."

"No. I saw you looking at it."

"Yes. And when you gave it to me, it was more mine than any dress or hairpin Lucien gave me. I loved it."

A lump was forming in my throat and I swallowed it down, willing the tears with it. I wasn't going to cry. Not over something so small. I knew it was ridiculous.

"Could you forgive me?" he said, leaning in so his breath was caressing my cheek. "If I gave you something else?"

He stepped back, lifting my arm and twirling me so my back was against his chest. I gasped at the sudden shift in positions, not hating the way his hands held my waist. The music continued, but our movements had ceased.

When I felt Rune's lips on my neck, I trembled, my head falling back against his shoulder without even thinking. He moved his mouth softly down to the bend of my shoulder, the tips of his fingers dancing over my bare arm.

When he stopped, my pulse was already racing with such vigor that my skin was flushed and my mouth dry. I let out a shivering breath as his hands came around to my front and he unraveled a little gold chain.

"I've made a new necklace for you," he whispered, his hot words tickling my ear.

I let him place the chain around my neck and sighed, relaxing against his chest. Once the necklace was clasped, I looked down, taking the pendant between my fingers to look at it.

Except, it wasn't a pendant at all.

It was a tooth. A gold molar with a hole drilled into it so the chain could pass through. And surrounding it like a round frame was a dirty-gold ring with Lucien's crest on it.

It took me a second to understand what the gift meant, but when I did, my skin flushed again. I should have been horrified, but all I felt was excitement. I felt Rune's lips press to my neck again and closed my eyes, savoring his touch.

"This is Lucien's," I said.

"I *hate* the sound of his name on your lips," he hissed in my ear, nipping at the lobe.

That voice sent heat directly south.

What was wrong with me?

"I'll never say it again," I promised as his hands snaked around to my front, gliding up over my corset-bound breasts and across the front of my throat.

"Do you like your gift?" he whispered.

"Yes. That's where you went after you came to me in the woods, isn't it?"

"What I heard in the dungeon killed me, Briar. I couldn't stand it. I wanted him dead. I had planned to bring him back to you, but I just couldn't help myself."

"How did you do it?"

He reached around with his hand again and gently collared my throat so the tips of his nails barely grazed my skin.

"I tore open his mouth," he whispered. "He begged before he drowned in his own blood. And I made sure he knew *exactly* who I was." He kissed me just beneath my ear and gooseflesh rippled across my skin. "And that you..." He kissed me again. "Didn't belong to him."

"And..." I gulped, my body on fire. "Do I belong to you?"

I felt the tip of his tongue slide over the shell of my ear and I couldn't help myself. I whimpered lightly, wanting him to go further.

"Only if you want to," he whispered.

His fingers slid up my throat and gently clutched my jaw, turning my head toward him. I expected him to kiss me, but he didn't. He hooked me with his eyes and stilled, releasing me as if to give me the choice to continue. His gaze—his lips—begged me to put my mouth on his. To feel him and breathe him in. My pulse quickened at the thought and I could feel the anticipation racing down between my legs.

But then the dining hall doors swung open, pulling us both out of our trance. Elanor marched in with that sour look on her beautiful face and stood erect, hands clasped elegantly in front of her.

"Forgive me, my king," she addressed, ignoring my presence.

Rune slowly turned to glare at her, the faint traces of a snarl rising from his throat.

"Yes, Elanor?" he said.

"The excitement from the other day attracted a gripson. It's stalking the outer edge of the maze near the woods. I thought you should know."

"Can the hounds not take care of it? Or you, for that matter?"

"I do not think it's alone. You're needed."

I had no idea what a gripson was, but it made the king shift. He sighed heavily and released me from his arms, leaving my back cold in his absence.

"Escort her back to her room," he ordered, walking pointedly toward the door without looking back.

Once I was alone with Elanor, the heat that warmed me in the king's presence turned to ice and I stilled. She looked at me like I was a pest and I still didn't know why. It had been proven that all of my memories were gone, but she harbored some kind of disdain for me.

"Come," she demanded. "I will take you to your room."

I followed Elanor through the palace, feeling uneasy. But that was nothing new. Her presence was chilling and she hadn't gotten easier to be around.

When we arrived at my room, that uneasy feeling got the best of me. The palace creaked and moaned the way an old wooden house would and it made the feeling worse.

The castle never creaked…

Elanor glanced at her shoulder as if she was trying to see me in her peripheral. I squeezed my hands together, wondering where Naeve and Lura had disappeared. I would have much rather they escorted me to my room instead of Elanor.

We were almost there and I couldn't wait to be rid of her. When I saw my open door, I skirted past her.

"Thank you," I said quickly. Elanor glared at me and cocked her head in the most bird-like manner I'd ever seen from the raven. "I'm feeling a bit ill," I lied, closing the door just as she seemed to step toward me.

As soon as the latch clicked, I heard the heavy lock turn. I stepped back with a start.

Petris had mentioned the palace being alive and I never questioned it. It did things like it had a will of its own and somehow I knew that it thought it best to lock Elanor out.

That made the cold chill almost painful. It was a warning. The palace knew something I didn't. Or, at the very least, it knew I wanted to be rid of Elanor's company.

Gripsons. They were grotesque things. A smile that big and toothy on the body of a doe would give anyone chills. They were a minor inconvenience unless they were in a herd. Of all the things that souls evolved into outside of the Labyrinth, they were the most annoying. Children, mostly. They were curious and destructive and, regretfully, unable to be saved once they fully gave into the hunger inspired by the woods.

This one had been small. It was easy to discourage it. So easy that I wondered why Elanor didn't do it herself since small tasks were a raven's job. Instead, she'd interrupted my time with Briar at a most important moment. I wanted to be irritated, but perhaps I needed to step away. I so badly wanted to press Briar onto the table to feel every inch of her in ways she likely wasn't ready for.

Ways I had to accept she might never be ready for.

Blood was splattered on the front of my tunic as I landed on the porch outside the main bathing chamber. The gripson wouldn't stay dead for long, but it would be discouraged from wandering so close to the Labyrinth for a while at least. Taking a leg or two got my point across very well. No point in taking the head since it could grow another with even more teeth.

I folded my wings in tight and let them fade from physical existence as I walked through the bath chamber doors. My wings were big. Too big, sometimes. Too heavy to drag around with me through the halls of Farrothorn.

I stripped off my tunic and shirt, dropping them to the floor as I headed across the slick tile floor to the long bathing pool that stretched across the whole room. The water would be warm, even if it was rain caught from the open ceiling. Ferrothorn would make sure of it. Though not technically conscious, the palace was alive in its own way. The warmth spread through its walls like blood through veins.

Wasting no time, I stepped down into the water and sunk chest-deep to soak for a while. I needed the time to stew in my thoughts. Not because of the gripson but because my time with Briar had been cut short. I was making progress. I was feeling something between us. Trust. Passion. Lust. It made no difference. Anything besides pain and regret was more than I thought possible when I first discovered where she'd been the past fifteen years.

And the way she beamed when I offered her the necklace. It warmed me more than I wanted to admit, proving I was still so damn weak to her. I would do anything for her. More so now that I knew the truth of where she'd been.

I wished I could have found her sooner. I wished it with all my heart, but even a king could not turn back time. I wished for so many things that I could never go back and fix.

An hour soaking in the bath as well as my thoughts had me eager to see Briar. I got out and headed to my bed chamber, slipping into a loose shirt and pants and rolling my sleeves while I went over all the things I longed to say to her. Things I couldn't say before because my mind had been too clouded. My eyes had been too blind to the truth.

I should have been able to see it all.

I never should have let myself feel anything but love for Briar.

If I wasn't so selfish, I could admit that she deserved better than me. But I *was* selfish. Selfish and toxic.

Wings fluttering through my window took me from my thoughts.

"My king," Elanor's melodic voice filled my chamber.

I looked toward my shoulder, but not quite at her where she stood behind me. She was the only one so bold as to enter my space without knocking. And she'd been doing it since Briar disappeared. Since I had fallen apart. She was the only one to have seen me at my best and my worst and she remained by my side.

Maybe because I had *made* her when I was at my worst.

I slowly turned toward her, finding her eyes momentarily fixed on my body.

"I assume the gripson was no trouble," she said.

"They never are," I said. "It was a small one. I have no doubt you could have handled it yourself or let the hounds loose." I sighed. "Would have allowed me more time with Briar."

"I didn't want to take any chances and I thought you would want to focus more on your kingly duties."

"My duties," I scoffed. "You know my duties better than I do, do you?"

"Not at all. But for over a decade, you've been distracted—"

"Did you bring Briar back to her chambers? Is she well?" I asked, walking to a small table with a wine pitcher and glass sitting on a tray.

I poured myself a cup and sipped from it as Elanor contemplated her words.

"She's in her room, yes."

"Good. It's been a long few days. Maybe she could use the rest."

"So could you."

"Indeed."

Elanor continued to stand at my window, watching me as I sipped my wine. I glanced at her, waiting to know what more she needed to say.

"Speak your mind," I said.

"It's just... I wonder if you will continue to need my company now that she is here."

"Your company. You mean when I sleep."

The corner of her mouth quirked ever so slightly like she wanted to smile, but was forcing herself not to.

"No," I said plainly. "I will not." Her spirit seemed crushed by that response. "I appreciate the way you've consoled me these years, Elanor. You know that." I took a few steps toward her, placing my hand against her cheek. "But my focus will be Briar, now. Now that we know the truth, I need her to be alright."

"What about what she wants?" she said, a hint of tension in her voice.

"We don't know what she wants yet." I dropped my hand, gulping down the last of my wine and setting the cup aside.

"And if she chooses not to stay?" Her eyes flicked to a plain wooden door past my bed. The door didn't fit. It was old and dull and unneeded now. Perhaps I had never needed it.

"I won't imprison her if that's what you're asking," I sighed.

Walking to a chair near my desk where I'd draped my clothes from the previous day, I fished out a fold of paper that was stuffed into one of my pockets. The sleeves of my coat were still crusty with Lucien's blood. I would need to clean it to get the stench out or I'd have to throw the damn thing away. I would have no trace of him in my home.

Tossing the folded paper on my desk, I explained, "This is the deed to Lucien's home in Cragborough. His signature was as boring as he was. It was easy to duplicate."

"And?"

"And the estate is Briar's… if she decides she does not want to stay with me."

Elanor took a deep breath, carefully reaching out to take the deed. When she unfolded it, a small smear of blood had browned on the corner, but no one would care. Humans cared for nothing but the exchange of wealth.

"She would have security, then. If she were to return," Elanor said.

"She would. *If* she chooses it."

That seemed to make Elanor happy. She had cared for Briar before. Everyone at Ferrothorn did. I just wished Briar knew that. I could have made it clearer for her if I wasn't so fooled by such a stupid trick. Such a stupid lie.

"Don't," Elanor said, placing her hand against my shoulder. "I can see you thinking about it. Humans are fools. It was easy for you to think she left you for the wonders of the mortal world. They're such treacherous things, humans. Anyone would have seen that letter and thought as you did."

"No," I shook my head. "I should not have been anyone. I should have been better. I was her protector and I did anything but protect her."

"It wasn't—"

"Leave me. I must rest. Soon, I'll have a real talk with Briar."

With that, Elanor set the deed on my desk and stepped away. While I was without Briar, she had barely left my side. Between our combined efforts to find her and her attempts to calm me at my lowest of times, she'd even slept in my bed. That nearness had become a habit... for both of us.

But I needed my space, no matter how much it might hurt her to give it.

BRIAR

I had changed into a black, silk nightgown and a blue robe after dinner with Rune. I wasn't tired, though. I'd gotten plenty of sleep and my mind was tied up in the way I felt when I was dancing with him. The skin on my neck still tingled where his lips had touched me and as I sat on the balcony staring over the courtyard, I toyed with my new necklace.

It was a morbid comfort to know I was wearing Lucien's tooth and ring, both of which had been taken from his corpse if the king had been honest with me.

He killed for me. Violently. Something about it set a fire in my core and I didn't care if I was messed up for feeling it. I'd been treated like I was crazy since I could remember by people who taught me to respect them. Love them. Obey them. Bile rose in my throat, but mostly because I hated myself for folding under their manipulations. I'd imagined my perfect past to replace the one I'd forgotten and I had always hoped I was strong before they broke me.

It was apparent that I wasn't. I was as weak as they came and I'd bent to each and every demand.

I thought back on all the uncomfortable dresses, rules, and limitations Lucien forced on me and ground my teeth.

I regretted that I didn't see Rune kill him… which confused me. I thought I loved Lucien, but I felt nothing but hate now like something in me had been waiting for me to finally catch on.

Stupid girl.

During my time alone in my room, I found myself worrying about Rune. If the kelpher was capable of hurting him, what could a gripson do? Of course, without me there to be a distraction, I wondered if it was even a contest. The way he had moved and swung his sword before was evidence enough that he could take care of himself. And though I didn't know what a gripson was, I wanted to think he could best one or more with ease.

But I still found myself worrying.

It was a strange feeling. Worry. I wasn't used to it. I wasn't sure I liked it. Then again, wanting someone was new, too. And that part I was beginning to enjoy.

"Stop this, Briar," I whispered to myself.

Unable to sleep, I closed my robe and tied it off at the waist, heading for my bedroom door. It was unlocked and that made me feel a bit more at ease. I looked around first before leaving, searching for Elanor, but I saw no sign of her so I headed barefoot through the palace to the library. That place felt more like home than anything else did and I needed its calming atmosphere. I needed a book to distract me and fill my head with fantastical things.

The very first book I grabbed had a stunning red cover, but I didn't bother to read the title. I flipped it open to find sketches and anthologies about knights and monsters. It would do.

I curled onto the sofa, book in hand, and tried to lose myself in the stories, but to no avail. Every five sentences, I thought of

Rune and every ten sentences, I found myself toying with my necklace again. Frustration coiled its sticky fingers around my thoughts and I was feeling even more restless than before.

I needed a book with more excitement. Something that could truly distract me.

Standing, I walked to the shelf and placed the anthology book back before skimming other titles. A blue book with gold trim caught my eye and I reached up toward it. My fingertips barely touched the bottom of the leather spine. I huffed with effort, standing on my toes to try and nudge the book from its space. I nearly had a grip on it when a hand swooped over me and slid it off the shelf with ease.

I spun around with a start, biting my tongue to suppress a squeak. Petris was standing so close to me that I had to press my back against the shelf to keep from touching him. He brought the book down slowly and handed it to me.

He was wearing coffee-brown leather pants, boots, and a cream-colored shirt that fit his figure loosely and was lazily tucked into his belt. It was late and his attire told me he was ready to turn in, but somehow, he found his way to the library.

I slowly took the book from him, finding my composure.

"Thank you," I said.

I took a deep breath to calm the stutter in my heart, catching a whiff of cedar and roses. I paused a moment, glancing down at the book in my hands.

So he and the king smelled the same, too. I wasn't surprised.

"It's late," he said. "Wouldn't you rather be sleeping?"

"I…" I hesitated, clutching the book to my chest. "Truthfully, I was worried about Rune. He went to the woods and I know he just barely recovered from his last tussle with a beast."

"You worried for him?"

"Well... yes." I reached up, touching my necklace. "I suppose I'm seeing things a bit differently now since I..." I swallowed. "Since I spoke to Father Eli."

"I imagine it might be overwhelming to open yourself to possibilities outside of what you've been told."

"Very."

"Well, worry no more. The king is fine."

"He returned then?"

He nodded once, finally giving me a bit of space. "Driving away a gripson is nothing to fret over. They're mere pests."

"Perhaps I should see him," I said, stepping forward to move past him.

He sidestepped and blocked me. My eyes darted up to his expressionless mask.

"Give him time," he said. "I'm sure he would want to bathe. And it is late."

"I don't mind. And I know where his rooms are. I wandered there by accident once already."

I moved the other way and Petris cut me off a second time. "I assure you, he'll want to dine with you in the morning to apologize for his early leave."

My brows furrowed for a split second before I chased the expression from my face. I'd learned to keep emotions out of my eyes to avoid questions and ridicule a long time ago and I put that skill into practice. But something was definitely strange about the way Petris was acting.

"If you're worried, I can relay the message tonight and you can see him in the morning," he added, further tickling my curiosity.

"No," I said softly, shaking my head.

Subtly, my eyes skimmed down Petris's long body and back up, noting his figure. For a man who claimed he was hideous beneath his mask, he had a flawless silhouette.

"Briar," he muttered. "You're blushing."

I moved a hand to my cheek to feel heat beneath my palm. I had no excuse for it. None that would be believable or worth the time it would take to sound convincing.

"Thinking of the king?" Petris said, his tone deep and quiet.

My heart jumped a little and I pressed my lips together, unable to fabricate a response.

"Would you," he said, stepping toward me. "Like me to relay that bit of information to the king as well?"

A shuddering breath crawled out of me and I felt my insides melt at the implication.

"I don't think there's a need."

"No?"

"No. I think the king will figure it out soon enough."

"Figure what out?"

"That... I don't hate him."

"Is that all?"

"And... I felt things tonight that perhaps I wasn't expecting. I discovered things."

He took another step toward me and if I could see his eyes, I knew they'd be searing into me like hot pokers to the ice wall I'd built around my heart. Another step caused me to back into the shelf again and he didn't stop. He moved in close and I could smell those familiar scents on him again. Gently, his fingers came up and hooked the chain of my necklace, lifting it.

"He gave you this," he said.

"Yes."

The word was soft and breathy. All I could do was stare at Petris's mask, wondering what was under it that he truly didn't want me to see.

"You like it, then," he said.

I reached up, carefully taking his wrist and dragging his hand slowly down over my breast. I trembled when his fingertips skimmed my pert nipple. But it wasn't a frightened tremble or a regretful one. I liked his touch.

I knew I would...

"Yes," I whispered.

I could have released his hand. I could have pushed it away and rejected his touch. My thoughts were full of the king, but at the moment, I had Petris. And his warmth was infecting me and turning into desire. It was sweet and addictive and I hardly knew how to sate it.

Without truly thinking, I held Petris's hand to my breast and encouraged him to touch me. The moment I did it, he tilted his head and shook it once like I was somehow torturing him. Like he was begging me to stop.

"Briar," he exhaled warningly. "This isn't what you want."

"Don't tell me what I want. It's all anyone ever does. You were the only one to have asked before. So ask me again."

He took a deep breath, his hand burning against me. Even if he seemed conflicted, I knew he was capable of pulling away, but he wasn't. Instead, he moved in, his body so close I could feel the vibration of his pulse.

"What do you want, Briar?" he murmured.

"I want..." my voice trailed off. I looked up at the unmoving shape of his lips. "To take off your mask."

He stilled, taken aback.

"You know I cannot let you do that," he whispered.

"Then touch me. The way the king wants to touch me. You said you know him better than anyone."

"This is dangerous."

"Would he be angry?" I slid his hand down my belly, my body aching for the kind of caress I could not get from myself.

"Not the way you might think."

"Then, you don't think he'd want this?"

"Oh, I can tell you he does. Without a doubt, he wants to be touching you right now. More than anything. He fears... you may not be ready."

"Show me how he would be touching me if I was."

He groaned softly, pressed himself against me, and then abruptly backed away with a shake of his head. With a deep breath, he composed himself and lifted his chin.

"It's late. You need rest. The king will see you in the morning."

Spinning around, Petris headed for the door. I almost didn't say anything. I watched him march away from me and nearly choked on my tongue trying to swallow down the words I wanted to say. But then he turned the corner into the hall and my feet rushed forward without thought.

"Petris, wait," I said, one hand on my doorframe to keep me from sprinting desperately toward him. He wasn't stopping. But I didn't want to let him go. "Rune!" I called after him.

He was mid-stride when he froze, his body rigid. My heart was galloping in my chest when I realized what I had just done. I'd stolen his secret. I'd allowed my words to escape me when I used to be so skilled at keeping them at bay.

I'd taken off the mask and broken the one rule he'd given me.

But I was past the point of no return. "Thank you... for wearing it. The mask, I mean. It's been so easy to talk to a face with no judgment. No emotion. Nothing to rival my own. It's been easy to confide in him. In Petris. But... you can take it off now. I'm not afraid anymore. Not of you. Only... of the things I want you to do to me."

He turned toward me, staring with his eyeless gaze. I knew I was right. I knew it. I had to be.

But I wanted confirmation so badly. I wanted to see his face. The face that had been behind the metal veil since the beginning.

Turning directly toward me, I could see his chest heaving with deep breaths.

"What is it you want me to do to you, little bird?" he said gruffly, cocking his head to one side.

I shook my head, unable to settle on anything in particular. I just wanted *him*.

"Whatever you want," I whispered.

He wasted no time in answering that plea. He started toward me, pulling his mask up as he walked. In an instant too fast to track, the black ponytail became long, silky blue hair and I saw Rune's strikingly beautiful face focused on me. His metal mask fell to the ground with a loud clank and bounced toward the wall, discarded. I sucked in a breath just as Rune's hand came up to rake through my hair and tug my head back. His lips were on mine in an instant, hot and demanding. I fisted the sides of his shirt to stay upright as I lifted onto my toes to meet him. The kiss was harsh. Demanding. Deprived. He parted my lips with his tongue and delved inside, devouring me like he'd been starving for days. Years.

No one had ever kissed me like that before. It was so full of desire. Need. Passion.

Rune drove me back into the library, kicking the door closed with his heel. I moaned into his mouth and as I did, his hands slid down my body, his fingers biting into my hips.

I just wanted to be closer.

I reached up and grasped his face between my hands, pulling him into me. It wasn't enough. He continued to back me into the room until my back hit a wall. His hips rolled forward and I felt the evidence of his desire press into my stomach. I sighed into our kiss and with a low, sensual groan, he took my lip between his teeth and bit down lightly.

Somehow, I was amused by that. A bit of revenge for the bite I'd given him in his room.

But I needed more. So much more. I wrapped my arms around his neck and at the very same moment, his arms coiled around my waist and he hoisted me off the floor. My legs wound around his hips and I kissed him again, claiming his mouth with my tongue.

Pressed between Rune and the wall, I did not feel fear regret, or sorrow. I felt elation and anticipation. I *wanted* him. Mask or no mask, I hungered for his touch. And he did not hesitate to give it now. His hand slid around to my front where my skirts were gathered at my hips and he delved between us. When his fingers slid between my folds, I whimpered, so desperate to feel him that I was getting impatient. And he could tell. He groaned again and pulled me from the wall, making his way to the sofa where he laid me down on my back.

We'd already crossed the line. There was nowhere else to go but forward and he knew it as well as I did. He tugged at the laces of his leather pants and slid them down, his lips never leaving mine. When I felt the heat of his bare flesh between my legs, the anticipation burned like fire in my core. I kissed him one last time and then pushed him away. He hesitated, opening his eyes to look down at me, that same fire burning in his gaze.

We were both fully clothed and he had his cock poised at my entrance. I didn't care. We both needed each other and we couldn't fathom sparing another minute. But I wanted to *know* it was him.

"I want to look at you," I panted, my palms on his cheeks.

He nodded, taking deep breaths to calm the hunger enough to linger for a while in the moment. Then, he slowly rocked forward. I was slick with need. I couldn't remember ever being that way for Lucien. But it did not distract from Rune's size. He stretched me more than he ever had.

Thinking his name made me sick. I stared deep into Rune's eyes to remind myself where I was and who I was with. The tooth and ring slid down my shoulder and was buried in my hair as he slid deeper. My back arched at the pinch of pain and I hissed, loving every aching second of it.

"I will be the last face you ever see," he breathed, pulling out only to push in again, plunging deeper. "If you let me."

I nodded, my hands moving to his arms as he braced himself against the sofa, rocking inside me again and again.

"Yes," I sighed. "No more masks. No more lies. Not ever."

"Not ever."

I took another breath, biting my lip when I felt myself wanting to cry out. The brief twinge of his thickness forcing its way into me had disappeared and I was consumed by pleasure. A kind of pleasure I had convinced myself did not exist. I dug my nails into his arms, certain I was going to tear through the fabric of his shirt.

"Harder," I muttered, barely aware of my voice. I craved the pain. The sweet pain that made me realize I had conquered it all. I'd survived every bit of it and could now choose how I felt. What I enjoyed. How I took it. I looked up into Rune's blazing eyes and steeled myself. "Rune," I said. "Fuck me. Hard. I want to feel this. *Only* this." I pressed a hand to his cheek again and lifted my head to press my forehead to his. "I want you to feel it, too."

There was a brief hesitation in his movements like he was processing what I was saying. I feared I would have to explain it to him or let the moment pass us by unanswered.

But then he understood.

His hand darted up to my throat and he held firm, his teeth clenching with a growl. He pushed my head down with his own and rocked into me with a brutal thrust that stole my breath away. Then another. Another. I gasped each time and then my gasps turned to moans. My core burned from the abuse as he picked up pace and I reveled in it. I was panting, my fingers tugging at the fabric of his shirt until I could feel his bare chest against my fingers. I curled them in, my nails piercing into his skin and with a hiss, his movements became more aggressive.

I could feel his anger. His sorrow. His frustration and his passion. It all flooded into him and trickled through me. And I found regret and rage. Relief and vengefulness and confusion. Our emotions created a storm between our bodies and neither of us could resist its pull.

"Yes," I rasped.

He squeezed my neck just enough to make me feel a brief sense of panic and then released me, letting the air back into my lungs in a rush of hot breath. I gasped and he devoured it with his mouth, kissing me hard and mercilessly.

My body swelled with pleasure. It sprouted in my core and its roots fanned out over my whole body, trapping me in a cruel knot. It was torturous in a way that I craved. He drove into me with a forceful thrust, hitting my center. I gasped at the painful invasion, gritting my teeth, but I loved it. I needed it. Because pain could only be felt if I was still alive. And I was *still* alive.

"Come for me, Briar," he panted gruffly. "Scream for me. I want to feel you unravel beneath me."

"Harder," I whimpered.

I barely expected him to comply, but somehow, he did. He thrust into me with the force of a tempest. I speared my fingers through his hair, watching his eyes become so bright, they were like stars. Again and again he proved that he could take it further, devouring every moan. Every rugged breath I took.

And then I was falling. He forced me far beyond my threshold and when I began to topple over, everything around me disappeared. I saw Rune and I saw myself in the reflection of his vivid blue eyes. Pleasure danced across my face. Tears glistened on my cheeks. I gripped him hard, nails biting deeper into his skin. I smelled blood, but I didn't care. I liked it. It drove me into a freefall.

My orgasm was dizzying. It took my breath away and I arched beneath Rune's hard body. I choked out a cry, my muscles and nerves tangled in bliss. Rune kept moving as the storm devoured me, forcing me to endure his ruthless thrusts until he was rigid with his own, powerful release. Liquid heat filled me and still he kept pumping into my languid body, taking everything. Giving everything. He left nothing untouched, nothing unanswered until my climax had finally ebbed and we were spent. Satisfied. At peace in a way I didn't think I was capable of.

The Past

I didn't know what I'd done wrong. I said the wrong thing. Looked the wrong way. Perhaps I hurt someone. I tasted blood in my mouth. Maybe I bit someone again. Whatever I did, they didn't like it. I heard screaming. Their fingers bit into my arms as they hauled me down the tile hallway. Something was inside my head, pounding on my skull with a hammer and it shook my vision. The tops of my feet were scraping on the floor, but I couldn't pick them up. The pain was excruciating and I couldn't move to relieve it. I couldn't speak.

Shouting voices struck my ears, but I didn't understand the words. And then my body dropped to a hard floor like a bag of potatoes, limbs flopping all over on a thinly padded surface.

Not this room. Anything but this room.

No… it's better than the cage. Be thankful.

The voices grew louder until words turned to boisterous laughter. They were mocking me. I was in pain, every bit of my body stinging and aching and on fire and they were mocking me as they slid my tired limbs into thick, fabric sleeves.

I knew where it was all leading. I'd been here before.

And now it was coming back to me. Blood stained the chest of my white shift before they covered it up. Licking my lips, I tasted the sickening tang on me.

As I pieced together what happened, my arms were crossed over my body and fastened with painful force. I was strapped into a tight, constricting jacket that allowed no movement at all. I thought my limbs wouldn't comply any further and yet they forced them to every time, folding them unbearably tight against my chest.

More laughter. More mocking. And screaming. Terror-filled screaming. I squeezed my eyes shut in shame and disgust.

"We're helping you," they always said, but all I felt was agony.

I peeled my eyes open just a crack to see the stained padded walls of my little cell all around me as two sisters scurried out of the room, their task finished. The door was open and through it walked a nurse in her white dress and one of the attendants. He was a strong man in a meticulous vest and trousers. He had overpowered me many times before. Outside the door, another sister held a hand to the side of her face where blood was gushing between her fingers and down her neck. She was in tears, her eyes downcast.

The coppery taste of her blood flooded my mouth.

I'd bitten off her ear.

The poor thing.

They're killing you. They deserve to die. Every last one of them.

No, they're helping me, and look what I put them through.

They're changing you. Destroying you.

I can't fight anymore. I don't want to. It hurts too much.

Resist.

Give in.

Fight.

Give up.

After scanning me with angry, revolted eyes, the nurse and attendant left me there. The door swung closed and darkness devoured me. It had been waiting. It knew I'd return and it had been waiting.

I drowned in my anguish and helplessness on the padded floor, sucking in as deep a breath as I could manage against the tight constraints of the straitjacket, and let out a scream so loud, my body shook at the force.

Present

. . .

I screamed my way out of sleep with visions of Southminster behind my eyelids. Visions that looked much different now after Father Eli's confessions. My face was drenched in tears. My body was sticky with sweat. The room was spinning when I came to and the darkness gripped me like claws sinking into fresh meat.

Where was I?

Frantic, I scrambled to find something familiar and felt arms around me. I screamed again, thrashing against a strong grip.

Not again. I was being good.

"Let me go!" I bellowed, kicking and scratching at whatever I could find. "Please!"

My voice broke and my throat was immediately torn to pieces. But I wouldn't be bound again. I couldn't. I threw an elbow at the first chance I got and it collided with someone's jaw. I dug the fingers of my other hand into pliant flesh and dragged them sideways, feeling skin gather beneath my nails.

"Please," I begged, unable to raise my voice any louder.

The strong arms pushed me down onto a soft surface and pinned me. I couldn't break free no matter how I struggled. A muffled voice spoke, but over my heavy breathing and shouting, I couldn't understand. Not right away.

"It's me!" I finally made out. "Briar, look at me!"

I opened my eyes, hoping to see something—anything—besides padded walls. Without thinking, I swung my hand and slapped someone across the face. Then I saw... Rune.

Blue eyes stared down at me, blazing in the darkness. His scent woke me from my crazed hallucinations and I sighed a breath of relief. Once it fully registered that I was not bound and was not going to be bound, I sobbed, tears flowing from my eyes uncontrollably.

"Rune," I choked out, emotions flying around inside me and colliding with each other. Shattering. Crashing about in ways I couldn't even process. I just... wept.

I'd hurt him. I scratched him. Hit him.

Father Eli would have been whipping me with his wooden stick. On my knuckles, most likely, where it would hurt the most.

"P—Please," I begged. "Don't. I can't go back. I..."

I was speaking nonsense. I wasn't at Southminster. I was at Ferrothorn. I knew that.

But I had hurt Rune...

His brows knitted together and immediately, he released my arms, wrapping me up in his embrace. He sat up, pulling me into his lap and cradling me against his chest. Trembling, I tucked my head under his chin and gripped him as if I would fall into an ocean and get lost otherwise.

"Never," he hissed, his lips pressing to the top of my head. "Never, little bird. Never again."

"I—I'm sorry. I'm sorry. I didn't mean to."

"I don't care." His hand swept across my cheek, pushing my hair behind my ear. "I don't care. I'm here and I've got you. I'm here. I'll never let you go. Never."

I curled even tighter into his arms, needing his touch. His protection. The comfort of his words. I needed it all to drown out the infection festering in my soul. The one left by all those who had hit, cut, and tortured my memories out of my head.

"Don't stop," I hiccupped. "Please, keep talking. Please. I need to hear you."

"Always. I'll do whatever you need me to. I'll talk to you." He kissed my forehead, his hand rubbing up and down my back. "I'll kiss you. I'll hold you forever if that's what you ask." He paused a moment, taking a couple of deep breaths. His heart sang against my ear and I relished it, letting the rhythm sing my madness back behind its thick walls. "I'm sorry," he finally said. "I will never regret anything more than not being there. I thought you the villain as they were hurting you. Torturing you. The gods and heavens alike know that you should never forgive me. I should have protected you."

Since the day we met, I hadn't heard him sound so broken. His voice was so tense and strained and as he spoke, his grip tightening like he was afraid I'd slip away. I wrapped my arms around him, unable to get close enough, and closed my eyes. I wasn't sure what to do. I couldn't remember who he was before or who I was. And if I was a different person now, then what did I have to forgive him for? We'd only just met.

For hours, I sat against Rune's body, wrapped in his arms and his heat. His protection. His breathing had slowed and so had mine. I could have fallen back to sleep in that position, letting his pulse and the hum of breath in his lungs lull me back into my cruel dreams. Instead, I found myself wondering something. Something I had a feeling Rune would know the answer to. I stared at the windows out to the balcony where the cerulean light outside bled into the library. I wasn't even sure that he was still awake, but then his thumb moved back and forth a few times over my arm as if to assure me he was still there. I blinked slowly, taking a deep breath to still myself.

"What was on my back?" I whispered. "The scars. I know you've seen them. What did they cut away? What did they take?"

His thumb stopped stroking.

Perhaps I didn't want to know.

"They clipped your wings, little bird," he said, pain turning his deep, velvet voice to something tired and wrecked.

"I had wings..." I said, feeling a familiar numbness clawing its way through my consciousness. One that often showed up when I was too much of a coward to face something. I hated it, though. I was tired of not feeling.

"I gave them to you," Rune whispered. "So you could fly. So you could feel as free as you were meant to be."

I blinked slowly, a single tear dragging down my already stinging, raw cheek.

"They took my wings," I said, my voice barely audible.

I knew they hadn't only taken my wings, but it felt like it was everything. My freedom. My choices. My spirit.

Rune renewed his embrace and coiled his arms around me tighter, his lips pressing to my hair.

"I will give you new ones."

I didn't expect Rune to be so gentle and affectionate. Or maybe I did. After confirming he was the very same man behind the mask, I suppose it was natural to associate him with Petris's traits. Petris was tender. Caring. Understanding. Rune had been forceful. Angry. Wound up.

As I walked behind him through the palace halls, I couldn't stop thinking about it. About his mask. About the way he carried himself differently. Even though I knew, it was strange to wrap my head around the idea that he'd been playing two roles since I arrived in the Glyn.

When we came to the foyer at the bottom of the steps, I paused a moment, taking in the thick vines along the walls like I did on my first night there. The flowers really were a sight, the fuschia and white were rich against the glass and black marble.

"Sweetbriar," Rune said, drawing my eyes to him. He reached out and plucked one of the flowers off the vine and slowly walked it over to me. "Do you like them?"

I nodded, watching him lift the flower to my hair and stick it in the binds of my loose braid.

"They were your favorite," he said, drawing my mood down a notch.

I dropped my eyes, feeling the pang of those lost memories in the dark void where they had once been. Rune nudged the knuckle of his finger under my chin and lifted my face to look at him again.

"I do wonder what your favorite might be now," he said as if catching on to my discomfort.

"I don't know," I admitted. I reached up and pulled the flower from my braid, twirling it between my fingers to get a good look at it. "These are beautiful, though. I can see why I—*she* liked them."

Referring to the woman he knew as "she" seemed to strike a nerve in him, but I was thankful that he didn't say anything. He breathed deeply and then forced a crooked smile to his lips.

"Come," he said, taking my hand. "I'm hungry."

We entered the kitchen and Rune, in his loose shirt from the previous night, strode over to the cold storage and returned with a platter of fruits and cheese already sliced up into bite-sized pieces. He set it on the table and stood on the opposite side of me, leaning on his elbows while he began picking at a pile of purple grapes. I took what looked like a dried apricot from the platter and bit into it, sitting on a stool. I still had the flower in my other hand and kept turning it gently, glancing at it now and then.

"So," I asked. "When you said you were close with the king, what you meant to say was that you *are* the king."

He flashed another heart-melting smirk, one of his sharp fangs peaking from behind his lips.

"Perhaps," he said. "But I also said it's complicated."

"You're one and the same. How's that complicated?"

He took in a long breath and stood up straight, chewing on a grape while holding three more in his hand.

"I have been here a long time," he explained. "Although sovereigns don't die, we do transform when there is a need. When we endure too much. When we grow tired. We are reborn in a way. But those past lives still exist. I knew I'd made a mistake when I assaulted you that first night. But I couldn't stay away. Petris... he was someone I thought you'd talk to. Someone I thought you could trust."

"So, you wore a mask."

He paused a moment, putting his last two grapes back on the platter. "I could not be gentle with you, Biar," he confessed. "I was angry. I have been spending my days hating you since I was fooled into thinking the worst of you. And I've been plotting the ways I would make you pay for years. But... I wanted to know. A part of me could not believe..."

His words tapered off and I felt my hands beginning to shake. I hid them under the table, pinning them between my thighs to warm the chill that had wrapped around them.

"I wanted to think the best and I ended up thinking the worst," he continued. "I was weak. I could not face you as a king. I hurt you too much. I frightened you. Petris could be all that I was incapable of being. He could be kind. Understanding." Another pause. He bent forward again, leaning on his elbows. "When you began to confide in him, it hurt, but I didn't want to let that go."

"Did you contemplate taking the mask off earlier? Did you consider telling the truth?"

His eyes met mine and I stilled, my breath catching in my throat.

"Yes," he muttered. "The night you came to my room. The night you let me touch you. You showed bravery that night. I know what I did to you. I know how I made you feel when you first came here and yet you came to me. I wanted desperately to tell you then, but a part of me thought you'd still need Petris."

I bobbed a shoulder. "Maybe I did. But I also need more truths than lies. Especially now."

"And you will get them. You will know all sides of me, Briar. I swear it. And I will get to know all sides of you if you allow it."

32
BRIAR

Rune and I polished off the whole platter of fruit and cheese when a loud storm began beating on the outer walls of the palace. I loved storms. Thunder and wind had always been a soothing sound to me on nights when silence was too unnerving to stand. I listened to the music of rain pelting the windows before Rune walked around to my side of the table and ushered me toward the door.

"Come," he said. "There is a greenhouse across the courtyard that will have a better view of the waterfalls than anywhere else. They rage when it storms."

"Outside?"

"Yes. Where else?"

Lucien despised rain. I didn't want to say that to Rune considering his reaction every other time I mentioned the man whose tooth was around my neck, but I was thinking about it.

He led me up to his room and I memorized the path from the kitchen. The memory of our first kiss tickled my lips when I saw his chamber again and I felt a familiar heat pool between my thighs. It was alarming to feel so much hunger for a man. I was unfamiliar with the sensation, but I adored it nonetheless.

Leaving me near the bed, he disappeared into a giant walk-in closet. When he came out, he was holding a purple coat with a soft fur lining. Once he handed it to me, he disappeared again.

"Put it on," he said. "It will be cold out."

I slid off my robe, careless that I was still in my silk nightgown. Smiling, I slid my arms into the coat and pulled it over my shoulders. I was swimming in it. It hung on me like a blanket and dragged an inch or two on the floor. But for some reason, it made it warmer to know it was Rune's. I hugged it around myself and caught my reflection in a large, wood-framed mirror standing by the bed. Turning one way and then the other, I mused over how childish I looked in the oversized coat.

But something else caught my attention in the mirror's face. That other door. It was barely cracked open, but something about the door made me stiffen. It was made of thick wood with a sliding lock on it that reminded me of the ones in Southminster. That kind of door didn't have a handle on the other side and it made my heart stop to remember how many doors like that I'd been locked behind.

I turned around to face it and slowly started toward it, too curious and suspicious to let it go uninvestigated. When I reached it, I gently pushed it open to find darkness beyond that smelled like roses and sage. It didn't smell like a prison at all, but as the light from Rune's bed chamber flooded the shadows, I saw a bed. A dresser. A window through which I could see the courtyard below and the raging storm outside. But the window was barred.

Beautiful red sheets laid neatly across the bed and intricately decorated pillows leaned against the headboard. It was a gorgeous room except for two very disturbing details.

Next to the window hung a dress, the hem of which was stained with dried blood. The gold gown brought back every memory in all their detail from the masquerade up until the point when the ravens slaughtered all the guests. It was the very dress I was wearing at the time and it was in that room as if that room was meant to be mine. And on the stone wall behind the carved, wooden headboard were chains with wool-lined iron cuffs locked to the ends.

That place was indeed meant to be a prison. One decorated and disguised as a beautiful, luxurious room. The room that was meant to keep me inside.

Fear, anger, and betrayal danced within me and made my stomach churn. My legs itched to run and my voice ached to burst free in a scream of rage and hurt. I could already feel the cold steel of the cuffs around my wrists, chafing my skin and keeping me immobile and trapped.

I felt sick. Panic licked its familiar rough tongue up my spine and I spun around, my body shouting at me to flee.

Rune stood in the doorway dressed in a fresh pair of black leather pants. He was barefoot and a dark blue tunic was draped in his hands as if he was about to put it on. His eyes were wide and his jaw was set tightly. He was upset.

"You..." I forced. "Was this meant to be for me?"

He slowly shook his head but said nothing. When he took a step toward me, I moved sideways, glaring. I silently warned him and pleaded with him at the same time.

"You were going to lock me away?" I said, my voice cracking.

"Briar—"

"Because you hated me? Because you wanted to torment me?"

"When you disappeared, all I had was a letter in your handwriting telling me never to look for you. Telling me that you wanted to be mortal after I gave you everything. When I found you, yes, I had every intention of punishing you until the end of your days just to show you an ounce of the pain I felt when you abandoned me."

He moved closer and as soon as I tried to run, he shoved the door closed with a loud clash. As I suspected, there was no handle on the inside. I clawed at the slick wood for a second before moving away as quickly as I could, retreating to the opposite side of the bed.

"You said no more lies," I said.

"I did not lie. When I brought you here, this room was forgotten. I couldn't bring myself to lock you in here, even before I knew the whole truth of your disappearance."

"Let me out of here." I was starting to feel an all too familiar rhythm in my heartbeat. It was dizzyingly fast and panicked.

"Briar—"

"Open the door!"

Next to me was a dresser and on it was a thick, glass vase. I grabbed it. I would have grabbed anything, but I was lucky it was a heavy vase. I threw it straight at Rune, hoping to hit him in the head. He effortlessly slapped it aside with his hand and it shattered against the stone wall. He marched forward, molten eyes focused on me.

"Listen to me."

I climbed quickly over the bed to avoid him and felt his hands grip the hem of the oversized coat. Once I was on the other side, I slid out of it and tossed it over his head, blinding him for a split second. Without thinking, I grabbed one of the manacles and slapped it over his wrist before backing up against the wall. Rune tossed the coat away and got to his knees on the mattress, panting with frustration. His eyes settled on me for a moment before he looked down at his cuffed wrist and he huffed out a humorless laugh.

"You're being irrational," he said.

"My mind is clear for once. You said I deserved freedom."

"I chose not to lock you in here!"

"But it was your intention! No matter what you thought I'd done, you are the kind of man to lock a woman away like this? To take her choices from her?"

He stepped off the bed toward me and by the length of his arm, I knew that if he reached out, he could touch me. I reacted without thought again and slammed my open palm across his cheek. His head snapped to the side and he stilled, but I was certain that the fire kissing my palm was more than the pain I'd inflicted on him. He slowly turned his gaze back on me, his expression dark and sharp as knives.

His eyes grew brighter when he met my stare and I wanted to will myself through the wall and out of that room. Terror invaded me like a million needles across my skin and I could hardly breathe through it.

"Again," he hissed.

Brows furrowed, I regarded him with confusion and failed to move. My hand was still tingling and not even a red mark had appeared on his face. My assault didn't affect him at all. Not physically at least.

He inched forward, finding the limits of the short chain, and tugged on the links loudly, startling me.

"Again!" he repeated.

I jolted and reacted immediately, my other hand swiping toward him and hitting him across the other cheek. He dropped to his knees beside the bed, his cuffed hand relaxed against the restraint in surrender. I stared down at him, unable to decipher the emotions flitting across his face. Both of my hands were stinging and my body was trembling with rage and fear, but then I realized that I was not the one trapped. I was not the one locked in chains and screaming and begging helplessly. He was.

My hatred for all the years I was a prisoner, both in a cell and within myself, overflowed into a tidal wave of action and I hit him again. Harder.

I didn't even recognize myself when I lunged forward, wrapping both hands around his throat and driving him onto the bed. I knew his strength far outweighed mine, but he allowed me to feel in control and fell under my weight. Stradling him, I reached for the second cuff and locked it around his other wrist only to stare down at the man beneath me. He was beautiful. Strong.

A liar.

Restrained and at my mercy. Powerless.

A king and a would-be captor.

My lip twitched with the urge to take out all of those frustrations on his pretty body. I saw his throat, exposed to me when he lifted his chin. It bobbed when he swallowed and I mimicked him, gulping down a swell of desires that had suddenly surfaced upon seeing him cuffed and disarmed.

"What are you waiting for?" he said, jerking against the chains. I jumped but stayed put, watching him. Trying to find answers to my puzzled thoughts. "I wasn't there for you," he continued. "When they were hurting you. When they were tearing into your mind and making you forget me. Forget yourself. I wasn't there, Briar." My eyes burned with threatening tears, but I refused to let them fall. "And then I was going to lock you in here like an animal and force you to see the pain you'd caused me without a thought to what you've been enduring all these years."

"Stop," I said through my teeth.

He shook his head. "Maybe I'm the villain. Maybe I'm just another cage."

Fury overflowed in my chest, spilling over every muscle until my hands jutted out to collar his throat again. That time, I squeezed. I pressed my thumps into his windpipe, putting my weight into it and gritting my teeth with a growl. He didn't struggle. His eyes remained on me, challenging and unblinking. I wondered how long he could go without breathing. He was not human. What could his body take that mine couldn't?

When his eyes finally closed, I questioned if I was going to really hurt him, but I couldn't let go. Not yet. I was enjoying being the one holding the reins for once. I pressed harder, watching his hands clutch the chains and squeeze.

And then I released him.

Taking Father Eli's life was easy in a way. Years of suppressing the desire to avenge myself made me enjoy watching him burn to death at my feet. But the idea of killing Rune did not have the same effect. When I heard him suck in a strained breath, I sat back against his groin. I watched his chest heave up and down, but he didn't struggle. Not once.

When his eyes opened and peered up at me, my hands were pressed to his chest.

"Don't be a coward, Briar," he rasped. "Hurt me."

"Stop," I shuddered.

"Why? You're in control."

"You're not the one that destroyed me."

"But I did nothing to stop it."

"You didn't even know where I was."

"No."

"Then how could you have stopped it?"

He shook his head. "I should have protected you. I know you're angry that I didn't."

"I don't even remember you. How can I blame you?"

He lifted his head, his jaw muscles pulsing. "I was here, loathing you, while they were cutting you up, inside and out."

"Don't."

"While they were twisting your thoughts and slicing into your memories. Taking and taking from you. I could have looked harder. I would burn the world for you. I have told myself that so many times and yet I failed to burn it down to find you."

"Stop!"

"Hit me! Punish me, Briar. Do it. Of all the men who have wronged you, I am the last still standing so hurt me."

I swung, upset that my body was giving in to his demands. The sting came back twice as bad on my palm. That time, I didn't feel good about it.

"Again," he exhaled.

"You're angry with yourself because you were a fool and believed a note over the woman you loved." I hit him again, raising my voice. "You left me for dead. Worse. You left me to suffer!" I paused, my hands trembling and red. "Her... you left *her* to suffer. I..." My thoughts became tangled and lost. Puzzle pieces were being shaken out of place. "But I'm not her," I whispered. "I'm..."

"Don't stop, Briar. Show me your anger."

I looked into his eyes, letting those blue gems pull me back before I sunk too deep into the holes Southminster had left. I couldn't go back. I didn't want to. I needed to stay and that meant remaining in control. Not only of Rune but of myself.

And I didn't want to beat my hands against him like others had beaten me. I much preferred the way he made me feel wanted. Safe. I cursed the room we were in, but for a moment, it disappeared.

"No," I whispered.

"I am at your mercy. You can do any—"

I leaned forward, my mouth devouring any other words he wanted to say with a deep, aggressive kiss. It took only seconds before Rune's mouth was moving against mine with the same vigor. I moaned, rubbing myself against his groin as I welcomed his tongue into my mouth. I felt him get hard beneath me until it was like grinding on stone. Over and over I rocked against his leather-covered length, wishing it was inside me but enjoying the suspense too much to stop.

When I felt him press up against me, I was panting, heat pooling between my thighs and making his leather trousers slick with my desire. Rune groaned and I answered that with a little bite to his lip, reminding him that I was not a gentle flower in need of coddling. At the moment, I needed intensity. Heat. Pain. Anything to keep me right where I was instead of in the pits of my hate.

"Move up, Briar," he panted against my lips.

"What?"

"I want to taste you. Gods, I've been wanting to since I saw you at the masquerade."

He raised his hips, forcing me to fall forward, and then he pulled the chains to their limits until his hands were under my knees. With one hoist, I was straddling his face. My hands slapped against the headboard for balance.

"Lift your skirts," he said.

"Rune…"

He turned his face into my leg and bit down, causing a shock of pain to shoot through me. I yelped, sitting back against his throat to pull my nightgown up and over my head. My hair fell down my bare back and when I realized I was naked, that familiar, fiery passion that I felt in the library returned twice as hot.

I leaned forward, hands on the headboard again, and lowered to Rune's mouth. The moment his tongue slid over me I gasped, my body shivering with pleasure. He began to suck, his face buried deep between my legs, and all I could do was grind against him, chasing the feeling.

I couldn't remember ever letting him or any other man kiss me down there, but something familiar about it made my body sing with anticipation. I whimpered, my stomach fluttering with pleasure when his tongue slid into me. I heard him growl with the same desire as he continued to lap at my arousal. I rocked against him, desperate to feel that high that I felt in the library when his teeth grazed my clit. I jolted, my breath coming in clipped gasps. Without much warning, the tension in my core started to unravel, spilling through me like a soft, unexpected caress in all the right places. I moaned, a mixture of satisfaction and hunger coiling deep inside.

But I wanted more.

Pulling away, I heard Rune groan out his frustration like he wasn't done either. I moved down his long, hard body until I was sitting on his thighs and worked my fingers against the laces of his pants. When I loosened them enough, I tugged at the waistband, shimmying them off his hips until his thick length sprung free, erect and eager. But I wanted all of him just like he was getting all of me.

"Gods, Briar," he breathed, lifting his head to look at me with a hunger that could have made me come again without touching him. That glint in his eyes could eat me live. "You're perfect."

"I'm broken," I corrected.

He shook his head, licking me off his lips. "You're perfect. Every bit of you."

I pulled his pants all the way off and ogled at the excellence of his form for a moment, swallowing. My body throbbed to feel him again. To let him fill me and occupy all the empty places inside me.

"Fuck," Rune swore. "I need to touch you."

I shrugged, biting my lip. "I don't know where the key is."

With that, he gave the chains a little tug and the links snapped with a metallic clink. In one swift motion, his arms were around my waist and he rolled me onto my back, his hips between my thighs. I gasped with surprise, arching against the hot length of him as he slid between my slick lower lips. I felt both exhilarated and betrayed to see that he could have broken free whenever he wanted. I should have known.

"I was never in control," I said bitterly.

He shook his head, his teeth sliding across my jaw up to my ear. "You are *always* in control," he rasped. He rocked into me again, coating his cock in my arousal. "If you tell me to stop, I will. If you tell me to please you until you're dizzy and breathless, I will. Just tell me, Briar."

I would scream if he stopped. I knew that much.

I slid my hand down between us, gripping his thick length and nudging it down until the head of it was notched at my entrance.

"Please," I sighed.

One word was all he needed. He slid his fingers through mine and lifted one hand above my head as he drove into me in one long, deep stroke. I gasped, my head snapping back at the intense pinch of pain and pleasure that burst through my core. I wondered if I'd get used to him.

I wondered if I wanted to.

Folding one leg under his arm, he began to rock, burying himself to the hilt every time. Every thrust made me gasp for air, hitting me so deep I could focus on nothing else.

"Replace what they took, Rune," I whimpered. "Fill me."

His lips crashed against mine, swallowing my moans as he plunged in and out of me. Our tongues danced together, laying claim to each other's mouths.

"There will be no space for nightmares when I'm through with you, Briar," he said, releasing my hand to grip a thick handful of my hair.

He tugged my head back, exposing my throat like a predator looking for a place to bite, and then he assaulted my neck with his mouth. I gripped his thick biceps, fingers squeezing until my nails were scoring his flesh again. He hissed at the burn and began to drive himself into me faster. His movements became desperate. merciless. I was crying out my pleasure with every thrust, my mouth agape and still barely able to catch a breath. I dragged my hooked nails down his arms, feeling his flesh give under my grip. The scent of blood filled my nose once more and I smiled, closing my eyes at the strange ecstasy I felt over it all. Whatever I'd done to him in the library had already healed and the idea that I could abuse his body like he was abusing mine just made me want more.

"Tell me what you want," he panted, his tongue preceding his teeth when he bit my neck.

I sucked in a sharp breath at the jolt of pain and plunged my nails against him harder in retaliation.

"I want you deeper," I confessed.

"Do you know what you're asking me?"

"Yes." *No.*

I didn't care.

"Then deeper I will go. I know there are places they haven't touched and so do you. Places only *I* can touch you."

Before I could process what he said, he lifted his wrist to his mouth and tore into the flesh with his teeth. I was almost snatched out of my pleasure-filled daze until he pressed his open wrist over my mouth and continued to drive into me, one hard thrust after another.

Bittersweet heat trickled over my tongue and down my throat and I suddenly felt weightless. I was woozy in a way that made my mind overflow with excitement. My skin vibrated with awareness, every nerve inside me dancing to a tune I couldn't even hear. My heart pounded, uncontrolled and wild. Something about his blood made me wild and I felt everything more potently than ever.

My eyes snapped open just as two giant black wings spread behind Rune, arching around us. His cock stretched me to my limits, leaving no room for me to think of anything else. Sitting up astride my legs, he gripped my hips with claw-tipped fingers and pulled me back and forth on his length. I slapped my hands to the sheets, balling the fabric in my fists as I lost myself in whatever heavenly paradise I was in.

"I know you want to come," he huffed, his thumb circling my clit. I arched up, crying out when the first trickle of my release teased my core. He pulled his thumb away, toying with my pleasure. "Command me, Briar. Tell me you want to come."

"I want it. Please," I panted.

"No," he grunted, thrusting hard. "*Command* it."

I lifted my head to look at him and the glorious wings splayed behind his back. His gaze ripped me open and seemed to see everything I had always wanted to hide. His skin was so white it nearly glowed.

"Make me come," I forced between moans.

"As you wish," he said, his lips spreading into a crooked, sinister smile.

He swiped his thumb over my clit again, massaging it as if he knew exactly where and how to touch me. As if he knew my body better than I did. I couldn't deny at that point that he did.

Within seconds, I was falling apart. I cried out, bursting with pent-up tension until no part of my body went unnoticed by the sensation. I shuddered, wave after wave of release pitilessly suffocating any pain or doubt from my thoughts. Just as it began to lessen, I reached up to touch Rune and like he was pulled toward me by invisible ropes, he leaned into my hand, bracing himself over the top of my body.

"Kiss me," I said, taking his face between my hands and claiming his mouth. He was still hard. Still grinding into me. "Come inside me," I panted, hooking my legs around his waist.

"Fuck," he breathed, riding me harder, his wings spreading again just before I felt his muscles go taut.

He groaned, his hands fisting the blankets on either side of my head. Streams of his burning seed filled my core, almost too hot to stand and yet so unbelievably wonderful. When his climax had finally subsided we were both panting, our skin slick with exertion. Trembling, I kept his face close, my fingers twisted in his hair as we shared breath.

Finally, I felt his cock go lax inside me, but he didn't move. He remained there, joined with me as the intensity slowly faded, and reminded me that the room was actually a bit cold. Rune's heat combined with my anger and passion had been keeping me warm, but now I was shivering. He slowly moved off of me and onto his side, pulling the blankets over both of us. With his arms wrapped around my naked body, he caged me close.

But this cage was different. This cage was soothing and locked all the demons out. This cage was perfect.

33
BRIAR

I eased out of one of the best nights of sleep I'd had in ages, reaching an arm out across a soft mattress in an unconscious search for the warm body that had been wrapped around me. I felt the heat on the blankets where Rune had been lying, but he was gone.

That immediately encouraged my eyes open and I turned over to see him perched on the side of his giant bed. He sat still as a statue, elbows on his knees, staring at the big windows across from him. His wings were tucked away into whatever magical place he kept them, out of sight, so I had a clear view of his bare, moonlit back and all the iridescent markings that decorated it.

Naked and tangled in sheets, I sat up, clutching the blanket to my breasts. I wasn't well versed in consoling others, but I wanted to console Rune. For some reason, his uneasiness was radiating off of him like a stone that had just come out of a fire.

"What is it?" I muttered.

He finally moved, proving to me that he hadn't spontaneously turned to stone in the night. His head turned slightly to acknowledge me, but he said nothing.

I couldn't remember ever being affectionate toward anyone. Lucien had asked me to hold him before like a child in a man's body, but I was beginning to understand that nothing between Lucien and I had been genuine or a good standard to judge any other relationship on. I wanted to do what felt natural between Rune and me and what felt natural was being close to him.

I moved myself against Rune's back and slid my hand down the back of his head, raking my fingers through his hair. He took in a deep breath at my touch and turned his head further, showing me the side of his face with a sensual hum. Gooseflesh rippled across my skin and I leaned in, moving his hair aside to press my lips to the back of his neck. I felt him shiver against my body and smiled at the control I was finding I had.

"That is dangerous, little bird," he whispered.

"Your thoughts are wandering," I answered, repeating words he'd used on me.

"They are loud today," he said, turning his glance toward the windows again.

"You're talking about the Labyrinth."

With a groan, he stood off the bed and out of my reach, grabbing a pair of pants off the floor and slipping them on.

"I need to tend to them," he sighed, shrugging on a black leather tunic and lacing it up the front.

"Now?" I asked.

He turned to face me. "Soon. After breakfast, perhaps. Would you eat with me, Briar?" he asked with a smirk that he knew would melt me.

I narrowed my eyes at his coyness and swung my legs over the side of the bed to stand, noting the broken metal cuffs on the floor. When we had moved to his bed, he'd broken them off with his bare hands and dropped them. I kicked one lightly with my toe and unfolded from the bed, still clutching the blanket to my bare breasts. The way Rune's gaze trailed over me said he was having trouble trying not to flick the blanket off of me and I found that I wouldn't have minded if he did. I liked the hungry way he looked at me. The way his eyes appreciated every inch of me. It was different than the way others had regarded me. I'd felt like an object before. A soulless, empty thing to be passed from one pair of hands to another. Rune looked at me like a priceless, wonderful treasure.

He said I was in control and the way his breath quickened when I was near made me believe it.

"I will have breakfast with you," I agreed. "If you let me come with you into the Labyrinth."

His brows furrowed at that, his head canting to one side.

"You want to join me?"

I nodded, part of me regretting that I asked and another part of me overly eager to experience it.

"I think I should," I said. "Could I get lost?"

He stepped in close and reached down, taking my fingers lightly between his and raising my knuckles up to his warm lips. His hot breath sent a slow shock through me that went straight to my chest and then descended downward.

"Not if I'm there," he whispered. "I would never allow it. Never again. But, the Labyrinth is filled with things you may not want to see."

"What do you mean?"

"I mean that it has a way of uncovering things that we sometimes wish stayed locked away. The mist inside those hedges can be cruel."

I bristled at that. "Things... like memories?"

He shrugged. "It is different for everyone. The Labyrinth keeps what we've lost and only what we want to find."

"Could I find what they took in there?" I asked, both nervous and excited.

Rune seemed conflicted about the idea. "It's not always so straightforward. It could break you more than you've already been broken or it can reveal ways to heal."

"Is that why you never told me what the Labyrinth is capable of before?"

His hand came up to brush my cheek. "If you come with me, you must be sure."

There was so much packed into those words that it nearly stole my breath. The way his eyes pierced me, drowning me in the truth of his statement, made my heart sore. I didn't think it was possible for my heart to ache that way and yet Rune had it in a vice grip. He kissed my knuckles again and then leaned in, bringing his lips to mine in a slow, tender kiss that somehow felt deeper than any kiss we'd shared before. It was filled with promise and desire and the sweet taste of it lingered on my tongue even after we parted.

"I'm sure," I whispered. "I... I trust you'll find me if I get lost. You did once, right?"

"And I'd do it a thousand more times. But, you won't get lost. I will not lose you."

I believed his reassuring smile. I trusted it as if I was already used to it. Like my soul knew he spoke honestly and would make good on the promise.

"Perfect," Naeve said, smoothing out my skirt.

I wore a deep purple dress with gems and lace inlaid on the neckline. I stared at myself in the floor-length mirror in my room and barely knew who I was looking at. Since I'd arrived at Ferrothorn, I'd been changing. My hair was in a twist over my shoulder, one wavy tress hanging on the other side and tickling my collarbone.

But my fashions and the way Naeve did my hair didn't matter to me. It was the gold necklace around my neck that made me feel the most beautiful.

After sliding my feet into a pair of black leather boots, I made my way downstairs with Naeve's hand hooked casually around my arm like I'd seen her walking with Lura.

"Can I ask you something?" I said.

"Of course, sweet."

"How well did you know me, exactly? I mean, *her*. Who I was before."

"I knew you for a bit," she sighed. "I was made to be your closest friend, but regrettably, I didn't get the chance.."

"So, you don't really know what the king and I were like before?"

"Not very well, no. But Elanor does."

I raised a brow at her, disbelieving.

"Elanor?"

"Yes. You two were great friends, actually. That was back when Elanor knew how to smile," she chuckled. "At least, that's what Elanor says."

My spine stiffened at the implication that Elanor and I had once been friends. All she'd done since we met was frown at me like I was a spot of dirt on her shoe. Then again, the king had not started out pleasant either.

"Don't dwell on it," Naeve said. "The king seems to understand now that you did not leave because you wanted to. In time, Elanor will, too. But she's a woman." She leaned in with a whisper. "We take a bit more convincing. That, and I do think she loves him too much to..."

She quickly pressed two fingers over her lips like she said something she didn't want to, but I couldn't unhear it.

"Yes?" I asked. "You can tell me. I don't have another soul to spill secrets to if you haven't noticed."

"It's just that she is closest to him out of all his subjects. She and him only got closer when you disappeared. She tried to fill the emptiness you left. But, between you and me, I don't think anyone can do that."

I was growing increasingly uncomfortable when Naeve referred to a past I didn't know as mine. But discomfort was part of living, I supposed. If I wanted to live, I would need to face the unknown with more steel in my spine than I ever had before.

Rune was one of those unknown things. There was an ache in my chest that grew more prominent the longer I was around him. Lifting a hand, I stroked the ring and tooth hanging around my neck, reminding myself that he'd slayed one of my many demons. That wasn't something that just anyone would do for another. That meant something.

But then I reminded myself there was a past that only one of us remembered and it turned the ache into an uncomfortable sting. Never before had the empty voids in my soul stung like fresh wounds. They'd always just been there, hollow and numb. Now they were injuries with torn stitches and they seemed to be bleeding.

"What are you thinking?" Naeve asked. "You've got a look about you."

I threw her a glance and tried to school my features. "Nothing," I lied.

"Come now. You may be good at hiding your emotions, but you have a tell."

"Do I?"

"Yes. It's subtle. Your eyes glaze over like you've run off somewhere and left your body behind."

I blinked at the imagery because it felt entirely too accurate. I often retreated into thoughts and forgot myself. I'd just never heard anyone put it the way she did.

"So? What are you thinking?"

"I just..." I paused, trying to stay present and honest. "I worry the king's affections toward me are based on the woman I was before. The woman I can't remember."

We stopped just inside the large doors leading outside and turned to each other.

"And you worry that will anger him? That he will abandon you?"

I shook my head, "Abandonment doesn't frighten me," I said, part of me realizing right there and then that I wasn't being entirely truthful with myself on that front. "But I do worry the king will hurt when the realization hits. The realization that, even if he thinks he found the woman he loves, she isn't me."

My own words made my heart ache and I had to bite my lip hard to distract from the unfamiliar pain.

"Briar," Naeve said with as sweet a smile as her oddly beautiful face could conjure. "I can't tell you what the king is thinking. But you know who can? The king. You have questions and you have concerns. Express them."

Father Eli had forced the rule of not expressing myself at Southminster. With pain and demand, he made the concept of communication sinful. Punishable. I winced internally at the memories and closed my eyes, willing him out of my head.

I couldn't let them dictate my thoughts anymore.

Reaching out, Naeve grasped the door handle and pulled one of the two doors ajar. She did it with more ease than I had, but much less than Rune. We both stepped out onto the landing and I peered across the courtyard toward the maze entrance, which was lit up under a bright moon that day.

Rune was standing with Elanor near the arched entrance to the Labyrinth. Her chin was as high as ever. After what Naeve said, I was feeling a bit heavier under her gaze, but I kept my shoulders straight, forcing myself not to shrink in her overbearing presence. I didn't know her past with the person I supposedly was and therefore I couldn't apologize for it.

When Naeve and I reached them, Rune's gaze settled on me and the tenseness he was clearly feeling with Elanor slowly dissolved from his face. To think that my presence was what relaxed his demeanor had my pulse fluttering with pride.

I wasn't used to it.

None of my reactions when I was around Rune made sense, especially after the initial shock and aggression he displayed when I first arrived. I gulped silently and inclined my head in greeting.

"My king," Elanor addressed. "We will patrol while you are occupied." She raised a brow at me before she turned and accompanied Naeve down the path.

Alone with Rune again, I felt both at ease and anxious. For a fleeting moment, he just looked at me. But the way his eyes took me in was so different from what I was used to. Lucien looked at me like he was wondering which way to position me for his pleasure. Father Eli looked at me like a sculpture he had molded proudly. Rune regarded me as if he barely believed I was real. Somehow, that made me feel seen.

My heart skipped a beat and it made me tense for a split second enough for him to notice. He narrowed his eyes at me and moved forward, closing the space between us.

"Are you sure?" he asked.

"Sure?"

"That you want to go in. Elanor has been trying to convince me not to bring you for the past half hour."

I looked past him into the dark, swirling mist beyond the maze's arch.

"Should I be afraid?"

"Everyone should be afraid of that place. It's eternity. It's a path that does not end for most. And it's the darkest parts of ourselves."

I took a deep breath and let it out on a controlled sigh before glancing down at Rune's hand. Reaching out, I slowly slid my fingers into his grip. Taking my bottom lip between my teeth, I bit down and used that twinge of pain to ground me before my damaged mind started to drift.

"If you don't let me go, I can't get lost," I said.

"Very true," he smirked.

I glanced over my shoulder to see that all the ravens had left and we were completely alone.

"Will Elanor be here when we come out like she was last time you returned?"

Rune sighed, the smirk dripping from his face. "I suspect not."

34
RUNE

15 Years Ago

Briar was buzzing with excitement. When I told her we were visiting the human realm, she lit up. If only she remembered her human life, she might not have been so elated. A human who enjoyed their life was a rare thing to come across in the Glyn. They passed through the Labyrinth so quickly, their conscience vacant of guilt or unfinished business.

But perhaps the human world looked different through the eyes of someone who couldn't remember their mortality. I would never know for sure. I was never mortal. Of course, I'd seen my fair share of foul human cruelty to know it didn't matter. Humans were as vile to each other as they were to themselves. Part of me didn't want Briar to see it, but I promised I'd take her and I promised I wouldn't leave her. And the only times the realms came close enough to cross between them was the week of Allhalloween.

"Are you sure about this?" Elanor asked.

My newest raven, Naeve, stood behind her looking like a lost puppy. She would be good for Briar. She needed someone with as much enthusiasm as she had and Elanor often lacked the energy. I tossed her a glance and nodded.

"Yes," I said. "And it will give you time to show Naeve more of the Glyn. You'll need the help to keep things peaceful here while I'm gone. She seems to like the hounds. Let her bond with them. It will do them all good."

"How long will you be?"

"Only a few days. Briar's grown obsessed with the art museum she saw in one of my books. I'll take her there and then we will roam a bit."

"Aren't you afraid she'll want to stay? All she talks about is seeing the mortal world."

"Are *you* afraid she'll want to stay?" I retorted.

"Of course not, my king. She loves you. But you love her, too. Which means she distracts you. I fear that you're getting distracted from…"

I narrowed my eyes at Elanor with a low growl. I didn't fancy being questioned by someone who'd known the Glyn and my responsibilities for a fraction of the time that I had.

"It will be fine," I assured her. "I've been away from the Glyn before. This is no different. And I trust you. You'll tell me if anything urgent happens. Ravens can cross realms far quicker than anything or anyone else and at all times. It's one of the many reasons I keep you around."

"I know," she complied. "Forgive me. I think you two deserve this. I just worry."

I chuckled lightly at her reservations. "Why?"

"Because…" she trailed off. "Because you are my king. I care for you. Perhaps more than I should."

I raised a brow at that, not wanting it to mean what I thought it might. An uneasy silence swelled in the room and Naeve, smart as she was, quietly ducked her head and slipped out the door.

"Elanor," I said, walking slowly toward her. A pink hue spread across her pale cheeks. She never blushed. "Are you well?"

"Very well, my king," she said, raising her chin.

More silence. I took a deep breath, knowing Briar was upstairs choosing her outfit.

"You are bound to always be honest with me," I said gently. "To never lie."

"And I have never lied," she said, her tone seeming defeated.

"But... you are not saying everything."

"Do you want me to?"

I didn't. I didn't because living in ignorance made things less complicated.

Elanor cleared her throat and straightened, veiling whatever glimpses of emotion she'd shown me with a stoic expression.

"I understand what my role is here better than you think," she said. "And more than that, I understand how you feel about Briar. She is a candle in the dark, Rune. One even I can see. But... something in my soul knows that light can be an addicting comfort. When someone blows out the candle, we've already forgotten how to live in the dark."

I furrowed my brows. I'd created Elanor during a long stretch of time when I was unhinged. Violent. She reflected bits of that every day, unable to change the same way I had since Briar appeared. And she'd inherited some of my magic. She never chose to use it, but she had it, I was sure. Her emotions could change the temperature in a room.

I swallowed, giving her a small nod before I stepped back.

"My king," she said, her voice soft. "You are becoming soft. I think it might hurt you one day."

293

I shook my head. "Say no more. Pain, my beautiful raven, is abundant. We must all feel it. In life. In death. In this place in between."

The way her shoulders relaxed, I wondered if she was giving up or simply pretending to. Either way, she appeared willing to drop her reservations and flashed a gentle smile at me.

"Of course," she said. "I wish you and Briar a safe and wonderful trip. I hope you show her everything she desires to see."

I reached out, placing my hand lightly against her cheek. She was cold. All ravens were. I'd given them purpose, but I had never given them life. They were soulless, made from my flesh and bone to exist for me. Briar had a soul and I didn't have to create any part of her. She was her own and I loved her for it. Briar had become a piece of me. My blood. My immortality. My everything.

• • •

Art. Music. Food. Weather. It was all different in the human realm. Norbrook was elegant, the history of the great city preserved in the walls of every building. In the fashions of every civilian. I chose to bring Briar to Highburn because it was where I preferred to visit if ever I had an itch to spend time among the mortals. They had the best of everything and the giant city was a melting pot of cultures that I knew Briar would enjoy.

And she did.

Dressed in a beautiful sunset red dress, she walked beside me, her arm hooked over mine. I'd glamoured us both, hiding the features that would turn heads. For me, it was my blue hair, which I turned black. My wings. My pointed ears. For her, it was her wings. In the Glyn, they were a beautiful blue-to-black color with glimmers of green at the tips. I didn't design them. They simply *were* as soon as I gifted them to her. Made from my blood, my essence, and our bond.

They were the only thing Briar was sad to say goodbye to when we stepped into the human world, but she was quickly distracted by all of the wonderful sights in Norbrook. The red-brick roads. The tall street lamps. The sun.

She loved the sun the most. The brightness. The warmth. And she looked absolutely stunning under the yellow glow. Her curious eyes lit up more than I believed possible and she wanted to look at everything. Every fountain, statue, park, and building.

"You're laughing at me," she said.

"Am I?"

I was. Because she brightened my soul with the way everything mattered to her. Everything was perfect and exciting. Thousands of years had taken that appreciation for the mundane from me.

"It smells so strange here," she noted as we walked down a narrower street filled with taverns, restaurants, and markets. She took a deep breath. "No flowers. No water. Just food and drink."

"You'd have to find nature to smell the flowers."

"I wonder where I lived. Before, I mean. Before I died."

"By the looks of you, you were from the north. From any place with no sun," I chuckled. But in truth, I never even tried to figure out where she came from. As far as I was concerned, she was born the day I found her. "If we stay in Norbrook too long, you're fair skin might burn."

"Burn? Really?" She shielded her eyes to look up at the bright sky. "It's like the solstice room but so much brighter. And this place is so much bigger."

"It only looks bigger because you haven't been far beyond the borders of Ferrothorn yet. The worlds are the same size."

"But you said beyond the border is too dangerous."

"It is. The world here is dangerous, too. But I don't intend to let you go."

She shrugged a shoulder. "It doesn't seem very dangerous."

"You have barely met any of the people here," I smirked. "Hungry creatures. And you," I quirked a brow. "Are exactly their taste."

Narrowing her eyes, Briar tried to read into my meaning. "I know you're warning me about something, but I don't want to know what it is."

"And you will never have to." Pulling her in, I kissed the top of her head. "Now, the one thing humans do well is eat. Let's find something."

She nearly hopped with excitement. "I'd love that."

In truth, I was talking of the shameful practice of trading fae in dark markets to high bidders. Fae were beautiful and their blood was valuable to those who knew how to harvest it. If anyone knew we were not human, we'd be targets. Especially Briar, who looked sweet and just innocent enough to snatch right out of my grip.

We found ourselves a patio restaurant with white, metal chairs and small glass tables meant only for two. Briar was so fond of the sun that we took advantage of the outdoor seating and had ourselves a lunch of stuffed goose breast and a dessert of fruit tart, which Briar particularly enjoyed. She had always loved food and every time she got her hands on something new, she peeled it apart in search of the ingredients.

"So I can make it myself," she always said.

But I had yet to see her make anything successfully.

Once we'd finished our meal, we continued down the strip where horse-drawn carriages clopped down the streets. People in elegant fashions walked with their lace perusals over their neatly coiffed hair. Briar tried not to be obvious about her staring, but I couldn't help but notice.

"These things are really quite eye-catching," she said, running a hand down her cinched waist. "But not comfortable in the least."

"The trends will change soon," I said. "They always do. Perhaps the next one will not require ladies to be bound so tightly behind corsets."

"Perhaps," she said. "So? What shall we do next?"

"You have not seen a ballet yet." I slid my arm out of her grip and instead tangled our fingers together. "And I have a feeling you will love it."

"If you think I will love it, I will love it," she smiled. "You know me so well."

When we arrived at the theatre in the early afternoon, lines of carriages were arranged along the street around a giant fountain. Briar touched every single horse, whether it was a small pat or a long stroke, she wanted to feel every giant beast under her fingers and she refused to wear gloves for that reason. She was addicted to feeling and I was addicted to *how* she felt. I was addicted to *her*.

She'd changed into another gown with equally rich colors, that time in jewel purple and gold. I dressed to match with a black and gold suit and knee-length coat with purple lining. Hand in hand, we entered the grand ballet house where crowds of eager onlookers filed in to take their seats.

"Ahh, Count Mortis," a man with a graying beard greeted us, tipping his top hat.

"Yuri," I inclined my head.

"It's been quite some time since you've graced our ballet house with your presence. Gods above, you don't look like you've aged a day."

I chuckled softly as he averted his attention to Briar. She greeted him the way she greeted everyone. With a beaming, too-trusting smile.

"This is my wife. Briar."

Yuri had a kind disposition and bowed his head at her and she returned the gesture with a small curtsy.

"So, this is where you've been all these years. Finding the most beautiful woman in the world to inspire even more envy in the rest of us."

Briar dropped her eyes, her cheeks flushing. My heart leapt at the pink forming on her face. It was my favorite thing to do to her, make her blood rush and her skin heat. When her eyes found me, my cock twitched behind my breaches and I almost wished I hadn't brought her to the ballet. It had been a long couple of days and she looked absolutely delicious in the corset she found so uncomfortable.

Yuri escorted us both to a box above the main seating and though a good half dozen people could fit in it with us, I slipped Yuri a few coins to make sure we were the only ones. When I closed the thick red curtains behind us and looked back at Briar, she was standing at the edge of the box staring out at the giant stage.

"I've read about these," she said. "In the library. I can't wait to see them dance."

It didn't take long for everyone else to find their seats and for the show to begin. The orchestra just in front of the stage took their positions and the building filled with the gentle sounds of them tuning their instruments. Violins. Pianos. Cellos. Briar was entranced as soon as she heard them. It wasn't until the music truly began that she finally took a seat beside me. Multiple sun lights gleamed down onto the stage, lighting up an intricate set of painted trees and silk fabrics that rippled across the background.

And the moment the music picked up, a slender woman in layers of flowing white silk skipped onto the stage like she was floating. I glanced at Briar and saw exactly what I wanted to. Her lips stretched into a smile.

I'd seen ballets. Operas. Horse shows. And I had seen everything in between a hundred times, searching for the excitement she was feeling at that moment. Finally, I was feeling it again and it was because of her. My glowing little bird. My candle in the dark. My flame.

Our hands twined together, we watched the ballet progress through a story of two lovers divided by war. The tragic and beautiful dance turned Briar's emotions into a symphony. I could hear her happiness and her sorrow through every flutter of her pulse and I devoured it, wishing never to lose it. The untainted, unused, unbroken beauty of her soul was my life. My everything.

When a man on stage in black tights and a flowing shirt caught the woman now wearing a black dress and lifted her above his head in a graceful spin, the music reached a climax that sent Briar's heart into a frenzy. I squeezed her hand and she turned her eyes to me, showing me the little diamonds of tears glinting unashamed in her gaze.

No words passed between us. Just a look. Just one, all-consuming stare that made both our hearts jump. Why were her tears and her smiles so potent? My heart punched the inside of my chest and I flared my nostrils, smelling the sweet jasmine perfume on Briar's skin.

"Keep watching, little bird," I said, a sinful smirk on my lips.

Her pulse raged as she slowly turned her head to the stage again, watching the dancers illustrate their tragic love on pointed toes. As she did, I began crawling my fingers along the layers of her skirts, dragging the heavy fabric up her legs. She shifted slightly, doing her best to keep her eyes on the show like I'd told her. The music began to pick up again as a slew of dancers in masks fluttered onto the stage, tearing the lovers apart in a sea of movement.

When my fingers found Briar's stocking, I dragged my nails upward across the soft fabric until I felt her bare skin. Those thigh stockings instantly sent quivers to my cock. Imagining her in only those stockings made me hard in seconds.

Sliding my hand further, I glimpsed Briar's chest. The way her breasts were pushed up with her tight corset made every breath look exaggerated. I licked my tongue across my lips, wanting to taste her, but also wanting to feed on the way she looked flushed and overwhelmed watching the show and absorbing my touch.

Continuing, I could feel her thighs part ever so slightly to welcome me. When I met bare, wet heat, I paused and glimpsed Brair's mouth as she bit her lip to conceal a naughty smile.

No undergarments. My breath hitched and she spread her legs further, completely aware of what she'd just done to me.

The dancers began a wild, chaotic number, crowding the stage with movement, and as the lovers met again in the middle, I plunged two fingers into Brier's slick entrance. She gasped, biting her lip again and gripping the arms of her chair. The way she trembled around me made my cock strain even tighter.

I slowly worked my fingers back and forth, my thumb stroking over her clit until she was squirming, doing her best to stay still as the dancers rippled in exaggerated patterns below us. I watched her throat bob and then her lips parted in a silent cry.

Gods, she was beautiful when she was in a sexual haze. And I wanted her. I wanted all of that untamed wonder. Leaning over, I spoke in her ear, my fingers curling upward and making her jolt.

"It's far too loud in this theatre for anyone to hear your cries," I said, nipping at the silver earring in her ear.

I slid out of my seat and knelt before her, pulling her to the edge of her chair and tossing her stockinged legs over my shoulders. When I brought my mouth down between her thighs, she shivered, her breaths coming in short, uneven whimpers. I licked over her swollen bud and then devoured her. My fingers worked in and out, steady at first and then desperate and hard. Her hands came down on my head, her fingers spearing through my hair to press me against her.

She was as hungry as I was.

I sucked and licked and moaned against her sex, eventually adding a third finger. The stretch made her legs shake and she dug her nails into my scalp, causing a delicious jolt of pain. The orchestra bellowed its tune, filling the theatre with the same level of passion. And I kept taking and taking until Briar shattered against me. I felt her clench around my fingers, her legs squeezing my head as she came. And no one could hear her cries of pleasure but me.

You have shown me more of the world than I could have ever hoped to see. You have been kind and gentle, and you did what no one else could ever do. You made me free. You gave me wings. You gave me everything. I thought that what I wanted in my new life was to be with you... but then I saw this world. This wonderful world full of wonderful things. There is something beautiful in mortality. In knowing you will die soon. And I want to know that excitement. I want to breathe the air, soak in the sun, and experience all that life did not let me experience the first time. Maybe this time will be different. Maybe, if I enter your Labyrinth again, you'll find me again and we can go on the way we left off.

But until that day comes, I need to be where I belong. Among humans. With all that you've given me, I can be *queen here. Me, queen of the sun, and you, king of the moon.*

I will miss your Glyn. Your touch. But if you truly wanted me to be free, you'd let me soar. You'd let me live.

I believe I loved you, Rune. I truly believe I did. And I believe I'll find you through that love again, but not yet. I know you kept me because I made you feel, but I cannot always make you feel. I cannot always be the cane on which you lean because your immortality has taken all of your empathy away. This world is simply a place to you. To me, it is everything and I wish to stay. But I know you cannot.

I pray you let me go. I pray you don't come looking for me. Let me spread my wings. We were never truly meant to be and you know it. We were meant to always be apart. Like darkness and light, we can never be one.

Your little bird,

Briar

I stood in front of the hearth where the flames had become pulsing red embers. I'd read the note a hundred times and each time, the pain lessened, replaced by emptiness. Numbness. I had wanted to show Briar everything. To revel in her excitement. I gave her a part of me. My love. My life. My very essence. And she dared to say she wished to live among humans again, only now she was not a mortal. I'd given my heart to her. It would make her live longer. It made her different and she knew it.

She could be a queen among humans. She could live out her long life indulging and experiencing all the world had to offer... without me. And it was what she wanted. The handwriting was clear enough.

Elanor was right. But my flame had not only gone out. It had betrayed me. It had set me on fire and I was burning.

I knew better than to get attached to things and people. And yet a little bird landed at my feet and I forgot everything. I disregarded my own rules. I broke down my walls and let a snake into my heart. She likely didn't even know the severity of her betrayal. She was so innocent. So caged behind her own inexperience.

But now she'd set herself free.

And part of me wished she'd break her lovely wings. The wings I gave her in blood. A part of me. My life. My soul. I'd given her a piece of all of it.

And she left me, taking it all with her.

"My king," a voice said, gentle and whispery.

I knew the voice, but it didn't quite register at first. I wasn't thinking straight. When I finally turned, I saw Elanor standing in my room at the inn. I wasn't surprised to see her. She must have picked up on the things I was feeling.

"What are you doing here?" I said flatly.

"There is a herd of kelpher ripping at the hedges of your labyrinth. But... I also sensed you were unwell."

My hand shook, the letter crumpling between my tight fingers before I let out a low snarl and closed my fist around the parchment.

I was the King of the Glyn. Rune Merikoth. I was all those things and more and I'd been distracted by some childish infatuation. Love. I'd let it infect me and that infection grew until I was weak and wounded. Useless.

Sever the rotting limb.

My lip twitched and I stood, dropping Briar's shallow, traitorous letter to the floor at my feet.

"I'll have to go hunting," I growled.

Elanor's eyes wandered around the room.

"Where is Briar?" she asked.

I hardly emoted at the sound of her name. For now, it was just a name and I couldn't let it strip me of who I was. I was the king. I had a whole world of souls to look after and perhaps she'd been too much of a distraction.

I refused to believe what Elanor had said. I refused to think I couldn't exist in the dark after I'd existed with my bright little flame for a few years. Compared to the centuries I existed in the shadows, it was nothing. *She* was nothing.

While my thoughts ran rampant in my head, Elanor bent to pick up the crumpled paper and unfolded it in her hands. I looked up at a small mirror on the wall to see a man I barely knew staring back at me. Black hair. Fair skin. He was the count. A mask I wore when I visited the human world. But I was not him. I was *Rune*. I watched as I shed that husk. Black hair turned blue. My eyes blazed bright.

"She… she has left," Elanor muttered, dropping the paper to the floor again. There was a long pause as I felt the full weight of my wings spread from my back. "I told you this would happen," she spoke, her words small and timid. "I wanted you to be prepared."

I slowly turned to face her, rage bubbling up in my chest. A low growl vibrated in my throat and I thrust a hand out to grasp her slender throat.

"Search the city," I said. "*Find* her."

"But… in the letter, she said—"

I tightened my hold, my fangs lengthening before her eyes. "Find her," I hissed.

Releasing Elanor from my grip, I stepped away, spreading my wings wide. They covered the length of the room, ready to carry me back to the Glyn. Back to the world I'd neglected. Back to the place that held no depth for me without *her*.

Fuck. I needed her, but it was all a mess now.

But there was blood to be shed and I was very much in the mood to shed it.

Present

I stood at the archway leading into the Labyrinth, doing my best to keep my breath slow and steady. In truth, I was timid. Inside was unknown. A place filled with the emotions of thousands of souls all seeking something different. All dealing with their own burdens and turmoil. But maybe my memories were in there. I wasn't sure I truly wanted them, but Rune told me it would only show me what I wanted to find. Perhaps if I found anything at all, it would give me perspective.

Or it would all suck me under in a current of pain and solitude.

Then I felt Rune squeeze my hand and my thoughts stilled. I found my breath and turned to look up at him, the burning unease in me immediately quelled with the embrace of his eyes. The way his hair was tightly braided back with smaller, conforming braids on each side accentuated his pointed ears and made him look more otherworldly than ever. His wings were folded behind him, but perfectly visible. He looked different. Regal. Terrifying. Bigger with all the parts of him exposed that he usually kept tucked away.

"You don't have to come with me," he said.

"I think I do," I whispered, turning my eyes toward the dark, misty entrance before us. "I came from there. How awful could it be?"

He squeezed my hand again. "Only as awful as you make it."

I wasn't sure what my mind was capable of creating or the things it could bring to light. I swallowed, staring again into the foggy darkness. The first step we took toward the archway caused a flurry of uncomfortable feelings inside me. Feelings that formed a wall in front of me. I suddenly couldn't move. I stopped, my stiffness causing Rune to tug against my grip before he realized I'd frozen. He turned back to face me, concerned but unsurprised. I couldn't find his eyes. Instead, my gaze was set on that monstrous blackness behind him. Standing so close, I realized the last thing I wanted was to enter that place.

Why had I thought I could? Why did I even suggest it?

"Briar," Rune said, his voice tender and soft.

I blinked, but I still didn't look at him. The darkness ahead… it had teeth. It was waiting for me to get lost inside and I wondered if I could ever find my way when I didn't even truly know who I was. What if Rune let go of my hand? What if I couldn't see where I was going?

"It's alright," Rune said, sliding his fingers from my grip. "The Labyrinth shows us things we must be ready to see. Perhaps another time, I will take you. But not today." He cupped his hands against my cheeks, letting his warmth wake me from my stupor. "Stay here. I will return soon."

I didn't want him to go. Something about the situation burned a hole in me like the Labyrinth was sucking something out. Exposing me. Stripping me of armor and skin. I watched Rune walk toward the entrance with confidence. He'd done it countless times. Why would he fear the Labyrinth? He didn't look back once as he slipped through the fog and disappeared into the shadows.

It was then that I realized I was shaking. Why was I shaking?

I was cold. So, so cold. I looked down at my hands and saw pale, ashen palms like the hands of a corpse. No color. No heat. I blinked a few times, trying to convince myself that I was ok, but I felt anything but alright. I was empty. Embalmed. Stripped of what I was until I was just a shell with no heartbeat.

What is this?

"As beautiful as the day you were gifted to us," a chilling voice said.

I spun around to see Father Eli standing only feet away, his robes pristine. He smiled at me, but that grin filled my stomach with jagged stones. I felt sick seeing him there, alive and standing.

I killed him. I watched him burn. I heard his screams die.

"You're dead," I huffed out.

"Dead?" He looked down at himself, his face going white as powder. "I suppose I am."

A laugh sputtered from his mouth, but there was no depth to it. No humor.

But then he was gone. In a way, at least. His robes disappeared in a whisp of white smoke and what was left was a translucent, gray figure. Naked. Aged. Hunched over like an old man. Or, more like a beaten dog with its tail between its legs. He walked, eyes down and vacant. Empty.

Dead.

I watched him walk right by me, mumbling things to himself. Searching. Treading as if he was desperately looking for a path to follow.

The Labyrinth is for wandering souls.

But I wasn't in the Labyrinth. I didn't go in.

Confusion gripped me like a snake coiled around a mouse. It suffocated me. But I was no stranger to being drowned in confusion. I straightened, trying desperately to keep my head above water, when, from the darkness, wandered another figure. Another soul, perhaps.

Or perhaps not.

She was... me.

Pale hair was tied in a half-ponytail, frizzy and unruly as ever. She wore robes as if she'd just woken from a refreshing sleep. The brightness on her face was what set her apart. I saw trust. Excitement. An innocence I couldn't even imagine myself ever possessing. To see her trot through the mist, unseeing and unconscious of my presence, was almost horrifying. Horrifying because it was me in a form I could not remember. Me in another lifetime. Me... if I was happy and whole.

Only something rigid in my gut made me certain that smile was about to be stripped from her pretty lips. Those brown eyes were soon to go dark. Those rosy cheeks would eventually be gaunt and chalky.

"I'm so happy you came to see us," she said, bouncing toward someone unseen in the mist.

"What is this?" I whispered, watching a broken past replay before my eyes.

The innocent Briar opened her arms to embrace someone and when that figure came into view, ice filled my veins. I couldn't see them beneath the large, lace-trimmed hood over their head, but I knew something was off. Something was so, so off.

"Of course," the woman said. "Come, before Rune wakes. I want to show you something only a lady would appreciate. And after, I have a wonderful gift in mind for you to give him. He'll love it."

She took the hand of my innocent little twin, leading her through the mist. I should not have followed. I didn't want to, but my feet moved anyway. There was something wrong and my aching heart needed to know what it was.

I watched the figures stroll what I had to assume was a street judging by the occasional street lamp. I was seeing everything as if through a very narrow lens, catching glimpses of the surroundings only when they came close to the subjects of the vision.

"Wait," I said aloud, getting an uneasy feeling the further the hooded figure and my mimic walked.

Something in me knew they were wandering too far from protection. Too far from something important.

My world fell apart when the two figures stopped in an alley and a man stood in the shadows, cloaked and hooded.

That innocent smile flattened off my mimic's lips. Even she knew something was not right at that point. She trembled as the man removed his hood and revealed a face I knew too well. A face I last saw only moments ago.

Father Eli. He had a wicked grin on him. One I couldn't help realizing was younger. Fewer lines were scattered on his cheeks. I froze, watching everything play out and full well knowing in my soul that I couldn't intervene.

This has already happened.

Innocent. Curious. In love. I felt those things bleeding off of the woman standing between Father Eli and the hooded woman. She was confused. Stunned.

So was I.

"You're sure that the king will not hunt me down and kill me?" Father Eli asked.

The cloaked figure shook her head. "I will direct his attention elsewhere. He won't want to save her."

311

"What are you talking about?" my mimic said, her voice trembling.

I felt that fear and betrayal inside me like I was there.

I *had* been there.

The woman didn't even look at her. Whether it was shame or disregard, she didn't turn her eyes from Father Eli. Instead, she handed him a roll of parchment tied closed with a thin, black ribbon.

"Instructions on how to use her," she said.

My mimic laughed, her tone laced with disbelief.

"Use me? What is this?" she said, trying to approach the hooded figure. The woman swiped her gloved hand over my mimic's face and in an instant, she fell to the ground in a heap of silk fabric and curly blond hair.

"Bleed her," the hooded woman continued to instruct. "But not too fast. She's pure fae from the Glyn, but Rune bonded with her, so she's strong. She can still die, though. Her blood will add years, but kill her and it will cease to help you."

"And, if she tries to escape?" Father Eli said, not an ounce of remorse or second thought in his words.

"Clip her wings," the woman sighed. "And then do what you do best."

"What I do best?" he jeered, cocking a brow.

"You run an asylum, I understand. One where you *help* people."

The word sounded so venomous on her tongue.

"I do," Father Eli said, crouching down beside the body on the ground.

He twirled his finger through a thin strand like he was handling a doll.

"Then condition her," the woman said. "Make her behave. Make her forget. Do whatever you need—whatever you *want*—to get her to comply."

A sinister smile spread across Father Eli's thin lips. "It's doable," he said, standing to face the woman again. "But how do I know the king won't find out and destroy me?"

"Oh, if he finds out, he'll do worse than destroy you. But he won't know a thing."

"And, what is it you want in return?"

Finally, the woman removed her hood, revealing a head of silky black hair pulled tightly into a neat bun. I knew that pale skin and those sharp eyes anywhere. I'd endured the way they cut into me since I saw her at the masquerade.

Elanor.

Raising her sharp chin, she said, "In return, you'll keep her away from my king. That is all I ask." She stepped closer to Father Eli, looking down her sharp nose at him. "Take her far away from here. If she dies, she will just end up in his Labyrinth and he'll find her again. Break her. You're a man. You should be quite good at it. Make her unrecognizable. Use her as you wish, but I want nothing of this pitiful flower to remain. I want nothing left of her for my king to love."

Another demonic smile crossed Father Eli's lips. "Ahh. You want him for yourself."

Elanor winced at that, but otherwise kept her composure, her face as dangerous and straight as a viper's.

"He just needs time to realize he loves me," she said, her voice uncharacteristically small. "I've been there for him. He…"

She trailed off and Father Eli, bending to scoop up the limp body at his feet, chuckled.

"Your secret's safe with me," he said. "I suppose, if this works, we might cross paths again. A century from now, perhaps," he laughed, draping the unconscious body over his shoulder like a corpse.

"Hopefully not," Elanor said. "But no matter what, as soon as I leave here, you will never recognize my face."

"What do you mean?"

"Exactly that. You'll know you acquired a fae girl, but you will not remember how and you will not try to find out. Take care of her."

Fury, sadness, hate, and confusion stormed the gates of my heart and I felt like a volcano on the verge of erupting. I balled my fists tightly against my sides as Elanor turned to face me, eyes fixed past me into the fog as she lifted her hood.

"Rune," I whispered

I needed him. I needed to feel him. To see him. To tell him all that I'd just witnessed. Whether they were memories or some twisted insecurities cooked up by my mad, scrambled mind, they existed and they had just torn my heart to shreds. I needed an anchor. A touch. A voice. Anything to pull me from that hell.

"Rune!" I screamed as Elanor's image marched toward me and passed right through me like vapor. I fell backward, my hands hitting something hard. Stone. Brick. I didn't know. "Rune!" I screamed again.

I rolled over onto my hands and knees and looked up to see a square room before me. There was only one window, barred and small, that let in dusky light. It shined down on a figure laying on a narrow bed. Her wrists and ankles were wrapped in leather cuffs and secured to the bedframe. Her face was turned away from me, but the shaved head was too familiar.

My golden locks had been shorn and I looked skinny, exactly how I remembered when I was in Southminster. Weeks of rebelling and denying food. Of fighting. Of wishing for death. It carved me down to a fraction of what I was. I was dressed in a white, cotton nightgown that was too thin to keep me warm. It was bunched up to my hips and my bare legs were spread while a man pumped himself between them.

"So beautiful," Lucien chanted, running his fingers down the side of my vacant face.

I could feel every thrust like I was still there, strapped down and stripped of my freedom. The pain was hardly physical. It was mental. It tore my mind and soul to ribbons. Hot tears stung my eyes, blurring the image before me as I—the woman on the bed—turned my head and I saw death on the face staring back. Emptiness. Hopelessness.

I closed my eyes and sobbed, clutching my stomach as a wave of nausea churned within. Lucien had been there since the beginning, just as Father Eli confessed. I felt sick. The only man I'd ever trusted had lied from day one. He didn't take me in as a kindness. They'd all groomed me to be quiet. To be beautiful. Still and compliant.

And I'd been broken enough to believe it all in the end.

Looking up, the room had changed. Instead of seeing myself strapped to the bed, I was curled upon it, my back against the wall. I was strapped tightly into a straitjacket, my chin-length hair unkempt and oily. Shadows pulled at the base of my eyes and I stared, void of anything. Joy. Anger. Sadness.

I was a piece of something that had once been whole and I wasn't sure how I ever thought I could be more.

I couldn't take it. I couldn't keep looking. I collapsed on the cold ground and folded in on myself, holding my knees to my chest. The darkness devoured me like a hungry animal that had been waiting for me to enter its trap for a hundred years. And I finally had.

My madness had me in its clutches and it was eager to tear me apart from the inside out.

37
RUNE

I carried Briar's body out of the mist and into the courtyard. She was slight in my arms, her fingers loosely gripping the front of my tunic. Elanor, when I came into the courtyard, was nowhere to be seen. Instead, Naeve was standing there, concern evident on her face.

"My king," she said, eyeing Briar in my arms. "Is she—"

"She is alright. I'm taking her to my room. You will care for her." Lura fluttered down in a drop of shadows, transforming from a raven to a woman in a blink. "Where is Elanor?"

Lura shrugged. "We went separate ways. I sensed distress so I came back from patrol."

I didn't care to waste time walking into the palace through the heavy front doors. Instead, I expanded my feathered wings and with one beat, I was on the balcony outside my chamber. I walked inside and set Briar down on my bed. Lura and Naeve were close in tow.

"My king, what's going on?" Lura asked. "You're scaring me."

She was always so sensitive to my moods, often letting them dictate her behavior. Sometimes it was irritating, but my youngest raven couldn't help herself. She was empathetic. With everyone, but understandably more with me.

And I was upset.

Briar sat up on the bed, eyes rounded with concern when she looked at me like she just realized where she was.

"Rune," she gasped, her gaze finding me. I knelt by the bed as she swung her legs over to sit on the edge of the mattress. "I— I saw... I saw..."

I took her hands in mine and squeezed. "I know. I need you to stay here with Naeve and Lura."

As I stood, she tugged on my hands, shaking her head. She knew fear well and yet this fear seemed difficult for her to process. She was shocked and overwhelmed.

"Lura and Naeve will take care of you. I need to do something."

"Please," she begged softly, but I couldn't stay. I slowly slid my fingers from her grasp and marched back to the balcony.

"Rune?" Naeve said as I passed her.

"The palace will lock you in until I return," I said.

I knew both my ravens were distressed. Without Elanor, who they'd always looked up to, my behavior must have seemed alarming, but the instructions were simple. Stay with Briar until I returned.

Once on the balcony, Naeve closed the doors behind me and I heard the lock click. Good girl.

I spread my wings, my muscles ready to take flight to one place I was certain to find what I was looking for.

High up in the cerulean skies of the Glyn, I could see my Labyrinth below where the mist had revealed the truth. A place never imagined I would take Briar, but when she chose to venture into that piercing fog, I couldn't deny her. Something was missing. She knew it. I knew it. And the mist knew what it was.

Now I knew, too.

I sored high, scanning the shadowy woods below. My realm was vast and most of it never saw the light of day. In the darkness, the most wicked and vile of souls lurked to suffer an eternity of self-torment.

But I didn't care about them. I was looking for only one monster.

I felt her long before my eyes found her.

Elanor was standing in the middle of a clearing. Where an old temple once stood proud, there were now ruins overgrown with moss and vines. The Glyn had once been the center of all things. The in-between. The place no soul could avoid, whether it was being torn from the mortal realm or introduced to it. Now, so much of it was a wasteland. Forgotten, even by me.

Even its temples where all manners of beings gathered to commune with the worlds and souls beyond were rubble. And Elanor stood within the carcass of the Temple of Larien like a relic from its dark past. She was staring up at the broken statue of the king before me. Ishkarin Merikith. Half of him, at least, for his torso and head lay separate from his legs.

I landed loudly on the ground, sending a whirlwind of leaves up in the gust of my wings. Elanor didn't react. She never had. Around her stood three black hounds, one with a broken horn. Purity always had a soft spot in his heart for Elanor, especially because he used to accompany us on hunts before Briar came into my life. The others? They dispersed to the broken stone walls when I arrived.

Slowly, Elanor turned around to face me and Purity, his lips trembling with an oncoming growl, pierced me with his red eyes. As always, Elanor's face did not betray her thoughts, but I was certain she knew everything. My nose twitched. My fingers curled into fists. Rage had become such a familiar feeling to me that I hardly knew where to direct it anymore.

Wordlessly, Elanor stared at me, her eyes a reflection of mine.

"Say something," I hissed.

The silence swelled like an ocean around us, letting no other sound past the wall.

"What would you like me to say, my king?" she said calmly.

I took a step forward and Purity snarled, his long toes curling on the dusty stone floor.

"Tell me the truth," I said.

"You know the truth."

"I want to hear it from your lips."

I took another step and Purity matched it. Still, I saw nothing in Elanor. No regret. No fear. No anger.

"I trusted you," I continued. "More than anyone, I trusted *you*. How could you—"

"She was a distraction," Elanor said, still even-toned. "You could have sent her into the mist, but you didn't. You let her lead your mind astray, Rune."

"Astray." I flared my nostrils, staring deep into her cavernous eyes. "And where did my mind wander when you took her from me?"

My voice was soft. Defeated. But the anger seared beneath. I knew she could feel it.

Elanor raised her chin at me, feigning confidence, but I knew it was fading. And that fire inside me was focusing somewhere I prayed it would never have to. Upon one of my own ravens.

"I do wonder, Elanor, what part of me you truly came from. Because I never would have betrayed Briar the way you did."

"What part?" Finally, I saw tears glistening in those vivid blue pools. An emotion. "I…" her lips trembled. "I am the part that hasn't forgotten your duty to this place. The Glyn. You have lost your way, Rune. You are meant to be the hunter. The protector. The *king*."

"What we did together was a betrayal of my true duty here. I meddled. I am not meant to be the judge. Only the keeper."

"You always thought the realms would balance themselves if you went too far and they never did. Maybe what we were doing was right all along?"

And then it clicked. The moment I saw Briar for the first time flashed before my eyes. I had suspected she was another soul who had wandered out of the mist... but there had always been something about her that was not like the others.

"The realms did correct things," I muttered. I met Elanor's eyes again. "The realms gave me Briar."

She snorted. "She was just a lost soul from the Labyrinth."

"No, she never came from the Labyrinth. She was made for me. To balance me because I was wandering too far."

She shook her head, eyes reddened. Purity snorted, taking a step back now when I took another forward. I slowly spread my wings, letting them cast a shadow over Elanor and putting her right in the center of my darkness.

"Love has distracted you," she said, her voice breaking. "You are not meant to love others. Others are meant to love you."

The corner of my mouth quirked at her words. They were words I'd never said but still, they were familiar.

Because Elanor was me.

"If I do not love, I cannot guide. And to be king of this place, I *must* love."

Elanor took an angry step forward, showing the emotions she'd always been so skilled at hiding.

"Phariel doesn't love! Phariel corrupts and manipulates."

"This isn't about my brothers."

"You are different. You are better than—"

"Enough!"

When I finally raised my voice, Purity shrunk under my tone. Elanor remained tall, watching me as I unlocked all that I was. All that I'd suppressed. All that I had become over centuries and centuries of existence. The monster. The devil. My wings spread wider. My skin became ashen. My eyes drowned in a black and blue storm of power I hadn't touched in a hundred years.

"Don't," Elanor said, shivering in my shadow, but staying planted where she was. "You made me to be your companion. To guide you. To help you. I *am* you."

"And I can take it all back."

"Briar could not remain. She would have destroyed you. Love is the death of duty. You must see it."

"I created you for love!" I roared the words so loudly that the remaining foundation of the temple shivered. "And I see now that I got you all wrong."

Slowly, I took another step forward, my eyes seeing Elanor for what she truly was. The piece of my soul that did not see anything outside of that skewed idea of justice I'd cooked up when I created her. She was the part of me that was a machine with no capacity to love anything but herself. Me.

"The day you surrendered Briar to Father Eli," I said. "Did you feel anything? Regret? Empathy?"

She hesitated and I knew exactly why. I had not given her those things when I made her.

I had been such a fool.

"Answer me, Elanor," I whispered.

She remained silent, the tears in her eyes conveying something I doubted had anything to do with regret.

"I felt…" she began. "Relief."

I wanted to ask why. I wanted to choke the false life out of her just to get an answer, but in the end, I was to blame for all of it. I made her and not with enough precision and thought to prevent her betrayal. She had wounded me so deeply and still, I hated *myself* for it.

"Please," she whimpered, her shoulders hunching for the first time since the day she rose out of the shadows of my essence.

"You do not fear punishment," I muttered, my hand slowly raising to her cheek. "You fear being nothing. And I cannot and will not try to make you understand how wrong you've been because I was too stupid to give you the capacity. I never thought it necessary. But I see now that when I created you, I had no need for a raven with empathy or the ability to care. It was not jealousy or hatred that drove you to condemn Briar to human hands. It was this fucked up self-obsession I gave you. The idea that you are the universal right and not to be questioned. I created a zealot... and I'm sorry for that."

My hand clamped around her slender throat and I watched her blue eyes go wide with shock. But her hands remained by her side. As I took in the fast flutter of her pulse under my fingers, I watched her. She was obedient as ever even in her last moments. Slowly, I raised her up, feeling her weight tug on my grip when her feet left the ground. She was so beautiful. At one time, I even thought her perfect. A flawless creation made from my magic, but I'd given her too much of it and not enough of what made a thing whole. I realized that now.

"There is no sense in making you suffer, as much as I long to see the fear and pain in your eyes that you caused Briar these fifteen years," I said. "But it no longer matters. I am as much to blame as you, Elanor. And you feel my pain just as I feel yours. And you must feel it so strongly now. I will be your prison where you can wade in that guilt and heartache forever." I paused to let those words sink in. For both of us. "I am sorry," I said, watching her tears slide down her white cheeks.

Purity growled, her body rigid as she watched my hand tighten around Elanor's throat. But the hound would not attack. She was mine just like everything else in the Glyn. A fact that Elanor had seemingly forgotten. I was *king*.

I watched as black veins formed like tiny threads under Elanor's skin. They moved up from the collar of her dress toward my hand and bled into me. I could feel it. It was a needle-like sensation that crept along my fingers, through my palm, my wrist, and straight into my heart from which Elanor had come. Little by little, the existence I'd woven for her returned to me and the harder I squeezed, the faster I took it back. Until finally, her body began to shrivel. Her skin turned ashen. Her eyes glazed over until they lost color completely. Her hair grayed and then began to dissolve on the gentle breeze.

Finally, there was nothing. A dress vacant of a body to fill it slid to the ground in a heap of black fabric. There was no soul to drift to the Labyrinth. Nothing remained of Elanor, the raven who'd been with me for two hundred years listening to me shout and rage and laugh and cry. She'd seen every part of me and somehow I had failed to see every part of her.

Opening my fist, I saw slight traces of Elanor's ashy remains dusting my palm. I had so easily destroyed something I created and I didn't feel nearly as bad about it as I should have. Or perhaps I didn't feel it because I had always known something to be wrong with my first creation. I'd always felt an emptiness in her that reflected mine. It was why I could never love her the way I loved Briar.

She simply wasn't enough.

I wasn't enough.

I turned to look back in the direction of Ferrothorn. I could not see it from that ruined temple, but I could feel it. It was the heart of the Glyn and my heart was inside of it. My everything.

38
BRIAR

Soon after Rune disappeared, sleep claimed me. I had no control over it. My body betrayed me, but despite the rest, I woke filled with worry. Rune had been gone for some time and after a bath and some much-needed rest, I was feeling anxious. I paced in his room, biting my nails and throwing constant glances at the balcony where he had disappeared, hoping to see him. Lura seemed just as nervous as me. She sat in a chair in the corner, eyes focused on the floor, but I knew she was worried. Naeve sat opposite her, her legs propped up on a stool. She looked quite bored.

"Stop your pacing," she said. "You two realize you are worrying about the king, right? He could ruin this entire realm with the snap of his fingers if he wanted. Venturing out into the untamed forest lands will not be his downfall."

"I'm not worried about that," I admitted. "I am worried about Elanor."

Naeve narrowed her eyes and rose from her seat. "What did you see in there, sweet?"

I stopped pacing and faced her, trying to take deep, calming breaths and only succeeding in taking too many too fast. I blinked away a bout of dizziness and shook my head.

"Things I needed to see but wish I hadn't," I said.

"Like what?"

"Elanor," I revealed. "Selling me to the men who broke me. To Father Eli. They took my blood. Used it. For years."

I didn't think Naeve's face could get paler until it did. "Elanor," she muttered.

I nodded. "I don't understand her motives and I may never understand them, but she gave me away so I'd break. And she made your king believe I'd betrayed him so he would break, too."

Lura stood up to look at us. "But he didn't break. He searched for you. I should know. He created me so I could help. Worrying over his happiness is all I've ever done."

Naeve was still staring, her eyes rounded with realization. "She has loved him more than any of us. She has wanted nothing more than to help him be king. A most effective king."

"Then she thought it best I did not exist," I said.

Maybe she was right...

I was nothing but a lost soul that Rune had kept around. One he'd given life to. One he'd fallen in love with.

Love.

That word should have been harder to say, even in my head, but my gut knew it was right. He loved me. He loved who I used to be, at least. I knew it to be true but didn't know how.

Even more, I didn't know why thinking of him triggered emotions I didn't think myself capable of feeling. Without my complete memories, why was my heart crying out for him? Why was my body aching for him to be by my side where I could see him and touch him and hear his voice?

"Briar," Naeve said, reaching out to cup my face with her hand. My eyes met hers and pain lassoed my heart, squeezing. Her gentle smile somehow brought me back. "It is alright to feel."

That statement anchored me. I felt it in my bones and nodded, blinking away any tears that might fall so I could continue to think clearly.

"I want to tell him," I whispered.

Her eyes flicked up over my head at the open balcony doors just as a gust of wind blew through his chambers. Naeve lowered her hand and inclined her head, which prompted me to turn. Before me stood Rune. He stepped through the doors, folding his massive wings back. On his head stood two thick antlers that swept back along his scalp, black in color and adorned with silver rings. It reminded me once more that Rune was not just a king. He was more like a god. A god of his realm and everything in it.

"Elanor?" Lura muttered.

Rune's eyes zeroed in on me and did not stray as he spoke. "Gone," he said.

I sensed some pain in Lura, but Naeve only sighed, accepting the situation.

"Should we—"

"Leave us," he said softly.

Naeve and Lura stepped toward each other and linked arms, walking calmly out of Rune's bedroom. Our eyes remained locked together. My heart was racing too fast for me to breathe without a noticeable shudder. I was in awe of his beauty and for the first time ever, I felt like I'd seen him before. Long before. This fully magnificent creature with claw-tipped fingers, fangs, wings, and eyes that could burn right through me was suddenly familiar. He was so terrifyingly beautiful I thought my heart might fail.

"I've seen you before," I whispered.

He took a step forward, never blinking. There was a tightness in his jaw like he was suppressing something. Passion and anger. Pain and regret. Mostly, he looked tortured. The feelings were all the same in the end. They were all destructive in their own ways.

But I longed for that destruction now. I longed for *him* and all the ways he could abolish the bars I'd been trapped behind for fifteen years.

Break them, I pleaded silently.

But he didn't. Not the way I'd hoped. Reaching toward his cluttered desk, he pulled out a folded piece of parchment and handed it to me. The heat in my core faded and I held my breath at the way he walked past me and kept his back turned.

I wanted to say something, but words were lost to me. Feeling let down, I opened the parchment to find a stained document with Lucien's signature at the bottom. I skimmed over it and furrowed my brows.

"This is the deed to Aedon Heights," I said. "And it's... signed to me."

"It's yours," Rune finally spoke. "All of it. If you decide to go back and live a life of your own, you can do it comfortably. He had assets that would support you for the rest of a mortal life."

I turned around to see his folded wings and the back of his head. Why wasn't he looking at me?

Too many thoughts were storming the gates of my self-control. The loss of important memories. The images and the pain that remained like ghosts on my body and mind from Southminster. The bitter taste of all the lies that they'd fed me was strong. The feeling of being incomplete. The warmth of the love I was starting to feel for the beast before me. The sickening idea that Lucien had been tainting my body long before I was in his care. Cuffs. Screaming. The overwhelming desire to die so many times. It all rushed back at me like a debris-filled flood, cutting, slicing, and bruising.

I was fae because the Devil in Blue made me fae. Because he loved me once. He'd given me wings and just as quickly, they were shorn. I was so unbelievably incomplete and wrecked that perhaps the king had finally come to terms with the idea that I was not his Briar. I was just... me. A ruined, ugly, broken creature made scrawny and sickly from the cages I'd been locked in for fifteen years.

Tears stung my eyes. My hands trembled and I wished he would turn around and face me. Face the biggest mistake he'd ever made.

I crumbled the paper in my hands. The sound made Rune turn. He eyed the deed first as I let it fall to my feet. Then his gaze met mine and he caught the moisture gathering there.

"You wish me to leave," I said softly. He said nothing. His jaw clenched like he was wrestling back his voice. His silence was a spear to my heart. "To go back to the place that will haunt me until the day my eyes close for good."

"You can sell the estate. Go anywhere you like," he said flatly.

The notion made me shake with anger.

"I wasn't talking about the estate," I said through my teeth. "The whole world is my nightmare. All good memories were stripped and you will never know what that feels like. And now I know that I was not just lost. I was given away by someone you trusted. Someone *I* once trusted."

I stepped forward, shoving my hands against Rune's solid chest. He stepped back as if my effort affected him, but I knew that was a lie.

"And now you tell me to leave," I continued. "You tell me I can be free, but you know nothing about being free or caged."

"Briar, stop," he muttered.

My hand flew across his cheek, but he did not retaliate.

"They mutilated me," I said. "They tortured me with words and whips and chains and ice. They raped me. Defiled me. Shamed me." My fist connected with his chest. Once. Twice. "They stole me from you and you found me and now you are giving up!"

"I am not giving up!" he finally shouted, grabbing hold of my flailing wrists.

I tugged from his grip and moved toward the door, but when I tried to open it, I found we were locked in.

"Let me out," I growled.

"I did not lock it."

I spun to face Rune again to see that he'd veiled his antlers and wings, which made him look less beastly and more dangerously handsome. But it was a venomous beauty.

"If you want me to leave, you need only tell me," I said, defeated. "Spare me the ache of your half-truths and tell me. Stab me with real honesty and get it over with." His lip twitched with frustration as he glimpsed the deed on the floor. "You miss the woman I was. I know you do. You want her back, but I can't give you that."

I took a long pause to gather myself. No matter how many times I rehearsed what I wanted to say to him in my head, getting the words out was like trying to dislodge a ball of thorns from my throat.

"All I want is to be free, as you said, but freedom for me is not as simple as fluttering out of some crate," I continued, my voice quivering. "I haven't been in a cage in a long time, but that doesn't matter. I'm the cage. But you made me wish I could be trapped with you. I… I wouldn't mind that so much."

I stepped toward him, taking a deep breath. "The day we met in the catacombs, you saw it. I wished to die. I longed for it."

"If you die, you don't go to the Labyrinth."

I scoffed. "Everyone goes to—"

"You were never human. I should have realized it sooner. You were given to me to correct something I broke in the realms. To balance me. Even when you were gone, the mere thought of you kept me from destroying the world around me."

I paused a moment, taking another deep breath in a desperate attempt to absorb Rune's scent.

"And... you would give that up? I'm trapped in thoughts of you, Rune. I ache for you. It's an ache I can't ease unless I'm near you. Touching you. Listening to you speak." Reaching up, I pinched my necklace between my fingers. "So, I remind you that I am not the woman you knew. The one who balanced you. There is nothing of her left." Tears stung my eyes again and I knew I was losing a battle against myself. "I have but one question and the answer you give will dictate whether or not I take your offer of so-called freedom. Could you love *me* without *her* was the offer to return to humanity your way of pushing me away?"

There was nothing for me to read on Rune's face. I was starting to think it was a mistake to even try to break the last barrier between us. I was a woman with half of her memories and if what he said was true, I didn't even have a past life. I was nothing and he was a king with many lifetimes behind him. Nothing about *us* made sense and maybe I was a fool for thinking it ever could.

"The truth is," I whispered. "The few good memories we've made since I've been here are more important to me than that necklace you gave me and crushed. More important than living a wealthy life outside this realm. They mean more to me than anything and perhaps it is because I had nothing, but it is true either way. You are a monster and I should not love you for all that you did to me. I should hate you, but I don't. I *need* you." A tear slid down my cheek, burning like acid.

Rune's eyes softened. The tightness in his lips relaxed a fraction and finally, I knew something was finally registering.

"Love," he murmured.

My heart skipped when I realized what I'd said. Love. I wasn't sure I even knew what love felt like, but there was something so potent forming between Rune and me, especially after all the lies and all the masks had been taken away.

Except for one. The one he was still wearing to shield me from what he was really thinking.

"I don't know how I felt before or if it was love," I said. "I don't even know what it should feel like, but my heart burns when I am around you. My pulse quickens. I want to touch you. Feel you. I want to scream at you and kiss you and..." I paused for a breath. "I want you to help me create memories in place off all that I've lost. You. No one else. You held me when I was falling. You slept beside me while I wept. No more masks, Rune. Please. I have torn myself open for you to see and if you cannot do the same then I will leave. I will waste away praying for the day I perish for good because there is nothing else for me."

Pain finally whispered across his eyes. I watched his broad chest expand time and time again as he breathed, but still, he had no words for me.

He didn't need them.

Rune stepped toward me and fell to his knees. He looked up at me, all the guilt and regret and hatred he felt, either toward me or toward himself, seeped through the glow of his eyes and went straight to my heart.

"The truth," he rasped. He flicked his hand at his side like he was swiping dust off a shelf and the crumpled deed burst into blue flames and disintegrated on the floor. "Let that manor be a home for spiders and bats. Your place is here."

Closing his eyes, Rune wrapped his arms around my legs and pulled me against him, his mouth pressing to my stomach. Hot breath penetrated the fibers of my dress and I shivered, raking my fingers through his hair.

"I would kill a thousand men if a thousand men had wronged you. And I'd bring you a piece of every one until your necklace snapped."

My heart galloped at the thought as Rune craned his head to peer up at me.

"I loved the woman you were," he continued. "The sweet, curious, mischievous little bird who wanted to see everything. Whose light flooded my darkness. Whose smile infected my soul." Slowly, he began to stand, making sure his palms traced every curve of my body as he unfolded to his full height. He'd gathered my skirts at my thighs and with no effort at all, he lifted me so my legs were wrapped around him. "But this—who you are—is who I love now. Wounded. Fierce. Unrealized and perfect. Beautiful." He began walking toward his bed, one hand lifting to comb his fingers through my hair and pull me close. "Violent," he growled, pulling me into his mouth.

Our lips crashed together in a heated kiss. There was no easing into it. Both our bodies had caught fire, fed by the heat rising between us.

"Kind," Rune said between kisses. "And still so curious even when the world has torn you apart."

Setting me down on the bed, he stepped back, watching me as he began to unlace his tunic. When he slid it off, I traced his body with my eyes, certain I would never get bored of seeing him like that. I watched him discard one thing after another until he was naked in front of me, white as the moon with smokey blue hair and eyes that burned. From his broad shoulders to his strong legs and even to the thick cock standing proud toward his navel, he was utter perfection.

I bit my lip as his wings slowly came into view again, large, regal, and dark. They filled half the room when they stretched out at full length. And those antlers returned, swept back like branches. This was him truly without a mask.

I stood up, watching him boldly as I unbuttoned my dress and slid it off my shoulders. The silk caressed my sensitive skin as it slipped to the floor in a heap. I was bare, every scar and marking branded on me for him to see. But if he'd shed his mask, then it was my turn to do the same.

Rune's eyes skimmed slowly down my body. There weren't many scars there. A scratch or two made from my own nails when I had been driven so mad in my solitude that I needed the pain to remind me I was still alive.

Reaching out, Rune placed his hand on my shoulder and gently spun me around so he could see my back. I trembled at the thought as he cleared my hair to the side and draped it over one shoulder. My eyes swelled with tears as his hand lightly brushed up my side. His thumb crossed over the brand on my hip and I could almost feel the passion from the moment it was created. The real one. Even if I couldn't remember, I knew.

Then his fingers traced the long, jagged markings on each shoulder blade. They still felt sensitive. They had since the day they were made. I took a deep breath, realizing that I felt more than naked now. I felt like I didn't even have skin anymore. I was just a heart and a soul, vulnerable and exposed.

"They still hurt," I whispered. "Like they've never healed."

"Because they never have," Rune answered, bending forward to press his hot lips to my shoulder. I closed my eyes to savor that feeling.

And then I felt something else. Something painful and jolting. I sucked in a breath and whimpered, but the pain wasn't like other kinds of pain. It was like a big stretch that relieved tension but hurt at the same time. I squeezed my eyes shut tighter, my pulse racing as the nerves of my spine seized. Gasping, I nearly fell over, but Rune gripped my shoulders, keeping me upright. One arm snaked around to my front and he took my chin gently in his hands. He turned my face to look at him and pressed his mouth to mine again in a deep but gentle kiss.

"They cannot take what isn't theirs," he whispered.

There was a new weight on my back, one that I felt proud to bear. I opened my eyes and found wings spread out behind me. Not black like Rune's, but a combination of green, blue, and black like a peacock stone. I stared for a long moment in disbelief until the reality of it settled and I realized those wings were mine. They did not feel too heavy or too strange. They felt familiar and freeing. They were... perfect.

"I gave a part of myself to you," Rune whispered into my ear, his teeth grazing my lobe. "And that will always remain."

I folded my wings in and turned to face him, wide-eyed and shaking with the most wonderful shock. Controlling them was natural like they were limbs I'd always had.

I sunk into his blue eyes and couldn't breathe. He'd filled me with his presence until the only thing that would relieve me of that emptiness was him.

Reaching up, I took his face in my hands and kissed him without abandon. I hooked one leg around him and then the other, climbing onto his hips as my tongue plunged into his mouth. Rune let out a soft chuckle against my mouth and then kissed me back with as much need, his fangs pricking my bottom lip. I moaned, grinding myself against his hard length.

"I feel you," I panted. "Everywhere."

"I know," he said, turning and pressing me up against the wall.

My wings spread, knocking stacks of books to the floor. "Sorry."

He chuckled again, rocking his hips so his cock slid between my folds.

"There is a reason I keep mine tucked away," he said, moving his mouth to my neck and assaulting my skin with his tongue.

"Should we—"

He bit down on my flesh, sending a jolt of excited goosebumps all across my body.

"Keep them out," he said, his hand sliding between us. His teeth nipped me again and I whimpered just as his fingers slid over the swollen bud between my thighs. "No more masks, remember? I want you as you are. And I want you to have all of me."

I writhed against him, my body thirsting for him to be inside me. When I kissed him again, two of his fingers plunged into my wet heat. He pumped them. Once. Twice. Then he added a third, stretching me wide. I gasped, throwing my head back at the delicious sensation when his thumb grazed my clit. He began to move his fingers in slow, long strokes and then withdrew, bringing them to his mouth. I watched him suck my arousal off his fingers and every nerve in my body lit fire from the sight.

"You taste so good," he groaned.

His hand slid across my cheek and back into my hair, gripping a hefty handful before he pushed his tongue into my mouth and devoured me. I locked my hands around the back of his neck and melted like a wax candle on a hot summer day. I needed more. I needed—

My thoughts paused when I felt the thick head of his cock at my entrance. He pushed inside in one thrust, stretching me wide and filling me so completely that I could hardly breathe. One of my hands slid over his chest, my nails biting into his skin as he rocked against me. He growled at the sting of my touch against his flesh and I loved it. I hungered for it. I dug deeper, dragging three lines over his sternum. Pulling away from our kiss, he snarled, tugging harder against my hair as he began to pump into me, one possessive thrust after another.

Hooking one arm under my knee, he raised my leg, driving deeper than ever. Even if I tried to think of something else, I couldn't. Our union blinded me to the world and all the horrors of my past and I relished it. Gods, I didn't care how or when I came to be. I didn't care if I was once human or if I was created solely for Rune. None of it mattered because I had him and I was so blissfully content thinking that from that point on, the only direction was forward.

"Rune," I moaned. "I'm going to—"

His hand moved from my hair to grip my chin, his thumb pressing between my lips and pinning my tongue to the bottom of my mouth.

"No," he breathed. "Not yet. You haven't even begun to know true pleasure."

He plunged deeper, his lips once more against my neck. I was a mess of heavy breaths, whimpers, and moans, my mind in a euphoric fog as he ravaged me. He changed rhythm, his fingers finding their way to my clit. I bowed against the wall, my legs shaking as my climax raced up on me.

"Say it," Rune grunted, stealing his hand away from my clit and leaving me to suffer. "I want to hear you say it."

"I…" I paused, uncertain and hardly able to focus on words.

He pulled me from the wall and, still buried deep, laid me down on the table where I'd cleared the books away with my wings. Whatever was left, he swiped away with his hand, leaving the room a mess. Hands braced on either side of me, he slowed his thrusts to long, gentle strokes that had me squirming with need.

"Rune," I said. "Please. I need…"

"I'm yours, Briar," he smirked, his eyes devilish. "What do you need? Command me."

I let out a strained breath, grasping for something I could not find. I needed friction. Intensity. *Everything.*

I lifted my head, pressed my hands to his chest where slight traces of blood had marked his skin, and finally found my voice the way I needed to.

"Make me come," I moaned.

That smirk returned, even more devilish than before. He stood up, wings spread wide, and took my hips in his hands, pulling me down his shaft. I gasped at the harshness of the thrust, but I ate up the pain. The way it took my breath away. The way he devoured my nightmares with his presence and gave me something to replace them. *Him.* I basked in all of it because it was all mine now.

He will look for you.
He will find you.
He will destroy you.

Those words rang in my head as I climbed that rope to the very top of ecstasy. He did search for me. He found me. He was destroying me in all the ways that I needed to be destroyed. He ripped at the chains that had shackled me and gave me wings. He set me free. He gnawed at the invisible prison and melted the bars of my cell.

The rope snapped and I began to fall, tangling in the delicious pleasure of my climax. It was a euphoric descent. One that Rune did not intend to end fast. He bent forward, his tongue tracing up between my breasts to my throat as a breathless cry forced its way out of me.

Nothing remained at that moment. Lucien's clammy touch was gone. All that was left of him was a charm on a necklace. Southminster was ashes. Father Eli was charred bones.

Rune's hand slid around the back of my neck and he lifted me against his body, devouring my voice with his lips. I was a trembling mess, my thoughts in wonderful shambles. He kept moving inside of me, chasing his pleasure only when I'd experienced mine. I braced myself on my palm, leaning back to watch his cock piston in and out of me. Then our eyes locked and a whole new world opened up. One where I was loved. Cherished. Free.

Those tears I'd desperately tried to keep at bay began to sting again and the moment one slid down my cheek, Rune went rigid with his climax. He groaned loudly, thrusting deep and staying there, locked inside me as his heat flooded my core. I was ridden raw and so wonderfully spent, my skin glistening with sweat.

Panting, Rune leaned forward and pressed his forehead to mine, his thumb sweeping across my cheek to dry a tear.

"I weep too much," I whispered shakily. "I'm sorry."

He cupped my face between his hands and shook his head. "I adore your tears. They make you so unbelievably beautiful to me, Briar."

Slowly, his wings and antlers faded out of existence, and as soon as I imagined my wings doing the same, they did. Rune slid his fingers through my hair once more and pressed a gentle kiss to my cheek, moving his cock just enough to remind me he was still buried deep inside me. He was still thick and hard and it almost renewed my arousal before I'd even caught my breath.

"Were you always this way?" I asked. "This unrelenting?"

He let out a low, handsome chuckle and pressed deeper. "Actually, it was you that was more voracious."

I smiled at that. "The way you make me feel, I am not surprised."

"And now? The woman you are now, will she be as insistent?"

"Maybe. Or perhaps I'd enjoy a good chase." I traced my fingers over his lips. "That day in the woods with the kelpher, violent as it was, made me feel..."

I stopped myself, wondering if it was wrong to admit the things I felt that day amongst all the blood and brutality.

"Tell me," Rune whispered.

I stared into his gaze, savoring the way his eyes made me feel so defenseless and invincible at the same time.

"I burned for you then," I confessed. "I worried for you when you left. But more than that, I wanted you. More when you bled for me. When you cut down that beast in front of me. And when you brought me this," I touched my necklace. "I would have done anything you asked. Not because I felt obligated. Because for the first time in my life, I wanted to fold for someone. To be at someone's mercy. Because in my gut and my soul, I trust you would never abuse that power."

"You did not feel that way when you saw the chains."

"No. I tasted betrayal yet again... until you allowed me to pour my anger upon you. And you did not judge me or condemn me for it. I had so much anger to give. Maybe I still do."

"I will take every drop of it if it means you no longer have to bear it alone, Briar. Know that."

The corner of my lip curled. "Does that mean we can keep the chains?"

Rune's brow quirked. "If you'd like," he smirked. "I would build a whole room dedicated to indulging your desires if you wish."

I pulled him into another untamed kiss, savoring the taste of him.

"My desires are clear," I breathed. "I desire you."

"That is the easiest wish I could ever grant you. You already have me. You've had me since the day you first saw me covered in blood and filth. And you have me now. Your mind has changed, but your soul remains the same and that is what I fell in love with, Briar. *You.*"

I slid my ankles around the back of his legs and pulled him tighter against me, reveling in how his cock was still so hard and eager.

"Then show me again what wonders I have to look forward to," I said, biting his chin lightly. "I should need frequent reminders."

He leaned forward, bracing his fists on the table as he bent to lick over my taut nipple.

"Be careful what you ask for, little bird," he rasped, biting down against my breast and making me yelp. "We have both changed in fifteen years."

That promise in itself nearly made me come. I shuddered at his words and held him close, content to have him inside me all night long.

Epilogue
RUNE

Briar was a natural. She wasn't squeamish or afraid of much after her experiences the past fifteen years. When I told her I wanted to start cleaning up the woods and make them more hospitable for the other inhabitants of the Glyn, she was all too eager to help.

But she was going to need her own familiar and I had no doubt she was strong enough to create one now.

A sacrifice of blood, bone, and tears could create one, but it wasn't just about what was given physically. I feared that Briar felt too much and would put too much into her creation as I had with Elanor, but she had convinced me she was in a good place. A place of confidence and control.

We sat in a clearing in the woods where Briar had arranged a circle of white stones on the mossy ground just as I'd taught her. Naeve and Lura stood off to the side, anxiously watching as Briar placed her molar in a bowl. She'd pulled it herself earlier in the week in preparation. Another would grow back, but bone was hard to grow back. Even for sovereigns.

She was tough as nails now and I admired the hell out of her for it.

Briar crushed her tooth into a stone bowl until it was gritty powder.

"Now, the blood?" she said, looking up at me for guidance.

I nodded, watching but not intervening. Creating something from your soul was not a simple thing. It was deeply personal and sometimes difficult and came with risks. Risks I was certain Briar could handle.

She'd become so strong. Months of reading, learning to fly with her new wings, feeding our lust-filled escapades, and learning about our world had built an entirely new woman and I loved her all the same.

Briar brought the tip of a small dagger to her palm and made a straight, slow incision across her skin, barely even wincing. Then she squeezed the blood over her crushed tooth and from a little vial she had tucked in her coat pocket, she poured a few drops of tears into the mix.

I was there when she collected them. She was so enamored by the waterfall down the mountain that she wept. She'd been drifting further and further away from the restraints Southminster had burdened her with and she was allowing herself to feel more and more. Her emotions often overwhelmed her, but she was learning to control them rather than suppress them. It was a process I was more than happy to be a part of.

"Alright," she sighed, carefully sliding the bowl into the middle of the stone circle.

"You remember the words?"

"Yes." Taking a deep breath, Briar stood, eyes fixed on the bowl.

"The familiar will take physical form from the contents in that bowl, but speaking the words will give it a mind."

Briar nodded and took a few more breaths, letting them out slowly the way she did when she was about to take flight. Then she closed her eyes and began to speak words from the old tongue exactly the way I'd taught her. And ever since the idea of getting a familiar occurred to her, she'd been buried in books of sovereign history and how the realms worked. And with that came her interest in the old language.

So when she spoke the incantation, she did it with more heart than I had. She felt the words and she poured them into her creation, one trickle at a time. Her accent was pure and her intentions were even more so.

In the middle of the circle, the stone bowl was smoking and filled the clearing with the scent of rain and orange peel. It was an odd scent, but distinctive... which meant something was forming. Something that would be a part of Briar and its own entity all at once.

Lura whimpered behind me. She had never seen the creation of a familiar and I was sure it was a bit jarring since she was one herself. Naeve pulled her close and patted her hand.

Briar glanced up at me, her eyes asking if she'd done things right. I gave her a soft smile because she did wonderfully.

And then we heard it. The first breath of life. It echoed within the ruins as specks of white began to gather around the stones, dancing in a swarm of smooth, white vapor. Briar watched anxiously as they started to swirl upward into a smoky column. Reaching out, she took my hand and squeezed, showing me a tiny glimpse of her nervousness.

As the smoke cleared, before us stood a man, tall and shredded in lean muscle. His skin was as white as smoke and his hair was long and pale silver. He dawned eyes in a slightly lighter shade than Briar's and a face with young, handsome lines, full lips, and expressive brows.

Briar was staring…

So were Lura and Naeve.

The clearing was silent and warm with the man's presence. I regarded him closely, astounded at how well Briar had done. She'd done a little too well because Naeve's heartbeat had just doubled in speed. I could hear it.

I glanced at her and raised a brow but she hardly noticed.

"It worked," Briar said, slowly letting go of my hand and walking toward her new companion.

I followed a step behind, watching as she lifted her fingers to touch his face. It was her way of proving things were real and I found her doing it to almost everything she believed was too beautiful or too fantastical.

The man's eyes were curious, reflecting Briar's personality immediately. He watched as she stroked his cheek and then circled him, taking in every detail of his very real, very handsome, form.

I tossed Naeve another look and caught her snapping her lips shut like she'd been drooling.

"Do you have a name or shall I give you one?" Briar asked.

The man's lips stretched into a crooked grin, flashing one of his sharp incisors.

"I don't have a name," he said, his voice just as perfect as his face. "But, if you wouldn't mind, I'd like to choose one myself."

Briar beamed at that request. "Of course." Then she met my gaze, her wide smile full of pride and excitement. I reached out and she took my hand, coming back to my side. "He's handsome, isn't he?" she whispered.

I gave him another glance and found his eyes had finally discovered Naeve ogling him from across the clearing. But once Briar addressed him again, his attention was hers and no one else's.

"I'm Briar. And this is—"

"The King of the Glyn," he finished, staring right at me with eyes that seared right through. "You love him so very much."

Fuck.

The way he said those words felt almost as potent as when Briar said them to me. I broke eye contact and glanced down at her with a forced smile.

"You've done a bit too well," I muttered.

Briar chuckled, but when she caught the seriousness in my face, she stilled.

"Really?"

"I—I can show him around," Naeve volunteered, stepping forward.

She seemed nervous. I'd never seen her nervous before.

What in the realms had gotten into her?

"Of course," Briar said, her gaze narrowing on me.

"Good idea," I said. I braved another look at the very naked man standing in the clearing.

"Shouldn't I bond with him or something, though?" Briar said.

"No need. He *is* you, little bird."

"He's right," the man said. "Even now I can feel your heart beating." His eyes found me again and that time they drifted slowly down my body in a way that reminded me far too much of his creator. "It's beating quite loudly for him," he said softly.

A soft tickle in my groin made me shift my feet and divert my eyes.

"Briar," I said, gaining my composure. "We may need to talk."

She giggled as if she'd already caught on to what was happening.

"You mean to tell me that I never looked at Naeve like that when you created her? You said you created her at the height of our infatuation."

"You barely knew Naeve before. I made her—"

"She kissed me," Naeve cut me off. "Just before your trip."

My wide eyes found hers. "What?"

She bit her lip and shrugged. "It was a small kiss. Said she had to get it out of her system. That was probably meant to be a secret, but I think that goes out the window in the current situation."

"Well…" Briar said. "That's interesting." She tapped her chin with her fingers, her gaze darting between her new familiar and me. "Alright, so kiss him."

I groaned and pulled her against my side.

"Naeve, if you'd be so kind," I said.

She didn't hesitate. Naeve waltzed forward, pushing her chest out to show off her cleavage as she caressed the man's arm.

"Can you fly?" she said.

The man quirked his brow and smiled, thinking about that for a bit. Then, with a step back, he dissolved into a swirl of white smoke and beat his big, white wings until he was perched on a branch overhead. He was the biggest white owl I'd ever seen in my Glyn, his eyes surveying the scene below. Naeve chuckled girlishly and leapt into her raven form, ascending toward him. As she climbed higher, the owl followed.

"Alright," I said chidingly. "What have you done?"

Briar was laughing. There was no remorse at all in those brown eyes of hers.

"If you didn't want him to love you, perhaps you should have forced me to make him when we were fighting."

I growled, brushing my hands through my hair.

"Lura," I said. "Would you head back and draw us a bath?"

She nodded, always so anxious to please, and leapt into the sky on her black wings. As soon as she was gone, I collared Briar's throat and drove her back into a tree, watching the excitement burst across her face.

"Well, you've gone and made me very turned on," I rasped.

Her hand slid down to the front of my pants, cupping my hard cock through the leather.

"Have I? Or do you have a little crush on my familiar?"

I leaned down and crushed my mouth to hers, grinding my lips so hard against her that our teeth met. She moaned, her hips rolling forward to meet the thrust of mine.

"Take me back," she panted.

I shook my head. "Or maybe I will take you right here, on the forest floor."

"Even better. As long as it's rough and desperate."

"Oh, I can assure you it will be those things and more."

I kissed her again, gathering her skirts in my hand so I could feel her bare thigh under my fingers. Her arousal coated the air and it made my pulse run wild.

"I will never stop wanting you," she said. "Gods, it's infuriating."

I chuckled, biting down on her lip just enough to make her gasp. That fury was what I loved. That intensity fed my soul and I longed for her never to stop.

She was the only thing I wanted. The only thing that could destroy me, again and again.

"Show me that fury, little bird," I breathed, knowing full well what she could do to me. "Ruin me."

"A bold request, my king."

I growled against her mouth. "Mmm, I love when you call me that, *my queen.*"

~ The Devil in Blue ~

Made in the USA
Middletown, DE
19 May 2024

54559453R00210